The door crashed open behind Jake, and the sound of hissing filled the corridor, drowning out the sound of his footsteps.

Jake skidded to a stop and raised the gun to his shoulder. Through the night vision scope he saw a creature with the upper body of a woman and the lower body of a snake bearing down on him at an incredible speed. He aimed the gun in the other direction and saw a corner fifty yards ahead. Dropping the weapon on its strap he sprinted, his boots pounding the tile floor.

The hissing grew louder and more frantic.

Jake turned the corner and slid to a stop. He freed the ATAC's strap from around him and raised the weapon to his shoulder. Through the scope he saw the creature whip around the corner and look in his direction. He lowered the barrel over his stump and lunged forward, thrusting the knife on the barrel's edge.

The knife cut into something solid, and the beast unleashed a hideous sound. Jake drew the blade out and thrust again, cutting into her sternum a second time. He pulled the blade out again, but this time something smacked the ATAC out of his hand with a whiplike snap, and he knew the monster had used her snake body to disarm him.

Jake backed up, ready to run, but something ensnared his ankles and jerked his legs out from under him. He landed on his back with a grunt, then clawed at the floor as the creature dragged him toward her. Lightning flashed outside the windows, illuminating her as she released Jake's ankles and wrapped her snake body around his legs and torso, pinning his arms to his sides.

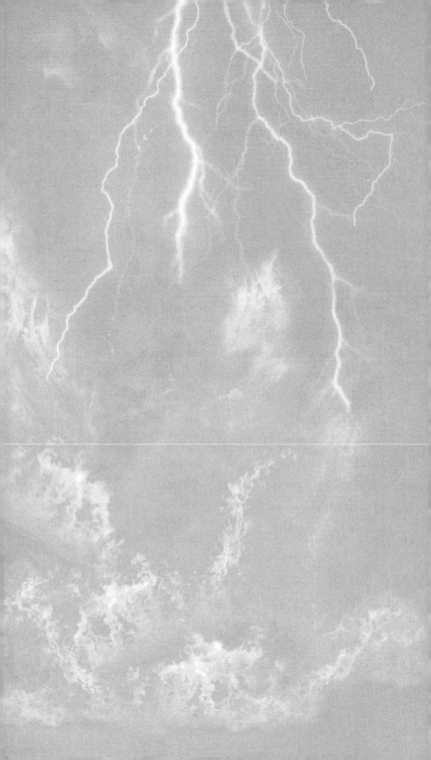

THE JAKE HELMAN FILES
STORM DEMON

Gregory Lamberson

MEDALLION
P R E S S

Medallion Press, Inc.

Printed in USA

Dedicated to my pal Joseph Fusco

Published 2013 by Medallion Press, Inc.

The MEDALLION PRESS LOGO

is a registered trademark of Medallion Press, Inc.

Typeset in Adobe Garamond Pro

Printed in the United States of America

ISBN 978-1-60542-746-1

10 9 8 7 6 5 4 3 2 1

First Edition

"She wanders about at nighttime, vexing the sons of men and causing them to defile themselves."

—Zohar, 19b

"Someday a real rain will come and wash all this scum off the streets."

—Taxi Driver

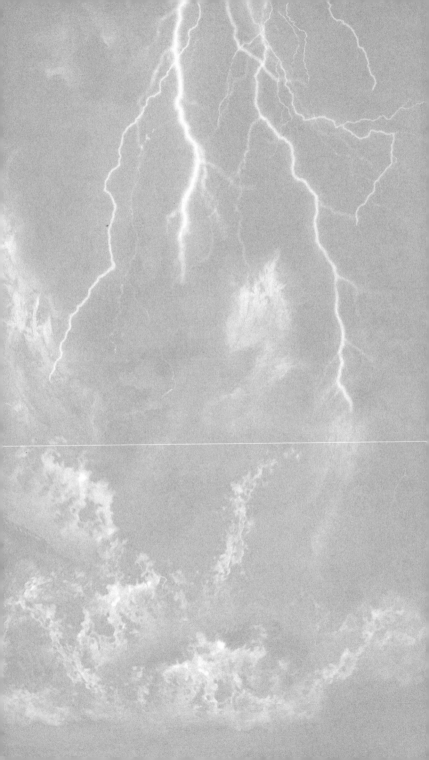

ONE

Laurel Doniger awoke alone in her windowless bedroom. Except for one night spent in the arms of Jake Helman, she had lived in seclusion for three years. She met with clients, of course, and Jackie Krebbs, the building's engineer, saw to her needs as far as food deliveries went, but otherwise she experienced no human contact. Worse, she had not set foot outside the storefront property, which served as her home and business, during all that time. But at least she was alive.

In the kitchen, she turned on the radio and the television. She had no difficulty processing the separate streams of information. The weatherman on *The Today Show* predicted clear skies and a beautiful day in New York City, while on the local radio news station a commercial for therapeutic cloning ended.

Lying on a mat on the floor, Laurel stretched and performed forty-five minutes of calisthenics, including jumping jacks, squats, crunches, sit-ups, push-ups, calf raises, lunges, and running in place. She followed this routine every day; confined to her apartment, she got no other exercise.

With a sheen of sweat clinging to her body, she showered, dressed in a simple green summer dress, and prepared egg whites and a fruit salad. After breakfast she swallowed numerous vitamins, a necessity because sunlight no longer touched her skin.

At 9:00 a.m., her front door buzzed, another routine. Laurel slipped on some comfortable shoes—she only wore them when she had visitors—and crossed the sunken parlor. The five-inch monitor mounted next to the door displayed a short, wiry man with a full head of bushy white hair and a mustache that hid his upper lip. He looked like a character in a Dr. Seuss book. Using the keypad, she shut off the alarm system and twisted the four locks on the door. She stepped back as Jackie entered.

"Good morning," he said.

"Good morning."

"Do you need anything?"

"No, thanks. I'm all set."

"It's going to be a beautiful day."

"That's what I hear."

"Jake still isn't back."

Laurel already knew. She would have sensed Jake's vibrations in the building if he had returned. "Maybe today."

"I hope he's all right."

So do I.

"Holler if you need me."

"I will."

Jackie stepped out into the sunlight, and Laurel closed the door, relocked it, and reset the alarm. She knew Jackie had a crush on her, so she was careful not to encourage him in that respect, but she depended on him for too much.

Stepping down into the sunken parlor, she passed the only furniture in the room: a round table covered with a red cloth and two chairs. She never saw more than one client at a time.

One hour later, Laurel studied the pretty brunette in the monitor. The woman had introduced herself as Janet Rogers over the telephone. Laurel unlocked the door and stepped back, then pressed the intercom button. "Please come in."

Janet opened the door, allowing sunlight to flood the inside of the parlor. Laurel remained in the shadows as the woman entered. Janet appeared as a silhouette until the door closed, shutting out the light. "Miss Laurel?"

"Yes." Laurel locked the door and gestured to the table. "This way."

Laurel stepped down into the sunken room and sat on the far side of the table, and Janet sat opposite her.

"Have you had a reading before?" Laurel said.

"No."

"How can I help you?"

"My husband, Alex, is missing. He works in Manhattan and commutes from Long Island every day. We've been married for six years. The only thing we don't have is a child. Last year I learned I can't conceive. He's been drinking a lot since then—I guess we both have—and we've been arguing."

Laurel didn't want to think about Long Island. "Couldn't you find a psychic out there?"

"I wanted to go somewhere I wouldn't be recognized."

"I told you my fee over the phone."

Janet reached inside her purse and took out some folded money. "It's all there. You can count it if you want."

Laurel closed her fingers around the money and felt Janet's vibrations strengthened through the twenty-dollar bills. She saw the woman counting out three hundred dollars and sticking the money into her purse several hours earlier. "That isn't necessary." She set the money on the table.

"I'll need a receipt."

"When we're done. You'd like me to tell you where your husband is?"

Janet offered a weak smile. "You read my mind."

Laurel rested the back of her hand against the table's surface between them. "Take my hand."

Janet slid one hand over Laurel's, and Laurel closed her other hand over it. A low electric current passed through Laurel, who tried to show no reaction. A barrage of images assaulted her at blinding speed, and conversations Janet had engaged in echoed in a cacophony. Years earlier, Laurel would have found it difficult to sort through the visual and audio data, but now she did so with ease while Janet gazed at her with curiosity. Light blossomed through pleasant moments and darkened over unhappy experiences.

Laurel pushed the light aside and traveled through the darkness. A ticking grandfather clock loomed before her, showing 1:00 a.m. Janet's Suburban occupied the driveway of her Long Island home. The clock struck 2:00 a.m. A man's face filled her vision as he called Janet crazy. In the garage a shovel struck the back of his head with skull-rattling force.

Flinching, Laurel looked down as she pulled her hands away from Janet's. "I can't help you."

"Why not?"

Laurel looked into Janet's eyes. "I just choose not to."

"That's it? What about my money?"

Laurel slid the money across the table and left it there. She did not want to reengage her connection with this woman.

"I came a long way to get here. I don't want my money back; I want my reading."

Laurel's jaw tightened. "And you want a receipt?"

"I want to know where my husband is."

"You already know where he is: four feet underground in woods a quarter of a mile from your house. You put him there after you buried a shovel in his skull."

The color drained from Janet's face.

"He was leaving you for another woman, so you killed him. You're a suspect in the case, but the police haven't found any evidence yet. You only came here today for the receipt for my services, so you can claim you're doing everything you can to find him."

Janet leapt to her feet, almost knocking the chair over. "You're a freak."

Laurel watched her scramble out of the sunken room. "The police will find Alex's body eventually. Things will go better for you if you turn yourself in now."

Janet twisted the doorknob, and when the door wouldn't budge she fumbled with the locks. Then she jerked the door open and fled into the bright sunlight.

As soon as the door closed Laurel turned the locks and reset the alarm. She didn't cry, which was something at least. Janet had only left her feeling nauseous. Laurel had no idea if the police would find Alex Rogers's body; she did not see into the future. She could only hope her bluff would shake Janet enough to drive her to confess her crime. Sadness for Alex crept over Laurel, who dared not call the police.

As she crossed the parlor an explosion caused her to jump. Spinning, she gazed at the curtained front window. Seconds passed, and then light flickered through the fabric, followed by a second explosion, this one closer to the building.

Thunder and lightning, she thought. But that was impossible. She had just seen sunshine outside, and the weatherman had predicted clear skies. She ran to the door and switched off the alarm, then reached for the top lock.

She froze, rigid with fear.

Then she reactivated the alarm and hurried across the parlor. She reached as far as the table when thunder exploded again, producing a boom that reverberated through the walls. Laurel lost her balance and fell to the floor. She wanted to curse herself. How had she been so clumsy?

The whole building shook. Grasping the table's edge, she climbed to her feet.

Thunder roared again, so loud it sounded as if it had originated inside the parlor. The lights blinked and went out.

Standing in the dark, Laurel glanced at the keypad on the far wall. Its power light had gone off as well. She knew the emergency generator would kick on in less than one minute.

Lightning flashed outside, briefly illuminating the parlor, and when the thunder followed Laurel knew she was no longer alone.

TWO

Jake Helman held his breath as murky green water pressed around him. No more than ten feet away, a splotched tentacle, as thick as a killer whale and as long as a city bus, stretched. The sight filled him with awe as much as fear. This was not a genetically engineered monstrosity born in a laboratory but a creature that had existed almost since the dawn of man. It had survived and evolved into a god. He wanted to flee, but there was nowhere to go: this was the giant creature's domain.

Other tentacles uncurled around Jake, creating multiple currents that tossed him. He spun in the water and swam the way he had come, but two tentacles arched before him in opposing directions, forming a giant *X*. He swam between them, but another tentacle shot past his head like a spring, and another ensnared his feet and tugged him toward the creature. He kicked with all his strength, but the creature held him like a grasshopper.

Another tentacle ensnared his sternum, its great suckers fastening onto his flesh. The tentacle raised him before all four of the creature's ancient eyes.

With his heart pounding like vodou drums, Jake inhaled water, his lungs filling with icy death.

Jake sat upright in a king-size bed, gasping for air, his heart still pounding. Moonlight unspooled through the slats of the blinds, and an air conditioner hummed. It took a moment for him to remember he was in a hotel in Mooresville, North Carolina.

Soft fingers slid up his naked right arm, caressing him. "Are you all right?" Maria Vasquez said.

He raised his left arm to wipe sweat from his forehead, only to remember he had lost his hand on Pavot Island. Setting the bandaged stump aside, he lay back down. "Yeah."

"Avademe again?"

He nodded, his head whispering against the pillow. Of all the horrors he had faced, Avademe clung to his subconscious, refusing to release its hold.

Maria curled up beside him, her nude body warming him.

Swallowing, Jake stared at the stucco ceiling. Despite his fatigue, he did not wish to fall asleep again. Sleeping meant waking in a cold sweat.

Jake slept after all and did not awaken until morning when Maria stroked him to full attention and they made love. They took separate showers, and Maria changed the dressing on his stump.

"I can't wait to get out of these clothes," he said.

"You just got into them."

"I want to wear some other clothes. My wardrobe's been pretty limited this last month and a half. I wasn't expecting such a long trip."

"It was worth it, wasn't it?"

Jake thought back on the war they had fought together on Pavot Island—the lives lost and the souls freed. He thought about Edgar. "God, yes."

Maria rubbed his beard. "When are you going to shave this off?"

"Never."

"You're starting to look like a hillbilly. That won't fly in New York."

"I'll trim it."

She gave him a sympathetic look. "You don't need to hide who you are."

"I just want to hide these scars."

A few months earlier, one of the humanoid children of Avademe had raked the left side of his face with its claw, leaving four deep trenches. The beard masked half of each scar, although the scars sliced through the facial hair as well.

"You're a good-looking man."

He grunted. "Once upon a time maybe."

"You're conceited and self-pitying at the same time." Maria placed one hand on his chest. "It's what's in here that matters."

He smiled. "It's a good thing."

Jake took their luggage out to her Toyota, which they had retrieved from New Orleans, where she had left it before flying to Miami and then Pavot Island. The July sun rose early, humidity dampening his shirt.

Crossing the parking lot, he saw Edgar standing at the curb near the hotel entrance, gazing at the sky. They had booked adjoining rooms, but he had kept to himself after dinner. Edgar appeared to have aged several years during his ordeal: gray hairs appeared in his mustache, and he had lost at least twenty pounds.

Joining his former partner, Jake followed his sight line to several birds soaring in the sky. Edgar watched them with such intensity that he didn't even notice Jake.

"How was your night?" Jake said.

Edgar turned to him as if awakening from a daydream. "I spent a lot of it online in the business center, catching up on news. You've been a busy man: taking down Prince Malachai's drug empire, almost getting killed in a spiritualist assembly upstate, and overthrowing Malvado's government on Pavot Island."

"It all sounds so simple when you say it."

"It was hard for me not to call Martin. I miss him so much."

"You'll see him soon enough."

"Tell me again about that cult."

"The Dreamers. They lured Martin through a science fiction website and promised to make his life complete. Maria and I broke him out."

"Then their founder, Benjamin Bradley, turned up dead in a Brooklyn shipyard, murdered with Mayor Madigan and some real heavy hitters."

Jake shrugged. "When you run with the wrong crowd . . ."

Edgar returned his gaze to the birds. "They look so free. Watching them, I can *feel* what it's like to fly."

"Your flying days are over, pal. You try that at home and you're likely to bust a wing."

Edgar continued to stare at the birds.

"Come on. Let's get Maria and have breakfast. I want to hit the road early. We've still got a lot of driving to do."

With Jake crippled and Edgar prone to staring out the car windows at birds, Maria did the driving. Edgar sat beside her and Jake rode in the back.

They stopped for lunch at a diner located at the northern tip of Virginia. Edgar picked at his food.

I could always get some birdseed, Jake thought. He had bought enough of it during the preceding nine months.

"I can't believe we're going home," Maria said. "I'm

almost afraid of what we'll find waiting for us in the real world."

"It will be good to be back," Jake said. He felt as though he had been gone for a year, not six weeks.

Edgar looked up from his food. "Do I still have an apartment?"

"You were AWOL for a long time. I covered your rent for as long as I could, but when your lease expired I moved your stuff into Joyce's basement."

"Let's hope she'll let me stay with it."

"I'm sure she will. She missed you as much as any of us did."

"She did more than that," Maria said. "She spent all her free time looking for you: putting up flyers, posting videos online, joining outreach groups. It's because she was so pre-occupied that Martin fell in with the Dreamers."

Edgar hesitated before answering. He seemed to process every bit of information that came his way, blinking like the raven he had been. "Thank you for helping Jake get him away from them."

Maria glanced at Jake. "We weren't exactly working to-gether at that point."

"You thought I was public enemy number one," Jake said.

"I thought you were hiding something and I was right."

"I'm still finding it difficult to accept you two as a cou-ple," Edgar said.

"You're the one who tried to fix us up," Jake said.

"We went on our one and only date with you," Maria said.

Edgar's face tightened even though Maria had not mentioned Dawn DuPre, his girlfriend at the time of his disappearance. The name had turned out to be an alias used by Katrina, the vodou priestess who brought the drug Black Magic and the zonbies it created to the United States. Katrina had also turned Edgar into a raven.

"I've lost almost a year of my life," Edgar said, "plus my apartment and probably my job."

"You've got Martin," Maria said. "We all have to move on after everything that's happened. We'll get through it."

Jake stayed quiet. The past year and a half had taken such an emotional and physical toll on him that he couldn't bring himself to tell Edgar everything was going to be all right.

On the road again, Jake took out his new phone and entered a number.

The phone rang twice before Carrie, Jake's office manager, answered, "Helman Investigations and Security."

"I'm coming home," Jake said. "I should be there tonight."

"Boss, that's great!"

"Do me a favor and take whatever's left in petty cash and get some groceries. I won't feel like shopping anytime soon."

"What petty cash? This office has expenses, you know."

"Then use the company card. Live it up." He had depleted his savings looking for Edgar in New Orleans and Miami, and Maria had depleted hers following him. "I also want you to call Larry Metivier and have him come to the office first thing in the morning. He'll try to get out of it, but don't let him."

"Understood. I can't wait to see you."

"Well, you'll get to see me soon because I don't have keys anymore, so I need you to stay and let me in whenever I arrive."

"The good news keeps coming."

Jake ended the call.

"Larry Metivier the mob doctor?" Maria said.

Jake looked at her. "Well, he is a doctor, but as far as I know he isn't in the mob."

"He treats criminals under the table. He patches them up so they don't have to go to the hospital and report their injuries."

"He treats cops, too," Jake said.

"Dirty cops."

"Do you two want to let me out here?" Edgar said.

They drove through Maryland and New Jersey, and when Manhattan came into view at last Jake drew in his breath. Despite everything that had happened to him there, it was where he belonged. As Maria drove through the Lincoln Tunnel the green fluorescent lights comforted him. The city withstood everything thrown at it; maybe that was why he loved it. It felt the same, but as he looked around he felt different.

Edgar stared at every person, car, and building they passed. "I feel like I was asleep and dreaming the entire time. There are no scarecrows walking around and no breadlines on the sidewalks."

"The economy's turned around," Jake said. *Now that the Order of Avademe is gone.* But the mention of Black Magic caused him to dig his fingernails into his palm.

Maria took the Fifty-ninth Street Bridge into Queens and headed toward Jackson Heights.

"You've got to be looking forward to seeing your mother and getting back to work," Jake said to her.

"My mom's in AC," Maria said. "Are you trying to get rid of me already?"

"No way."

They entered the neighborhood where Joyce and Martin lived: congested streets, jammed sidewalks, and bustling shops. Multiethnic music issued from the open windows of apartments and vehicles, and pedestrians passed each other in the heat.

Maria double-parked. "This is as close as we should get."

Edgar unbuckled his seat belt while Jake exited through the side door. Standing outside, breathing the aromas from a shish kebab cart, Jake opened the passenger door and Edgar got out. They looked at each other for a moment and then embraced.

Edgar pointed at Jake's stump. "Take care of that." Then he melded with the crowd.

When Jake slid into the passenger seat Maria stared in the direction where Edgar had disappeared. "He's loose," she said.

Edgar followed the sidewalk to Joyce's house, which had

seen better days. Even though none of the people passing him had any idea who he was, he felt self-conscious, as if he had done something wrong. He spotted a traffic light with a camera at the corner, then opened the gate and mounted the steps to the front door, which he knocked on. He had rehearsed this scene in his head countless times.

Locks turned and a chain lock clattered against wood. The door opened and Joyce stood there, looking as beautiful as Edgar had ever seen her. They had dated for two years and lived together for two more before splitting, and Martin had come along in the middle of those two periods.

Joyce's lips parted. She looked like she wanted to speak, but instead she threw her arms around Edgar and held him tight.

He had not expected such an emotional reaction from her, and he patted her back, which produced weeping spasms from her.

"Thank God you're all right," Joyce said. Then she let go of him and guided him inside, where she shouted upstairs, "Martin, come down here, please." She wiped the tears from her eyes. "Where have you been?"

"It's a short story," Edgar said. "I don't remember."

A tall boy Edgar almost failed to recognize appeared at the top of the stairs. Edgar's heart beat faster as the boy's eyes widened.

Then Martin ran down the stairs. "Dad!" He threw himself at Edgar, who caught the boy and held him. "Where have you been? What happened?"

Edgar's eyes watered. "I really don't know."

"Is Jake with you?"

Edgar faced both of them. "I'll say this only once: neither Jake nor Maria had anything to do with me coming home. That's our story and we're sticking to it. As far as you two are concerned, I just showed up here out of nowhere." He looked at Joyce. "I know you know I don't have anywhere to stay—"

"You're staying right here with us. We wouldn't have it any other way, right, Martin?"

Martin grinned through his tears. "Right."

Edgar hugged the boy again, then held one arm out for Joyce, who came to him.

Maria drove Jake to his office building on East Twenty-third Street, one block away from the Tower, headquarters to Tower International, and pulled over to the curb. Jake glanced at Laurel Doniger's storefront psychic parlor. When he turned to Maria, her expression seemed cool.

"Here we are, back in the real world where we started," she said. "It's like nothing ever happened."

"That isn't true," Jake said. "A lot's happened. A lot's changed."

"Pavot Island is a long way from here. Hell, even Miami's a long way from here. We both got caught up in that Caribbean heat."

"It feels pretty hot to me right here."

"You know what I mean. We're two very different people . . ."

"I think we're two of a kind."

"Maybe that's what I'm afraid of."

"You don't have to be afraid of me."

"I'm not. I'm afraid of this crazy world you live in."

"It's the same world you live in."

"You wanted to bring Edgar back, I wanted to bring Edgar back, and together we brought him back. Mission accomplished. Now we're home, and our lives have to go back to normal."

"Manhattan's hardly a haven from abnormal occurrences. Remember Avademe's warehouse in Brooklyn? The zonbies you cleaned up? Crazy shit doesn't only happen on Pavot Island."

"You killed Avademe. This city is never going to see an invasion of zonbies again because we cut off the supply of Magic. What's left?"

Jake swallowed at the mention of Black Magic. He was trying to keep his mind off the drug. *Then why did I bring up zonbies?* "What's any of that got to do with us?"

Maria looked at Jake. "I just don't see us working as a long-term item, that's all. You've got your life, I've got mine, and now that Edgar's back the two don't ever have to meet again."

Jake leaned over and kissed her. She responded, and when they separated he ignored everything she had said. "I'll call you tomorrow. Good luck at work."

Jake got out of the Toyota and took his new traveling bag from the trunk, and Maria drove east. He watched her join the traffic, then turned to Laurel's parlor. He wanted to tell her that Edgar was okay.

When he and Maria had flown to Pavot Island, Maria carried a romance novel written by Erika Long, who resembled Laurel, albeit with a different hair color and style. Maria told him Long had been missing for three years. He had conducted some cursory research online at Miriam Santiago's house in Miami, and he had questions for Laurel.

Finding the door locked, he checked the time on his phone: 6:37 p.m., earlier than he had anticipated arriving.

He rang the doorbell but no one answered. Whoever she really was, Laurel never left her apartment.

Something's wrong.

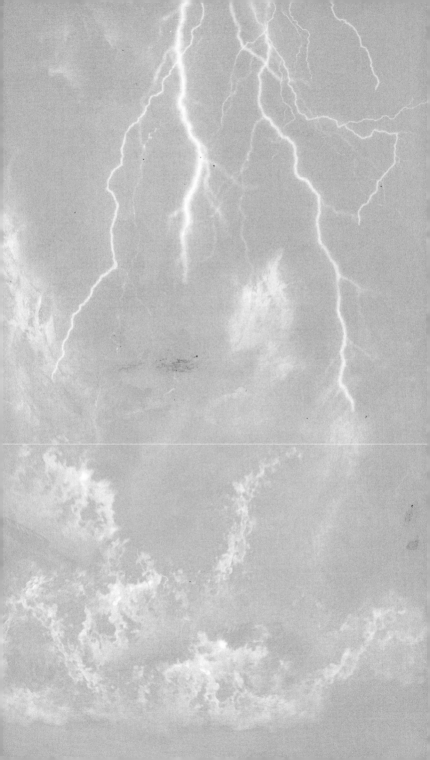

THREE

Jake pressed the button for his suite, and Carrie buzzed him inside. He had installed cameras in the building that permitted anyone in his office to see the lobby, stairwells, and corridors of the building. Passing the recessed mailboxes, he boarded the elevator. He hadn't been in one since his time on Pavot Island.

The door opened, and he walked the long corridor to his office at the end, the dying sunlight behind him casting his shadow over the sign on the door: Helman Investigations and Security.

The door opened and Carrie threw her arms around his waist. "Boss!"

Setting his hand on the goth dwarf's back, he gazed inside the suite. Ripper, Carrie's boyfriend, stood by her desk. The Korean man had dreadlocks, and a gold tooth glinted in the fluorescent light. Jake disliked Ripper, and he had forbidden Carrie to let him inside the office.

Carrie released her hold on Jake, took his right arm, and led him into the office. "Nice beard," she said, looking up. "I asked Ripper to come wait with me since I didn't know how late you'd be. You don't mind, do you?"

Jake closed the door. "No, I don't mind."

Ripper's eyes widened. "Yo, what happened to your hand?"

Carrie gazed at Jake's stump and screamed. "Oh, my God."

Jake held his arm close to his side. "I had an accident."

"Bullshit. Who did this to you?"

"It doesn't matter. He isn't around anymore."

She raised her eyebrows and opened her mouth wide. "*Okay . . .*"

"Let me see you in my office before you leave." Jake passed Ripper and the kitchen and entered his office. He set his bag down and glanced at the floor-to-ceiling cage that ran from one end of the wall to the other. The cage served as an uncomfortable reminder of Edgar's time in another form.

Carrie entered and closed the door. "I'm sorry about Ripper."

"Don't worry about it." He picked up a four-foot box on the sofa.

"That came by special messenger yesterday. I'm sorry I forgot to tell you."

The return label listed Jorge De Jesus in Miami, but Jorge did not live in Miami. He had fought side by side with Jake and Maria on Pavot Island, his homeland. Jake set the package down and crossed the room to the safe, which he kneeled before.

"Did you bring Edgar back?" Carrie said.

He hesitated. "No, I found a good home for him in New Orleans."

"Oh." She sounded disappointed.

He manipulated the three combination locks on the safe. "Were there any security issues while I was gone? Any irregularities with the alarms?"

"No, I would have told you if there had been. Wait. The power went off for about a minute during a storm. Why?"

Inside the safe, a laptop dedicated to Nicholas Tower's Afterlife project rested upon a small stack of file folders, with memory cards and flash drives scattered around it. Jake scooped out a ring with three keys on it, then shut the safe and spun each lock. "No reason. You can leave now. Lock up." He took the Glock .9mm he kept in the safe in case he was ever forced to open it by an intruder and tucked the weapon into the back of his khaki shorts beneath his shirt.

"I have some accounting issues to go over with you," Carrie said.

He had originally hired her to do his bookkeeping before he promoted her to office manager. "Tomorrow."

Edgar sat on the sofa in Joyce's living room. He had lived in the house when they were still together before the relationship had gone south. Martin sat beside him with a wide smile.

Joyce crouched before him and touched his cheeks. "You look different."

"I know. I got old." He took her hands away from his face but continued to hold them.

"You've lost weight, too."

I ate like a bird, Edgar thought.

"I don't understand how you can't remember what happened," Martin said.

Edgar looked at his son. "Maria and I were working the Machete Massacres case, which dovetailed with the Black Magic epidemic in the city. I was getting close to finding out who was behind it, and that's all I remember. I woke up in an alley today and made my way here."

"Black Magic's gone. So are the scarecrows. There was a big gang war when you disappeared."

"The big players were killed," Joyce said. "It was all over the news."

Prince Malachai and Papa Joe, Edgar thought.

"Do you think whoever was behind those killings abducted you?"

"It's possible." Katrina had imprisoned him in her heartless way.

"Are you in danger?"

"No." He could tell she wanted to press the issue, but she wouldn't for Martin's sake.

"Nine months of your life gone." Her voice warbled. "Have you called Maria or Jake? You have to go to your squad and tell them. The department had so many detectives looking for you."

"I haven't called anyone yet. I don't even have a phone. I just wanted to see you both. I'll deal with the fallout tomorrow. I want one relaxing night to get my thoughts together." He didn't like lying, but he had to protect Maria's job.

Joyce bowed her head against his thigh. "We've missed you so much."

Martin hugged him. "I really did, Dad."

Edgar stroked the back of Joyce's head with one hand and held Martin with his other arm. He had never needed them more.

Emerging from his building, Jake cast a furtive glance at the Tower, where he had once worked for Nicholas Tower, the genetics king. He had moved into this particular building to keep an eye on the structure.

Turning his back to it, he faced Laurel's parlor, then unlocked the four locks on the door. When he had moved into the building, he accepted an offer to supervise its security in exchange for a big rent discount. Although Laurel's space was part of the building, she had given him the keys herself.

He opened the door, and city light filled the dark space as the alarm box whined. Allowing the door to close behind him, he switched on the lights and punched his code into the keypad, silencing the alarm.

Jake descended two steps into the sunken parlor and

moved to the table in its center. Drawing the Glock from his shorts and hoping he wouldn't need to fire it with one hand, he moved into Laurel's living quarters in the back. "Laurel?"

He used the Glock's barrel to flip the switch for the ceiling light in the kitchen. With his heart beating faster he drew in a breath and moved to the windowless bedroom, where he flipped another light switch. He noted nothing out of place. Then he crossed the kitchen to the bathroom. It was also empty.

What the hell had happened to Laurel? In the time Jake had known her, she had never left this storefront home and business. He knew she was hiding from someone. But who would a romance novelist have to hide from, and why did Erika Long adopt the alias Laurel Doniger, psychic healer? He knew her powers were real because she had used them to heal his injuries when Katrina worked her own magic on his psyche and lower back.

The hair on the back of his neck stood on end, an instinct he had developed while still in NYPD. As he turned to leave the bathroom he glimpsed a flash of dark color moving behind him in the mirror.

Maria entered her one-bedroom Bronx apartment feeling exhausted from three and a half days' worth of driving. Setting her bags down, she looked through the mail her mother had stacked on her table. The apartment looked cleaner than she had left it.

All she wanted to do was take a shower and change, but she had an important call to make first. Sitting on the sofa, she kicked off her sandals and entered a number into her phone.

Bernie Reinhardt, her partner, answered midway through the third ring. "Please tell me you're in a New York state of mind. These guys Mauceri keeps partnering me with are driving me crazy."

"I just walked into my apartment."

"That's good since you're supposed to work tomorrow morning."

"You don't have to remind me. What's the latest on Alice and Shana?" Alice Morton was the surviving sister of Papa Joe and the mother of Prince Malachai, two powerful drug dealers killed during the Black Magic epidemic. Joe's wife had been killed, too, leaving Alice to care for his daughter, Shana. Maria had felt a bond with the seven-year-old girl and wanted to see her escape the family business.

"Big Alice has definitely taken over Papa Joe's franchise," Bernie said. "She's got half a dozen lieutenants and a powerful street operation. She and Shana moved into a condo on Thirty-fourth and Ninth."

"Is there any activity in their condo?" If Alice was using her condo for business around Shana, Maria could convince the court to take the little girl away. *And then what?*

"Negative. She's playing it smart."

"They all do until they get stupid."

"Speaking of which, how's your vacation partner?" Bernie disapproved of Jake.

"I don't want to talk about him right now."

"Good. Besides overthrowing a Caribbean country, did you have a nice leave?"

"Mission accomplished."

"I'm glad to hear that. What was your mission again?"

"Good night, Bernie."

"Good night, kid."

Ending the call, Maria selected some clothes from her bedroom, then went into the bathroom and ran the shower.

Jake aimed his Glock at the man who stood behind him.

"Whoa, whoa, whoa!" A short man with shock-white hair raised his hands.

Exhaling, Jake raised the Glock, aiming it at the ceiling, then at the floor. "You almost got yourself killed."

Jackie Krebbs lowered his hands. "Well, that would have been pretty damn fucked up."

Jake slid the Glock into his shorts.

"What the hell happened to your hand?"

"I lost it."

"I can see that."

"Where's Laurel?"

"You got me. She disappeared a week and a half ago."

"Do the cops know?"

Jackie shook his head. "Miss Doniger left me specific instructions not to notify the police if she disappeared."

"That happens to be illegal."

"I do what she tells me. According to her no one will even notice she's gone, except Eden, Inc. when her rent is late."

"If the alarm didn't go off she left on her own," Jake said.

"Maybe."

"You don't think so?"

"Nope."

"Why not?"

"Let's go to my office and talk."

Jake was not accustomed to Jackie calling his work space in the basement of the building his office. "Lead the way."

Edgar pushed his dinner plate aside. "That was great."

"I would have made something special if I'd known you were coming home," Joyce said.

Home, Edgar thought. "No, this was delicious. I don't remember the last time I had a home-cooked meal."

"Are you sure that's all you want? You hardly touched it."

"I've been having trouble digesting my food."

"You need a physical."

"I don't know if I have a job, let alone medical benefits."

"Everyone has medical coverage now. If you get caught up in some bureaucratic quagmire, I'll dip into my savings."

"I couldn't let you do that."

Joyce glanced at Martin, who watched them like a spectator at a sporting event. "You can't account for your whereabouts for nine months. You have no memory of why you disappeared, where you were, or how you got back. You need a physical and you probably need therapy."

Edgar raised one hand. "First things first: I need to go into work and learn the status of my job. I'll worry about the rest after that."

"Martin, finish your dinner and do your homework."

Martin pushed his plate aside like Edgar did. "I'm done, too."

"That's what you think."

"Dad didn't have to finish his."

"Listen to your mother, please," Edgar said.

With a sullen expression, Martin returned to his food.

"I don't need you to undermine my authority with him," Joyce said.

Edgar raised his eyebrows. "I didn't do that."

"Yes, you did."

"I was just backing you up."

"I don't need you to back me up. I've raised him alone or close to alone for most of his life. If I tell him to do something, I need him to listen to me."

"I'm sorry. I didn't realize I did anything wrong."

Giving him a stern look, Joyce rose. She picked up her plate and his and carried them into the kitchen.

Edgar glanced at Martin, who shrugged. He stood and followed Joyce into the kitchen, where she scraped the uneaten food into the garbage. He took the plates from her hands. "I'm sorry." Then he took the plates to the sink and ran water over them.

Joyce moved beside him and crossed her arms. "Our son joined a cult."

Edgar tried to look surprised.

"The Dreamers. They pose as a science fiction fan club for a company called Sky Cloud Dreams. Martin got sucked into their shtick over the Internet. Jake and Maria got him out of it, but I've had to keep my eye on him."

"I'll have to thank them."

"You have to speak to Martin."

"Okay, I will."

She narrowed her eyes. "You already know this, don't you?"

"How would I?"

"Jake went to Louisiana looking for you a month and a half ago. I don't know why he chose there, but he told Martin he was getting close. Then he went to Miami. During the same time, Maria took a leave of absence. Less than three weeks later, here you are."

"I told you, they had nothing to do with this."

"Why do I have the feeling they're both back now?"

Edgar said nothing and she returned to the dining room.

Jake followed Jackie through the basement to his office. As they passed the garbage compactor, he recalled battling zombies and disposing of their sawdust-filled cadavers in there.

Jackie opened the door to the windowless office and threw a heavy set of keys onto a wooden desk covered with papers. Jake sat opposite the desk.

"Miss Doniger told me this day might come, and if it did I should tell you what I know, which isn't much."

Jake had believed he was Laurel's sole confidant. "You've got my attention."

"Miss Laurel moved in here almost three years ago. Her tenancy was arranged through Eden, Inc. Eden had just bought the building and kept on Monde Building Management, the company I work for. I don't deal with Eden, and I've never met any of the suits there. Everything they need is communicated to my boss, Jeff Wilson."

Jake had met with Wilson when he agreed to supervise the security for the building. He never enjoyed meeting with corporate types, but he couldn't complain considering the dirt cheap rent he paid in exchange for his services.

"I worked here fifteen years before Eden took over. MBM was worried their contract wouldn't be renewed. Jeff told me he had the feeling Miss Doniger was an important tenant, and I laughed when he told me she was a psychic. Then he sent me to meet with her. As soon as she shook my hand she knew exactly how to talk to me."

Laurel was a psychic but only when she touched her subject or spent prolonged periods of time near him, which allowed her to read his vibrations. She had read Jake several times and knew him better than anyone else on earth.

"Miss Doniger told me she never intended to leave home and I would be in charge of arranging her grocery deliveries to my office, then I would bring them to her. Security was a big concern of hers, and she would only see clients who made appointments. She was nice and I liked her, and I had the feeling she was hiding from someone, that she needed protection. I did everything she asked. It wasn't an imposition. Two weeks later, I learned Eden was keeping MBM."

Jake had the feeling Jackie had fallen in love with Laurel. "Do you think Laurel had that kind of pull?"

"I don't know how, but yes." Jackie opened a drawer, took out a bottle of scotch, and held it for Jake to see.

Jake shook his head. In Miami, he had drank a beer with Maria and had felt fine, then Malvado's goons had forced him to ingest Black Magic on Pavot Island. Even though the Mambo Pharah had drained the addiction from his body, thinking of Black Magic made him antsy.

Jackie filled his glass and gulped the alcohol. Setting the glass down, he sighed. "Then you came along and you hired Carrie. I guess I didn't think about how weird the building had become because things were weirder outside with the scarecrows. Now they're gone and so is Miss Doniger."

"Tell me how she disappeared."

"The last time I saw her was one morning a week and a half ago when I checked in on her. Everything seemed fine. When I checked in on her the next morning she didn't answer the door, so I used my keys. She was gone but the alarm was on. Only three people had the code: her, you, and me. I checked with Central Alarm Station, and they told me the alarm hadn't been turned off during the night."

"She's a psychic, not a magician. She didn't vanish. She had to walk out that door. Maybe there's another exit neither one of us knows about."

Jackie smiled. "I know every square inch of this building."

"Do you know her by any other name?"

"No, just Miss Doniger."

"What about her background?"

Jackie took another gulp of scotch. "Nothing. But here's the thing: after you left, she told me that if she disappeared she didn't want me to notify anyone and she didn't want you looking for her. I thought it was a weird thing for her to say, and then she was gone. But she was clear that she wanted us both to forget all about her."

Rising, Jake made eye contact with the engineer. "She knows me better than that."

Jackie smiled. "I was hoping you'd say that."

FOUR

Jake stood at his office window and gazed at the Tower glowing in the night sky. Then he closed the blinds, shutting the sight out, and sat at his desk and booted his computer. He spent forty minutes going through his e-mails, which he had avoided checking on the road because he didn't want to take a chance on his location being traced.

After first meeting Laurel Doniger he had conducted an online search, but it had turned up no useful information about her. In fact, he had found no evidence that the psychic even existed. But now he had another name: Erika Long. He located the same biography online that he had seen in the back of the novel *Stormy Sands*.

New York Times and *USA Today* best-selling author Erika Long is the creator of over 20 romance novels, including the High Seas trilogy and the award-winning *Love Runs Deep*.

Erika is the winner of multiple literary awards, including eight from the Romance Writers of America, for which she served two terms as president, and two from *Romantic Times*. Erika grew up on Long Island, New York, graduated with honors from Vassar, and worked as an assistant editor at Random House before selling her first novel to Lilian Kane's Eternity Books. She enjoys sailing, skydiving, and horseback riding.

This gave Jake plenty to go on. As he expected, the author of twenty books generated a lot of interest online, with over one hundred pages of links turning up on Google. The most recent dealt with her disappearance. From the *New York Daily Post*:

Police are investigating the disappearance of romance novelist Erika Long, last seen leaving her Upper West Side condo on Saturday.

"We're terribly worried about her," said Harla Soto, president of Eternity Books. "It's not like her to just leave like this without telling anyone." According to Soto, Long is not currently seeing anyone and has never been married.

Long is the best-selling author of 20 romance novels, including six for Eternity Books under her real name and fourteen for Harlequin under the pseudonym Kelly Lion. She is best known for the award-winning *Stormy Sands* and the High Seas trilogy.

Jake had always suspected Laurel Doniger had been in hiding, and now he knew it.

He probed deeper into her background. Erika Long was now thirty, three years younger than Jake. She had grown up in Hicksville, Long Island, where her father operated a chain of movie theaters and her mother worked in the same office. She had graduated high school with honors, then Vassar. While in college, she sold several romance novels to Harlequin under the pseudonym Holly Rebell.

After a one-year stint at Random House, Erika sold her first novel under her real name to Eternity Books, which published her next five books, including the best-selling High Seas trilogy. The books were *New York Times* best sellers, and she followed them with *Stormy Sands*, her greatest success. All six books had been optioned by Hollywood, and the High Seas trilogy was currently being produced as a TV miniseries.

After Erika's disappearance, Harlequin reprinted her first fourteen titles under her real name. All her books remained in print, and if anything, the mystery of her disappearance had increased her sales.

Jake scrolled through the links and stopped at a newspaper headline. He clicked on the link.

Sidney Long, the owner of a Long Island movie theater chain, died on Saturday after being struck by lightning outside his Hicksville home. Long, 59, died one week after the disappearance of his daughter, romance novelist Erika Long. He is survived by his wife, Helena, 56.

Jake continued to dig.

A Long Island woman drowned on Saturday when waves capsized her boat in waters off Long Island Sound. Helena Long, 56, set sail alone with the purpose of spreading the ashes of her husband, Sidney, 59, who was killed by lightning one week earlier, at sea.

The Longs' daughter, romance novelist Erika Long, disappeared two weeks earlier and has not been heard from since.

Jake paused. Two parents killed one week apart, and within two weeks of Erika Long's disappearance. A tragic streak or something more nefarious?

Laurel was psychic; she had read his conscious and subconscious mind when they had sex. She possessed healing powers. She had absorbed the curse Katrina put on him. She had advised him with regards to Katrina's zonbies and the transmogrification curse that transformed Edgar into a raven, and she had sent him upstate to the spiritualist assembly Lily Dale in search of information on Avademe. She was as embroiled in the world of the supernatural as he was.

He skimmed through interviews with Erika, who came off as more genuine before her success with Eternity Books. The interviews she gave during her six years with that publisher seemed rehearsed and showed less personality.

Jake did a search on Harla Soto, the president of Eternity, which led him to the company's slick and sexy website and to another figure: Lilian Kane, the owner of the publishing house. Jake had never heard of Erika Long before seeing Maria's copy of *Stormy Sands*, but he *had* heard of Lilian

Kane. He knew her as the author of trashy romances and soap operas, and he had seen her name above the titles of cable TV movies and on perfume commercials that ran on network TV. As he recalled, his late wife, Sheryl, had kept several paperback editions of Kane's novels in their bedroom.

He clicked on Kane's image and it filled the screen: black hair, blue eyes, and a sensuous mouth. She fit the bill for a romance queen. She radiated glamour and could have passed for a movie star. The photo must have been old, because Kane appeared to be thirty-five, forty at the oldest, and Jake was sure she had been around for thirty years. Or maybe she had spent some of her millions on the best plastic surgeons.

He moved the cursor over the Upcoming Appearances tab and clicked on it. A full calendar of events for the rest of the year appeared, and Jake zeroed in on the one at the top:

Lilian Kane, the Queen of Romance, will sign copies of her latest novel, *Love Knows No Lust*, at the Eternity Books booth at World Book Expo in the Javits Center, Wednesday through Sunday from 1:00 to 4:00 p.m.

Jake double-checked his calendar: the convention had already been running for two days, not that it mattered to him.

Next, he located a quote from Kane on Erika's disappearance in the *New York Times*.

"Erika is a true talent," Ms. Kane said. "She knows how to write, she knows how to entertain, and she knows to give the public what it wants. Please note that I'm using present tense; that's because I refuse to believe she's dead. She's alive, and I vow to use Eternity's resources to find her."

Jake clicked the Back button and returned to the Eternity Books website, where he clicked on the About Us tab and stared at the company's address.

His eye widened and his heart beat faster. He leapt out of his chair and ran through his office.

In the corridor outside, he allowed his office door to close and he charged up the stairs to the fifth floor, then sprinted up a final stairway to the roof. He opened the door and staggered into the warm night air, compounded by heat radiating from the rooftop. Moving to the safety wall at the roof's edge, he gazed one block and a half west, where a twenty-two-story building blocked his view of the city behind it: 175 Fifth Avenue: the Flatiron Building, home to St. Martin's Press, Tor/Forge—and Eternity Books.

Staring at the famous triangular building, Jake drew in a deep breath. Why the hell had Laurel—Erika Long—chosen to hide just one block away from the headquarters of her publisher? He shifted his gaze to the Tower, glowing in the night.

For the same reason I chose an office so close to the Tower.

Edgar knocked on his son's door, then opened it.

Martin looked up from his bed, where he had spread schoolbooks before him.

"It's getting late," Edgar said. "I'm going to bed. Shouldn't you do the same?"

"I just want to finish this chapter."

Entering the room, Edgar saw no dirty laundry on the floor, a surprise. "What are you reading?"

Martin frowned. "*The Adventures of Huckleberry Finn.*"

"You don't like it?"

"It's hard to read. Nobody talks like this."

"They did back then."

"Then I'm glad I'm alive now."

Edgar moved over to a wall shelf and picked up a gleaming gold-plated athlete clutching a basketball. He turned the trophy so it reflected light. "Congratulations."

"Those games with you and Jake really helped."

Setting the trophy down, Edgar recognized the object next to it: a replica of the black falcon prop from *The Maltese Falcon* he had given Jake when Jake became a private eye. He picked up the heavy falcon and stared at its features. "What's this doing here?"

"Jake gave it to me. He told me to hang on to it and never give up faith that he'd find you."

Edgar put the falcon down. Jake had used the statue to brain a scarecrow, a former snitch who had stabbed his eye. Edgar had disposed of the body. "Then you can give it back to him."

"You'll probably see him before I will, right?"

Edgar took the falcon again.

"Tell him I said thanks."

Smart kid. He sat on the edge of the bed. "Your mother told me about the Dreamers."

Martin stared at him.

"I'm not going to tell you what you should have done. I'm only going to tell you what to do if they ever reach out to you again or if you're tempted to contact them: talk to me. Understand?"

Martin gave a slow nod.

"I love you."

"I love you, too."

Edgar took the boy into his arms and held him. The falcon felt heavy in his hand.

Sipping home-brewed coffee, Jake checked his security log. According to the data the electricity in the building went out at 10:45 a.m. due to a thunderstorm. The system restored forty-five seconds later when the emergency generator had come on.

Accessing his e-mail, he located the ticket confirmation for his flight to Pavot Island. It was the same day Laurel disappeared. In fact, he and Maria had been airborne when the power on East Twenty-third Street went out. Jake might have been looking at Erika Long's author photo in Maria's copy of *Stormy Sands* when Laurel's alarm had failed.

Jake focused on Lilian Kane, the owner of Eternity Books. She was fifty-nine, even older than Jake had thought. She had made her mark as the author of trashy soap operas and over time moved into the arena of sensational novels about empowered women. Studying the photos, headlines, and articles about her, Jake thought she portrayed herself as a commonsense feminist and sex symbol at the same time.

Lilian's name was so synonymous with her genre that she had turned it into a brand. Her high book sales attracted Hollywood, and the movies based on the books increased sales further. Ten years earlier she had turned down a small fortune to re-sign with her publisher and had instead founded Eternity Books. In the intervening decade she had become the wealthiest private owner of a publishing company in the world. During the same period Erika Kane disappeared, she made headlines for donating ninety million dollars to assorted charities.

Jake brought up images of her Eastchester mansion, thirty minutes outside Manhattan. Surrounded by floral gardens and statuary, it resembled a palace from the Roman Empire. The mansion had been featured in magazine spreads, and Lilian had conducted a televised tour for a syndicated entertainment news show. Jake studied satellite photos of the estate, nestled in a wooded area and overlooking a valley. He guessed a long building parallel to the driveway was a garage and a smaller square structure located near the property's gate was a security station.

The buzzer to his office sounded.

Unaccustomed to late night visitors, he clicked a button

on his intercom. He looked at the security monitors above his safe, opposite the front of his desk. One showed an overhead view of the vestibule, where Maria stood. He pressed the buzzer button, unlocking the downstairs door, and released it when she entered.

Jake bookmarked the web page and shut down his computer, then went to the safe, unlocked it, and returned the Glock to its resting place. There was no need for Maria to know he had already gotten himself into another situation.

He crossed the office and unlocked the front door as Maria exited the elevator, a duffel bag slung over one shoulder. Apparently she intended to spend the night.

"This is a surprise," Jake said.

"I have to keep you on your toes," she said as if she hadn't tried to blow him off just hours earlier.

Maria gave Jake a light kiss on the lips.

He closed and locked the door. "That's a big purse," he said.

"I carry a big toothbrush." She looked around the office. "I feel strange—antsy. Like part of me is still back in Miami or on Pavot Island. Do you know what I mean? It's like I can't readjust to a normal environment."

"I do know what you mean." But he felt antsy for a different reason, and he pushed Black Magic out of his mind again.

"You haven't changed your clothes yet. That means you haven't showered, either."

"Excellent police work."

She walked down the hall and entered his office. When Jake joined her, she stood staring at the giant cage he had installed for Edgar.

"I don't know how you do it. Everything here is a reminder of the trouble you get into."

He shrugged. "We are what life makes us."

"The wisdom of Jake Helman. Here's some wisdom from Maria Vasquez: get rid of that cage before someone thinks you're keeping people in there."

"I don't get many visitors."

"The first time I came here we were enemies."

"We were never enemies. You were just confused about your feelings for me." *Sort of like now.*

Maria snorted, then moved to the sofa and pointed at the long package on top of it. "What's this?"

"A thank-you card from Jorge."

"Aren't you going to open it?"

"I don't have to. I already know what's in it: an ATAC 3000, courtesy of our friends the freedom fighters. Libération de l'île Pavot." The ATAC 3000 was a high-tech machine gun developed by one of the military subsidiaries of the Order of Avademe. An entire shipment of the weapons had made its way into the hands of the Pavot Island criminal underground before providing the freedom fighters with an advantage over their oppressors.

Maria picked up the box and weighed it in her hands. "This has to be illegal ordinance. How do you think they got it here?"

"They could have smuggled it from the island, or they could have a supply somewhere in Florida waiting to be smuggled."

She set the box down on the sofa. "Don't you think you

should take it out of the box?"

"After everything we went through on Pavot, I need a break from guns."

She wandered over to the bookcase and examined his small library. "Books on tape?"

"For stakeouts."

"It's hard to believe there is such a thing in your life."

"They're few and far between."

Bending sideways, Maria examined the titles. "Legal thrillers? For shame, Jake."

"They're no worse than your romances."

"Touché." She stood before his safe. "Crown jewels?"

"I'm a private investigator. I have sensitive files."

"I bet you do." Maria gestured at his bag. "You haven't even unpacked yet?"

"Who unpacks on their first day home?"

"Your suitcase is going to smell like dirty laundry." She made a face, then set her bag down and took off her trench coat. She wore the same tight green dress she had worn to Sylvia's restaurant in Harlem when she and Jake had gone on an abbreviated double date with Edgar and Dawn Du Pre. The dress matched her eyes and emphasized her figure. "Remember this?"

"How could I forget?"

Maria walked to the office door and closed it. Then she turned and walked to him, swinging her hips. "I need your help, Mr. Helman," she said in a breathy voice. "You're the only man who can save me." She walked to the back door, opened it with exaggerated movements, stepped inside, and turned on the light.

When Jake joined her in the windowless storeroom that served as his bedroom, it occurred to him that he hadn't set foot in here since his return.

"Oh, my," Maria said. "I've seen bigger jail cells. Cleaner ones, too." Turning from his cot, she flipped on the light in his shower stall. "Now this is interesting."

"The toilet and sink are by the kitchen."

"That's convenient if you cook a lot."

"I don't."

"I didn't think so." She moved closer to him, which did not take much effort. "You're going to have to upgrade."

"I'm willing to consider it."

She draped her arms over his shoulders. "Are you going to show me how glad you are to see me?"

Jake slid his hand over her waist and kissed her.

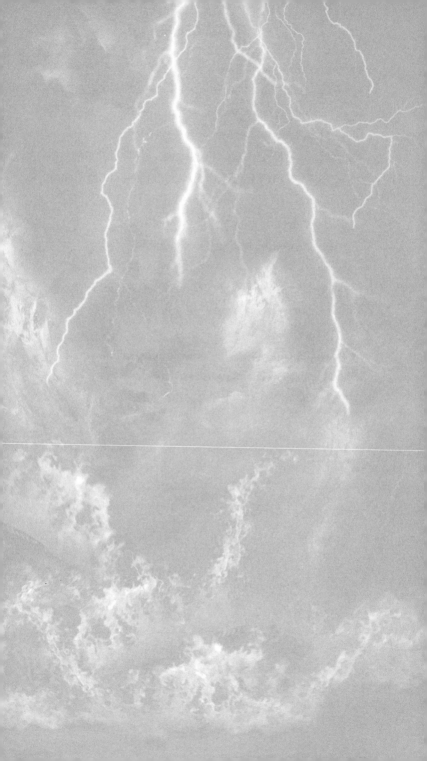

FIVE

Edgar lay awake on his bed in Joyce's basement, surrounded by his furnishings and belongings. Staring at the ceiling, he listened to every sound outside: music from passing cars, pedestrians chatting, birds lighting on tree branches. He finally fell asleep sometime after 2:00 a.m., only to awaken at 7:35 when he heard movement in the kitchen upstairs. He got dressed and joined Joyce, who wore a bathrobe. Bacon sizzled in one frying pan, scrambled eggs in another.

"What are you doing up so early?" Joyce said. "You don't have to go in at any special time."

"I couldn't sleep last night, and I wanted to see Martin off."

"You're too late. He just left."

"That must have been what woke me up."

"I reminded him not to say anything to anyone at school. Are you nervous about today?"

"Yeah, I guess. I'm sure someone is going to want to speak to you both after they're finished with me."

"I'm sure but we don't know anything." She fixed him with a knowing look. "That's why you're keeping us in the dark, right?"

He felt the ends of his mustache turning up. "I plead the fifth."

"You do that." Joyce served the food onto plates, then turned to him. "I missed you."

"I missed you, too."

"I couldn't sleep last night, either. I wanted to go down into the basement, but it didn't feel right with Martin in the house."

"I know what you mean." But he wasn't sure what to do about it, and uncertainty had never been part of his character.

"I'm so glad you're okay," Joyce said. Then she kissed him and he pulled her closer.

Maria climbed the stairs of Detective Bureau Manhattan on East Twenty-first Street. A uniformed PO passed her without saying anything. Familiar scents filled her nostrils: old wood, peeling paint, and musty rug mats. She had not felt at home in her own apartment, but she felt at home here.

She entered the squad room of the Special Homicide Task Force just before the start of her shift. Seeing Bernie at the coffee station, she nodded to him and went into the women's locker room. It didn't surprise her to see graffiti on her locker door: Welcome back, zombie lady. Ignoring the taunt, she spun the combination dial on her lock, which she removed, and opened the locker door. At least the inside had not been vandalized. She set her duffel bag in the locker, closed the door, and snapped the lock shut.

Then she returned to the squad room, where she gave Bernie's shoulder a gentle squeeze.

"Hallelujah," Bernie said.

"That's right. You can relax now. The cavalry has arrived." Maria knocked on Lieutenant Mauceri's glass door, and the short man looked up from his monitor and beckoned her forward. When Maria entered the office and closed the door Mauceri peered at her over bifocals. "New glasses, L.T.?"

"Yes, Vasquez, life has gone on while you were gone."

"I'm glad to hear it, sir, but I'm back and ready to get busy."

"Is your personal situation resolved?"

"Yes, sir." She had taken a leave of absence after using up her vacation time shadowing Jake in New Orleans.

"That's a nice tan you've got."

"I always tan in the summer. You should know that."

L.T. reached into his desk and took out Maria's holstered Glock, which he handed to her. "Reinhardt will be glad you're back."

She slipped the holster onto her belt. "Yes, sir, I'm sure he will."

Maria went to her desk and sat opposite Bernie. Once upon a time, Jake had sat in the same seat, and Edgar had called Bernie's desk his home away from home. Scanning her desk, she noticed several of her personal items were out of place, and she moved them back where they belonged.

"The world kept turning," Bernie said.

"So I hear. Are you working on anything?"

Bernie shook his head. "Just some paperwork for the ADA. Do you care to help me?"

She booted her computer. "I'd love to, but I've got six weeks' worth of memoranda to read."

Jake stood on the Third Avenue sidewalk, savoring a hot dog with the works for breakfast. How he had missed the Big Apple. A fountain gurgled foamy water outside the angular office building, and the sun shone in the clear blue sky. A man wearing a blue suit and an obvious toupee passed him.

"Wilson."

Jeff Wilson turned around and Jake walked over to him. Wilson's eyes showed recognition, but Jake doubted the man remembered his name.

"Jake Helman. Your Twenty-third Street building."

Wilson relaxed. "Right, our security consultant."

The innocent comment stung Jake. Wilson didn't know that Laurel had disappeared, but if Jake had been in the city instead of flying to Pavot Island, maybe she would be in her parlor now. But then Edgar would still have feathers.

"I didn't recognize you with that beard and . . ." He made a circular motion in front of his face. "What happened?"

Jake slipped his stump into his pocket. "It comes with the territory. I need to ask you a few questions about Eden, Inc."

"You couldn't call?"

"Nope."

"Okay, then, come on up to my office."

"Thanks but I'd rather speak out here."

"Why the cloak-and-dagger routine?"

Jake finished his hot dog. "I like to work in the street, that's all."

"I don't want to be late, so make it fast, will you?"

"Who's your contact at Eden?"

Wilson's expression changed into one of mild concern. "Why do you ask?"

"They're a client. I need to know."

"No, Monde Building Management is your client. I hired you."

"I like to know where my money comes from."

"You're not getting money. You're getting a huge discount on your office rental. Plus, we're looking the other way as far as your living arrangement goes."

"It's all of value, and I'd like to know who's making it possible."

Wilson moved closer. "Eden, Inc. is a dummy corporation. I know because I've checked. Eden, Inc. exists for tax purposes and licenses and permits, but it doesn't really exist;

there's no office. Every paper trail leads to another dummy corporation and another one after that. The pattern gets more and more complicated, like a spiderweb, with different strands leading back to the starting point. You want to spend two years going nowhere with it, be my guest."

"How does the corporation get in touch with you?"

"Usually by certified letter from different points around the world. Sometimes by e-mail."

"I want that e-mail address."

"Forget it. Eden pays us to run that building, and they pay us well. Every move they make is legit, but they're an international company with a reason to be secretive, and I've signed a confidentiality agreement."

"One more question. How did Laurel Doniger get her space? You obviously didn't do much of a background check on her because there's no real information on her available."

"Simple: Eden told me to rent that space to her. And you know what? I'm glad we did. She may be eccentric, but she's always on time with her rent and she's never any trouble."

Jake raised his eyebrows. "You've met her?"

"No. That's why I've got Jackie Krebbs there."

Jake watched Wilson enter the building.

Darryl Hughes sat on the concrete steps of an abandoned

church on Fifth Street near Avenue B. Three people worked in his crew: A-Minus, who ran the money; Ferret, who ran the crack; and Kiss Rock, who stood lookout. A-Minus and Ferret were black teenagers, and Kiss Rock was a white girl who looked Hispanic. Darryl was black, too, and at twenty, the oldest member of the crew, which was why he ran the spot.

He had worked for an independent crew last year until the Black Magic war between Papa Joe and Prince Malachai drove the independents and their product off the streets. Now Joe and Malachi were dead, the Magic was gone, and crack, coke, and heroin had made a strong return. The economy was booming for everyone, and Darryl liked not having to worry about scarecrows anymore; the world was a better place without those zombies.

Darryl and his crew had just started the day shift, and business was brisk. He watched a Buick glide to the curb, white boys in the front seat and rap music blasting over the speakers. Darryl looked at Kiss Rock, who nodded, and he in turn nodded to A-Minus, named after the best grade he ever scored in school, probably in the fourth grade.

A-Minus ran to the Buick and leaned close to the open window. Then he reached inside the car, grasped some money, and hid it in his fist. Turning from the car, he gave a hand signal to Ferret and sprinted to the mailbox on the side of the building and dropped the money into it. Ferret ran to the car, put some rock candy into it, and turned away. The Buick drove off.

In and out, just like every drive-thru in America. It was going to be a beautiful day.

Kevin Wilmont and his friend Sapo sat in the front seat of a black SUV watching Darryl's crew rake in the dollars.

"Amateurs," Sapo said.

"The crew boss might know what he's doing, but they're all lazy," Kevin said. "They think the cops are the only ones they need to worry about. That's just wrong thinking."

"Stupid little hoppers."

"Like you never hopped."

"Yeah, I hopped. I slung. And I was a stupid little hopper and a stupid little slinger."

"Good thing you wised up."

"You got that right."

"You ready to do this?"

"I was born ready, homes."

Kevin shifted the SUV into gear, turned into the street, and angled toward the drug spot. He lowered his window as he pulled over and made eye contact with Darryl, who scrutinized every potential buyer.

A-Minus ran to the vehicle and eyed its occupants. "What's up?"

"Not much. What's up with y'all?" Kevin shoved his Glock against A-Minus's skinny chest and squeezed the trigger twice.

A-Minus staggered back with a disbelieving look on his face.

As Kevin aimed past the youth at Darryl, who leapt to

his feet, Sapo got out of the SUV. Kevin fired three times, but only one round struck Darryl, and that was just a graze. Sapo fired twice over the hood, both shots hitting Darryl in the chest. Darryl dropped to the steps, grimacing as he clutched at his wounds. Ferret and Kiss Rock took off.

"Get back in the car," Kevin said.

But Sapo walked around the vehicle and over to the church steps, where Darryl gave him a pleading look. Sapo aimed the gun at Darryl's head and squeezed the trigger. The impact slammed Darryl's head against the steps. He stopped moving and blood flowed from his head.

Sapo returned to the SUV and got in. "Let's go."

Maria took her time reading her e-mail and departmental memos.

"You must be a lot more popular than me," Bernie said. "It would only take me half an hour to read six weeks' worth of e-mail."

"If you want to know how popular I am, go read the welcome back note on my locker."

"What's it say?"

"The usual."

"Luck of the draw. Any one of them could have been the primary on that case, and they'd be cooking in the same stew."

"Well, they didn't catch that case, did they? I did."

"Did I tell you how happy I am that you're back so I don't have to work with the assholes around here?"

Maria smiled. "Thanks. It's good to see you again, too."

"How about dinner tonight to celebrate your home-coming?"

"We're already having lunch. Isn't that enough?"

"Let me guess: you've got a hot date with a certain morally questionable private eye."

She offered him a polite smile. "I know quite a bit about Jake's morals, and they aren't the least bit questionable."

"If you say so. I didn't mean to offend you."

Her smile broadened.

"Oh, my God, you're in love with him, aren't you?"

Maria shrugged. "I don't exactly know what my feelings are for the man, but I'm not about to work them out with you."

Bernie remained expressionless. "You're doomed."

Maria felt herself blushing. "Maybe I am."

Bernie's mouth dropped open.

"What?"

He pointed past her. "I don't believe it."

One by one the detectives in the bull pen looked across the squad room, and Maria knew even before she turned around that Edgar had arrived. He stood in the double doorway, framed by lime-green paint, staring at his colleagues as if they were ghosts. It was strange to see him wearing a sports jacket and a tie again, and the clothes hung loose around his diminished body.

The telephones rang around the space as she rose from

her seat as if in a daze, playing her role to the hilt, and crossed the squad room. She felt the eyes of the other detectives on her as she moved toward Edgar and gave him a big hug.

"This is some bullshit," a male detective said behind her.

SIX

Entering his suite, Jake made eye contact with Carrie, who glanced at the corner waiting area. He followed her sight line to where Larry Metivier sat with a bored expression. Jake had forgotten he had told Carrie to bring Larry in. "Good morning."

Larry stood. "First you order me here, then you're late? Come on. I do have a career. Speaking of careers, that's a good new look for you. Are you a lumberjack now?"

Jake offered his hand. "Good to see you."

Larry shook it. "Same here. That's some sunburn, by the way."

"I went fishing in Florida."

"What did you catch?"

Jake entered his office, a silent indication for Larry to follow. He turned at his desk and remained standing. "Close the door."

Larry closed the door, and Jake took his stump out of his pocket and raised it.

Larry did a double take. "Holy shit. What the hell happened? That must have been some cookie jar."

"A bad guy chopped off my hand with a machete."

"I thought machetes were going out of style." He gestured at the stump. "May I?"

"That's why you're here."

Larry unhooked the clasp on the bandage, which he unwrapped. "When did this happen?"

"Two and a half weeks ago in another country."

Larry tossed the bandage onto the desk. "Whoever dressed it did a good job."

Jake said nothing. Maria had been dressing the wound since the revolution on Pavot Island.

Larry pressed on Jake's stump. "Does this hurt?"

"No."

"Then what do you want me to do?"

"I've got fresh bandages. You can start by rewrapping the stump."

Larry shrugged. "The cut point has healed, and there's no sign of infection. Bandaging the stump won't serve any purpose at this point."

"Great, then your trip here wasn't a waste of time. What are my options now?"

"You can get a prosthetic hand or a hook. There are some good bionic models on the market now, too. Maybe you need to find a new line of work while you can still walk."

"Are you so eager to lose a patient? I'm not likely to call

you if I just pass a stone."

"You're one of my few patients who isn't a crook. I wouldn't mind seeing you stick around in this world for a while."

"I'm touched." Of course, Larry, who took large portions of his fees in untaxed cash, was a criminal himself. "What do I have to do to get a prosthetic?"

"I'll have my office manager send you a list of facilities that will take care of you. You'll need to have your arm cast so the prosthetic will fit you like a glove. Are you right-handed?"

"I would be now anyway, right?"

"I'm trying to use my best bedside manner, and you're not making that easy."

"Get that list sent over, will you?"

"Sure thing. I know you didn't file a local police report if you were in another country, but you should notify your insurance company and apply for disability. You could be on easy street now."

"Not interested."

"Suit yourself." Larry stood there, waiting.

"Is something on your mind?"

"My fee."

"Send me a bill."

"This is a house call."

Jake raised his stump. "I'm not trying to cover this up, so it's a legit visit."

Frowning, Larry shook his head. "You see? That's what I don't like about you—the gray areas. Pick one side of the law and stick with it."

John "Ramses" Coker pulled his black Escalade into the Fifth Avenue parking garage and drove to the second level, where he backed into a space. He had the local news on, not rap music, and he wore a button-down shirt, no jewelry. So far, there was no reporting on Darryl Hughes's murder, which either meant that Kevin and Sapo had failed or the media had deemed the killings of minority drug dealers not newsworthy.

Lowering his window, he switched off the engine but allowed the news to continue. "Today the United Nations is voting on whether or not to readmit Pavot Island as a member now that Miriam Santiago has succeeded dictator Ernesto Malvado as the island nation's president. Malvado was killed by freedom fighters two weeks ago during Pavot's revolution."

Another black SUV rolled into the garage, and Ramses flashed his brights. The second vehicle went by him, its tinted windows preventing him from seeing its occupants. Ramses watched the SUV pull into a parking space. He didn't carry a gun, but he had one hidden inside the door if he needed it.

The doors of the SUV opened and Kevin got out. The assassin crossed the garage and stood before the Escalade.

"Did you do the deed?" Ramses said.

Kevin looked around the garage. "Yeah."

"What was the count?"

"Two down. Two got away. K isn't getting up."

"Good but letting two witnesses get gone isn't news to my ears."

"We didn't know either of them, and we don't think they knew us. It all went down fast, and they were out of there."

Ramses nodded at the SUV. "Is Sapo in your ride?"

"Yeah, he's listening to tunes."

Of course. "Drop that ugly little motherfucker off somewhere. The cops could be looking for a pair of hit men fitting your descriptions traveling in one vehicle."

"Yeah, I'll do that. You going to send a crew to that church?"

"Don't worry about what I'm going to do. Go lose Sapo."

Kevin returned to the SUV.

Ramses rubbed his chin. Alice wasn't going to be happy that the triggermen allowed two of Raheem's hoppers to escape, but hopefully she would be pleased enough with the rest of the outcome to let that oversight slide.

Maria looked out the window as Bernie drove the unmarked Cavalier down Third Avenue.

"That's quite a coincidence, you and Edgar showing up the same day like this."

"Maybe it was God's plan," Maria said in a flat voice.

"Was he on Pavot Island?"

She looked him in the eye. "God?"

"Edgar."

"No."

"But you know where he was, don't you?"

Maria said nothing.

"You go to a Caribbean island looking for information on your former partner, civil war breaks out, and two weeks later you both walk into the squad room on the same day."

"We didn't walk in together."

"No, you weren't that dumb. Where the hell was he? Is he still in trouble?"

"Don't ask me any questions that I can't answer."

"Let me put something into perspective for you: Edgar was a detective working a high-profile case when he disappeared. The department spent a lot of time, manpower, and money looking for him."

"You don't have to tell me. I was involved with a lot of those efforts, remember?"

"So was I. I was right there with you."

"So what's the problem?"

"You're involved with the investigation. You were his partner. Now that he's back, there will be a lot of questions. If you withhold any information, they're going to come after you hard."

"Some codes are more important than regulations."

"Whose code? Helman's?"

"No. *My* code. You don't have to worry about any of this coming back on you. I would never do anything to jam you up."

"Oh, kid, that isn't what this is about. I'm worried

about you and your career."

"I appreciate that, really."

Two parked squad cars and an ambulance flashed their strobes over a crime scene: an abandoned church on Fifth Street at Avenue B.

"You ready for this?" Bernie said.

"I saw more action on Pavot Island than I'll see in my entire NYPD career."

"Braggart."

They got out of the car and joined a PO who stood between one body on the sidewalk and another on the church steps. Bernie showed his shield and so did Maria. A crowd milled behind two strips of crime scene tape, watching with interest.

Maria scanned the observers: hard-faced teenagers and disapproving adults. A young boy rocked back and forth on his bike.

"What have we got?" Bernie said.

"Two male perps," the PO said. "This was their spot. No witnesses."

"Except for whoever got away," Maria said. "Two guys didn't run this spot alone."

"We usually saw four of them here at a time."

Bernie leaned over the corpse on the steps. "I know this guy. Darryl Hughes."

"Who did he work for?" Maria said. Before partnering with Maria in the Special Homicide Task Force, Bernie had worked in Gang Prevention.

"I don't know. He worked for a small fry a year and a

half ago. Then his crew got whacked in the Machete Massacres."

"This is Raheem Johnson's spot," the PO said.

"Not anymore." Bernie turned to Maria. "Alice Morton owns this corner now."

Edgar sat in the interview room for the Missing Persons Squad, located on the fifth floor of the same building as the Special Homicide Task Force. A table separated him from Detectives Dave Setlik and Jonathan Knopf. Both men were in their late thirties. He had seen Setlik around; Knopf was new to him.

"Mr. Hopkins," Setlik began.

"*Detective* Hopkins," Edgar said.

Setlik gestured at the air. "Where have you been all year?"

"I don't know."

"You don't remember?"

"That's right."

"Where were you yesterday?"

"I came to in Queens late in the afternoon."

"What part?"

"Astoria, maybe. It's hard to tell with all those triangles. Thirty-eighth Street, Thirty-eighth Road, Thirty-eighth Avenue . . . I think I was lying in an alley. I had someone else's clothes on and no wallet, money, or ID. Once I figured out where I was, I walked to the house where my son and his mother live in Jackson Heights."

"What's the last thing you remember?" Setlik said.

Edgar faced the mirror. He knew L.T. stood on the other side. "I remember working the Machete Massacres and other killings related to Black Magic. I remember playing basketball with my son."

"Anything else?"

"Not really."

"Who was behind the Black Magic?"

"In my opinion? Prince Malachai."

"Do you have any proof?"

"It wasn't Papa Joe. He was killed."

"So was Malachai. He turned up dead in the foundation of a construction site, along with a woman named Ramera Evans. Do you know who she was?"

"No."

"How about Dawn Du Pre?"

Edgar spoke in a slow cadence. "She was my girlfriend."

"Past tense?"

"I broke up with her."

"Tell us about that."

Here it comes. "I didn't trust her, so I went to her apartment and broke up with her."

"Why didn't you trust her?"

"She just didn't seem trustworthy. She was always excusing herself to make calls. She said they were for her PR clients, but I never saw any evidence that she even was a publicist."

"How did she take the news?"

"She got angry. I didn't care."

"What happened then?"

"I don't remember."

"Is that where your amnesia comes into play?"

"Yes."

The Missing Persons detectives looked at each other.

"Do you remember leaving Miss Du Pre's apartment?" Setlik said.

"No."

"Do you remember anything from the last year before you became aware of your surroundings yesterday?"

"No."

"Dawn Du Pre and Ramera Evans were the same person. Did you know that?"

"No."

"And Ramera Evans was Prince Malachai's squeeze. Did you know that?"

"No."

"We have evidence that you went into her apartment the last time you were seen but no evidence you ever left it," Knopf said. "How do you explain that?"

"I don't."

"Did you kill Malachai and Evans?"

"No."

"How do you know if you can't remember anything?"

"I know I didn't kill anyone. Why would I? I broke up with her, not the other way around."

"Some sixty corpses turned up all over the city the same week you disappeared. Those we were able to identify were dealers and addicts. Their bodies were packed with sawdust, their fingertips and toes were cut off, and their teeth were pulled out to make identifying them hard, but we used DNA testing. In every single case, the vic was shot in the head with a high-powered rifle."

"I've never owned a rifle."

"Let's review what we have. You were on the Black Magic Task Force and believed Prince Malachai was behind the Black Magic epidemic. You were dating Dawn Du Pre who was really Ramera Evans, who was banging Malachai, the target of your investigation. You say you broke up with Du Pre, and then you disappeared without a trace.

"While you were MIA, someone put down sixty scarecrows, many of them dealers in Malachai's operation. Malachai and Du Pre turned up dead, and you stay missing for almost a year. Then you turn up out of the blue, and you don't remember anything that happened after you broke up with Du Pre. You don't remember anything from the last nine months of your life."

"It's pretty crazy," Edgar said.

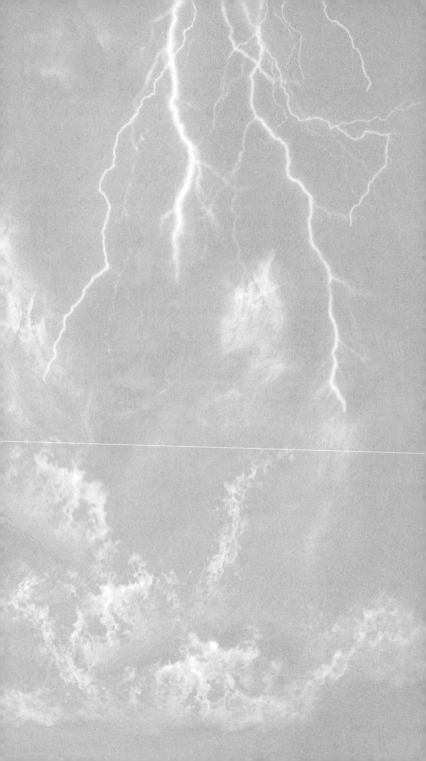

SEVEN

Jake exited his office and stood before Carrie. "I have a task for you."

Carrie looked up from her desk. "Good. I need a break from these numbers."

"Dig up everything you can on Eden, Inc."

She gave him a disbelieving look. "You mean our landlord who gives you such a sweet deal? Did you come back just to make us homeless?"

"We're not going to be put out on the curb. I just need some deep background."

"Uh-huh."

"I'll be back in a few hours." Jake left the suite and took the stairs down to the lobby, where he opened the front doors and breathed in warm air. Sunlight caused him to squint at the New York Edition Hotel, formerly the Met Life Tower, looming above him.

With his hands in the pockets of his slacks, he walked west, one pedestrian of many. As he passed Madison Avenue he didn't even glance at the Tower on his right; instead he studied the Flatiron Building straight ahead. The building had always been a curiosity for him because of its unique architecture, and it had become part of the landscape he saw daily since opening his business in the neighborhood. Unlike the Tower, the Flatiron's chief attraction, aside from its design, was its old New York feeling.

Jake bought a pretzel from a street vendor and crossed Broadway, which sliced the city grid at a forty-five-degree angle, and entered the building's shadow. An aluminum skeleton supported a construction awning along the building's eastern face, and construction workers jackhammered the sidewalk. He wandered over to the northern corner of the triangular island the landmark building stood upon. Chewing on the pretzel, he watched the busy traffic at the intersection for several seconds and then turned to face the building's entrance. Smokers lingered outside, and other people passed through the glass entrance in both directions.

The hair on the back of his neck did not stand on end. In fact, he experienced no physical reaction at all to the building. His gut told him Laurel was not inside. Finishing the pretzel, he crossed Fifth Avenue and continued west.

Maria and Bernie sat in their Cavalier, which Maria had directed him to park on Thirty-fourth Street at the corner of Ninth Avenue. Looking past him, she stared at the awning extending from the entrance to 356 West Thirty-fourth Street. Sloane House had once been the largest residential YMCA in the country before being converted into condos. The uniformed doorman stood at attention.

"Doorman service," she said with a disgusted tone.

"What are we doing here?" Bernie said.

"Alice Morton ordered those hoppers killed and you know it."

Bernie pushed his glasses up his nose. "I also know there's no evidence to prove it; there were no witnesses. So let's head to the medical examiner's office, get a statement, and go back to the squad room and fill out our preliminary report."

The doorman opened the door, and two people exited: a black woman and a little girl.

Maria's stomach clenched. "That's her. That's Shana."

Papa Joe's daughter.

Bernie sighed. "At least she's got a nanny."

The nanny and Shana crossed the street, passing right before the unmarked police car.

Maria stared straight ahead as Shana passed her so as not to be seen. Then she looked into the side mirror as the nanny hailed a taxi behind them. "Follow them."

Bernie scrunched up his face. "I know you care about the kid, but how does this fit into our investigation?"

"Just do it."

Bernie started the engine just as the taxi passed them, then pulled into traffic and made a U-turn. "This is highly irregular."

"We're not going to get into trouble."

"I'm not convinced." He followed them to Tenth Avenue and made a left turn.

Maria focused on the back of the yellow taxi.

Three minutes and four blocks later, the taxi pulled over and discharged its passengers. As soon as the taxi sped away, Bernie took its spot. The nanny led Shana into Chelsea Park.

"I think the nanny's kosher," Bernie said. "I don't see her peddling rock in that playground."

Maria got out. "Park the car and find me." She closed the door before Bernie could protest. Crossing the street, she circled the fence protecting the park.

The nanny sat on a bench, and Shana ran over to the playground and joined other children in a sandbox.

Bernie walked up to Maria. "Cops are supposed to scare away people who do what you're doing."

"You see where the nanny's sitting? When I get over to the other side of the fence, you distract her. All I need is thirty seconds."

"You're pushing the boundaries of our partnership."

Ignoring him, Maria followed the fence to the other side, which afforded her a closer view of Shana. The nanny watched the children play, looking bored. Bernie stood twenty feet behind her, his lack of enthusiasm radiating from him. Maria curled her fingers around the chain-link fence and nodded.

Bernie circled the bench, then pointed beneath it and spoke to the nanny. He made a show of crouching and reaching beneath it.

"Shana!"

Shana looked around while Bernie stood, blocking the nanny's view of her charge.

"Over here!"

Shana looked straight at Maria. Behind her, Bernie held paper money before the nanny.

"Come here quick."

Shana glanced over her shoulder at the nanny.

"Please come here."

Biting her lip, Shana ran over to the fence.

Maria crouched so the girl blocked her from the nanny's view. "Do you remember me?"

"Maria."

"That's right. Are you okay?"

Shana nodded.

"I know you had a birthday a few weeks ago. I'm sorry I couldn't call you."

"That's okay."

Maria stuck a card through the fence.

Shana took it.

"That's my business card. It's got my number on it. Keep it safe. Don't let anyone see it. But if you ever need anything at all, call me, okay?"

Shana nodded again.

"Now put it in your pocket or your sock, and don't forget to hide it someplace safe, like far under your mattress."

"Shana!"

Shana looked over her shoulder at the nanny, who stood beside Bernie. She ran to her without saying good-bye to Maria.

On the fifth floor of One Police Plaza, located on Park Row, Edgar opened a door labeled Major Crimes Unit.

Inside the office, a fiftyish woman looked up from her desk. "Can I help you?"

"Detective Hopkins to see Lieutenant Geoghegan."

"Just a moment." The woman picked up a phone and pressed a button. "Detective Hopkins is here." She listened for a moment, then hung up. "He says to have a seat. He'll be right with you."

"Thanks." Edgar sat in a wooden armchair near a water cooler.

A few minutes later, Ted Geoghegan, a lieutenant with MCU, exited his office wearing a short-sleeved white shirt with a too wide striped tie. He was short, and his military crew cut gave off a conservative 1950s vibe. "Come on, Hopkins."

Edgar followed the lieutenant down a side hall where Geoghegan stopped and opened a door. Edgar entered the interview room, and Geoghegan closed the door and sat on the far end of a metal table. Edgar sat on the remaining chair.

"Can I get you anything?" Geoghegan said. "Water?"

"No, thanks."

"This interview's being recorded."

"I know the drill. I've already been through it with Missing Persons and IAB today, and I've conducted an interview or two in my time."

Geoghegan announced the date for the benefit of the recording device. "Subject is Hopkins, Edgar, detective second grade with the Special Homicide Task Force based in Detective Bureau Manhattan Midtown South. Conducting the interview is Geoghegan, Theodore, lieutenant, MCU." He glared at Edgar. "Where have you been the last nine months?"

"I couldn't tell you."

"I've read the transcript of your interview with Missing Persons this morning. Are you maintaining you have no memory of the last nine months?"

"That's right."

Geoghegan smiled. "You used to be partners with Jake Helman."

"That's right."

"And yet you interviewed him when he was a possible suspect in the murder of the Cipher. Not exactly by the book, was it?"

Edgar had done more than sit in on Jake's interview; he had destroyed video security footage that showed Jake entering Marc Gorman's apartment building, then departing after the serial killer's execution. "He wasn't my partner then, he'd already resigned from the force, and I didn't conduct the interview. My partner Maria Vasquez did."

"It was irregular as shit."

"Talk to Lieutenant Mauceri about that. I was the primary on the Cipher case, and Vasquez caught the DOA call before we knew who Gorman was. She was new to the unit. I just sat in on the interview to make sure she covered every base."

Geoghegan's smile tightened. "Helman resigned rather than take a simple drug test, and you disappeared while running down a wannabe drug lord. Are you sure Helman didn't drag you down with him?"

"My disappearance had nothing to do with Jake."

"How do you know?"

"Because I know Jake."

"Did he have anything to do with your reappearance?"

"No."

"How do you know that?"

"Because I know Jake."

"You must have a theory about what happened to you."

"I was working on two big cases: Black Magic and the Machete Massacres. When they converged, I got close to figuring out who was behind them."

"So whoever was behind Magic and those massacres had you kidnapped?"

"I'm not about to guess, but that's a pretty solid theory."

"Except we know Prince Malachai was the big mastermind behind those operations, and he got killed along with your girlfriend."

"Maybe she was in on it, too. We both know that Malachai was just one link on a long chain."

"Vasquez was your partner when you were conducting these investigations."

"I hope she still is."

Geoghegan gave him a long prosecutorial look. "That's up in the air. A lot of questions need to be answered."

"We'll see what the union says about that."

The older man chuckled. "Yeah? I can't wait to hear it. Let's get back to Vasquez. I've read her reports at the time of your disappearance. She never mentioned anything about you closing in on the head of the Black Magic ring."

"That was almost a year ago. I can't remember anything since then, and I can't remember every discussion me and Vasquez had at the time."

"The department has your notes. They're notably thin."

"I don't waste a whole lot of time writing down speculation."

"Do you expect me to believe you had no idea your girlfriend was also doing Malachai? That the three of you weren't working together?"

Shit, Edgar thought. "I figured it out when I confronted her. That's why I broke up with her."

Geoghegan stood and circled his desk. "An NYPD detective investigating drug-related murders disappears for almost a year and then mysteriously shows up with no memory of what happened to him or where he was. This isn't a Missing Persons case. It isn't an Internal Affairs case. It's a Major Crime Unit case, and I'm making it mine."

Edgar rose. He stood a full foot taller than Geoghegan.

"Good, because I want to know what happened to me more than anyone else."

"You're on indefinite suspension pending a full investigation. I want you to get a physical today, and I mean a complete workup, including genetic drug testing and psychological evaluation. If you're hiding something we'll find it."

EIGHT

Walking along Eleventh Avenue, Jake observed police officers directing traffic onto Thirty-third Street because Thirty-fourth had been closed off.

As he drew closer to the Javits Center, the voices of young women standing at the corner and along a raised walkway grew louder. "Thank you for coming to World Book Expo. If you already have a ticket or a wristband, go to the first two sets of doors. If you do not have a ticket or a wristband, walk to the far doors. Remember to keep reading."

Jake merged into a group moving at a snail's pace and realized he had joined a line to get in. Over a hundred people stood ahead of him. He caught a mixture of aromas: hot dogs, shish kebabs, and sweat.

"Thank you for coming to World Book Expo . . ."

Inside the convention center, Jake gazed at enormous banners draped from the ceiling, some of them thirty feet high, trumpeting books and publishers. One banner dwarfed the others; it was forty-feet high, and a giant Lilian Kane stared down at him, smiling with one hand on her hip and her latest book in the other: *Love Knows No Lust.*

Standing in one of two dozen lines to buy tickets, he found himself admiring Kane's figure and wondered how much photo manipulating the fifty-nine-year-old's image had required for the display. The caption on the banner read, *Lilian Kane presents her most passionate novel yet. Exclusively from Eternity Books.*

Twenty minutes later Jake purchased a day pass for sixty dollars.

"That's more than I expected," he said to the ticket agent, a young woman with long dark hair and large frame glasses.

"You'll walk out of here with that much in free books," she said.

It took him five minutes to locate the entrance to the show, and then he entered a different world. Five thousand publishers and book vendors had set up shop—some with simple booths but many with elaborate setups involving portable living rooms, miniature libraries, and re-creations of settings from books. Sales reps greeted readers and industry professionals and handed out business cards, catalogs, and bookmarks. Patrons stood in line to purchase books from publishers and have them signed by authors.

Jake saw books of every type on display, and he couldn't believe the number of zombie novels with similar titles and covers. He felt certain that none of them referenced Black Magic, vodou, or the demon Kalfu. Reps smiled at him to get his attention; at first he smiled back and waved no thanks, but as his first hour in the center drew to a close he learned to ignore them.

He spent another half hour wandering the aisles. A new hardcover caused him to chuckle: *Where's Old Nick? The Life and Times of Nicholas Tower*. Jake picked up a copy and leafed through it. He had seen some of the photos before, but many were new to him: Nicholas Tower at construction sites and ribbon-cutting ceremonies decades before he went into self-imposed exile in the Tower. Near the end of the book, a two-page spread showed a collage of Anti-Cloning Creationist League members protesting outside the Tower.

"That's expected to be one of our best sellers this year," an attractive saleswoman with bright teeth said.

"Old Nick keeps making money," Jake said, returning the book to its display.

He rejoined the mass of people walking the expo and saw a horizontal banner promoting Lilian Kane, Eternity Books, and *Love Knows No Lust*. At last he reached the wall at the far end of the mammoth convention center, where dozens of authors sat side by side on raised desks, signing books for anxious readers. He passed the lines at a slow speed, glancing at each author, searching for the Queen of Romance.

Then Jake spotted a trailer with *Lilian Kane* and *Eternity Books* painted in giant cursive letters on the side, separated by Cupid's arrow. As he circled the trailer, which was protected by security guards and red velvet ropes, he saw the setup on the other side: two booths for Eternity Books and two for Lilian Kane. Two female sales reps manned each pair of booths, and at least two hundred women stood in a line extending from one. He gathered that Lilian Kane signed books at her booth, blocked from his view by her adoring fans. Feeling a little self-conscious, he joined the line.

A heavyset woman in her early twenties, not unattractive, turned to him. "You don't look like the average Lilian Kane fan."

Did she hope to find love at a book signing? He smiled. "I'm here for my girlfriend."

Gazing at his face, she offered a skeptical expression, as if to say, *Who the hell would date you?* "Lucky her." Sarcasm dripped from her voice.

Jake decided to do some man-on-the-street research while waiting to meet the main attraction. "Have you read many of her books?"

"I've read all of them. She's the best."

Jake hid his doubt. "Have you also read Erika Long?"

"Yes. She was good before she wrote for Eternity, but under Lilian she became great."

"My girlfriend read *Stormy Sands.*"

"I liked the High Seas trilogy better."

"What do you think happened to her?"

"I think she was kidnapped. Someone that famous doesn't just disappear for three years. *Somebody* would have seen her."

He agreed with her. "How long have you been reading Lilian?"

"Since I was a teenager. My mother left her books lying around, and I picked one up out of curiosity. It caught my attention because of all the sex, but I read them now for the romance."

"I've seen her name above movie titles."

"You're going back twenty years. Now they become TV movies and miniseries. They're all okay, but they tone down the sex too much." She winked at him.

I thought you read the books for the romance, Jake thought. "*Love Knows No Lust* sounds pretty racy."

"It's supposed to be her hottest one yet."

I can't wait. "My girlfriend reads e-books. I hope she appreciates this."

"How could she not? This is a first edition hardcover signed by Lilian."

The line moved and Jake looked behind him. Another hundred women had joined them, most of them in their twenties.

"I'm so nervous," the woman said. "I can't believe I'm actually meeting her. This is my third time trying; the other two times were at bookstores, and they cut the line off before my turn. I'm so glad she's here for the whole expo."

They stood close enough to the booth now for Jake to observe the activity behind it. One woman at the table on the left sold copies of the book, and another stood beside Lilian Kane at the table on the right. The author had shoulder-length dark hair, and her bangs looked razor sharp. She looked down at the book she was signing. As soon as he saw her, Jake felt perspiration forming on his forehead.

The woman beside him moved to the table and purchased her book, then approached Lilian Kane.

Jake stepped up to the booth.

"Hi," the sales rep said, beaming at Jake. She made Jake

feel as if she knew him.

"Hi, there." An uneasy feeling grew in his stomach. "I'm getting a copy for my girlfriend."

"What's her name?"

"Maria."

The woman wrote *Maria* on a Post-it note, which she affixed to the book cover. "Here's a free sample of Lilian's new perfume, Real Eternity. That will be sixty dollars."

Jake raised his eyebrows.

"Thirty for the book and thirty for the autograph. That's a bargain."

"Oh." Jake took out his wallet, set it on the table, opened it, and managed to slide three twenty-dollar bills out, which he handed to the saleswoman. Tucking the rest of the contents back into his wallet proved a little more challenging. He returned the wallet to his back pocket, slid the sample perfume bottle into his side pocket, and picked up the book.

"Have a nice day," the saleswoman said.

"You, too." He took his place at the front of the line.

The woman he had stood beside fawned over Lilian Kane. Then the woman turned away with a big smile, clutching her copy of *Love Knows No Lust* to her ample bosom. "Oh, my God, oh, my God . . ."

Jake stepped before Lilian Kane, and she looked up at him, a slight smile on her lips.

"Hello." She extended one hand for his copy of her book.

Looking into her eyes, Jake froze. His heart skipped a beat and then sped up. He felt the color draining from his face as his limbs turned numb.

Everything about Lilian's features resembled a great work of art, an exaggerated example of impossible perfection: her oval face was as smooth as glass, like a porcelain statue, her lips were full and inviting, and her cheekbones were high. But her eyes unsettled him the most. The whites lacked veins, and her irises were as blue and clear as the Caribbean waters off Pavot Island, her pupils like black spheres suspended in that water. He saw in her eyes the same thing he had seen in the saleswoman: recognition.

Despite the flawless configuration of her body, the thought that she was not human slammed into him.

"It's easier for me to sign a book when I actually have it in front of me," Lilian said. Her voice had a strange echo, as if she were speaking in a cave.

"Oh, I'm sorry." Jake handed her the book. The temperature grew hotter and his breaths came faster. What was happening to him?

Lilian glanced at the Post-it and smiled. "You don't look like a Maria."

"It's for my girlfriend." Nausea crawled up from his stomach.

Lilian opened the book and inscribed its title page. "It was brave of you to come here."

Her words were in perfect synchronization, and Jake heard them without the echo at the same time he heard them with the echo. He found it hard to concentrate as he battled the feeling of sickness spreading through him. "Oh?"

Looking up from the book, Lilian gestured at the

women behind him. "I mean, it was brave to stand in line with all these women. I don't get many men at these events. They're too embarrassed to be seen waiting for a romance novel." She held out her hand. "I'm happy to make your acquaintance, Mr.—?"

He realized that while he heard her words properly with his ears, his mind heard them a split second before she spoke them, creating the overlapping effect.

"Helman." *But you already know that, don't you?* "I'd better not shake your hand. I have a cold." Jake knew better than to make physical contact with people with supernatural powers. Katrina had put a curse on him by using the oil from his fingertips on a business card he had given her. Laurel knew his most intimate secrets because she had touched him numerous times. And Miriam Santiago controlled his car from a distance and sent him on a high-speed ride because he had given her a card as well.

"You sound fine to me," Lilian said. "And I use hand sanitizer after every reader leaves the booth. Come on. I won't bite."

Something about him amused her; she was playing a game.

"I'd better not. Thanks all the same."

She pouted. "I'm sorry if I frightened you, Jake. That wasn't my intention."

He swallowed. "How do you know my name is Jake?"

"Isn't that what you told me?"

"No."

Her smile returned as she held the book out to him.

"Oops."

Jake tried to take the book from her, but she held on to it.

"I think we'll see each other again."

She released the book, which grew heavy in his hands. All he wanted to do was get the hell out of the convention center.

"Maria's a lucky woman. I could just eat you up."

Jake's stomach twisted and he grimaced. He took a step backwards and stumbled into the crowd of waiting women. His limbs seemed to melt and he collapsed. Someone cried out, not with very much urgency, as he struck the floor.

Lilian chuckled, but when he glanced at her, her lips weren't moving. She stood, a look of mock concern on her face.

Darkness swirled around him until he embraced it like an old lover.

NINE

The sickness spread from Jake's stomach to his throat, and his head felt like it was swinging upside down on one end of a pendulum. Voices murmured above him, and the floor spun in a circle, like a carnival ride. His eye was open, but the figures bending over him appeared blurry. He blinked several times but couldn't shake the sensation of movement.

Lights so high above . . .

Jake couldn't remember where he was or how he had gotten there. He remembered going into the bathroom of Kearny's Tavern to do some blow, then getting into a shoot-out with two thugs who had tried to rob Kearny, an ex-cop.

Dread and Baldy . . . I killed them both.

His heart had gone into overdrive as he heard the sirens of approaching police cars, and then he had taken a nosedive onto the floor. For some reason this comforted him now.

I didn't resign from the force and I didn't go to work for old Nick at the Tower and the Cipher didn't kill Sheryl and Cain and Abel are just two characters in the Bible and no woman named Katrina ever turned Edgar into a raven and Avademe never existed and I didn't save Maria from Kalfu on Pavot Island . . .

Maria.

The shapes looking down at him and the high ceiling of the convention center came into focus. He raised his left hand to his face and gazed at his stump, and the scenario in which the past year and a half had never occurred evaporated from his mind.

Lilian Kane . . .

Using his right arm for support, Jake managed to sit up. His head felt like a sponge that had absorbed too much dirty water.

"Are you all right?" The voice was so muddled that Jake couldn't tell if a man or a woman had uttered the words.

He nodded or at least he thought he did.

Gentle hands clasped his arms and helped him stand. The crowd swelled, and concerned-looking people pressed around him. He could no longer see Lilian.

"Sir, are you all right?" A woman with long auburn hair stood at his side. He recognized her from the Eternity Books booth.

"Yes, I think so." He looked into her eyes, which appeared normal. Human.

She held an unopened bottle of Evian. "Would you like some water?"

He did want water but he waved his hand. "No, thanks."

"Are you sure? It might make you feel better."

"I'll be fine. I just need some air." The last thing he needed was to drink some concoction that would turn him into a frog or a puddle of bubbling ooze. "Excuse me."

As he turned away, a woman standing in line held out his copy of *Love Knows No Lust*. "Don't forget this."

He took the book from her. "Thanks." Then he staggered away, unsure of his bearings. People heading in the opposite direction cleared out of his way, which told him his scarred face showed too much panic.

He didn't care.

Lilian Kane knew who he was. Worse, she wanted him to know that she knew him. She reminded him of a cat batting at a mouse like a toy. His instincts had told him she was responsible for Laurel's disappearance ever since he had gazed at the Flatiron Building, but the sight of her pretty estate had tempered his feelings. Now there could be no denying it. Laurel had warned him that because he had made supernatural forces aware of him, they would never leave him alone. How could he ever hope to live a normal life again?

Crossing the massive sunlit lobby, he broke into a run for the doors and emerged outside, where hundreds of people milled about, smoking and devouring food purchased from street vendors. Clutching his book, he pushed his way through the crowd to the curb, where he raised the book in the air, signaling a taxi, which pulled over. He jumped into the backseat and gave his office building address.

I could just keep going, he thought. But that wasn't

exactly true. He had no money to survive on—he had spent his savings searching for Edgar, and now he was living on credit.

I can live on credit anywhere.

But he couldn't go off the grid living on borrowed money, and it was hard to survive on a dishwasher's wage. Besides, he didn't intend to abandon Laurel. He had to know if she was alive before he did anything else. And he knew just where to begin his search, but it had to be right away, before Lilian Kane returned home from the expo.

She's got to be staying in Manhattan until it's over.

Jake looked at his stump. He had managed to fight without his left hand on Pavot Island, but he felt at a distinct disadvantage back in the States, where any extreme actions he took could have a negative impact on his future.

He needed help. Reaching into his pocket, he took out his phone. His first instinct was to call Maria, and he scrolled down to her name in his directory. His finger hovered over the call button and then moved away from it. The same instincts that told him Lilian Kane was a supernatural predator also told him not to involve Maria in his exploits again. She was a strong woman, a real warrior, but a person could only deal with so many monsters in the course of one month.

His finger moved up to Edgar's number, but he dismissed the thought even as it formed. It would be a long time, if ever, before Edgar had recovered from his experiences enough to help in the field again. He pressed another number.

"Helman Investigations and Security," Carrie said after the second ring.

"I need to know if Ripper is available to do some work today."

"What kind of work?"

"I need some backup on a stakeout. The pay is five hundred."

"Cash?"

"That's easiest."

"He's available. How soon do you need him?"

"I'll be there in ten minutes. I want to leave as soon as possible."

"I'll get him here as fast as I can."

Jake shut his phone down and slid it back into his pocket. Then he positioned *Love Knows No Lust* on his lap and opened it to the inscription.

Maria,

You're a lucky woman. Jake's got your back. Maybe we'll meet in person someday.

Eternally yours,

Lilian Kane

Maria entered the squad room with Bernie, and they sat at their desks.

"I wonder how much longer this will be my desk," Bernie said in a quiet voice.

"I wouldn't worry about it," Maria said. She doubted

the department would keep Edgar on under the circumstances, and if it did she knew the brass would reassign him to another spot.

Mauceri exited his office and came over to their desks. "What's the word on those DOAs?"

"We're filling out our report now," Maria said. "It's going to have a lot of white space."

"Witnesses?"

"None," Bernie said. "We canvassed Avenue B and Fifth Street."

"What's your feeling?"

Maria looked at Bernie. *You tell him.*

"It looks like Alice Morton is moving in on Raheem Johnson's territory," Bernie said.

Mauceri frowned. "Do you have any proof?"

Maria offered Bernie a shrug.

"Nothing specific but we know she's been moving downtown. With Papa Joe and Malachai—her brother and son—out of the picture, she's been consolidating what's left of their operations. Raheem was the next biggest player, and she's preparing to knock him down."

Mauceri turned to Maria. "If you don't have anything to go on, I suggest you watch your step around that woman."

"Yes, sir."

Mauceri handed a piece of paper to Maria. "Geoghegan from MCU requests your company at One PP."

Maria looked at it. "Both of us?"

"No, he specifically said he wanted to see you alone." He dropped his voice. "Edgar met with him earlier."

Of course, Maria thought. "Any particular time?"

Mauceri glanced at his watch. "At your earliest convenience."

"Ten-four."

Mauceri returned to his office.

Bernie stared at Maria. "Have you committed any major crimes I should know about?"

"In this country? None that I can think of."

Jake took the stairs two at a time and barreled into his office.

Carrie looked up from her desk. "Ripper will be here in an hour."

Closing the door, he looked at the watch on his right wrist. "Good."

Her cadence sped up as he rushed by her desk. "I spent all day tracing the chain of title on Eden, Inc. It got me nowhere, just one dummy corporation leading to another. It was kind of a waste of an entire day."

"Thank you."

He closed his office door behind him, tossed his copy of *Love Knows No Lust* on his desk, and removed the painting hanging over his sofa, revealing the secret storage space where he kept his arsenal: several different handguns, most of which he didn't feel comfortable wielding with one hand.

Looking over the weapons, he selected a Smith & Wesson Model 325 Thunder Ranch revolver with a black matte finish and set the six-shooter and a box of ammunition on his desk. He had fired a Glock one-handed on Pavot Island, but the action had left his arm throbbing; he needed something that would be easier to use because it packed less of a punch. Jake rehung the painting, then flipped the gun's cylinder open and loaded six rounds into it and another six into a speed loader.

He opened his safe, withdrew a bundle of five hundred dollars in twenties, and slid it into his pocket. After closing the safe, he went into his bedroom and selected a green nylon camouflage outfit from his standing wardrobe closet and tossed it onto his cot. He threw a duffel bag beside it and rifled through his belongings for accessories.

Back in his office he used a letter opener to slice through the tape on the long box that Jorge had sent him. In less than a minute he gazed at the ATAC 3000 inside the case he had pulled from the box. The assault weapon had a laser scope on top of its body and a grenade launcher beneath its barrel. Jorge had thrown in six magazines but no grenades.

Jake curled his fingers around a hilt and drew a long sword sheathed in a scabbard from the box. Setting the scabbard on the sofa, he held it down with one leg and freed the blade. Weighing the weapon in his hand, he recognized the blade that Ernesto Malvado had used to slay Andre Santiago and Jake had used to humiliate the demon Kalfu.

Jake slid the sword back into its scabbard, which was harder than drawing it, and left it on the sofa. He closed the case for the ATAC 3000, then opened his desk drawer and removed the Thunder Ranch in its shoulder holster and stuffed it into his duffel bag.

Sitting at his desk, he brought up the Eternity Books website on his monitor. He clicked on the About Us menu button and scrolled over the portraits and biographies that appeared beneath Lilian Kane's information. Studying the pictures, he furrowed his brow. Every member of the Eternity team was female. He recognized three of the women from World Book Expo.

Harla Soto, President. Long auburn hair and full lips. She had offered Jake the bottle of water.

Chloe Sanderstein, Vice President. Blonde with blue eyes. She resembled a model to Jake, and she had worked Lilian's table with Harla.

Jada Brighton, Director of Business Development. The black woman who had worked at the opposite table.

All three women looked beautiful and glamorous. Jake tapped a single finger on his desktop and scrolled through the other profiles. Every woman in the company must have turned heads in person, and each appeared to be under thirty-five. He wondered if this was normal in the publishing world.

The Order of Avademe had been the opposite: all old men. Until Jake joined their ranks and brought them down. Somehow he didn't see himself wearing a dress to do the same with Eternity.

He scrolled back up to Lilian Kane's photo. In two dimensions, her eyes appeared normal. On his screen, her photo could have been touched up, making her appear impossibly perfect. Face-to-face, she had looked even better. Her employees, if that's what they really were, appeared beautiful but not in the extreme manner she did. They also looked human.

What the hell *was* Lilian Kane? What were her followers? And what did they want with Laurel?

Are they all psychics?

He decided to listen to his instincts.

Witches.

After parking in a garage, Maria walked a few blocks to the fortified thirteen-level building known as One Police Plaza. Inside the lobby, she showed her shield to the police officers maintaining security and walked around the metal detectors.

Men and women in suits crisscrossed the gleaming floor of the opulent lobby as she made her way to the elevators.

"Maria!"

She turned as a man a foot taller than her, wearing a crisp blue suit, caught up to her: Arturo Delgado, an assistant district attorney with whom she had worked on numerous cases.

"Welcome back to the trenches," Arturo said.

"Thanks."

"Is everything okay? I know you took an emergency leave."

"Everything's good. What are you doing here?"

He smiled. "I had a meeting on the fourteenth floor."

One Police Plaza only had thirteen floors, but cops and other people in the know referred to the police commissioner's office as the fourteenth floor.

"You must be moving up in the world," Maria said.

"I'm trying. Hey, I just heard that Edgar's back. That's great news."

She felt her body tightening. "It's the best news I've had all year."

"Do you know what the story is? I mean, it's unbelievable, right? I thought for sure he was buried in a field somewhere in Jersey."

"I really don't know anything. I'm just grateful he's okay."

"Would you like to go out for dinner? I meant to ask you before, and then you were gone."

She had felt an attraction to Arturo when they worked a case together two months earlier and had sensed the same attraction in him, but she had been preoccupied with her caseload and the search for Edgar. Then she followed Jake to New Orleans.

"I don't know. I make it a rule not to date cops, and an ADA falls into the same category for me. We work to-gether."

Arturo didn't bat an eye. "I understand. Give me a call if you change your mind, okay?"

She smiled. "Yeah, sure."

He headed for the exit and she boarded an elevator. She got off on the fifth floor and walked to the door marked Major Crimes Unit.

Inside, she faced a receptionist to whom she showed her

shield. "Detective Vasquez, Special Homicide Task Force. Lieutenant Geoghegan's expecting me."

"One moment." The receptionist pressed an intercom button. "Detective Vasquez is here."

"I'll be right out."

The receptionist smiled at Maria rather than repeat Geoghegan's words.

A moment later an office door opened and Geoghegan stepped out. He wore a jacket over his button-down shirt, and the way he straightened his arms to rid the sleeves of wrinkles told Maria that he had just put the jacket on.

"Good to see you again," Geoghegan said.

Maria had met with him three times: to discuss the sixty sawdust-filled cadavers, the shipyard in Brooklyn where Mayor Madigan and several other power brokers were killed, and Edgar's disappearance. "Thank you."

The lieutenant looked at the receptionist. "What's open?"

"B."

Geoghegan gestured to the corridor lined with interview room doors. "Shall we?"

Passing the lieutenant, Maria turned the corner into the hall and moved through the open door to interview room B.

Once both of them sat facing each other, Geoghegan leaned forward, a degree of familiarity between them. "That's some tan you got. Did you just get back from vacation?"

You know my deal, she thought. "I was on leave. I just got back."

"Where did you go, if I may ask?"

There was no point in lying to him. If he didn't already know where she had been, he would find out. "I was on Pavot Island when the shit went down."

Geoghegan raised his eyebrows. "What the hell were you doing there?"

"I went with a friend. We were looking for a cheap romantic getaway. We didn't expect the package to include a Caribbean revolution."

"Holy cow. Were you ever in any danger?"

Maria reflected on her experiences battling soldiers and zonbies and evading a river full of carnivorous Biogens. "We were in danger the whole time."

"Who's the lucky fella?"

Maria met his gaze. "Jake Helman."

Geoghegan didn't blink. "You say that like I should know the name."

"He told me you've spoken a couple of times."

"How did you two meet?"

"You know I took his place in Special Homicide."

"And you interviewed him after Gorman killed Helman's wife, then turned up dead."

"So? There was no conflict of interest."

"You mean unlike in Hopkins's case?"

"I didn't say that."

"No one ever got pinned for murdering Gorman, did they?"

Maria's stomach tightened. "No."

"But Helman was a suspect."

"He was briefly a person of interest, but we cleared him

right away." On Pavot Island, Jake had confessed to the murder. She had never expected she would have to defend her investigation, which she had conducted according to regulations.

"How was that?"

You must have seen Jake's jacket. "His supervisor at Tower International provided him with an alibi. She came to the station and spoke to me and Edgar."

"But Kira Thorn disappeared right after that, didn't she?"

"Yes." Jake had killed her as well. "She disappeared after Nicholas Tower died."

"You think that's the connection?"

"Thorn was Tower's executive assistant. She could have had access to secret accounts of his."

"I guess that would be easier for you to accept than Helman killing her because she found out he was up to his neck in trouble."

"Did you bring me down here to ask me about Jake?"

"Gorman isn't your only unsolved homicide, is it?"

"You know it isn't."

"You've got a hell of a record." He looked like he wanted to smile.

"Why am I here?"

"Hopkins disappeared almost a year ago while you and he were investigating the Machete Massacres, which you tied to the Black Magic on the streets. Today you returned to the job and he showed up out of thin air an hour later. That's quite a coincidence, isn't it?"

"I called to arrange the end of my leave a week ago."

"Where were you then?"

"Miami."

"With Helman?"

"Yes, we stayed in Miami for a week after we got back from Pavot Island."

"Did you come straight here after that?"

"No, we went to New Orleans to pick up my car."

"What was it doing there?"

She disliked lying. "I drove to New Orleans to get away from things for a while. I was stressed out after I got tagged with those sixty corpses and the FBI took over the murders of Mayor Madigan and the industrialists. Those murders are unsolved too. I ran into Jake while I was in New Orleans. I didn't know he was there."

"How long were you there before you 'ran into' him?"

"A week, maybe longer. I wasn't ready to come home. Jake was heading to Pavot Island, and he drove to Miami to catch the flight. I decided to join him at the last minute, so I left my car in Orleans and flew to Miami to catch him."

"So it was an impulsive, romantic decision?"

Maria held his gaze. "Yes."

"And you wound up on Pavot in the middle of a revolution. That's some luck. Bad luck follows Helman around just like trouble, doesn't it?"

"I don't know. We haven't been dating that long."

"Did you happen to see Hopkins on Pavot Island?"

"No." It felt good to tell the truth.

"How about in Miami?"

"No, and before you ask, I didn't see him in New

Orleans, either. I haven't seen him at all until he walked into the squad room this morning, and we haven't spoken over the phone or communicated by text."

"Gee, you knew what I was going to ask and everything. Maybe I'm wrong about you. Maybe you *are* a good detective."

"Can I go now, or do you have a point to make?"

Geoghegan's smile seemed genuine. "You, Helman, and Hopkins are three of a kind."

Maria rose. "Yeah, we've all been murder police."

Geoghegan stood as well. "You've got more than that in common, and I'm going to find out what it is."

TEN

Jake opened his safe and took out the laptop inside it. Glancing out the window at the Tower, he set the laptop on his desk and raised the lid. Then he removed a battery from the charger beneath his desk and popped it into the laptop—he refused to connect it to AC power and he had disconnected Internet capability—and booted the file on the DVD-R it contained.

The laptop was dedicated to a single file: Afterlife. Nicholas Tower had funded the research project at a cost of millions of dollars over a period of a nearly two decades. The end result was a compendium of research conducted by scholars, researchers, theologians, and scientists—the most thorough exploration of the occult, supernatural, and existence of an afterlife.

Jake had downloaded the file from Kira Thorn's computer. As far as he knew, he possessed the only copy, although the concern that someone else had it tugged at his conscience.

One of the researchers for the Afterlife project had been Ramera Evans, a leading expert on vodou. Evans's work for Tower unearthed the secrets of reanimating the dead and performing transmogrification. Using the alias Katrina, she had unleashed the drug Black Magic on the streets of New York, created a legion of zonbies to do her bidding, and turned Edgar into a raven after Jake revealed to Edgar that she was consorting with Prince Malachai. She told Jake that she had gained her powers by agreeing to fornicate with the demon Kalfu. Jake wondered if Lilian Kane had done the same thing.

The laptop's screen filled with the Tower International logo, and then Afterlife's search engine opened. Jake keyed in *witch*, and the program jumped to a section entitled Witchcraft.

He had skimmed the content in the months after Ramera had transformed Edgar into a raven, hoping to find a way to return Edgar to human form. For selfish reasons, Ramera had withheld certain information from her contribution to the file, so Jake had found no usable data in the program. He only hoped that the six individuals who had contributed to the section on witchcraft had not also withheld critical information.

The glossary defined a witch as "one credited with supernatural powers, often with the aid of the devil or a familiar; an ugly crone; an alluring girl or woman; a practitioner of Wicca." While Afterlife dismissed Wicca as a harmless pagan religion, Jake gleaned plenty that aroused his interest.

Most religions and cultures referenced some form of witchcraft or sorcery. Although the concept of witchcraft existed for as long as mankind kept records, the belief in it blossomed in early modern Europe, where it was viewed as a conspiracy to undermine Christianity, which led to witch hunts. "Well-meaning sorcerers and healers" were considered witches. So were mediums and clairvoyants. All were burned at the stake.

Laurel's a healer and a psychic, Jake thought. *In ancient times, she would have been considered a witch.*

He read accounts of twenty people executed for witchcraft in New England between 1645 and 1693, and five others died in prison. Every execution appeared to be a case of public hysteria, but Jake had to wonder. Kira Thorn had confessed to studying witchcraft with a coven in Massachusetts, and through Tower's research project she had learned how to cast an energy spell preventing Cain and Abel from materializing inside the Tower unless summoned.

The geographic area of New York had become a focal point for psychic and supernatural activity because Avademe had lived in Lake Erie before moving to the waters off Brooklyn. Was Massachusetts a focal point for witchcraft, and if so, was it for a similar reason?

The intercom on his desk buzzed. "Ripper's here," Carrie said.

Jake pressed a button on the box. "I'll be right out."

He shut down Afterlife, closed the laptop, ejected the

battery, and returned the laptop to the safe. Then he stuck the battery into its charger, picked up the duffel bag, and opened the door.

In the reception area, Ripper stood at Carrie's desk, wearing his traditional long black duster despite the temperature.

Jake set the duffel bag down on the desk and held out the cash. "Five hundred, as agreed. If we run into any trouble, I'll make it a thousand."

Ripper eyed the cash. "What if I make it back and you don't?"

"Consider the extra five hundred an incentive to make sure we both come back."

Ripper nodded to Carrie. "Give it to her in case *I* don't come back."

Jake handed the cash to Carrie, who deposited it into her bag. He had already amended his will to give her the lion's share of his few assets. Now that he and Maria were getting closer, he wondered if he would need to amend it again.

Carrie fixed him with a stare. "Bring him back alive and intact."

"Will do." Jake had no intention of putting Ripper in harm's way. Jake returned to his office and picked up the case with the ATAC 3000 inside it. He carried the case into the reception area, where Carrie had risen on her high leather boots with the Frankenstein soles and kissed Ripper.

"Wait until I'm gone for that, will you?" Jake rested the box against the wall and picked up the duffel bag.

Ripper withdrew his tongue from Carrie's mouth and faced Jake.

"I'm going to get my car. Bring this down to the lobby in ten minutes."

Maria double-parked across the street from Sloane House. No cop would give her a ticket. She crossed the street and entered the lobby, her rubber-soled shoes pressing into the long burgundy carpet, and stopped at the doorman's station. "I'm here to see Alice Morton. My name's Maria Vasquez."

The doorman picked up a landline and entered a number. "Maria Vasquez is here to see you, Miss Morton."

"Tell her it's a social visit."

"Yes, ma'am." The doorman hung up. "She heard you. You can go up to 4B."

"Thank you." Maria passed him en route to the two elevators and pressed the button on the wall. When the elevator to her left opened she boarded it and pushed the appropriate button. The door closed and Maria watched the indicator count floors.

When the door opened, Maria stopped in midstep: a tall black man with facial hair stood before her. Their eyes met and she made him as a bad guy. She had to check herself to keep from reaching for her Glock.

"You getting off?" he said.

"Yes." She slid by him, expecting him to get on.

He didn't and the elevator door closed.

Alice Morton stood three doors and at least twenty-five feet away, half in and half out of her condo.

Maria looked over her shoulder at the man, who motioned her forward. "Can I help you?" she said in a tight voice.

"You can't help *me*," the man said.

Maria took out her shield and showed it to him. "Now you show me yours."

The man stared at her, then showed her his driver's license. His name was John Coker.

Maria took out a small notepad and wrote the name down. "You got an alibi for around 9:00 a.m. this morning when Darryl Hughes and a hopper called A-Minus got themselves killed?"

"As a matter of fact I do."

"I'm all ears."

"I was in bed."

"Can anyone corroborate that?"

Coker looked past her at Alice.

"Take a walk," Maria said.

Coker raised his eyebrows and Alice nodded.

Coker studied Maria, then turned back to the elevator and pressed the button. The door opened right away, and as Maria strode toward Alice it closed again.

"Don't you ever give up?" Alice said. "I thought I'd seen the last of you."

"Consorting with known criminals could be considered endangering the welfare of a minor."

"Why does he have to be a 'known criminal'? Because he's black?"

"I'll let his record speak when I check it out. I see you've moved up in the world."

"What do you care?"

"This building's board must not mind where their tenants get their income."

Alice's face tightened. "I'm the steward of my niece's inheritance from my brother. I can spend it however I like if it's in her interest."

"Is that bling you're wearing in her interest?"

"Somebody has to set an example for the child."

"What kind of an example do you think you set for that little girl?" She regretted the words as soon as she spoke them.

"Careful, Detective. I might have to file a harassment complaint against you."

Maria stopped two feet from the woman. "I'm not here to harass you, just to warn you."

"About what?" Alice almost sneered as she enunciated each word.

"Someone popped two of Raheem's hoppers this morning."

"So? What's that got to do with me?"

Maria knew her smile didn't show much amusement. "Raheem's going to come after whoever made that move, and he's going to come hard."

"That's none of my concern."

Maria moved closer. "Word on the street is that you've picked up where Joe left off, and you're making moves to take over Lower Manhattan's trade."

"Then the street talks too much."

Maria put her left hand on the doorframe. "You might

think you're safe from your enemies in this pricey condo, but you're not, and neither is Shana."

Alice stood still, showing no fear in reaction to Maria crowding her. "That little girl is safer with me than anywhere on earth."

"No, she isn't. She's in more danger here than anywhere else. You should just let her go."

"Go where? With who? *You?*"

Maria hesitated.

"I didn't think so. You said your piece. Now *you* take a walk." Alice entered her apartment.

Maria dropped her arm so the woman could close the door. Staring at the peephole for a moment, Maria bowed her head, drew her breath, and walked away.

Jake double-parked in front of his building and glimpsed Ripper standing inside the lobby. With the Maxima's air conditioner humming, he unlocked the doors and lowered his window as the Korean exited the building.

"Throw that in the backseat," he said.

Ripper opened the door and tossed the ATAC 3000 case on the backseat. Then he closed the door and got in beside Jake, who merged into traffic.

"What's the score?" Ripper said.

"Hopefully a damsel in distress."

"Your lady?"

"No."

Ripper stared at him. "I want to know what I'm getting myself into."

"We're going to a mansion in Eastchester. A friend of mine is missing, and I think she's being kept there. I'm going to go in and find out; you're going to sit in the car and wait for me to come back." He nodded at the box. "You're going to watch me through the scope on that gun. If you see anything I need to worry about, warn me. If it's more serious than that, shoot. When I come out, be ready to take the wheel."

"What makes you think this friend is inside the mansion?"

"A feeling in my gut says so."

Ripper snorted. "I can't get caught holding any gun."

Jake knew Ripper had served time for burglary. "Then you'd better keep your eyes open."

Maria saw Bernie still sitting at his desk when she reentered the squad room. She sat at her desk. "Let's run a check on one John Coker."

"What did he do?"

She booted her computer. "He looked at me the wrong way."

"Where did he commit this serious offense?"

"In the corridor of Alice Morton's building."

"Don't tell me you went back there."

Maria entered Coker's name into the system. "Okay, I won't tell you."

"Oy vey, why?"

"Because I don't want Raheem killing Shana when he goes after Alice."

"And here I thought you left to meet with Geoghegan."

"There was that, too."

"Was it over Edgar?"

"Nominally."

"Helman."

She didn't say anything.

"We can't all be wrong."

"Bingo."

"Huh?"

"John Coker, aka Ramses, has had his fair share of drug arrests, and Narcotics has linked him to Alice. He might even be her second in command."

"Really? Ramses?"

"Go figure. I guarantee he's sticking it to Alice."

"What if he is? That's got nothing to do with our investigation unless you think he was the triggerman this morning."

Maria bit her lower lip.

"Unless, of course, this has nothing to do with our investigation. Why would it? You just got back from one personal mission. Now you want to start another?"

"I know you're right but this is who I am. I'll try not to cross my wires, but that's difficult in this case. Everything ties back to Big Alice."

Bernie stuck a stick of Wrigley's gum into his mouth. "I got your back, partner. I just want to make sure I know your agenda—and that you know it."

"I appreciate that."

"At least this time I don't have to worry about you tagging along with Helman." His eyes widened. "He's not involved in this, is he?"

Maria chuckled. "No, he has no idea what I'm up to, and I have no idea what he's doing."

ELEVEN

Driving along a tree-lined road in a wooded stretch half an hour outside the city, Jake slowed down when the female voice of his GPS told him they were approaching their destination.

A high stone wall came into view, followed by metal gates that closed off a long driveway. Jake glimpsed the guardhouse one hundred yards away. Careful not to stare, Jake returned his attention to the road. A quarter mile later, he made a U-turn and pulled into a space behind some trees and bushes. The woods formed a sideways horseshoe around the Maxima.

"I bet cops use this spot to catch speeders," Ripper said.

"No doubt," Jake said.

"Then maybe it isn't the best place to park. They could roll up on us without even meaning to."

Jake lowered his window. "There's a white plastic bag in the glove compartment. Do you mind giving it to me?"

Ripper removed the white bag and handed it to Jake, who closed the window over it so it dangled outside like a call for roadside assistance.

"You really think that will work?" Ripper sounded unconvinced.

"There's a chance." Jake lowered the other windows an inch, then turned off the engine and gave the car keys to Ripper. "Don't lose these, and plan on being the one to drive us back."

Jake opened his door and got out, taking his duffel bag with him. "I'm going to change."

"I'm not going anywhere," Ripper said.

Jake went into the woods and changed into his green nylon running suit, which took longer than he had anticipated. He put on the shoulder holster with the Thunder Ranch snug inside it and took out an olive-green backpack stuffed with goodies. Then he attached a headset to the walkie-talkie on his hip and secured the earpiece to his right ear.

When he returned to the car, he opened the door and tossed the duffel bag into the backseat. Then he stuck his right foot, clad in a leather combat boot, on his seat. "Tie my shoelaces, will you?"

Ripper frowned but tied the lace on the combat boot. Jake removed his boot and set his left foot on the seat. Ripper tied that one as well.

Jake handed him the other walkie-talkie. "Switch to channel three and get that case out of the backseat."

Ripper adjusted the walkie-talkie, got out, and removed the case.

"Open it."

Ripper opened the hard plastic case and took out the ATAC 3000. Jake could tell by the way the younger man held the weapon that he knew what he was doing.

Ripper snapped the super machine gun's stock to his shoulder and peered through the scope, holding the gun ready to fire. Lowering the gun, he held it sideways and studied its features. "This is some serious shit."

"You're a one-man army."

"Why are you trusting me with this? I have your car keys, too. What makes you think that when you get inside that mansion I won't just take off? I could sell this artillery for a small fortune."

"I don't trust you. But I do trust Carrie and she trusts you."

"I got your back." Ripper slung the weapon over his shoulder, tossed the case into the backseat, and used the remote control on the car keys to lock the doors.

Jake spoke into the headset. "Walkie check."

Ripper pressed his thumb against the control for the walkie-talkie. "Good check."

"Then let's go."

They set off through the woods.

"Did you case this joint?" Ripper said.

"No time."

"Floor plans?"

Jake shook his head.

"Inside information?"

"We're going in cold."

"Then why do this now? Why not wait and do it right?"

"That isn't an option. The woman who owns this mansion is at an event in Manhattan right now. I need to get inside and find my friend before the woman leaves that event, which should be in the next hour."

Ripper scrunched up his eyebrows. "Does this woman have a name?"

"You're better off not knowing."

"Why, so I have plausible deniability? I'm an ex-con. There's no such thing. You've got me holding a gun, which could land my ass in jail."

Jake sighed. "The woman who owns this estate is Lilian Kane. Ever heard of her?"

Ripper shook his head.

"She's a big romance novelist and publisher."

"What does she want with your friend?"

"That's the million-dollar question."

"How do you know she has her?"

"When you're a cop you develop a sixth sense about bad guys."

"Did your spider sense go off when you met me?"

Jake glanced at his companion. "You bet your ass."

Ripper shrugged. "Then maybe there's something to this after all."

Reaching the edge of the woods, they crouched behind bushes overlooking a deep green yard spotted with floral gardens, which Jake recognized from the photos he had seen online. The breeze whispering across his face carried their sweet fragrance.

Two hundred yards away a white mansion with three

floors and columns gleamed in the sunlight. Columns in the front and back supported roofs. The windows were tall and narrow and reflected the sun. French doors on the side faced a wide patio that wrapped around to the rear of the mansion, which overlooked the valley below.

Ripper whistled. "You sure Julius Caesar doesn't live here?"

"I'll let you know when I come out."

"So many flowers . . ."

"They'll provide me with cover. I don't usually do this sort of thing in broad daylight."

"Neither do I."

Jake nodded to the front. "The guardhouse should be about two hundred yards that way. One guard, maybe two. If I come out and I'm not alone and any guards come running, shoot them in the legs."

"What if police come?"

"Stash the gun somewhere we can find it later."

Ripper unslung the ATAC, raised it to his shoulder, and peered through its scope.

Locating the zoom control, he pressed it. "I don't see any alarm stickers on the side door or windows."

"That doesn't mean anything."

"Someone's moving around in there . . . looks like a maid. She's fine, too."

Jake wasn't surprised that such a large dwelling required staff, and he told himself there might be more than one person inside.

"I count three cameras, which means there's probably more."

"Call me the Invisible Man." Jake checked his watch. "Let's get this show on the road."

Ripper sat at the base of a tree with the gun ready.

Jake pulled a lightweight green ski mask over his head with a single space for both eyes and a hole for his mouth, then a single green latex glove.

Jake circled the bushes to a clearing and glanced in the direction of the guardhouse. He got down on his hand and knees and lowered himself to the bright green grass and crawled toward the house. He moved with deliberation, sliding one limb through the grass at a time, squeezing the ground with his hand and pushing against the dirt with his boots. Sweat formed on his forehead, but the cotton mask absorbed it.

Fifty yards to the first flower garden . . .

He found the approach almost relaxing. The ground beneath the manicured lawn felt smooth, devoid of bumps and rocks.

Ripper's voice came over the speaker in his ear: "I can hardly see you."

Jake reached the garden and crawled inside it so he could not be seen by the cameras on either side of the great lawn. Water frothed from a stone fountain in the garden's center. He moved along the shadow of the shrubs for another fifty yards. The sweet smell of so many flowers sickened him somewhat, and he swatted buzzing bees from his face.

When he reached the edge of the garden, he gazed at another one spaced an even fifty yards away. He took a breath and resumed crawling. Halfway to the second garden an airplane droned overhead. Within the second garden, he passed an eight-foot statue of a nude goddess who gazed down at him with blank eyes, her arms spread wide, marble skin gleaming in the sunlight. The tips of her sculpted feathered wings pointed at the earth.

Fifty yards ahead lay the last obstacle before the mansion: a polished stone bench facing a concrete fire pit, with tall, sculpted ferns on either side of it.

Jake spoke into the headset. "Do you see that maid?"

"A few minutes ago she moved into what looks like a living room at the front of the house, facing the driveway," Ripper said.

Jake scanned the windows, which reflected the blue sky. He crawled the fifty yards to the bench, where he rested in the shade, and stared at long marks that started on the concrete and disappeared into the fire pit. They looked like they had been clawed by human fingers. He wanted to investigate the pit, but he knew his outfit would stand out against the hot concrete.

"The maid just went upstairs," Ripper said.

Jake resisted the urge to stand and run the final fifty yards to the house, so he settled for crawling faster. When he reached a patio surrounded by shrubs, he leapt onto the pink rock surface and sprinted past ornate metal furniture to the French doors at the side of the house.

Feeling better as soon as shade enveloped him, he gripped one of the gold handles and jerked it, but the door was locked. He drew the hunting knife from a sheath on his boot, forced the blade into the space separating the doors, and pulled it up with so much force that the door unlocked. He pushed it open with his stump before the lock could slip back into place.

Stepping inside with the knife still clutched in his hand, Jake used the blade to pull the door closed by its handle. He gazed at the interior: gleaming marble floors, black and white Italian furniture, and ceilings fifteen feet high. The room was thirty feet deep, and he saw no motion detectors or other sensors.

Five life-sized oil paintings with gold frames covered one wall: a woman with short curly hair; a blonde bombshell, her dress blowing up around her thighs; a rock star performing at Woodstock; an opera singer performing *Aida* in a red and gold opera house; and Lilian Kane reading one of her books to a circle of women gathered in a floral garden outside. Jake wondered if the mansion was large enough to accommodate Lilian's ego.

Moving toward the back of the house, Jake passed through a threshold with hand-carved wood and entered another large room filled with six pianos, a harp, and padded chairs and sofas embroidered with golden trim.

As he crossed the hardwood floor, he glimpsed a library on his left: floor-to-ceiling bookcases filled with hardcover books accessed by a long wooden ladder on a track. He crept to the threshold and peeked inside. Bookcases lined every available inch of wall space in the deep room, with six two-sided bookcases rising from the middle of the floor, creating aisles.

A noise behind him caused him to jerk his head back to the piano room.

Footsteps?

His gaze darted from one side of the room to the other, then turned to the ceiling. He heard the sound again, and a shadow glided across the floor. Jake snapped his head in that direction but saw nothing. Beneath his ski mask, the hair on the back of his neck stood on end. Moving away from the library with slow caution, he scanned the room. Out of the corner of his one eye, he glimpsed another shadow darting from view.

With his heart beating faster he crept into the middle of the room, where he could also see the kitchen in the opposite direction. In the gallery, forty feet away, a dark shape padded across the floor and blinked at him with green eyes: a black cat. Jake swallowed, and the cat took off like a shot.

Exhaling, he turned and entered the oversize country kitchen, which could have served a restaurant. Jake circled the room, taking in a breakfast nook, a long island, two dishwashers with German labels, a commercial oven, and a wooden table surrounded by eight chairs. Glancing through an archway to another room, he counted twelve plush chairs around an oval table carved of dark wood. Everywhere he looked he saw wooden fixtures and carvings of leaves or tree branches. Potted plants hung from the ceilings like lights, casting shadows of foliage on the walls.

Turning back to the kitchen, he zeroed in on a wide wooden door and approached it. He grasped the doorknob, which didn't turn, then slid the hunting knife back into its sheath and withdrew a lock-picking kit from his pocket.

He selected a stainless-steel tool with a curved head that resembled a dental instrument and inserted it into the knob, gave it a few turns, and withdrew it when he heard a click.

As he returned the instrument to the kit and the kit to his pocket, he spotted eight black cats in a perfect half circle on the floor, watching him.

TWELVE

Jake did a double take. Did the felines expect him to feed them?

Or do they plan to eat me?

He hissed at the animals to drive them off, but they didn't react. He hissed again, this time waving his hand.

The cats turned rigid, their tails puffing up as they pulled back their ears.

Jake lunged at them. "Go on. Get out of here," he whispered.

One cat growled, a low sound that grew shrill. Another hissed at Jake. A third leapt at his masked face.

He batted the feline away with his stump, and even before it struck the floor a second leapt at him. He meant to knock it aside, but his fist connected with its head, and it flipped over in the air, its legs spread out.

Before he knew it, four of the felines launched at him at the same time. He punched one in the head, driving it to the floor, then threw his right arm back, flinging another into wooden cabinets. Almost at the same time, he swung his left arm away from his body, hurling another cat across the kitchen. The fourth cat landed on his chest and sank its claws into the nylon fabric of his running suit. He seized the animal by the nape of its neck and tried to pull it away, but its claws dug into his flesh.

Another cat flew through the air at him, and Jake jerked the one on his chest away, using it to smack the newcomer aside. Then he threw the cat at three others that hissed at him from the floor and sent them scurrying.

A cat sank its teeth into his left forearm, close to his stump, and he cracked its skull with his fist. Another buried its claws into his thighs. He drew the Thunder Ranch from its shoulder holster and clipped the cat across the side of its head with the barrel, which he then swung into the hind-quarters of a cat sailing through the air in his direction, slamming it face-first into the wall behind him.

Three more cats ran into the kitchen, and Jake knew that if he didn't make it into the basement right then he would have no choice but to start firing . . . and he would run out of ammunition fast. Spinning toward the door, he reached for its knob with his stump, which accomplished nothing.

Damn it all!

As a cat clawed the space between his shoulder blades, he jammed the Thunder Ranch into its holster and seized the doorknob, which he twisted and pulled. A second cat sank its claws into his buttocks as he opened the door, and as he retreated into cool darkness both creatures sank their teeth into him. A third cat bit into his left forearm.

Balancing on a step, Jake slammed the door on the shoulders of the cat clinging to his arm. The cat yowled, and Jake opened the door just enough for the animal to fall to the floor, where he kicked it out of the way and shut the door. Then he rammed his back against the wall behind him until the cat fastened there dropped to the stairs and scrambled away.

Jake took two steps down, then dropped into a sitting position on the stairs. The cat on his buttocks screamed and twisted free of him. Jake sprang to his feet and fumbled in the darkness for the light switch. The instant the overhead light came on he saw both cats running at him with their ears pinned back. He took one step below and kicked the closest animal with all his strength. The cat struck the wall above the stairway and dropped motionless to the stairs. A glowing sphere of golden light rose from the dead feline and faded.

Animals do have souls, Jake thought. But why hadn't the killer cat's soul darkened with negative energy? Because it had not attacked him of its own free will.

The second cat—running on only three of its legs—attacked his ankle so he couldn't kick it. He grabbed behind its neck and lifted it a few feet away from his face.

The cat hissed and spat at him, twisting its body in a frenzied effort to reach his arm.

Jake tightened his grip on the animal and stared into its hateful green eyes. "Fuck you," he said through clenched teeth. Then he turned back to the door, intending to open it and throw the cat into the kitchen. The only problem was he couldn't open the door with his stump. On the other side of the door, the cats scratched at the wood. He stared at the door, listening and sweating, his heart pounding as the cat in his grip performed acrobatics in a desperate attempt to reach his flesh.

Jake pressed the cat between the door and its frame so hard the growling animal couldn't move its limbs. Then he set one foot beneath the cat's ass and in one fluid motion released his hold on the creature, twisted the doorknob, and kicked the cat so that it forced the door open and flew into the cats crouched for attack around the door, scattering them.

Even as Jake shut the door, black shapes sprang at him with their front limbs outstretched in attack mode. He flinched at the sounds of their bodies smashing against the door. The scratching on the wood grew frantic.

As he stepped over the still body of the cat he had kicked against the wall, he told himself the cats were not witches' familiars.

Which means that's exactly what they are.

He spoke into the headset as he descended the stairs. "I'm in the basement. Watch out for cats or any other animals for that matter. Where's the maid now?"

"I have no idea," Ripper said. "Any trouble?"

"Nothing a big dog couldn't handle."

Reaching the smooth concrete floor of the basement, he felt as if he had entered a bunker. The cinder-block walls were clean and smooth, and the floor lacked water stains. Perhaps as many as one hundred old wardrobe chests and wicker baskets filled the space.

He moved to a brown chest with black trim, and when

he lifted the lid a piece of it came away in his hand like brittle composite siding for a house. He set the broken piece inside the chest as a musty odor filled his nostrils. Clothing filled the chest two feet deep, and when he pinched a dark green article to inspect it, the fabric crumbled into dust. Setting his hand flat in the middle of the pile, he pushed down, and his hand went straight through the fabric, as if the clothing had been fashioned out of lint. A rising cloud of dust forced him to look away. Lilian Kane took the concept of vintage clothing to a new extreme.

Closing the chest, Jake surveyed the others behind it. They grew progressively darker, their metal components more corroded. Circling them, he stopped at one in the back. The dark shape almost resembled a piece of debris from a sunken ship resting on the ocean floor. He gave the chest a sharp kick, and his foot went right through the side. When he pulled his boot free, dust and sand poured out and the chest collapsed.

Jake drew in a deep breath and exhaled. Passing old-fashioned mannequins with Victorian dresses on them and stacks of large paintings with decorative frames, he faced the far wall, which seemed closer than it should have been. By his estimate, the basement occupied only one-third as much space as the house.

He stared straight ahead at a bookcase centered within the wall. There were five shelves, maybe fifty mason jars on them, all empty. Narrowing his eye, he followed the edges of the bookcase. Something about it troubled him.

Jake moved toward the bookcase, his footsteps echoing.

As he stepped onto a rubber mat, he thought how strange it was to have a single mat on such a large concrete floor.

When he heard a sound not unlike a bowstring launching an arrow his muscles had already tensed. His mind told him to retreat from the mat, but his momentum made that impossible, so he leapt forward off the floor, swinging his hand at a copper pipe that ran along the ceiling. Before his fingers closed around the pipe he heard a loud whoosh as a gleaming metal blade—eight feet long and anchored to the center of the bookcase one foot off the floor—whipped beneath him like a giant straight razor and snapped into the wall on the opposite side.

That could have chopped off both my legs at the shins!

His body swung forward and back, and he wrestled with his next move. He had to believe that there was at least one more giant blade higher up, but if he dropped to the floor the first blade might swing back.

Jake released the pipe. An instant later a second blade swished over his head, so close he felt wind in his hair. His feet touched the mat, the second great blade crashed into the wall, and he sprang off the floor, diving sideways, just as the first blade swung out again. For a split second the blade passed beneath him, and he held his breath, praying not to lose his remaining hand.

He landed on the cement floor, his right shoulder taking the brunt of the impact, just as the first blade hit the wall. When he looked up, the bookcase appeared normal again.

I could have lost my head and *my legs.*

Jake rolled away from the bookcase until he bumped

into a solid object. Turning his head, he gazed at a 1930s console radio with a chestnut body. He performed a one-armed push-up and stood, then studied the scratched surface of the radio, which had a gold-colored grill cloth. A metal plate identified the unit as a Philco Type 89 Lowboy.

The black plastic remote control on top of it was a Panasonic. As far as he knew, such devices didn't operate antique radios. He picked the remote up. Then he pivoted on one foot, aimed it at the bookcase, and pressed the Power button.

Nothing happened.

He pressed the Power button again, then Play.

The entire bookcase receded into the wall with a gentle motorized hum. As the bookcase continued to move backwards, tracks on the floor behind the wall came into view, and an overhead fluorescent light flickered to life, revealing a passageway six feet deep. The two giant blades remained in position, crossing the threshold like barriers.

Sliding the remote control into a pocket, Jake pushed the radio to where he had stood when the blades had threatened to sever his limbs and decapitate him. The blades remained in place.

He pressed the control for his headset. "I found a secret passageway in the basement behind a bookcase. It's possible I triggered an alarm so stay alert."

"I'm not napping," Ripper said with an edge in his voice.

He's growing on me, Jake thought.

Then he moved to the wall, grasped one edge of the threshold, and stepped over the lower blade while ducking beneath the upper one. He stood before a set of wide concrete steps and debated whether to leave the bookcase in place or return it to its position in the wall. He left it alone and descended the steps to a landing, then descended a second set facing the way he had come.

At the bottom Jake faced another threshold, this one ten feet wide, which opened into a chamber large enough to account for the space missing from the basement. Candles flickered on the floor ahead of him, reminding him of Mambo Catoute's chamber on Pavot Island.

Drawing the Thunder Ranch, he moved closer to the threshold. He estimated that twenty thick candles had been arranged in a perfect circle dead center on the floor, and he wondered if twenty corresponding zonbies lay in wait for him. The deep space was dark except for the glow provided by the candles, so he took out a Maglite with a magnet on it and attached it to the barrel of his gun, then passed its beam over round coffee tables covered with books, candles, and matches, and at least a dozen bookcases stocked with mason jars. Squinting at the jars, he noted they were filled with what appeared to be herbs, spices, and soil. Each jar bore a label.

Entering the space, he saw no sign of Laurel, and he doubted there was room for another secret chamber. He stopped at the candles. The circle they formed reminded him of the summoning circle in which he had battled Kalfu. Pieces of clothing were strewn around the circle, and Jake recognized the dress he had seen Laurel wear. Spots of dried blood appeared on the ripped fabric.

Dear God, no.

Water stained this area of the floor, and half the tattered dress lay soaking up a puddle of discolored liquid. The odor of urine reached his nostrils.

"Jake?" The voice sounded weak. "Up here . . ."

Tilting his head back, Jake saw only darkness. Then he aimed the flashlight above him. The ceiling was three times as high as that of the basement he had just left, and he realized that it must have continued at the same level beneath the house. The flashlight revealed a giant white spider on the ceiling, its flesh glowing white.

Laurel!

She was spread-eagle, her back pressed against the ceiling and her hair hanging straight down, obscuring her features. She had been stripped nude, and as far as he could tell, no bonds or supports of any kind held her to the ceiling.

Jake peeled off his ski mask, then shined the flashlight on his face.

"Help me . . ."

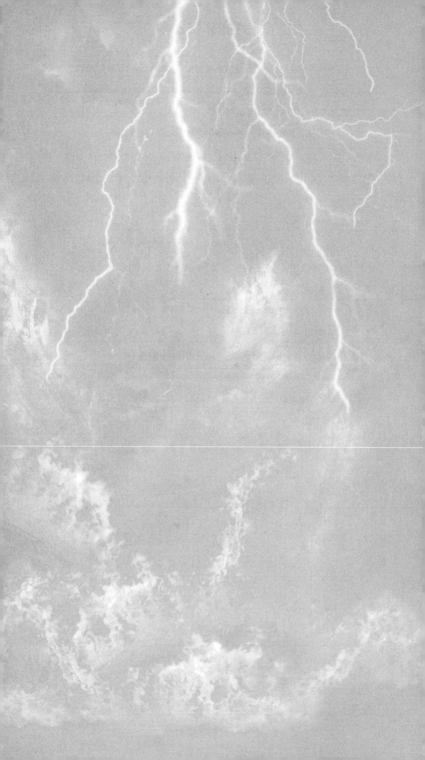

THIRTEEN

Jake moved as close to the candles as he could without touching them. He didn't notice any fire extinguishers. "What's holding you up there?"

"Lilian."

Jake swept his flashlight around the gloomy interior. Seeing no sign of Lilian, he returned his attention to Laurel. "These candles?"

He couldn't tell if she nodded or not. *The candles are used for different spells, not just for controlling zonbies.*

Going down on one knee, he licked his forefinger and thumb and pinched the flickering yellow flame of the candle, extinguishing it. Smoke curled up from the candle, and Jake tilted his head back.

Laurel lurched to one side, her left arm moving in a frantic manner. "Careful."

Standing, he went to the candle opposite the one

he had extinguished. Kneeling, he licked his fingers and pinched the burning wick.

Above him, Laurel sucked in her breath, her right arm free.

If he extinguished all the candles, Laurel would crash to the concrete floor, and he doubted he could catch her with one hand.

Using the two extinguished candles as markers, he approximated two additional candles that divided the circle into imaginary quarters. Crossing to one, he kneeled and extinguished it, and Laurel's left leg swung down, unencumbered. He moved to the fourth candle and put it out, and her right leg swung forward as well.

Jake rubbed his beard. Sixteen candles remained. "Any suggestions?"

"You're doing fine. Just take your time and do one at a time. You'll know when to stop."

"Your head is still pressed against the ceiling. If you drop while it's stuck there, won't your neck break?"

Laurel drew several deep breaths. "Take two steps to your left."

Jake followed her directions.

"Now kneel."

Obeying, he raised his hand over one candle and held it there, feeling its warmth.

"Move your hand one candle to the right."

He did.

"That's the one."

He extinguished the candle and watched Laurel rotate her head.

"My back, upper back, and ass are still being held."

Jake looked at the candles. He had extinguished 25 percent of them. Rising, he waited for Laurel to direct him.

"Move five candles to your right."

Jake shifted in the appropriate direction, kneeled, and held his hand over one candle.

"Yes."

Licking his fingers, he extinguished the candle's flame.

Laurel's upper body bowed forward. She moved her limbs as if underwater, pushing them against some invisible resistance. Her buttocks anchored her to the ceiling.

Standing, Jake spread his arms. "What now?"

With her arms outstretched before her, Laurel appeared to be fighting for balance. "Walk opposite that candle."

Gazing across the circle, Jake went over to the candle he believed was opposite. "This one?"

"Yes."

He kneeled and extinguished the flame.

Laurel's body dropped and she cried out. One foot into her descent the free fall stopped, and her entire body wobbled as she tried to maintain a level position, her stomach muscles straining in the flashlight beam. "I'm loose. Bring me down one candle at a time."

Jake extinguished a candle and Laurel descended by two feet.

Twelve candles left, he thought.

Laurel arched her neck and back with her arms at her sides like an airplane, her ankles together and her toes pointed. She resembled an Olympic gymnast or a diver.

With each candle he extinguished, her body lowered another two feet. Soon it quivered ten feet off the floor, and Jake noted dozens of scratches that covered her pale flesh.

Cat scratches, he thought.

Another candle, another two feet. Sweat beaded on her forehead, and Jake reached up to take her hand.

"No," she said with a grimace. "You have to break the spell completely."

He extinguished them one by one and watched her body draw closer to the floor, her buttocks taut. Even at this distance, she reeked of urine and filth. Dozens more scratches crisscrossed her backside.

Jake extinguished the final candle, and Laurel struck the concrete floor face-first, her palms making a simultaneous slapping sound. Grunting, she tried to push herself off the floor, but weakness had taken its toll.

"Is it safe for me to enter the circle?" Jake said.

Laurel nodded, her lips parted. "The spell's broken."

Jake put his latex glove on, stepped over the candles, and grabbed Laurel's left bicep. He didn't want her to touch his skin, which would have opened his mind up to her. As he pulled her upright, he balanced her with his stump.

She gaped at it. "Oh, my God. What the hell happened to you?"

"I could ask you the same thing, and I will, but let's get out of here first." Using one foot, Jake swept the candles out of their way, and they stepped clear of them.

Laurel stumbled beside him, and he maintained his grip on her bicep.

"I'm so weak," she said.

Jake slid the backpack from his shoulders and turned sideways. "Unzip the side pocket."

Laurel wavered as she unzipped the bag and took out a granola bar.

"I keep them for when I'm on stakeout," Jake said.

Chewing on the crunchy bar, Laurel zipped the backpack shut.

Jake dropped the backpack, then took off his nylon jacket and held it out to her. "I didn't think to bring a change of clothes for you."

Laurel pulled the jacket on and zipped it, and Jake led her out of the chamber to the stairway. Her weakened state and bare feet slowed their ascent up the stairs.

"Did you find a blood relative of Ramera Evans?" Laurel said.

"Yes, in Miami. Then I went to Pavot Island."

Laurel raised her eyebrows. "Is that where you were maimed?"

"It was worth it. Edgar's home and he's human."

"That's incredible."

"Let's see if I can get you out of here alive." At the top of the stairs, Jake led Laurel to where the trick bookcase remained parked against the wall. After the commotion with the cats, he half expected the maid to have found him out.

Ripper's voice came over the speaker in his ear. "Are you there, Jake? What's going on? I'm getting nervous."

Jake squeezed the microphone button. "Sorry about that. I'm not used to having backup. I'm coming out now, and I'm not alone, so be ready for trouble."

Laurel blinked at him.

"My office manager's boyfriend."

"Ripper's an ex-con and you don't like him."

Shrugging, Jake raised his stump. "I needed help. Your life matters more to me than the quality of the company I keep."

"Thank you for coming."

"You're welcome."

They stood before the giant blades in the secret doorway. Jake took the remote control from his pocket. He pressed Play and the bookcase moved forward on its tracks. He pressed Stop and it stopped.

"It should be deactivated." He unsheathed his knife and tossed it on the floor. The blades remained motionless.

"Come on." He stepped over the lower blade and beneath the upper one and helped Laurel do the same. Then he ushered her away from the mat before the doorway and pressed the remote control, triggering the bookcase to return to its proper place. While that happened, he lay on the floor and retrieved his knife, which he sheathed. Jake stuffed the remote control back into his pocket, and he and Laurel crossed the basement, passing the chests.

Jake slid the backpack off, reached inside, and removed a gas mask. "I didn't think ahead to bring you clothes, but I did bring this. Put it on."

Laurel stretched the insect-like rubber mask over her head.

"Now me."

She took out another gas mask and stretched it over

his head, then adjusted the rubber around his skin. They regarded each other through two layers of protective lenses. Jake took a metal cylinder out of his backpack and shook it; Laurel closed the pack and held it while Jake slid his arms through the straps.

They walked to the basement stairway, where Jake froze. The naked corpse of a man lay on the stairs, where Jake had left the cat he had killed. The man's penis bore the scars of long-ago mutilation.

He was neutered.

He didn't know why he was surprised. Katrina had turned Edgar into a raven, so there was no reason to doubt that Lilian Kane—whoever she was—turned men into cats. And then she had them neutered or performed the procedure herself.

"Come on," he said, his voice muffled by the mask.

They crept up the stairs, past the corpse.

Jake held the cylinder out to her. "Twist the top."

Laurel did as he said, and the cylinder belched tear gas. "Now open the door."

Laurel turned the knob and Jake kicked it wide open, revealing at least two dozen black cats waiting for them. He aimed the gas at the closest cats, spraying them, and they retreated, some yowling. Then he threw the cylinder into the middle of the pack, scattering the felines in all directions.

He and Laurel entered the kitchen, which seemed darker through the lenses of his gas mask.

A shadow moved to his left, and as he turned a woman in a maid's uniform screamed and lunged at him, cocking her arm high over her head, a butcher's knife gleaming. Her eyes were entirely black, like two lumps of coal.

Flinching, Jake raised his left arm in a defensive gesture just as the maid swung the knife. He deflected the blow with his stump, then clocked the woman in the jaw, slamming her against the pantry. The maid dropped the knife and cried out, a strangled sound that could have come from one of the blinded cats, then bent over to retrieve her weapon. Jake kicked the knife out of her reach, then pulled her up by her hair and punched her again, this time hard enough to knock her out.

As she slumped to the floor, Laurel shrieked.

Spinning, he saw her staggering in a circle with two cats clawing at her shoulders.

"Move into the dispersal area," he said.

She stumbled into the gas, and the cats leapt from her and fled, leaving claw marks in Jake's jacket.

Jake grabbed Laurel's arm. Dragging her behind him, he ran into the piano room. Three cats appeared ahead of them, hissing as their tails puffed out. Jake kicked one across the room, and it scrambled beneath a sofa. He stomped on another, breaking its back. The third ran up his body and clawed at his face, which the gas mask protected. He grabbed the cat by the nape of its neck and hurled it at the floor, where it stopped moving.

He didn't wait to see how long it would take for them to revert to human form. They rushed into the gallery, where he came to a sudden stop, his heart thudding at the sight of the woman standing before them.

Lilian Kane.

She looked just as she had at World Book Expo, except she had stopped smiling.

Jake felt the blood draining from his face.

Laurel ripped off her gas mask. "She isn't really there. Astral projection."

Unconvinced, Jake removed his gas mask as well.

Lilian continued to stare at him, blinking.

He passed his arm through her body, which had no mass. "She sees us, though."

Laurel tugged on Jake's arm, leading him through Lilian's image. When they reached the French doors, he looked behind him and Lilian had vanished. Staring ahead, he felt like he was gazing at an alien landscape. Darkness had fallen over the estate, yet sunlight still shone through the cloudy sky.

"We have to hurry," Laurel said.

"Stick the masks back in my pack," Jake said.

Laurel stuffed their masks inside it.

As soon as Jake heard her zip up the bag, he opened the French doors and they ran onto the patio. He closed the doors to prevent any of the cats from chasing them. Muddy clouds covered the sky as far as he could see, and the air crackled with electricity, causing the hair on his neck to stand on end. But the sky had been clear twenty-five minutes earlier.

A sound behind them caused Jake to turn around. The cats threw themselves against the French doors. Taking Laurel's hand, he ran off the patio and onto the lawn.

He could only run at half speed because Laurel's bare feet slowed them down.

"What did you do to piss off those cats?" Ripper said over his earpiece.

"Not now," Jake said.

They passed between the stone bench and the fire pit, and Jake glimpsed what appeared to be ashen corpses intertwined.

Human sacrifices?

Regulating his breathing, Jake frowned as he stared ahead. In the floral garden closest to them the arms of the goddess statue were raised before it like those of a wrestler. Jake remembered them being spread out, palms to the earth. As he slowed his gait, the statue's head turned in their direction.

Mother-father, Jake thought.

Laurel stopped in her tracks, halting Jake as well.

The statue stepped off its pedestal and crossed the garden, its angelic wings resembling weapons.

"What the fuck?" Ripper said.

The statue moved with mechanical consistency, crushing bushes as it walked onto the lawn, where it faced Jake and Laurel. Then it continued forward.

FOURTEEN

Releasing Laurel's hand, Jake squeezed the button for his microphone. "Shoot it."

Automatic gunfire exploded from the woods behind the statue, and Jake drew his Thunder Ranch and fired as well.

The statue stopped and looked over its shoulder in Ripper's direction, then turned back to Jake and Laurel and resumed its advance.

"Put your gun away," Laurel said.

Jake had fired half his load. "Are you crazy?"

"I need your hand."

Jake saw the seriousness in her eyes and holstered his gun. He held out his hand, which she grasped.

The statue stopped moving.

"Move eight paces to our right and stop," Laurel said under her breath.

Jake followed her lead like a twelve-year-old boy forced

to dance at school.

They stopped.

The statue moved forward, slower this time, turning its head from side to side.

"We're invisible to it," Laurel whispered.

Jake glanced at her. He saw her fine. He looked at their clasped hands: he saw them, too. "I don't understand."

The statue jerked its head in their direction.

Laurel pursed her lips, mimicking a shush.

Then it occurred to Jake: blind spots. Kira Thorn had created one around the penthouse of the Tower to keep Old Nick's location a secret from the higher powers, and Avademe had created several for the same purpose.

Laurel took soft steps toward the woods, and Jake attempted to do the same.

The statue studied the ground behind them.

With his heart pounding, Jake did the same. *It sees the tracks we're making.*

The statue broke into a run, its marble feet tearing up the lawn as it charged at them like an angry bull.

Jake shoved Laurel away, knowing he would become visible to the statue again. Laurel staggered backwards and fell on the grass.

The statue locked its blank eyes on Jake and moved in his direction.

"Keep shooting," Jake said into the microphone on his headset. He drew his revolver and fired his last three shots, each round striking its intended target and producing little more than a puff of white particles. He stuffed the empty revolver back into its shoulder holster.

Ripper continued to pepper the statue's back and wings with heavy firepower. "We've got company."

Good, Jake thought.

Two security guards in blue uniforms ran around the corner of the mansion with Glocks drawn, one heavyset with curly red hair and the other Hispanic with a bushy mustache. Their eyes widened as they skidded to a stop and gaped at the statue, which turned to them. The guards were too mesmerized to pay attention to Jake.

"Fire," Jake said.

The guards raised their weapons and opened fire. The rounds ricocheted off the statue's body, and Jake found it impossible to calculate where they would strike.

The statue's wings folded away from its shoulders. Jake knew the wings couldn't expand, but their pointed tips still made them deadly weapons. It ran at the guards, who stutter-stepped away from each other, then it pivoted, swiping at them with its wings. One wing crushed the redheaded guard's skull; the other shattered the hip of the Hispanic guard, who screamed as his broken body collapsed to the earth. The first guard's soul rose from his corpse and faded.

Laurel went to the redheaded guard and stared at his Glock.

The statue regarded Jake with unblinking eyes, then sprinted toward him. Jake fled toward the rear of the mansion. He knew the statue was in close pursuit when he heard the sharp cracking sound made by marble feet slamming onto concrete. Thank God the statue was too heavy to fly.

The footsteps grew louder behind him, closer. Turning his head, he glimpsed the marble monster out of the corner of his eye. It ran in perfect form, its hands balled into fists, moving with a single purpose: to destroy him. The statue bore down on him, and Jake feared it would leap, closing the distance between them.

Dodging to his right, he hid behind a stone column. The statue peered around the column to his right, and he feinted left. Then it peered around the left side, and he feinted right. Taking a single step back, he pivoted and sprinted for a statue of a lion perched near a flight of wide stone steps. The goddess statue's footsteps thundered behind him.

As he ducked behind the lion, Jake saw the shadow of the goddess statue swinging over the granite lion. An instant later, chips of the lion's mane rained down on the concrete. Jake stood behind the lion as the goddess positioned itself to pummel him. The female statue jabbed at him with each fist, and he ducked from side to side. Then the goddess swung at the lion's head with such force that fissures formed throughout the head. Another swing obliterated the head, and Jake flinched to avoid flying shards.

"Are you all right?" Ripper said over the walkie-talkie.

Jake ran to the far edge of the patio. Three flights of stone steps separated by landings descended the hill to a glass-enclosed swimming pool. He rushed down the stairs. The statue jumped on the first landing with what sounded like an explosion. Seeing the figure struggle to free its legs as if they had become entrapped in quicksand, he knew the impact had shattered one of the slabs that formed the landing.

"What the hell's going on, Jake?"

Jake pinched the microphone control. "I'm a little busy."

He ran down the final flight of stairs to the concrete that surrounded the swimming pool. Beyond the pool, the hill continued to slope to the valley. As Jake opened the wide door of the glass structure, he heard the statue's footsteps cracking the steps behind him. He hurried inside and closed the door.

Laurel appeared at the top of the steps, a Glock in her hand. Jake prayed she would not fire the weapon; it would do no good, and maybe the statue would see the gun even if it didn't see her.

He pushed a pool chair in front of the door, then searched for a weapon. To his left, a waterfall cascaded into an oval pool that appeared to have no shallow end. Next to it, a fountain frothed in the center of a pool three feet deep with curved stairs beneath the surface. And to Jake's right, steam rose from a hot tub. He grabbed a pool skimmer on a long aluminum pole and practiced lunging with it, but the device was useless with one hand, and he discarded it.

The sharp sound of glass shattering caused him to turn as the statue crashed through the door. The statue crushed the aluminum frame of the pool chair with a single step.

Jake picked up the pool skimmer and held it like a jousting lance. He swatted the statue's face with the skimmer four times in rapid succession.

Then the statue plucked it from his hand and bent it in half.

Big deal. I could have done that. Jake moved backwards,

keeping his eye on the pool's edge. Crouching, he drew his knife from its sheath and held it ready. He could run around the pool in circles until Lilian came home, or he could settle this now.

Jake charged at the statue. It swung its right wing at him, and he jumped back. The statue recovered its balance, and he charged at it again. The statue swung its left wing at him. He jumped back once more, and as soon as the wing passed him he kicked it, trying to drive the statue into the swimming pool. But the statue used its momentum to spin in a complete circle with far more grace than Jake had thought possible.

He heard a whooshing sound as the wing came back down, and he moved away just as the tip of the wing shattered a piece of the concrete deck. The marble goddess jerked her wing free and wavered for balance.

Even though Jake knew a single blow from the statue could crush his skull, he had no choice but to engage it. The statue tilted toward the pool, then regained its balance by dropping its right wing for support. Jake faced it sideways, with his back to the pool. The statue threw a left at him that he ducked beneath, saving his brain, then it threw a right, which he also avoided.

He sheathed the knife and threw himself at the statue's torso, knowing its reaction would be to crush him in a bear hug, then pressed his hand and stump against its chest and launched himself backwards off the edge of the pool. The last thing he saw before striking the water was the statue tottering on the edge.

Jake sliced through the water and took some up his nostrils. The statue fell in after him, engulfed in a field of bubbles. It attempted to swim after him, but it sank to the bottom. Jake rolled over and kicked both legs, rising to the surface, where he swam as fast as he could to the opposite side of the pool. He found the task difficult with his left hand missing, but he made it and grasped the edge. He tried to jump out of the pool and sank back beneath the water. Turning, he saw the statue rising on one leg.

He rose to the surface and swam along the edge until he reached the ladder, which he scrambled up, his right arm doing double duty. He sucked in air as he set both feet on the concrete.

The statue took slow steps toward him along the bottom of the pool.

Jake seized the fiberglass ladder and shook it: he couldn't remove it without tools. He ran around the pool, through the space where the door had been, and up the steps, water dripping from his nylon sunning suit, and met Laurel half-way up the steps.

"Move," Jake said, out of breath.

Laurel stared past him. "Look."

Jake turned. Inside the pool, the statue started pulling itself up the ladder, its wings breaking the surface. Then the steps on the ladder broke, and the statue sank from view.

"How did you know?" Laurel said.

"I didn't. I just guessed."

"Lilian controlled that statue from afar. Now that you've put it out of commission she'll find another way to come after us."

Jake guided her up the steps. "You don't have to tell me twice."

When they reached the patio, Jake tried his microphone. "Ripper, can you hear me?"

Ripper didn't respond; the water had damaged the headset's control.

"We've got to catch him before he leaves without us."

As they ran by the mansion, cats leapt into the windows, hissed, then jumped out of view to run to the next window.

Turning the corner, Laurel collapsed beside a garden. "I can't run anymore."

Jake helped her to her feet. "I can't carry you."

"Then leave me. Get the hell out of here while you still can."

"I came here for you. I'm not leaving without you."

"Now what?" Laurel stared at the sky, her body radiating fear.

The clouds turned green and grew denser, coalescing into a dark force. Then a swirling pattern formed, spinning in a downward funnel that twisted down to the earth, sucking dust and debris into it.

The guard with the broken hip and his dead partner lay between them and the tornado. The Hispanic guard rolled onto his chest and crawled toward them with a pained expression, dragging one leg behind him.

The tornado pulled the dead guard into its vortex, and Jake watched the corpse vanish into the swirling debris. He started toward the surviving guard, but Laurel held him back.

Two seconds later the tornado sucked the screaming

man into its fury. If the second guard's soul escaped, Jake could not see it. He looked over his shoulder at the pool.

"Forget the statue. She can't control it and the tornado at the same time from far away."

Jake stared at her with his eye widening. "You're saying she's behind *that*?"

The tornado, more than forty feet wide at its base and two hundred fifty feet wide where it met the clouds, roared toward them.

Laurel held out her left hand.

Grabbing it, Jake raised his voice. "Let's go back inside. If she's really controlling this, she won't trash her mansion." *I hope.*

Laurel dragged him toward the woods at a forty-five-degree angle. "That's exactly what she wants. We're safer out here."

Running, Jake watched the tornado tear through the lawn, passing within one hundred yards of them. He couldn't see the woods to determine if Ripper remained waiting for them, and he knew that even if the receiver for his headset still worked, he wouldn't hear the man's voice over the tornado's deafening roar.

As they passed the garden closer to the woods, the tornado stopped just short of the house and changed direction like a giant top: it pursued them at an incredible speed.

Laurel jerked his hand, changing direction again. Now they fled toward the driveway in front of the mansion at another forty-five-degree angle. The wind at their backs pushed them faster. They passed the front of the mansion and crossed the yard. Taking the lead, Jake pulled Laurel to the left. They stopped as soon as they reached the row of cherry trees. Behind them, the tornado zigzagged across the side yard, destroying the lawn.

Taking deep breaths, Jake glanced at Laurel, who nodded her readiness. Turning, they ran along the trees, parallel to the driveway. The woods beckoned two hundred yards to their left, but Jake knew Laurel wouldn't make it far in there on bare feet. They stood a better chance running for the road at the end of the property.

The roar grew louder, and as Jake looked behind him the tornado broke from its searching pattern and blew between the woods and the cherry trees, sucking branches, limbs, and entire trees into it. Laurel pulled Jake to her right, crossing the driveway. They ran onto the lawn without any protection except her invisibility spell, and Jake felt exposed and helpless.

The tornado shifted its trajectory to the right, ripping five cherry trees out of the ground and sending them flying in different directions. Jake and Laurel stopped, trying to calculate the trajectory of one tree that sailed over their heads and struck the lawn ahead of them. They went around it and veered into the driveway, running for the guardhouse ahead.

Behind them, the tornado resumed its zigzagging pattern, crossing the driveway and tearing up the front lawn. If Laurel was right and Lilian controlled the tornado, she wanted them bad. They reached the guardhouse.

"Keep going," Jake said, out of breath.

"No more . . ."

He slid his right arm around her waist and pressed his stump against her chest, holding her up. "Walk to the gates but keep moving. When you see them open, go through and hang a left, understand?"

She nodded, her hair a mess and her eyes dazed. He gave her a gentle push and she staggered forward.

Then he entered the guardhouse, where he saw a dozen monitors for cameras stationed around the property, all of them feeding into a digital recorder. He jerked the recorder away from its station, disconnecting it from cables, and dropped it on the floor.

A separate monitor showing the gates overlooked a manual switch, which he threw to one side. On the monitor he saw the gates open. Framed within the back window like a painting, the tornado raced straight toward him. He ran out the side door of the guardhouse and after Laurel, who had already vanished.

The tornado blasted through the guardhouse, destroying it in seconds like a model made of balsa wood. Jake pumped his legs faster. The roar of the tornado grew louder, and wind whipped at his back, debris stinging his legs. He ran through the gates and made a hard left turn onto the road just as his Maxima screeched to a stop in front of him.

Sitting behind the wheel, Ripper reached over and opened the passenger door for him.

Jake jumped in and shut the door.

Laurel sat in the back, one hand clawing each front seat. "Now back up slowly. We have to be quiet."

His face tight with fear, Ripper threw the car into reverse and backed up.

The tornado moved into the road where the vehicle had just been, spewing debris. It stood in place, like a runner debating whether or not to cross the street.

She made the entire car invisible, Jake thought.

The tornado veered away from the Maxima.

"Make a slow U-turn and get us the hell out of here," Laurel said.

FIFTEEN

Ripper executed a three-point turn and floored it, and the Maxima rocketed away from Lilian Kane's estate, trees blurring on each side of the vehicle.

Pressed against the seat by velocity, Jake checked his side mirror and watched the tornado move in the opposite direction. He fastened his seat belt, drew his Thunder Ranch, and popped its cylinder open. "How did you make the whole car invisible?"

Ripper glanced into the rearview mirror.

Still clutching the seats, Laurel stared ahead. "I created a blind spot around the car that makes it invisible to Lilian's powers, just like I did with both of us in the yard. Since she wasn't here she had to rely on her magic to see us, and that's what I was able to shield us from."

Jake fished his speed loader out of his pants pocket. "How the hell is she controlling that tornado?"

"She created it, just like she did these clouds, and whatever she creates, she controls."

With the revolver loaded, Jake snapped its cylinder shut and peered at the dark clouds overhead. "Lilian creates weather?" He holstered the gun and returned the empty speed loader to his pocket. "How does she do that, by rain dancing?"

"She's the most powerful witch alive. At least that's what she told us."

Ripper turned in their direction with an incredulous expression.

"Us?"

"The members of her coven."

"Eternity Books."

"You did some research."

"That's how I knew where to find you. Your letter to Jackie sure wasn't any help."

"I was trying to prevent you from doing anything foolish. I should have known better."

"Here we are."

"I said thank you."

"Clear skies ahead," Ripper said.

"Don't slow down," Jake said.

Gesturing through the windshield, Ripper raised his voice. "Will one of you tell me what the fuck's going on? I stuck around and saved your hides when I could have taken off, and I rode to the rescue when I saw the lady here run through those gates."

Jake peered at the clear, darkening sky. "Keep driving.

We'll piece things together for you as we go."

The car passed beneath the edge of the cloud cover.

"Slow down," Jake said.

Ripper eased up on the gas and the Maxima decelerated.

Laurel stared out the back window. "If I drop the shield while the clouds are still visible, she'll see us."

"You're a witch, too?" Ripper said.

"I used to be."

"This is some fucked-up shit."

"Cheer up," Jake said. "You doubled your pay."

"I should be getting a hell of a lot more than that for tangling with witches and shit."

"A deal's a deal. Besides, who believes in witches? There's no such thing."

"That statue came to life. I *saw* it. I shot it over and over, and that Robocop gun didn't do shit. Now she says the queen bee sent that tornado after us, and I believe her. You should have seen those clouds roll in out of nowhere. I wanted to bolt."

"You're awfully willing to suspend your disbelief," Jake said.

"I believe in the occult."

"I'd have asked you for help sooner if I'd known that."

Ripper glanced at Jake's stump. "I'm glad you didn't."

Jake turned to Laurel. "I know your connection to Kane but nothing else. What did you do to her that drove you into hiding and made her come after you?"

"If you want to spill secrets in front of a stranger, spill your own."

"Touché. That bag back there has my jeans in it. You're welcome to them. Just take my wallet out."

Laurel unzipped the bag and took out his jeans. "Good thing there's a belt."

"Are we going back to the office?" Ripper said.

"Yes," Jake said.

"That's the first place she'll look for us," Laurel said as she pulled on the jeans.

"No kidding. I paid her a visit today and she knew who I was."

"You can't fight tornadoes."

"I don't plan to."

"She'll come after us with everything she's got. Wait until you see what she can do face-to-face."

"If Manhattan's the first place she'll look for us, then she's going to do damage whether we go there or not. At least I have resources at my place. I'd rather take my chances facing her with them now than without them whenever she tracks us down."

"Why did you bother rescuing me if you were just going to take me back to where she found me in the first place?"

"It's in my nature."

"Did you two used to be married?" Ripper said.

Jake looked at Laurel and they smiled.

"We understand each other," Jake said.

"My girl's back in New York, so that's where I'm going." Ripper nodded at Jake. "You're not wearing your jacket anymore. Do you plan to wear your piece at the tolls?"

With difficulty, Jake leaned forward and removed the

shoulder holster, which he stuffed into the side compartment of his door.

"Uh, those clouds are following us," Ripper said.

"She knows where we're going," Laurel said.

Jake turned on the radio and searched for a weather station.

Edgar grabbed a slice at a corner pizzeria and walked to
Jake's office building. Streetlights came on as dusk settled
over the city, and he didn't think twice about seeing the
Tower reaching into the clear evening sky.

He passed a Cajun restaurant where he and Jake had
eaten several times, then stopped outside the psychic parlor
near the entrance to Jake's building. He had passed the
parlor every time he had come to see Jake and had never set
foot inside. Why would he? He didn't believe in psychics,
tarot card readers, or palm readers. But something drew
him to the storefront now. Gazing at his reflection in the
front window, which had closed curtains behind it, he felt
that he *had* been inside before. Had Jake taken him in there
during his time as a raven? If so, he had never said anything
to him about it.

Moving to the door, Edgar tried the doorknob, but it
was locked. *After business hours.*

Then he took out his phone and called home.

Joyce answered on the third ring. "Hello?"

"Hey, it's me."

"Where are you? I'm cooking pot roast."

He didn't want to tell her, but he had lost his taste for meat. "I'm standing outside Jake's building. I need to see him and then I'll come home."

"How was your day?"

He sighed. "About like I expected."

"The phone won't stop ringing."

"Reporters?"

"Word of your return is out."

Damn. "I'm sorry, babe."

"Don't be. It's a small price to pay to have you back. I told them I don't know where you're staying. I'm afraid that if I unplug the phone they'll just show up here."

"Do it anyway and don't answer the door. I'll call your cell when I'm close." He ended the call, stepped into the vestibule, and pressed the buzzer for Jake's office.

"Yes?" a woman said.

Edgar knew that Jake had a part-time bookkeeper, and Jake had told him Carrie now worked as his full-time office manager. "I'm here to see Jake."

"We're closed. He isn't here. Come back tomorrow."

"My name's Edgar Hopkins. I used to be Jake's partner."

A moment passed and then the door buzzed.

Edgar entered the lobby and rode the elevator to the fourth floor. His footsteps echoed in the corridor as he walked to Jake's office. He tried the door but it was locked, so he rang the bell.

A moment later the door opened, and a woman about

four and a half feet tall with piercings and tattoos stood before him. If Jake had told him Carrie was a dwarf, Edgar had forgotten that bit of information.

"Come in then," Carrie said, turning away from the door.

Edgar watched her walk to her desk in leather platform boots that added six inches to her height. She wore tattered fishnet stockings, a leather miniskirt, and a bright blue belly shirt.

Some dress code, he thought as he closed the door.

"Jake's on an assignment. I don't know when he'll be back."

"Are you working late?"

"No, I'm waiting for him."

"Then I'll wait, too."

"He could be a while."

"That's okay. I've got time." In truth, he wanted to get to Brooklyn to see Joyce and Martin, but he needed to see Jake. He looked around the sparse office. "I'd like to wait in his office."

Her smile oozed sarcasm. "I can't allow that."

"All right." He sat in one of the chairs in the corner.

As the lights of the Triborough Bridge gleamed in the settling darkness, Jake looked out his window. Clouds raced across the Harlem River. Water appeared to rise from the river, forming a cylinder that reached the clouds.

"Mother-*father*," he said. "We've got company."

The waterspout must have been two hundred feet wide and five times as high. It crossed the river parallel to the bridge, but halfway across it veered over at an angle, moving closer to the bridge.

Ripper weaved the car in and out of lanes.

"Stay steady," Laurel said. "She's looking for breaks in the traffic patterns to locate us."

Ripper drew in a breath and slowed down.

"That's better."

They got off the bridge and merged onto FDR Drive, and Jake lost sight of the waterspout. Glancing in the rearview mirror, Ripper sat forward. Jake and Laurel turned at the same time. Through the back window, Jake saw a tornado barreling down the FDR at one hundred miles per hour. "Crap," he said.

The tornado raced along the FDR and hurled speeding cars out of its path, scattering them like toys, throwing them as far as thirty feet away. It absorbed a Lexus, which vanished within it.

Ripper stepped on the gas, accelerating to one hundred miles an hour, shifting from lane to lane, racing the other speeding cars.

One hundred feet above the ground, the Lexus emerged from the tornado upside down and sailed spinning through the air.

Oh, my God, Jake thought.

The Lexus crashed onto the highway, its front end

flattening, and rolled several times, causing other vehicles to spin out of control. Jake glimpsed gold light flickering inside the demolished Lexus.

"Do you still want to go back to Manhattan?" Laurel said.

"The end game isn't just to rescue you anymore. It's to stop her," Jake said. "We can't do that unless we're close to where she is."

The tornado bore down on them.

"I can't go any faster without crashing," Ripper said.

Jake read the speedometer: one hundred and ten. The car shook.

He looked at Laurel. "Any ideas?"

With fear visible in her eyes, she shook her head.

"Slow down, pull a U-ie, and skirt along the edge of the highway in the opposite direction. Maybe we can squeeze by it without getting sucked in."

"You're bugging," Ripper said.

"You're our only hope."

Ripper took his foot off the gas and the Maxima decelerated.

The approaching tornado sucked an SUV into its vortex and spat it out in the opposite direction. The debris inside the cone filled the rear window.

"It's going to be on top of us before we slow down enough to turn," Ripper said.

Jake stared at the speedometer: sixty miles an hour. "Step on the brakes!"

Ripper screamed and slammed on the brakes, and the car shook from the force of the oncoming tornado.

Just when Jake thought the tornado would swallow them, Ripper jerked the steering wheel hard right and continued to turn it even as the car went into a spin so fast that Jake thought the tornado had them.

The view outside the window blurred, Jake's stomach lurched, and Laurel joined Ripper in screaming. The tornado's roar grew so loud that Jake couldn't hear anything else. The car settled on its shock absorbers facing the side of the highway, its windows covered with dust. The engine continued to run, and Laurel clung to the front seats. The roar moved away from them and faded.

"Is everyone okay?" Jake said.

"Yeah," Ripper said.

"I'm fine," Laurel said.

A sound like a thousand pebbles pouring onto concrete filled the car, and a downpour of rain washed the windows, revealing the cars racing by them.

Peering out the back window, Jake watched stunned-looking drivers get out of the vehicles that had been scattered to the sides of the highway and inspect them for damage.

"Follow that tornado," he said.

SIXTEEN

Jake directed Ripper to the parking garage where he maintained a space. Ripper switched off the engine, unfastened his seat belt, and reached for his door handle.

"Keep the doors closed," Laurel said.

Jake slid his arm through the loop of his shoulder holster, which he adjusted.

"What now?" Ripper said.

Laurel released Ripper's seat. "Take my hand."

Ripper took her hand.

"Now you can open the door. Get out and don't let go of my hand."

Ripper opened his door and got out. Jake helped Laurel into the front seat so she could follow Ripper sideways. Before she got out, she offered Jake her other hand.

Jake turned around in his seat, kneeling on it, and grasped Laurel's hand. "I'm lucky I still have one hand."

Laurel got out and Jake crawled after her, using his stump for balance. His jeans were baggy on her, and she had rolled them up. Ripper handed him the car keys, and he used the remote to lock the door. The three of them stood with their hands locked.

"Remember," Laurel said. "Don't let go."

"Don't worry," Ripper said.

They walked to a metal door, opened it, and entered a stairway. The door slam echoed behind them and they climbed the stairs. They emerged on the ground level and walked outside.

"Oh, shit," Ripper said, echoing Jake's thoughts.

Dense clouds filled the sky as far as the eye could see, cottony claws poised to rake the city.

"It could be a regular storm," Ripper said.

"The hell it could." Laurel turned to Jake. "You want to go to our building? Let's get there fast."

They moved down Twenty-third Street. Around them, pedestrians glanced at the sky and walked faster. Jake felt moisture and electricity in the air at the same time.

"Keep your eyes peeled for any women standing near the building," Laurel said. "They'll be looking for us, and they'll be able to see us. Stay close to the buildings so Lilian can't see us from the Flatiron."

"I expect a bonus," Ripper said.

Jake noted the Tower gleaming against ominous black clouds. They hugged the buildings on their left, and he couldn't see the Flatiron Building.

Gusts of wind assailed them, pushing them backwards,

and they leaned into the force, resisting it.

Propelled by the wind, a man staggered toward them, leaning his back against the force. He slammed into Jake's and Laurel's hands, but they held firm and wouldn't allow him to break their grasp. Jake moved behind Laurel like a swinging gate and the man blew by him.

The clouds above turned green, casting an eerie pall over the sidewalk.

"Oh no," Laurel said.

A funnel descended from the sky, touching down between the Flatiron building and the Tower. Garbage rose from the ground and blew out, newspaper pages floating in all directions and clouds of dust billowing away from the cyclone. Motorists slammed their brakes and honked their horns, bringing traffic to a calamitous standstill. The cars rocked on their shock absorbers. Windshields splintered and windows shattered. A woman pedaling her bicycle away from the force looked over her shoulder, then screamed as the tornado pulled her and the ten-speed end over end into its funnel.

The tornado hurled parked cars out of its way, and a Buick flew through the air and crashed through the glass façade of the Tower's second floor. Cars rolled across the sidewalk on either side of the street with great booming sounds. The tornado remained stationary, gyrating like a dancer, its funnel expanding.

Scores of motorists abandoned their vehicles and ran in the opposite direction.

Jake stood rooted to the sidewalk, debating their next

move. If they ran to the building, they might reach the doors before the tornado swallowed them. If they turned and retreated, it could devour them.

But we're supposed to be invisible to Lilian, he thought.

A heavy metal trash can dropped from the sky and crashed behind them.

Ripper sprang forward. Laurel did not protest, even though she had to run barefoot on the sidewalk, and Jake followed. They headed straight toward the tornado, which lurched forward and raced in their direction, blowing through four lanes of traffic.

Abandoned vehicles rose before Jake and his companions like a giant wave, crashing on top of each other, metal shrieking against metal. One car after another disappeared inside the twister's vortex, only to rocket back out. An SUV sailed over the street and slammed into a UPS truck, crushing both vehicles' front ends; a Nissan Sentra flew spinning into a corner of the New York Edition Hotel, where it flattened on impact and fell to the sidewalk below; a police cruiser shot upside down through the second floor of a building. Clouds of dust blew against the buildings, turning them chalky white.

Jake, Lauren, and Ripper sprinted through the dust, beyond the Cajun restaurant Jake frequented, and hit a wall of resistance when they reached Laurel's parlor. The tornado froze ahead of them, sucking a traffic cop into it.

Gritting his teeth, Jake leaned into the wind force, dragging Laurel beside him, Ripper pulling her from the other side.

The broken body of the traffic cop blasted out of the tornado like a missile and went through the third floor of Jake's building.

Jake planted one foot on the sidewalk, then the other, straining with effort.

A Hyundai blew onto the sidewalk in front of him, producing a shower of sparks. The car sped past them, crashed into the front of Laurel's parlor, and shattered its window.

Circling the car meant getting even closer to the tornado. Dust and other particles struck Jake's face. An airborne milk crate spun toward Ripper, who deflected it with his free hand, but one corner still struck the side of his head.

Jake reached the door first and turned his back on the force. A thick layer of dust covered the glass door. He pulled Laurel close to it, Ripper bringing up the rear. Ripper had the only free hand, so he opened the door. Even as Jake pushed them inside the vestibule the tornado increased its turbulence, its roar deafening. Jake realized that through the tornado, Lilian may have seen the door open with no one standing before it.

Ripper pressed the buzzer button, blood flowing from the gash in his head.

A projectile exploded through the door behind them, shattering the glass pane and slamming into the wall to their left at an angle with such force that it showered them in warm liquid: human blood. The broken, shredded form of a bald man collapsed on the floor, his shattered limbs as flexible as tentacles.

Laurel squeezed Jake's hand, her face spattered with

blood. Because Jake didn't see a soul rise from the corpse, he knew the man had been killed inside the tornado.

The inside door clicked and they rushed through it. Jake kicked the door shut, and a layer of dust formed over its glass panes. As he turned in the direction of the elevator, a human missile crashed through the door and slid across the floor, leaving a wide trail of blood, and came to a stop ahead of them. The alarm kicked in, adding to the cacophony of violent noise.

"Stay out of the blood," Jake said. "She'll see our footprints."

Still holding hands, they made their way to the elevator and ran across the narrow lobby to the stairs, which they climbed. As soon as Jake could not see the front door, Laurel released his hand and Ripper's.

"Lilian knows which floor your office is on," she said, panting. "I think she drove us here so she'll know where we are."

"We were supposed to be invisible to Lilian on the street," Jake said.

"We were," Laurel said, wincing with each step. "She must have had a search spell on your car. As soon as we left it, the spell located it and she knew we were in the neighborhood."

The ringing alarm echoed on each floor of the building. On the fourth floor they staggered to Jake's office. The alarm stopped as Carrie opened the door, and they ran gasping into the suite, covered head to toe in dust.

The roar of the tornado had dwindled to nothing when Jake slammed the door and turned its locks.

"I think it's over." Edgar stood at the dust-covered window.

"You're bleeding," Carrie said, her voice rising at the sight of Ripper's wound.

"It's nothing," Ripper said.

"Let me see."

Ripper got down on one knee and bowed his head.

Carrie's eyes widened. "Shit, you need stitches."

"Later," Ripper said.

Carrie embraced him. "I was so worried about you, and then that tornado came, and I was terrified you'd walk right into it."

"We did."

"You came through that?" Edgar said.

Jake gestured at his dusty clothes. "It wasn't easy."

"Who's this?" Ripper said.

"My partner." Jake faced Edgar. "What's going on?"

"Ex-partner," Edgar said, measuring Ripper. "Who are you?"

"He's my boyfriend," Carrie said.

Edgar looked at Jake. "I wanted to talk to you." He shifted his gaze to Laurel and his face and voice softened. "I didn't expect *this*."

Laurel stared at Edgar as well.

Edgar crossed the office and stood before her. He looked her up and down, then cocked his head and blinked. "You took care of me."

"I'm Laurel."

"Thank you."

"You're welcome."

Edgar embraced her. She hugged him back.

"I'm confused," Carrie said.

Sirens wailed outside and Edgar released Laurel.

"People are hurt down there," Edgar said.

"Some are dead," Jake said in a weak voice.

"We should go help."

Jake gestured at his companions. "We can't right now. Leave it to the emergency response teams."

Edgar narrowed his eyes.

Ripper stood. "If that tornado's gone, I want to get out of here fast."

Jake looked at Laurel, who shook her head.

"That isn't a good idea," he said.

"You've got to be shitting me," Ripper said.

"You want us to stay here?" Carrie said.

"You can leave," Laurel said. "But Ripper needs to stay with us."

"He needs to go to an emergency room."

"After what just happened, the emergency rooms will be packed," Jake said. "You'll just end up spending the night there. We have a needle and thread."

"I'm not going home without my man. If he stays, I'm staying, too."

"Then you can sew him up."

"My meter's running," Ripper said in a prison-hardened tone.

"Shut it down. I'm not charging you for protection."

"You're the one who put me in danger."

"Let's not play the blame game. We've got more

important things to worry about."

"What's going on?" Edgar said.

Carrie sniffed the air and made a disgusted face. "Damn, what's that stink?"

"I'd like to take a shower," Laurel said.

Jake gestured down the hall. "The shower's behind my office. I'll get you some—"

"I know where everything is." Laurel strode across the office on bare feet, leaving bloody footprints behind her.

Carrie made a sour face when she realized the source of the foul odor. Then she looked at Jake. "I suppose you expect me to mop that up."

"Later," Jake said.

Carrie's expression grew more disgusted. "Boss, your eye is dirty."

Blushing beneath his beard, Jake faced Ripper. "I'll get you what I owe you so far. Just wait here. Come on, Edgar."

Jake went into the kitchenette, where he poured tap water into a mug, then led Edgar into his office. Jake closed the door, then the bedroom door, which Laurel had left open. The number of sirens outside multiplied.

"What the hell's going on?" Edgar said. "You're dressed to go behind enemy lines."

Jake set the mug on his desk next to a washcloth. "I'm in the middle of something." He mixed a clear cleaning solution into the mug and used his thumb and forefinger to remove his glass eye. "I guess you could call it a new case."

"Say the word and I'm here for you."

"I appreciate it but no." Jake dunked his eye in the

water, which turned muddy. "You've got your hands full. Just get better and take care of Martin. Go back to work, if that's in the cards."

"I don't think it is. I don't know if I want it to be, either." Edgar picked up the sword from the sofa. "What are you doing with this?"

The ATAC 3000, Jake thought, grimacing as he set his eye on the washcloth. He had forgotten the gun in the car. "It's a gift from a friend." He picked up a small bottle of eyedrops and applied the fluid to his empty socket.

Edgar unsheathed the sword partway and gazed at the reflection of his eyes in the blade. "A thank-you card from Pavot Island?"

Jake returned his glass eye to his socket. "You should be a detective." Kneeling before the safe, he spun a dial on it. "Speaking of which . . ." Maybe he could deflect Edgar's curiosity.

Edgar snapped the sword in its scabbard, which he returned to the sofa. "No real surprises. Mauceri threw me into the system. Missing Persons met with me, then your friend Hammerman from IAB, then your other friend Geoghegan at MCU."

Jake opened the safe. "Teddy's a real sweetheart, isn't he?"

"He puts the *G* in 'gruff.' I had the distinct impression he has a hard on for you."

"I make friends wherever I go." Jake counted out some cash, then closed the safe. "I'll be right back." He went into the reception area and found Ripper and Carrie standing at her desk.

"Here's your balance *and* your bonus," Jake said. "Good work."

Ripper accepted the cash without counting it. "Thanks but I'd like to go home."

"It isn't safe. We all need to stay here tonight."

"A real pajama party, huh?"

"At least we have food." He looked at Carrie. "Right?"

"Right." Carrie picked up a note from her desk. "Lieutenant Geoghegan called earlier."

Jake took the note. "Thanks. Call Jackie and make sure he knows what just happened outside. Warn him there are two bodies in our lobby."

Two innocent people, he thought. How many more casualties had Lilian caused?

When Jake returned to his office, Edgar stood at the wall-length cage he had occupied as a raven, swinging the door back and forth.

"I don't think this is legal," Edgar said.

"It served its purpose."

Turning from the cage, Edgar took an object out of his pocket and set it on Jake's desk. "This belongs to you."

Jake recognized the replica Maltese Falcon that Edgar had given him when he received his private investigator's license.

"You gave my son a murder weapon?"

Jake had used the statue to brain AK, a scarecrow sent by Katrina to kill him. AK was a former informant of Jake's who had taken out Jake's eye with a knife before Jake managed to crush his skull with the falcon.

"You make it sound so twisted. You were a raven. He

was lost. I gave that to him to keep his spirits up."

"You have no idea what it's like to be a parent. If you had a kid I'm sure you wouldn't give him evidence from a homicide."

"I appreciate that."

"Geoghegan ordered me to see the department shrink, so I did. She thinks I'm suffering from post-traumatic stress disorder."

"You are." *That makes two of us.*

"She wants to hypnotize me."

"You aren't."

"Of course not, though it's tempting." Edgar gestured to his head. "I don't feel like I'm all here. I don't feel like a man. Human. I feel like something else."

Jake moved closer to his friend. "Miriam said it would take time. You've only been yourself again for less than three weeks. If I was in your shoes I'd be a drooling basket case."

"I wish I'd taken another month to pull myself together."

"It was your call to come home because you wanted to see Martin."

"I didn't expect to be treated like a criminal."

"I told you what to expect."

"I never take what you say seriously."

The office doorbell rang, and Jake glanced at the security monitors recessed in the wall above the safe. Maria stood at the door in the hallway.

"It's like Grand Central here tonight," Jake said, opening the office door.

"The three of us need a reunion."

Jake hurried through the reception area just as Ripper

opened the door for Maria, who registered surprise as she sized him up. She entered the office, her clothing dusty but not as bad as Jake's and Ripper's, and met Jake near Carrie's desk. Ripper closed and locked the door. Jake felt Carrie staring at Maria.

"What the hell happened to you?" Maria said to Jake.

"I was outside minding my own business when a tornado came by."

"Dressed like a commando?"

"I didn't say where I was coming from."

She nodded at Ripper. "It looks like you boys were out together. Are you all right?"

"I'm fine. How about you? You've got blood on your sleeve."

Maria glanced at her jacket sleeve. "I helped get a guy into an ambulance downstairs. It looks like a bomb site out there. There are two dead guys in your lobby, too."

"Edgar's here."

She raised her eyebrows. "Tell me you didn't drag him into anything."

Jake gestured to his office. "Ask him yourself."

Maria entered the office and Jake followed her.

"Long time no see," Edgar said.

"You were the talk of the station."

"Unlike Jake, I've always been popular. How was your first day back?"

"Same old, same old. I caught a couple of dead hoppers downtown."

Maria looked at Jake. "I was going to offer to take you out to dinner, but how about if the three of us go out instead?"

"Count me out," Edgar said. "I'm going home."

"I've got to stay here with Carrie and Ripper," Jake said.

"Carrie's your secretary, right?"

"Office manager," Carrie said from the other room.

Maria closed the door. "Who's Ripper, that perp with her?"

"I needed an extra person today."

"For what? Jesus, Jake, we just got back. Can't you take some time off?"

The bedroom door opened, and Laurel stepped out wearing Jake's robe, her hair soaking wet.

Jake stiffened and Edgar shot him a panicked look.

"I feel a lot better," Laurel said, noting Maria.

"Who's this?" Maria said in an icy tone.

"I'm Laurel Doniger."

"I told you about Laurel," Jake said.

Maria's expression tightened. "The psychic downstairs. What are you doing up here?"

"I'll be going now," Edgar said.

"Wait for me," Maria said.

"I'll wait out front, then." Edgar escaped to the reception area and closed the door behind him.

"Why don't you tell Maria what you want her to know?" Laurel said to Jake.

"You know my name?"

"I've told Laurel all about you," Jake said.

Maria flashed an angry look at him. "Why don't you tell me what you want me to know?"

"I'll just wait in the bedroom." Laurel returned to the

back room and closed the door.

"What the hell was that?" Jake said.

"You took the words right out of my mouth."

"Laurel's in trouble. I'm helping her. That's all you need to know."

"What kind of help are you giving her, a shampoo? She looks pretty comfortable in that robe, which looks familiar. Oh yeah, I wore it this morning."

"She needs my help the same way Edgar did. She's a friend, she's helped me in the past, and I owe her."

"Why is she in your bedroom wearing your robe?"

"She isn't safe anywhere else."

Maria moved closer to him. "You told me you never slept with her."

Jake swallowed. In Miami when Maria had asked him about Laurel, confessing his brief liaison with the psychic had seemed like an unnecessary complication.

"You fucking piece of shit." Maria stormed past him and opened the door, then stopped and turned back to him. "Just so you know, Geoghegan's got a major bug up his ass about you." She continued into the reception area and slammed the front door.

Laurel emerged from the bedroom again. "I'm sorry about that."

"It was kind of unavoidable."

"You didn't even try to stop her."

"I know. I'll pay for that later. But I wanted her gone for her own safety. Edgar, too. Neither one of them would have left if they'd had any idea what kind of trouble we're in." Moving behind his desk, Jake gestured at the chair on the other side. "It's time you filled in the blanks for me."

Laurel sat down. "What a switch, me sitting in your domain, like one of your clients. Are you sure you're ready for the truth?"

Jake lowered himself onto the leather chair. "I already know that you're Eden, Inc., and I'm pretty sure you stole ninety million dollars from Lilian."

SEVENTEEN

I was born in Hicksville, Long Island, where my father owned and operated a chain of movie theaters. Mother was a voracious reader, and left paperbacks of every genre lying around our house: Erle Stanley Gardner's Perry Mason novels, Reader's Digest Condensed Books, Jacqueline Susann novels, and romances. I got my love of the written word from her.

I got good grades in school, thanks to what was later determined to be a photographic memory. I related well to others, especially to my parents. I didn't have any siblings so we were a close trio. I felt the beating of their hearts and the regulation of their breathing. I felt their vibrations when they were nearby and experienced separation anxiety when they weren't. I had no idea that other children didn't share the same connection.

One winter when I was in third grade I was playing in

our backyard when I had the mischievous urge to throw a snowball at a sparrow chirping in our oak tree. I was terrible at sports and a pathetic shot, so it never occurred to me that I might actually strike it. My heart froze when the poor creature plummeted to the ground. I ran to where it had fallen and dug it from the snow with my mittens. The small bird quivered in my hands, its clawed feet moving in slow circles.

I raced to the back door of our house and banged on it, and when my mother opened it I showed her what I had done. Her expression told me the sparrow would not survive. Tears streamed down my cheeks and the sparrow turned still. I don't remember sinking to my knees, but that's where I found myself, still clinging to the sparrow, my teardrops spattering its feathers. Then a wave of nausea spread through my small body, and the bird kicked again. I sniffled, my eyes widening. The bird managed to right itself.

Sensing my mother's astonishment, I rose. In the blink of an eye the sparrow took off. I watched it soar away, and the motion increased my nausea. The world spun around me and I tasted blood. I felt a weight crushing me into the snow, a sickness pinning me down. My mother crouched beside me and helped me to my feet, and I threw up in the snow.

Inside, my mother wiped my face with a tissue and got me out of my clothes, a peculiar look on her face. The sparrow hadn't been dead but it had been dying. And it had flown away.

Two years later when I was twelve, our dog Bogie, a mutt with champagne-colored fur, slowed down. A tumor developed on his left side, and he walked with a limp, the tumor swinging from side to side. My father explained that Bogie would have to be put to sleep soon.

Bogie slept in my bed on what was supposed to be his last night, and I clung to him, weeping. I stayed up well into the night and awoke to Bogie licking my face. His new-found energy excited me, but when I sat up to embrace him my stomach lurched. I leapt out of bed and ran to the toilet just in time to vomit.

My mother kept me home from school, and I continued to vomit. At some point it occurred to me that I had thrown up more food than I could possibly have had in my stomach. I felt better by dinnertime, which was when we realized that Bogie's tumor had disappeared and he had regained his former spunk. My father chose not to take him to the vet's. Why spend the money? Bogie lived another three years and died of natural causes.

My period came when I was thirteen. A big deal in every young woman's life, right? For me it was more like taking a step forward in evolution. I became sensitive to my parents' presence and moods, even when I was alone in my room. I remember the first time I woke up because one of them had a nightmare; I didn't wake because I heard my mother screaming but because her thoughts and mental images intruded on my sleep. They almost suffocated me, and I awoke in a confused panic. I was even more disturbed the first time I experienced one of my father's dreams.

Over the next five years my senses developed. When I touched someone, their thoughts and emotions overwhelmed me, which made dating difficult; there's such a thing as knowing too much about a person. This all could have taken a toll on me. The temptation to drink or drug my awareness into submission was great, but I had a passion for learning, which dictated that I take care of myself and deal with my growing abilities. I researched psychic phenomena and spiritual healing and visited psychics to see what I could learn from them.

Most were frauds, but one, a psychic healer in Brooklyn, was the real deal. "You absorb the sickness and injuries of others like poison," Madam Selena said. "But then it's inside you like poison. That's why you throw up. It's important that you expel this poison because if you don't you can die. Don't ever make the mistake of thinking you can heal yourself. That's for physicians, not healers."

I had no intention of using these powers if I could avoid it, although I knew my experiences had already had an impact on my writing. My teachers said I had a superior grasp of character development and insight into human behavior, and I graduated high school with honors and won a scholarship to Vassar, where I majored in creative writing and minored in business at my father's insistence. I sold my first romance novel to Harlequin under a pseudonym during my freshman year and sold several more by the time I graduated. I had a number of relationships and learned to ignore the energies I read from my companions, at least short term.

One day during my senior year a sophomore boy collapsed in the cafeteria. His energy had been compromised, and I knew he had suffered a drug overdose. Someone called 911, but everyone basically stood around doing nothing, and I felt his energy fading. I had no choice but to help, so I kneeled beside him and put my hands on his chest.

He had been snorting heroin all night and then crashed, missing his morning class. He awoke for lunch, snorted some more, then wandered over to the cafeteria, a rich boy with a golden future as long as I intervened. But I could scarcely sit there and meditate, chanting while I sucked the poison out of his body. With all my fingertips pressed against his chest, I leaned forward and blew into his mouth. I drew the heroin out of his body through my fingers, but as far as the witnesses knew, I was giving him mouth-to-mouth resuscitation.

I heard his heartbeat and felt his blood streaming through his veins. I also felt my fingers sinking through his flesh and into his body, and a dreamy rainbow spread through me. Then I threw my head back and projectile vomited at the lunch lady, and it was my turn to collapse. I hadn't absorbed all the drug, but I saved that brat's life. His family pulled him out of school, and none of them even bothered to thank me. Bogie had showed more appreciation. That's what makes animals beautiful, isn't it? I guess that's why I felt so protective of Edgar when you brought him to me.

I went to Random House right out of college as an assistant editor. There's nothing like reading books for a living to take the fun out of reading. After six months in the corporate world, I decided to get back to doing what I loved. I wanted to write more than disposable romance novels; I wanted to remain in that genre but at a more prestigious level. I kept up my twelve-hour days, then wrote at night and somehow managed to find time to query agents. That's a fun process: send out twenty letters and wait for those self-addressed stamped envelopes to come back in the mail like homing pigeons.

Finally I got a nibble. A man named James Spider from a major agency invited me out for drinks and told me he planned to start his own agency and wanted to represent me. The only catch was that he also wanted to sleep with me. I declined his offer, and he became verbally abusive and told me I would never amount to more than I already was. It was the most humiliating experience of my life. That man broke my spirit.

One of my duties for Random House was to attend World Book Expo, and that's where I met Lilian. I waited in line to have her sign her latest novel for my mother. I sputtered like any overenthusiastic fan, and somehow she understood my babbling about who I was and what I did. Harla Soto, the president of the company, said she knew my work and thought it was good. Lilian invited me to come see them when I had something new. I was so elated that I didn't even realize I had sensed nothing when I shook Lilian's hand; I got no reading from her at all.

I spent every free minute writing *Love Never Sleeps*, then submitted it to Lillian and waited, which is such a big part of the process.

I didn't have to wait long: Harla called one week later and asked me to come in for a meeting at the Flatiron

Building. Eternity Books occupies the top floor. Lilian had held on to the electronic rights to all her books, and she released the e-books through Eternity and produced her own audio books. The money rolled in, along with fresh TV and movie interest. She and Harla also took on the best talent they could, hiring established authors from the other houses.

Walking into the Eternity offices was like stepping into high society for artists. Lilian had hired top designers to transform the odd-shaped office space of the Flatiron into a luxurious gallery, museum, and lounge all rolled into one. The receptionist knew my name, and Harla greeted me and took me into her office. She said my novel had great potential, and they wanted to sign me to a multi-book contract with a larger advance than I had ever dreamed of. I quit my job the next day.

I worked closely with Lilian and her editors, who made my writing better than it had ever been. Lilian mentored me herself; she said my characterization was top-notch, but my historical details needed greater attention. It amazed me how much she knew about the Middle Ages. We reshaped the book's structure, adding subplots and increasing suspense.

Eternity unveiled *Love Never Sleeps* at World Book Expo and treated me like a celebrity. Harla took out full-page ads in *Publishers Weekly* and hung giant banners in the convention center. Radio spots ran on stations across the country, and their in-house publicist booked interviews for me in every imaginable media outlet. Lilian made sure my book became a best seller, and within a year I was close to a household name.

I moved into a one-bedroom apartment in Manhattan, and Lilian shuttled me to the best and most exclusive parties, where I rubbed elbows with the rich and famous. Lilian thrived on glitz and glamour, and for the first time in my life, I was the object of attention from the media, the paparazzi, and men. Lilian encouraged me to date actors and musicians but to maintain an aura of mystery, playing coy when asked about my liaisons. Our publicist fed the information to the gossip columnists, and I was surprised anyone gave a damn.

I wrote every weekday, and every other weekend I went to Lilian's mansion. The Roman architecture is intentional, because debauchery was always on the menu. Lilian invited everyone from her staff on these retreats, but I was the only author besides herself. She considered the authors she had hired away from the other houses old hat. She had used them to help build the foundation for her success, to slap the other publishers in the face and send a signal that she had no intention of playing nice. She was ruthless in business and enjoyed twisting the knife with a smile.

We each got our own room when we stayed at the mansion. At first we imbibed expensive alcohol, imported from around the world. Later Lilian introduced us to exotic narcotic drinks, encouraging us to let down our guard and free our inhibitions. These drinks had powerful hallucinatory effects that stimulated my body in ways I had never known.

Marathons of sex followed, sometimes with men Lilian arranged for us and sometimes with each other. I had never been interested in drugs or women as sexual partners before, but under Lilian's careful orchestration both were impossible to resist; we held orgies that would have made Caligula envious. The pleasure was intense, mind-boggling, and exhausting.

After a weekend in Eastchester, I needed days to recuperate. The excursions had an unexpected side effect on me: I became more aware of my surroundings, more sensitive to the energies of the people around me. My mild psychic abilities blossomed, and I found myself looking forward to Lilian's concoctions and surprises. I evolved, and there was nothing I wouldn't do for Lilian, whose physical attention proved overwhelming. She encouraged us to explore each other in any manner of combinations, but she had one rule: we were never to engage each other beyond her walls.

In private we addressed each other as "sister," and Lilian referred to us as a "sisterhood," a secret, superior society. I grew to view our sisterhood as a cult, with myself as a willing participant. A year passed before I caught the first whiff of witchcraft. When I was high and Lilian had her legs wrapped around me, pushing God knows what inside me, she whispered obscenities into my ear, which, in my intoxicated state, drove me wild. But as time progressed, I realized Lilian's boastful proclamations had nothing to do with fantasy. Her goal wasn't to turn me on but to indoctrinate me into her coven, and she succeeded.

We didn't wear cloaks, we didn't worship Satan, and we didn't follow the order of Wicca. There were no Ouija boards in the house, no books of spells. Lilian never invoked the name of any deity; if anything, she set herself on a pedestal for us to kneel before. She dismissed any notion of an afterlife and pushed us to live for ourselves in the moment, to be brave enough to take what we wanted and feel no remorse.

The deeper I sank into her self-aggrandizing world, the more I came to realize that my sisters had been collaborators with Lilian the whole time, playing the roles of neophytes for my benefit to make me believe we were all falling under her spell at the same time. This should have made me angry but it didn't. I felt welcomed. Loved. And I knew that with the possible exception of Lilian, none of them shared my ability, which made me Lilian's favorite acolyte. At the time, nothing mattered more.

We practiced spells that increased our narcotized state and heightened our pleasure. It occurred to me that Lilian placed love spells on all of us each weekend. Then there were the cats, black and shiny. Lilian kept so many of them in the house that I questioned her common sense. I realized that she owned one for herself and one for each of my sisters. Every feline was a neutered male and wore a jeweled collar. I wondered when Lilian would present me with my own pet and whether or not I was hers.

On a sunny day in August, she took us onto the back patio, overlooking the valley below. She disrobed before us and stood nude in the sunshine with her arms raised. Clouds formed in the clear sky. Lightning flashed. Thunder roared. Rain fell. Then hail. And snow. *Only over the valley.* I stood gaping at the spectacle. Then Lilian lowered her arms and turned to me, and the sunshine returned. She strode past us back into the house.

My sisters and I exchanged looks of awe. I had no idea if Lilian had actually changed the weather—created weather—or if she had merely created an illusion. In that moment, it didn't matter; I believed she was a god. We followed her into the house and administered to her needs, reveling in her magic.

After my third book for Eternity was published, Lilian arranged for me to become president of the Romance Writers of America, a position I held for two terms. It was an honorary title as far as I was concerned. In reality, I was a puppet: Harla's staff drafted my agenda and posted my positions on the RWA message board. All I had to do was appear at functions and read the speeches Lilian wrote for me. But my time in office cemented my reputation as one of the real players in my field; I became a commodity. TV deals landed at my feet, all managed by Harla.

Lilian and Harla took me to a high-profile industry party thrown by Alicia Dormeyer, the head of The Love Book, Eternity's chief rival. Alicia had started out as a reader and progressed to editor like so many others in publishing, then switched gears and became an agent. She formed The Love Book as an independent publishing company and cultivated the careers of many greats in the genre, including Lilian, who eventually left to form Eternity.

Alicia was in her sixties, though she appeared to be a decade younger, and she and Lilian enjoyed a friendly, catty rivalry like two old movie stars. Seeing them together made it almost impossible to believe Lilian was close to the same age; my mentor looked only a decade older than me, which she attributed to plastic surgery and blood doping. When she appeared at many public events, she wore glamorous sunglasses, which hid just how youthful she appeared.

Alicia greeted us with open arms at the party, and as soon as she turned her back Lilian ordered me to seduce Scott Dormeyer, Alicia's son and second in command, which took little effort on my part. Scott hoped I'd spill Eternity's secrets. Instead, I absorbed from him every facet of The Love Book's upcoming four-year game plan. Lilian wasted no time destroying her rival's company.

At our next retreat, Lilian presented me with a gift to keep at the mansion: a beautiful black cat, fully grown. I named him Othello, and he took to me just as my sisters' cats took to them. I became Lilian's regular companion at the retreats, and we spoke for hours on every topic imaginable. I loved Lilian but so did all my sisters. She said she loved us. Rituals began to dominate our weekends, and she demanded absolute allegiance and obedience from us, which we gladly granted, refusing her nothing.

Almost three years ago, after the publication of my sixth book for Eternity, Lilian gathered us in the basement where we practiced our spells and named me her chief disciple, which made me second in command. Tears filled my eyes and I thanked her. I expected the others to be jealous, especially Harla, but they embraced me and made love to me. That celebration felt like the culmination of my life.

Then Lilian led us into a secret chamber illuminated by torches. A man lay naked on a round table, his wrists and ankles bound to the surface by an invisible force. He wore a black hood. We stood around the table as he strained against his invisible bonds.

Lilian handed me a long dagger with a serpent wrapped around its handle. "Kill him."

Even in my inebriated state I must have looked dumbfounded.

"Prove your love and loyalty. Sacrifice this man."

I stared at the blade in my hand, then at the man on the table. Lilian removed his hood, and it took several moments for me to recognize James Spider's horrified features.

"This man humiliated you. He treated you like dirt. He represents everything we despise in our industry and in life. No one knows he's here. No one will find his body. No one will ever tie you to this action, which is only a crime in the eyes of a system we reject. Do this for yourself. Do this for our sisterhood. Do this for *me*. Show us how much you love us."

Staring at Spider, I tightened my hands on the knife's handle. I had never forgotten him even though I had tried, and I had daydreamed about confronting him in public and belittling him as he had belittled me. But I always pushed such thoughts to the back of my mind, as adults are prone to do.

"Make yourself feel good. Make yourself feel powerful."

Swallowing, I hesitated.

My sisters rubbed my back and shoulders. "Do it," they said in unison. "Do it for us."

Spider's face trembled with fear, tears rolling down

his cheeks. His mouth opened and closed, and I knew he wanted to beg for his life, but Lilian had placed some spell on him to keep him silent.

Gripping the dagger in both hands, I held it over his heart, giving myself a target, then raised it over my head.

"Do it now," Lilian said.

I drove the dagger down with all my strength, piercing Spider's heart. Squeezing his eyes shut, he arched his back, a whistling sound escaping his nostrils. Releasing the dagger, I stepped back and Spider's body slumped to the table.

Lilian closed the fingers of one hand around the handle and drew the blade out, freeing Spider's dark blood to pump through the wound. His head rolled to one side and his body stilled.

For a moment I felt nothing, then shock. I had just murdered a man in cold blood.

"Now you're really one of us," Lilian said. Stepping closer to me, she ran her tongue over the dagger's blade, lapping the blood, and kissed me. Then she and my sisters pulled me down into darkness.

I awoke early the next morning, entangled in Lilian's limbs on a round bed, her thoughts hidden from me as always. Recalling little that had occurred after the murder, I slipped on a silk robe and descended the stairs to the gallery, where I gazed at the portraits on the walls. Lilian worshipped the women in those paintings. I cast my first solo spell, creating a tiny blind spot in my mind, where my thoughts and new suspicions would be safe from Lilian and my sisters.

A shadow glided over the tile floor. Othello blinked at me, and I knew he had been sent to spy on me. Turning my back on the portraits, I walked into the kitchen, selected my breakfast, and carried it out onto the patio. The cat followed me and rubbed against my leg.

My sisters rose in pairs, and soon we luxuriated on the patio and in the pool. I smiled and made conversation, laughing when it seemed appropriate, but inside I wanted to cry. I had committed murder, and that murder linked me to those witches forever. No one mentioned my actions the previous night; no one had to. They had me right where they wanted me.

Alone in my new condo, I wept. I couldn't write; the magic that came from creating was gone. Lilian called me to check up on me, and my sisters did as well.

My contract with Eternity was up for renewal. Everyone assumed I planned to sign on for another round, and I assured them I did. Harla mailed me a contract for ten novels that would have made me a multimillionaire. I signed the papers and mailed them, and Lilian made sure the announcement received great fanfare. I was on the cusp of being as famous as Lilian herself.

I enjoyed a weekend at home and dreaded returning to the mansion. To my relief, Lilian departed for a two-week publicity tour in Europe. I had two weeks to plan my escape. On Lilian's advice, I had invested most of my money in real estate and had little in the way of liquid assets.

The first payment on my heralded deal with Eternity would not arrive until the following month, and I knew that if I asked Harla to expedite it, red flags would go up. Then Harla called me: Lilian had requested that she take me out to a celebratory dinner in her absence. I accepted her offer with seeming gratitude and set my plan in motion. I went to my second bank and closed down my old college fund. I had kept it a secret from Eternity's accountants and had stuffed it with cash at every opportunity. If Lilian's team monitored my banking with the account they knew about, no sudden flurry of activity would alert them. I walked out of the location with a hundred grand.

I purchased a used SUV. Wearing a disguise and plain clothes, I rented a basement apartment. It was in a Staten Island house, so I didn't have to worry about paperwork or a background search. I returned to Manhattan, showered, and got ready for my dinner with Harla.

We met at Le Bernardin on West Fifty-first Street. We drank wine and ate fish and chatted like old friends. I made sure the wine kept coming. I drew the conversation out, prolonging our date, and by the time Harla paid the check with her corporate credit card she was drunk. When we left the restaurant she staggered and I caught her. Then I hailed a taxi. Sitting in the backseat, Harla closed her eyes and moaned. I slid my hand over hers and interlocked our fingers.

"We'll be there soon," I said.

Then I absorbed her thoughts, reading her like a book. I disregarded her life experiences; I didn't care about her. Instead, I focused on her duties and responsibilities at Eternity Books. No matter what Lilian said, Harla was her most trusted lieutenant. I committed dates, figures, bank account numbers, user names, and passwords to my memory. With Lilian's information in my grasp, I sifted through thoughts and mental pictures until I experienced a conversation in which Lilian discussed her intentions for me with Harla. My eyes widened and I nearly vomited. I released Harla's hand, and the taxi pulled over to her building.

Harla opened her eyes, as if sensing something had happened while she had been unconscious. I put her mind at ease, thanked her for a lovely girls' night out, and bid her good night.

Once home, I picked up my laptop with all my files, went into the garbage room, and dropped it down the chute to be compacted in the disposal unit. Then I drove to my Staten Island hideout, confident Harla suspected nothing.

I had nine days to pull off my scheme before Lilian returned to the States. I expanded the blind spot in my brain to encompass the house and set to work. I bought new clothes, hair dye, scissors, and a laptop. I created multiple aliases and over one hundred fictitious shell corporations with corresponding bank accounts. I was grateful my father had insisted I minor in business at college and that I had been blessed with a photographic memory.

I opened multiple Swiss bank accounts, then accessed Lilian's primary account. It took only six mouse clicks to relieve her of one hundred million of her hidden dollars. I donated 90 percent to charities in her name, sent 1 percent to James Spider's family, and nine million dollars for myself.

I caught a few hours' sleep, then dyed my hair blonde

and loaded my belongings back into the SUV, taking the blind spot with me. I drove to JFK and abandoned the SUV, then took a taxi back to Manhattan to begin my new secret life.

I'd like to say I thought out every detail, but that wasn't the case. I went straight to the Flatiron District, because I figured Lilian's own neighborhood would be the safest when she blew her top. Hiding under her nose appealed to me. I knew that would drive her crazy if she found out.

Surrounded by a shield, I walked into a psychic's parlor on Twenty-third Street. Madame Lisette greeted me in the sunken parlor, and I paid her for a reading. She was a fraud, and she was on the edge of being destitute: her husband had left her high and dry. Lisette desperately wanted to return to France, so I made that possible. I paid her thirty thousand dollars in cash to sign her sweetheart lease over to one of my new aliases and to leave me with copies of her documents and access to her nearly empty bank account.

I had my sanctuary, but I needed to buy myself greater protection. I had no idea how soon Harla would figure out I'd flown the coop or when Lilian would search for me. I assumed she already knew her money had disappeared and was on her way back.

From the safety of Laurel Doniger's parlor, I made plans to purchase the entire building.

Two days later, word of my disappearance dominated the media. I felt terrible for my parents and desperately wanted to contact them, but that was impossible.

I knew when Lilian came home, because a storm hit

New York that almost wiped the house I stayed at in Staten Island from the face of the earth. Lightning struck and killed my father in Hicksville, and stormy waves drowned my mother one week later. Lilian caused their deaths, but my beating heart proved I'd outsmarted her. I bought the building for five million dollars and readied myself for a life of solitude, biding my time.

EIGHTEEN

Tears rolled down Laurel's cheeks, but her voice did not waver. "I've waited so long to tell someone all that."

The sirens outside had stopped.

Jake gazed at Laurel. "It's not like I never asked."

"Knowledge is a dangerous thing. The more you knew about me, the greater the chances of Lilian discovering where I'd holed up. I knew the first thing she would do was cast a search spell for me; the thoughts of anyone who saw me and knew who I was would trigger her psychic alarm."

A helicopter hummed outside.

A TV news crew, Jake thought. "You stole one hundred million dollars." He disbelieved his words as he spoke them.

"Most of it went to good causes, even if you discount what I kept for myself. Thanks to me, Lilian was hailed as a world-class philanthropist. It was the best public relations she ever bought."

"The most expensive, too. If I've learned one thing about the wealthy, they don't take kindly to other people helping themselves to what belongs to them."

"I only depleted the secret account I knew about. I'm sure she has more that Harla didn't know about."

"You could have skimmed a million, and she might not have even noticed it was missing."

"She would have known, and she would have been just as angry. Powerful people don't like to be outwitted."

"So you made a public show out of it."

"She still would have killed my parents. It's a miracle she didn't kill Harla. I can just imagine what she did to her."

"You could have gone into hiding in Costa Rica or Tahiti or Belize . . ."

"The search spell would have been global. There's nowhere I would have been safe. I made the best play I could, which was to hide as close to her as possible."

"You can't just buy a building on eBay, even if you have the money."

"I used surrogates, of course. Middlemen. Money talks, and I knew the odds of a man recognizing a missing romance novelist—even if I hadn't changed my appearance—were slim."

"Does Jackie know any of this?"

"No. As far as he's concerned, Eden, Inc., views me as a favored tenant. He believes I have a medical condition that makes me sensitive to sunlight, coupled with agoraphobia. I came to rely on him, though, and we became good friends. Until you moved in he was my sole company."

Jake sat forward in his seat. "I remember when I first

checked this office space out. I saw your parlor before anything else. When the Realtor showed me the office, I knew I could never afford it, but something in the back of my head told me to make that offer to handle building security in exchange for a discount on the rent. Did you plant that idea in my head?"

"I don't have that ability. But I felt your vibrations as soon as you entered the building. At first I panicked that Lilian had come, but I could tell your energy was positive. When the Realtor posed your counteroffer to Eden, Inc., I accepted."

Sheryl's energy, Jake thought. "Why?"

"I needed a knight in shining armor."

Jake snorted. "I only set foot in your parlor because you sent Carmen Rodriguez to me. Was that a ruse?"

"No, I really wanted to help Carmen. That's why I kept the parlor open: to help people. I have a lot to atone for."

"You murdered a man."

Laurel lowered her voice. "We have a lot in common: we've both killed people, we both know that the supernatural exists, and we both set up shop near our enemy."

"I've only killed bad guys, usually in self-defense. You killed an innocent man."

"You don't need to remind me. Like I said, I have a lot to atone for."

The telephone rang, and Jake glanced at the light on the device. The hair on the back of his neck prickled.

"Don't let her answer it," Laurel said.

Jake stabbed the intercom button. "Don't answer the

phone, Carrie."

"I wasn't going to," Carrie said over the speaker.

The phone continued to ring. The answering machine picked up, and Jake listened to Carrie's voice. "You've reached Helman Investigations and Security . . ."

After the outgoing message ended, there was a click.

"Maybe she'll send an e-mail," Jake said.

"Lilian won't send anything that can be traced to her."

Lightning flickered through the dust-covered window, and two seconds later thunder boomed like an explosion, causing both of them to flinch.

"That was close," Jake said.

"She's angry."

Rain pelted the windows, streaking the dust, which soon vanished.

Jake rose and went to the windows. As he closed the blinds, he glimpsed the strobes of emergency response vehicles illuminating the disaster zone below. "That tornado threw cars around like they were Tonka toys. If she wanted you dead, she could send a Chevy through this window right now."

"Lilian could bring this building down if she wanted to, but she doesn't want me dead. If she did, she would have killed me when she found me or while she had me pinned to her basement ceiling."

He returned to his seat. "Then what does she want? To make you beg for mercy?"

"She needs me."

"She couldn't find another dime-a-dozen romance novelist?"

"Not one with precognitive senses and healing powers. She wants my body. I don't mean sexually. Lilian only uses sex for gamesmanship, to get the upper hand on someone or to mislead them. She always has an ulterior motive."

"I'm not going anywhere."

"Lilian's centuries old. Those portraits in her mansion are of women whose bodies she either possessed or copied. She took their identities until they grew old, and then she discarded them and moved on to the next one. She's already been in her current guise for too long, but she's built such an empire with Eternity that she decided to cultivate her next identity in-house. She didn't make me a best-selling author because of my talent. She wanted to lay the foundation for a continuation of the Lilian Kane persona, and my innate abilities made me desirable to her."

Jake pictured the portraits in Lilian's mansion and the collection of museum quality antiques in her basement. "Eternal life. Old Nick wanted the same thing."

"But he was willing to settle for a second lifetime. Lilian's already had that many times over."

"What does she do with her host bodies?"

"Every one of those women suffered a public death, no doubt arranged by Lilian. My former sisters are too young to know the details firsthand."

"There was a power outage in the building for less than one minute on the day you disappeared from downstairs."

"During a sudden storm."

"At that same time, I was on a flight to Pavot Island."

"Who knew that your girlfriend was a fan of mine? The

moment you recognized my author photo in the back of the book she brought on the plane, the search spell identified my location. The storm struck, the power went out, and they had me before you landed."

Jake drew in his breath. Laurel knew all his intimate moments with Maria. "I wore that damned glove for nothing. You know everything that's happened to me since I left for New Orleans."

She gave him an apologetic smile. "I couldn't help myself. We held hands all the way here. Latex doesn't stop vibrations and I can't help feeling them. If you had left Maria in Miami, we wouldn't be sitting here."

"And those security guards at Lilian's mansion and those civilians downstairs wouldn't be dead."

"I sent you a message not to try to find me. What else could I do? I guess we both have a lot to atone for now."

"No. Lilian did this. Even if you stole her fortune, she had no right to abduct you, and her designs on your body defy any weighing of right and wrong. Those guards were grunts, and those civilians had nothing to do with this."

"I've never seen her lose her temper, but I have seen her angry—fury bubbling below the surface. She won't hesitate to crush anyone to make a point, especially men."

"She's the one who needs to atone for her actions."

Now Laurel sat forward. "Have you been listening to me? She can't be stopped, not by you, not by me, not by anyone. She's the most powerful witch alive, because she's been alive for so long, growing her powers. I screwed up her plans before and now you have. She'll stop at nothing to get me back, but she doesn't need you alive."

"Then I'll have to take her out before she drops a house on me."

"You can't beat her."

"I brought Avademe down. He—*they*—scared me more than she does."

"You had help then."

Cain and Abel, Jake thought.

"As far as I can tell, the only backup you have now is that hoodlum, the dwarf, your girlfriend, and Edgar. I know you don't want Maria involved, and Edgar's in no frame of mind for action. You have no big guns to call on."

She was right. When Jake had called on his supernatural allies to help on Pavot, they had ignored him. So had Sheryl's spirit. "You said you've had a shield over this building since you moved in, but that didn't prevent Sheryl from appearing to me in this very office."

"The only witchcraft I know, I learned from Lilian. That doesn't extend to higher powers."

"Then we can assume she's human and has no power over them, either."

"Assume nothing."

"How does one kill a witch? By drowning them or burning them at a stake?"

"Old wives' tales propagated by religious paranoia."

"She must have an Achilles' heel."

"If she does, no one has found it in all this time."

"Maybe no one has tried."

"How do you intend to look for anything from here?"

Jake glanced at his safe.

"Afterlife," Laurel said.

Jake nodded.

"Katrina withheld information about Kalfu and vodou. What makes you think the other researchers didn't do the same? And even if the other teams recorded everything they uncovered, that doesn't mean anything in there pertains to Lilian."

"That's the beauty of research: you never know what you'll find." He paused. "Katrina and the dark Mambos on Pavot got their powers from Kalfu. It wasn't enough for them to get their hands on written spells. They needed to bargain with a demon. Yet you've cast spells without doing so."

"I made my bargain with Lilian. All of us in the sisterhood did. I don't know where Lilian got her powers, but she limited what she taught us so we could never become a threat to her. I'm sure she's kicking herself for teaching me what she did."

Jake drummed his fingers on his desk.

"Are you thinking we should summon Kalfu ourselves?"

Jake considered the idea.

"I don't think he'd be very receptive to that."

"Why not?"

She didn't answer, but he knew she knew he had made Kalfu angry.

"You should have reminded me to bring the ATAC 3000 since I forgot it."

"I was worried about other things."

"You held Ripper's hand, too."

"What would you like to know?"

"Can I rely on him?"

"I think so. He lives on the fringe to be sure, but he's got a code and he's loyal. He loves Carrie, too."

Jake did not articulate his thoughts.

"I can't tell you anything about her. I read your vibrations when you moved in because I picked up on Sheryl's energy inside you."

"How did Lilian know who I was?"

"I didn't tell her anything, but she used a spell to reverse the direction of my power. She knows everything about me and everything I knew about you before I was captured."

"Then she doesn't know about Maria?"

"I don't think so. The search spell tripped an alarm, but there's no way she could have read your mind or seen through your eyes from so far away. I doubt she cared, either: she had what she wanted."

Jake glanced at the sheathed sword on the sofa. "Then she also doesn't know I faced Kalfu or that he's royally pissed off at me for rattling his cage."

"Unless Kalfu or another demon tells her."

"*You* could summon Kalfu."

"I don't know how, and even if I did, would you really expect me to crawl into a summoning circle with that monster?"

"No."

"Good, because I'd rather deal with Lilian."

Jake thought about the ATAC 3000 in his car.

"Bullets won't stop a tornado," Laurel said.

Jake narrowed his eye. "Are you sure you aren't reading my mind right now?"

"I can't do that. I just know you well. Remember when you pulled a gun on *me*?"

"Good times."

"And because I know you and I read you out on the street, I know you're not up to taking on Lilian."

Jake raised his stump. "You mean because of this? Tell that to the guy who did this to me. Oh, wait, you can't. I killed him with my glass eye."

"Bill Russel was nothing but a thug with a CIA pedigree."

"I also overthrew a government since we last saw each other."

"You had an army to help you. I'm not talking about your hand, anyway; I'm talking about your spirit."

"My fighting spirit? Excuse me, but didn't I just break you out of that house of horrors?"

"You wouldn't have escaped alive if Ripper hadn't pulled up when he did. Your soul is tainted. You're not the same man you were when you left New York."

"You mean the Black Magic."

"If you'd used much more you'd have become a zonbie."

"A good witch removed it from my system."

"She absorbed it and expelled it. The drug may be out of your bloodstream, but the psychological damage was done. You need time to recuperate, just like Edgar."

"It doesn't seem like I have much of a choice."

"Lilian loves nothing more than to toy with weakened men."

Ripper cried out in the reception area.

Jake leapt out of his chair and ran to the door with

Laurel behind him. Opening the door, he saw Carrie draw a strand of thread attached to a needle through the gash in Ripper's temple.

Carrie turned in their direction. With her free hand she dabbed at his temple with a tissue, which turned crimson. "Sorry. He freaks out at the sight of blood."

"Gimme some booze to dull the pain," Ripper snarled.

"This house is dry," Jake said, though he would have had a hard time turning down a drink.

"There's your backup," Laurel said.

Carrie snapped her head in Laurel's direction. "What's that supposed to mean?"

Oh no, Jake thought.

"Nothing, dear."

Carrie slammed the needle down on the desk, which pulled on the thread stretching to Ripper's eyebrow, causing him to groan. Ignoring him, she stomped around the desk. "Don't speak to me like I'm a child, damn it."

Laurel looked down at Carrie. "Now why would I do that?"

Jake tried to get between them. "Can we just focus on—?"

"Don't disrespect Ripper and don't disrespect me, you white-skinned freak." Carrie wagged one finger in front of Laurel.

"Ladies . . ."

Laurel smiled. "You're calling *me* a freak?"

Ripper jumped to his feet. "Don't talk to her like that. I saved your ass today. The least you could do is—"

Jake raised his hand and stump. "This isn't getting us anywhere."

Carrie let loose a piercing scream.

Jake followed her sight line to the window, which he moved toward with disbelief. Through the rain, a shape levitated outside the window. Moving closer and bending forward, he blinked at Lilian Kane's twisted features.

"You've got to be shitting me," Ripper said.

Jake froze, gazing at Lilian. Her hair was not wet, and the wind did not wrap her dress around her body.

Laurel shut the blinds.

Jake faced his friends. "It's okay. Don't panic. She isn't really out there."

Then he glanced at the TV. A pink title card with white cursive lettering had replaced the news story.

Surrender Erika

Jake picked up the remote on Carrie's desk. He aimed it at the TV and changed the channel. The same message appeared. He changed the channel again, with the same result. He pressed the button again and again, but the message persisted.

Carrie glared at Jake. "You've got a lot of explaining to do."

NINETEEN

They cleared off Carrie's desk, arranged the waiting chairs around it, and sat down to a meal of frozen dinners, canned vegetables, and power drinks while the storm outside rattled the windows.

"Ripper already knows that Lilian Kane is a witch," Jake said.

"The romance queen?" Carrie said. "I thought she looked familiar."

"I wish I hadn't involved him, but I did, and now you're involved, too."

"I thought witches were old hags who flew around on brooms. She was just *floating* out there."

Jake looked at Laurel, who said nothing. He got the point: anything he told Ripper and Carrie was his responsibility. "That was just an astral projection. Lilian was sitting warm and dry up the street in the Flatiron Building while we were looking at her."

"Maybe it was a hologram."

"Science has nothing to do with this."

Carrie turned to Laurel. "Oh, my God, you're Erika Long! I have every one of your books."

"You, too?" Jake said.

Carrie composed herself. "I read them when I was in high school, all right? Cut me some slack." She aimed a thumb at her chest. "Tough bitch here, okay? I don't read romance novels anymore." Her voice softened. "But I really did love the High Seas trilogy."

"Thank you," Laurel said. "Erika Long is dead, just like her parents. She'll never write another book."

"Are you a witch, too?"

"Not like Lilian."

Ripper leaned close to Carrie. "She made us invisible."

"Holy shit, she's after you, isn't she?" Carrie looked from Jake to Ripper. "That's where you guys went, to rescue her." She snapped her fingers. "There was a tornado in Eastchester while you were gone and another one on the highway. Is that where you were?"

Jake formed a half smile. "You've learned a lot from me."

"Too much," Laurel said.

"I'm wasted on office work," Carrie said. "I tell Jake I want to go on stakeouts, but he always says no."

"I try to keep my few friends in a safety zone," Jake said.

"You didn't think twice about dragging me into this mess," Ripper said.

"I never liked you much."

"The feeling's mutual."

"I was wrong about you, and I was wrong to involve you. But if I hadn't, Laurel and I wouldn't be here. You're all right."

"Thank you, Ripper," Laurel said.

Carrie lowered her voice. "You're the psychic who works downstairs, aren't you?"

"Congratulations on hiring such a crackerjack assistant," Laurel said to Jake.

"I don't want you reading my mind. Please stay the fuck out of my brain. Some things are private."

Laurel gave a slight nod. "I have more important things on my mind anyway."

"So why is Lilian Kane after you?"

"I'd rather not say. Some things are private."

"Uh-uh. Me and Ripper are stuck in this mess with you. We're entitled to know why our lives are in danger."

Jake didn't think Ripper or Carrie would feel much sympathy toward Laurel if they knew she was a murderer who had embezzled one hundred million dollars from her publisher.

"We need to stay here until this blows over," he said. "Lilian is a witch, and she's behind those tornadoes and the storm raging outside. Laurel's made it impossible for her to work her magic on this building, but Lilian could destroy us easily enough if she wanted to. She won't do that because she wants Laurel alive. As long as we all stay here, we're safe.

"But we can't stay here forever. Sooner or later I'll have to take action. If we don't find a way to stop Lilian, Laurel and I could wind up dead. If that happens, you two will need to fend for yourselves. That means creating new identities and going underground. I don't intend for that to happen, but if it does, the less you know the better."

Carrie took a moment to consider what Jake said. "Can she know who Ripper is?"

"Maybe not," Laurel said. "He wasn't with Jake when he busted me out, and I cast a spell over the car that made it impossible for her to see inside it. It's possible she didn't see him."

"Then we could just walk out of here right now if we wanted to."

"You can do that anyway but I advise against it. I can't hide you from her when you leave, and she'll be suspicious of anyone exiting the building now. She won't hesitate to destroy you, just to let us know she can."

Carrie looked around the room. "So we're prisoners."

"For the time being," Jake said.

"Couldn't you have just dropped her off at the bus station? I mean, she can make herself invisible to this wicked witch's magic wherever she goes, right?"

"Lilian wouldn't have known that. She still would have unleashed this storm to make a point if nothing else."

"Damn. This is so fucked up."

"I'm sorry," Jake said.

"She's not even a client."

"I'd have done the same thing for you."

Carrie's expression softened.

Ripper took Carrie's hand. "So what's the plan?"

"For now we sit tight. We've got food, weapons, and

running water." Jake gestured to the security monitors on the wall, where two men boarded up the broken panes in the downstairs doors with plywood. "And we'll see if Lilian sends one of her people inside."

"She has people?" Carrie said. "More witches?"

"An entire coven," Laurel said.

"We are so screwed."

"For what it's worth, I'm sorry, too," Laurel said.

"Can't we call the cops? Two of them were just here."

"I don't want Maria or Edgar involved."

"Isn't that nice of you? What about that Geoghegan lieutenant who keeps popping up? Doesn't he have juice?"

"And tell him what?" Jake said. "That a famous author is a witch who created three tornadoes that killed several people?"

"Lilian kidnapped her. There are laws against such things."

"We'd have a hard time proving that."

"Laurel could go public, at least with the stuff people would believe."

Jake glanced at Laurel. "That wouldn't make a difference. It might embarrass Lilian but it wouldn't stop her."

"You're both hiding something. There's a reason why she can't go to the police."

"I think you're the psychic," Laurel said. "But Jake's right. We have no recourse through any system recognized by the rational world. Right now, Lilian holds all the cards."

Carrie turned on the TV. Lilian's message had disappeared, and an old black-and-white movie played. She switched to

Manhattan's twenty-four-hour cable news channel.

A woman in a rain slicker stood beneath an umbrella. "John, this downpour shows no sign of letting up, making it difficult to clear East Twenty-third Street, where the tornado struck two hours ago, killing six people and injuring a dozen others. Two tornadoes touched down just outside the city as well."

The broadcast switched to a newsman in the studio. "Thank you, Karen. We've just received word that JFK, LaGuardia, and Newark airports have shut down due to the extreme weather conditions."

"She's making sure we don't fly out of Dodge," Laurel said.

"We don't know how bad this storm is going to get," Jake said. "Let's all take showers and turn this office into a dormitory. We could be here for a while."

Jake showered first and changed into fresh clothes, then waited with Carrie and Laurel in the reception area. When Ripper emerged from the shower, the two men moved Carrie's desk across the room, then the sofa bed out of Jake's office to where the desk had been. The rain, lightning, and thunder continued.

"You can take my bed," Jake said to Laurel as Carrie made the sofa bed. "I'll sleep in my office. I plan to do a lot of research tonight anyway."

Ripper pointed at Thunder Ranch in Jake's shoulder holster. "I want a gun."

"So do I," Carrie said.

"You can't shoot the rain," Jake said.

They both stared at him.

"You don't want one, too, do you?" he said to Laurel.

She shook her head.

"I'll be right back." He went into his office and closed the door. As he removed the painting from the wall, he wondered if Carrie knew about his cache of weapons. He selected two weapons and the appropriate ammunition, then returned to the reception area and handed Ripper a Smith & Wesson .38 revolver and Carrie an M22 semiautomatic with a four-inch barrel, both in holsters, and set the ammunition on the desk.

Ripper slid the .38 out of its holster and snapped the revolver's cylinder open. "You don't have anything heavier? We should have brought that cannon back."

Jake regretted leaving the ATAC as well. "You're not leaving this office, right? These will do in here."

Carrie pulled the small gun from its holster.

"Do you know how to use that?" Jake said.

"I'll show her." Ripper tucked the .38 into his belt, then picked up the cartridge for the .22, took the gun from Carrie, and slapped the magazine into the gun.

"Do me a favor and don't sleep with those. Keep them on the floor under the bed."

"You got it, chief."

"Try to get some sleep. I'll watch the monitors from my desk. I may wake you to take over when I get too tired."

A weather map on TV caught Jake's attention.

"In addition to airport closings, we've just received an alarming report from the national weather bureau," the newsman said. "Unexpected storm conditions in the Atlantic are heading for the Northeast. According to projections, a category 1 hurricane could reach Manhattan by lunchtime tomorrow. Viewers are advised to batten down their hatches, stay off the streets, and stay tuned for updates."

Lowering the volume, Jake felt uncertainty swell in his stomach. The fear in Laurel's eyes told him he had reason to be afraid.

That only gives us until noon, he thought.

"It could be a coincidence," Ripper said. "That storm could break down or miss us altogether."

"It won't," Laurel said.

Carrie paced. "What the hell are we going to do?"

"Like the man said, we batten down the hatches."

Jake closed his office door, which he locked with as much discretion as he could muster.

"Maybe we should have let them go," Laurel said.

"I'm not taking any chances. I saw too many people killed on Pavot Island. There's got to be a way to deal with Lilian."

"You can't kill her."

"You keep saying that. I'm not convinced."

She looked around the office, stopping at the chair facing the empty space where the sofa had been. "You don't need to sleep out here."

"It's a small bed."

"We can manage. I really don't want to sleep alone."

He gestured at his computer. "I've got a lot of work to do."

"It will go faster if I help you."

He held her gaze. "That isn't a good idea."

A hint of a smile formed on her lips. "I'm glad for you but you could just hold me."

"I'm not sure Maria would view that as an innocent gesture between friends."

"Judging by the scene she made, I'd say you're right."

"She has a temper."

"You haven't made any commitment to her."

He didn't answer.

"All right, I understand. Try to get some sleep. If you need me for anything, you know where I'll be."

"Good night." He watched her go into the bedroom and close the door. Loyalty to Maria wasn't his only reason for declining Laurel's offer; he wanted to keep his thoughts to himself.

He walked to his safe, manipulated the combination dials, and withdrew the laptop. Leaving the safe door open, he set the laptop on his desk, popped in a battery, and raised Afterlife. He glanced at the security monitors, which showed empty hallways and a quiet lobby, then turned the television on and found the weather channel.

"The hurricane forming in the Atlantic has been upgraded to category 2," said the meteorologist standing before a screen that showed an animated depiction of the hurricane, "and appears to be heading to the eastern coast of the United States. Hurricane Daria will touch down in New York City sometime after rush hour and before noon."

Lightning flashed and thunder boomed, causing Jake to jump.

It was a dark and stormy night, he thought as he opened Afterlife's search engine.

TWENTY

Lying in bed half-asleep thanks to the storm, Ramses tried to ignore the ringing cell phone until Alice kicked his thigh.

"That's your phone," she said.

Sighing, Ramses sat up and grabbed for the phone but knocked over a bottle of Bacardi instead. "Shit," he said, grateful he had screwed on the bottle's cap.

"Just turn the light on, fool."

He hated when Alice spoke to him like that. It was hard enough playing second in command to a woman, let alone one he had to sleep with to attain that rank, but suffering her insults was a true test of his patience.

Switching on the bedside lamp, Ramses picked up his phone and glanced at its screen. He didn't recognize the number, which meant it was a new burner. He pressed the Talk button. "Yeah?" He spoke just one word so as not to give himself away to any unfriendly callers.

"Yo, it's me," said a boy with a high-pitched voice.

Ramses glanced at the clock, which flashed 4:45 a.m. "You just woke me, motherfucker. Be a little more specific."

"Sorry. It's me, Amazon."

Ramses had assigned the code name Amazon to Wonder Girl to use over the burners. She was seventeen and ambitious, so he had promoted her to corner boss at the new spot on Avenue B, located two blocks from where Kevin Wilmont and Sapo had killed Darryl Hughes and A-Minus.

"What up?"

"It's been raining all night."

"Yeah, so?"

"Business is down—*way* down—and there's a hurricane coming."

"So what you want me to do about it?"

"We're soaking wet out here and freezing. Can't we go home?"

"Hell no. We just *took* that corner. Now you want us to give it up without a fight?"

"I'm just asking. We cold and shit."

"Hold that corner and don't be calling me with any more bullshit." He ended the call, set down his phone, and picked up the bottle of rum.

"Take those ignorant motherfuckers some umbrellas and hot chocolate," Alice said.

"Now?"

"No, when the rain's stopped. Of course now. You've got to know when to show your people some compassion. Amazon's new. She don't know any better."

"So I got to go out in this storm because she don't know to bring a raincoat to work?"

"No, you got to go out in this storm because I *say* you do. You're the one who put her in charge of that corner."

Biting his tongue, he got out of bed and pulled on his clothes from the day before; there was no point in showering. He turned off the lamp and crossed the condo, ignoring Shana's bedroom door and cursing Alice beneath his breath. She wasn't even that good in bed.

As he strode through the rain to the garage—*he* didn't need an umbrella—Ramses reminded himself that he put up with Alice's abuse for the same reason he enforced her wishes: he intended to leave her corpse in an abandoned building in the Bronx for rats to feed on and take over her empire.

Hell, he would have done it already except Alice still had some moves to make, and her upscale life in this tony building had created a layer of security for her that he didn't feel comfortable penetrating just yet. That was the problem with so many players in the drug trade. They were in such a rush to escape the street they forgot that was where they made their money in the first place.

It took less than a minute for the downpour to soak Ramses head to toe, which only made him angrier. The rain striking the pavement reminded him of gunfire. He entered the paid garage, his sneakers squishing, got into his SUV, and pulled onto the street. Even with his windshield wipers going at full speed, he had trouble seeing ahead of him.

He drove downtown through the rain to an all-night pharmacy, where he bought four umbrellas. Then he stopped at Mickey D's and ordered five hot chocolates at the drive-thru.

Shopping for youngsters, he thought.

"Would you like whip topping?" a female voice said over the speaker.

Fuck the whip topping. "No, thank you."

"Drive up, please."

The cashier was a pretty black girl with straight hair. He gave her a tip and a smile and fantasized about coming back to see her once he had removed Alice from the picture.

With one hot chocolate snug in his cup holder and the others in a tray holder on the seat beside him, he encountered little traffic as he drove to Avenue B. He eased down the ratty street with caution, peering through the rain on the windows to find the stoop where Wonder Girl had set up shop.

A figure detached itself from the darkness: Wonder Girl's lookout. He didn't know the boy's name. Then he saw Wonder Girl standing inside the vestibule of a run-down apartment building, silhouetted by dingy yellow light from a low-wattage bulb.

A Puerto Rican boy appeared at the passenger window, which he lowered. "Whatchoo want?" the boy said, rivulets of rain running down his face.

Ramses flicked on the dome light. "You just opened this here shop for business. Is that how you talk to a potential customer?"

"Sorry. I didn't know it was you."

"Of course you didn't know. That's the point. Get away from my car. You're dripping all over the leather."

The boy stepped back, and Wonder Girl, who stood a

foot taller than him, took his place.

"You belong in front of the building, not inside it," Ramses said. "How are these fiends out here gonna see you?"

"What fiends?" Wonder Girl said. "Ain't nobody out here, and if they was, they'd be seeing me inside the building, not outside it."

Ramses knew she was right, but he wasn't about to admit it. He passed the umbrellas to her through the window. "Here. Distribute these to your people."

"Thanks." Wonder Girl took the umbrellas, opened one, and handed the rest to her lieutenant.

Ramses held the tray of the hot chocolates up as well. "This is for y'all, too."

"That's what I'm talking about." Wonder Girl beckoned to her second lookout up the street, who came running through puddles. She gave the hot chocolates to the boy, who wore a red hoodie. "Keep one of those dry for me."

The boy nodded and shuffled over to the one holding the umbrellas.

Wonder Girl turned back to Ramses, who gave the last hot chocolate to her.

"Things will get better," Ramses said. "Business will be booming."

"I hope so."

Thunder cracked and Wonder Girl's face split open, spewing blood all over her hot chocolate and Ramses's leather interior. As she toppled to the sidewalk, her two lookouts drew their Glocks.

In the rearview mirror, Ramses saw two figures running

across the street, firing handguns of their own, spilling the lookouts across the sidewalk. Ramses flicked off the dome light, shifted the SUV into Reverse, and stepped on the gas. Looking over his shoulder, he sped right into the shooters, hurling their broken bodies aside. Then he stepped on the brakes, which squealed.

A third shooter ran into the street and fired one shot after another at Ramses's windshield, which separated into three distinct networks of cracks.

Sliding down in his seat, Ramses shifted the gear again and stomped on the gas, roaring forward. The SUV slammed into the shooter, who rolled over the hood in a blur and crashed through the fractured windshield like a hit deer.

Ramses didn't feel the pain in his chest until he tried to sit up to shove the shooter's body off him, and then he saw blood fountain out of the hole in his chest.

Ah, shit, he thought as he lost control of the SUV.

Jake sat staring bleary eyed at his desktop with the TV on when Laurel emerged from his bedroom. He saved the Word document he was working on and closed it, then opened a file and sent it to his hard drive. Sheets of rain propelled by gusts of wind pounded the windows.

"Did you sleep at all?" Laurel said.

"It was hard with that wind and thunder, but I managed to grab a couple of hours." He burned the document to a disc.

"Did you have any luck with your research?"

"Maybe."

She gave him a look. "I had two and a half years to look for everything I could on Lilian online and found nothing. All I did was become an expert on the superstars whose lives she usurped."

He said nothing.

"Are you going to tell me what you found?"

"Not yet. It's more of a hunch than anything else." Jake ejected the disc and deleted the file from his hard drive.

On TV, Mayor Connie Krycek addressed reporters in the city hall press room.

"What's the latest?"

"Our mayor's telling people to get out of town or stay inside. The subways are already flooding and she's shutting them down. Hurricane Daria's scheduled to hit at 11:00 a.m. Daria." Jake grunted. "It should be Hurricane Lilian." He crossed to the safe and opened it.

Moving the Glock aside, he set the disc on top of the laptop, then closed the safe and stood. "Let's check on the kids and make breakfast." He rapped on the office door, then unlocked and opened it.

Carrie and Ripper sat at Carrie's desk, eating cereal and watching the press conference while thunder rumbled.

"You didn't wake me up for my watch," Ripper said.

"I knew we were safe until Daria touches down," Jake said.

Ripper checked the time on his phone. "That should be in three and a half hours."

"I'm going to make sure that hurricane never reaches the city," Laurel said.

Jake arched one eyebrow. "Oh?"

"I'm going to turn myself over to Lilian."

"The hell you are."

"Innocent people are dead because of me. That's not the kind of atonement I was looking for."

"None of those deaths were your fault or mine. Lilian bears 100 percent of the responsibility for them, and she needs to pay."

"That isn't going to happen, and I can't just sit by anymore. Those tornadoes and that waterspout were nothing; this hurricane could kill hundreds of people, maybe thousands. I won't have that on my conscience."

"You won't have to. I'm going to see Lilian."

"For what possible purpose?"

"To negotiate with her."

"That's a suicide mission. You have no leverage. Lilian wants me alive, not you. She'll destroy you without giving it a second thought."

"I think I *do* have leverage."

"Tell me what it is."

"If I tell you that, you'll only try to convince me I'm wrong."

"All the more reason why you should tell me."

Carrie stood. "Let her go. There's no reason why you should die for something that's between the two of them."

240

Jake smiled. "I'm not planning to die."

"What if you do?"

Jake turned to Laurel. "You'll know what to do."

"Do you want me to go with you?" Ripper said.

"I appreciate the offer, but I need you to stay here to watch after Carrie and Laurel—and to make sure Laurel doesn't come after me. For my plan to work, this is where she needs to be."

"The office opens in half an hour, but I'm sure Lilian's already there," Laurel said. "I'm willing to bet they all slept in their office, too."

"I bet theirs is fancier."

Maria entered the squad room dripping wet and blew hair out of her eyes as she hung her coat on a rack and set her umbrella beside it. "Sorry I'm late. The trains are crazy."

Reaching for his coffee mug, Bernie didn't miss a beat. "Be glad you made it in at all. Krycek ordered the whole system shut down within the hour. At least you only had to come across town instead of from the Bronx."

"I came from my place."

"Trouble in paradise?"

"I don't want to talk about it."

Bernie's expression turned to one of satisfaction. "Okay. Well, we're up."

"Can't I dry out for a few minutes first?"

"What's the point? You're only going to get wet again."

"Maybe I can avoid wrinkling."

"I guess I could pass it off to someone else, but the DATF boys specifically asked for us. They've got eight dead hoppers down on Avenue B."

Maria's expression hardened. "Let's get out of here."

Mauceri stopped at their desks. "You taking that call downtown?"

Maria nodded.

"I want you back here by the time that hurricane hits. If it looks like you need longer, call in and we'll figure out a safe location for you to wait it out."

"You got it, L.T."

Bernie put on his tan trench coat and held her coat for her.

"Thank you," she said.

They signed out an unmarked Cavalier and exited the building, each holding an umbrella.

"It's hard to imagine this getting worse," Bernie said, aiming his umbrella into the wind.

It took them a few minutes to locate the right car.

Bernie slid behind the wheel and started the engine, then pulled into the street. "At least there isn't much traffic."

Maria didn't answer.

"Do you want to talk about it?"

"No."

"Good."

When they reached Avenue B, Maria saw several red

and blue strobes in the distance. "It looks like we're late to the party."

A uniformed PO stood in the intersection, closing off the street to new traffic. Bernie pulled over to one side of the PO, lowered his window, and showed the woman his shield. She waved him through.

"The shooting occurred at 0530 hours," Bernie said as he coasted through puddles.

That gave the uniforms half an hour with the crime scene, the Detective Area Task Force detectives the same amount of time before they reached out to Bernie, and now half an hour for them to reach the crime scene.

Maria spotted a handful of POs in rain slickers standing near yellow crime scene tape that crisscrossed the street and sidewalks. Two detectives stood holding umbrellas.

"It looks like all the action happened out here," she said. "I don't think we're going to find much evidence after the vics have been in the rain for two hours."

Bernie double-parked the car and they got out. Maria opened her umbrella and heard her partner do the same. As they crossed the street she noted two bodies slumped against parked cars, one on each side. Farther up the street, an SUV jutted out at an angle from a parked car it had collided with.

They joined the Detective Area Task Force detectives, who stood with umbrellas of their own over four more corpses, one of them female.

"Dan Malcomb," one of the detectives from the 11th Precinct said.

"Jim Allcorn," the other said.

"Bernie Reinhardt. You spoke to me on the phone."

"Maria Vasquez. Thanks for calling us and thanks for waiting."

Malcomb pointed at the corpses at their feet. "We checked their IDs. They were all from the Bronx. The girl's the oldest, seventeen. The black kid's sixteen, and the Puerto Rican is fifteen. I don't know what that other one is, but he can't be older than fourteen."

Maria and Bernie exchanged looks.

"The two in the street are both fifteen," Allcorn said. "They're local boys from the project on Allen and Grand."

"If these six can be packed up I want to take you for a walk," Malcomb said.

"I think we're good," Bernie said, looking at Maria.

"Yeah," she said.

Malcomb led them back into the street, leaving Allcorn to watch over the bodies.

Allcorn beckoned to the waiting meat wagon, and two EMTs hopped out.

"Any news on Daria?" Malcomb said.

"She's coming," Bernie said.

"It feels like she's already here."

They stopped at the SUV and gazed through the shattered windshield at the two bodies in the front seat.

Malcomb spat into the street. "As near as we can figure, the shooter shot into the windshield of the oncoming vehicle, killing the driver, who managed to hit him anyway, and his body flew through the windshield."

"Where's the shooter from?" Bernie said.

"Different building but still the Lower East Side. It doesn't take a rocket scientist to figure out Raheem Johnson paid Alice Morton back for shooting up his corner yesterday, which is why we called you. We've already spoken to neighbors who say the uptown crew set up shop here yesterday."

Maria stared into the dead features of the driver, slumped in his seat with the other corpse's legs across his lap. "That's John Coker, street name Ramses. He may have been Alice's right hand." She knew it, but she didn't want her last visit to Alice to become part of the record.

"So, what do you say?" Malcomb said. "You want to team up on this?"

"These are your homicides," Maria said, provoking a frown from Malcomb. "We're here to assist you so far as it helps our investigation."

"That's better than nothing. You want to help us with the legwork?"

"Maybe."

"Do you want to shake Raheem or Alice?"

Maria suppressed a smile.

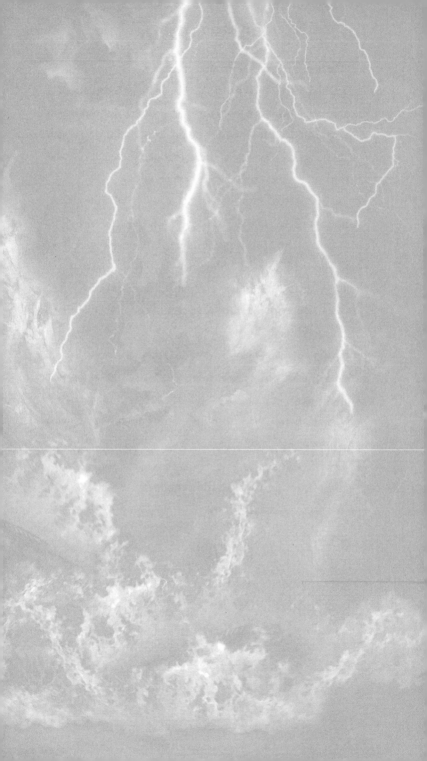

TWENTY-ONE

Jake exited the building's elevator carrying a closed black umbrella.

Jackie stood at the doors, supervising a man in the replacement of the glass panes in the two doors.

"You may as well leave the plywood in," Jake said.

"No kidding," Jackie said. "I came as soon as I heard the news. I was already in a taxi when Carrie called. Did you see those bodies down here?"

"I saw them."

Jackie whistled. "I never saw bodies messed up like that. You're not going out there, are you?"

"I've got to see someone."

Jackie leaned close and whispered, "You learn anything about Miss Doniger?"

"I'm still working on it. Keep the faith."

"Faith don't cost nothing."

"I'll see you later." Jake stepped around the worker and stood facing the plywood panels in the darkened vestibule.

Taking a breath, he opened the door, and the wind tore it from his hands and slammed it against the outside wall. Rain descended from the sky in a steady downpour. Jake triggered the umbrella, and as soon as it opened the wind blew it inside out. He aimed the umbrella at the wind, which blew it back into the correct configuration.

Jake turned his body as he closed the door with his stump, and a sudden gust of wind snatched the umbrella from his hand. He watched the umbrella spin away. The damaged cars had been towed, and the parlor's missing window had been boarded up. He flipped up the collar of his black trench coat, stuffed his stump and hand into his pockets, and walked away from the wind, which howled like a banshee.

After only half a block, his face felt numb from the cold and tears streamed from his eye. Litter moving across the sidewalk in waves made scraping sounds. The garbage spun around him, creating a cyclone through which he could not see, then faded as abruptly as it had formed. A cargo truck drove by, resembling a torpedo in the water.

Passing Madison Avenue, Jake saw a police car parked at the corner; three officers sat inside the car. Water sloshed into a storm drain and right back out again. An empty commuter bus headed east, splashing him with more water.

The wind blew him forward. He planted his feet, leaned back, and walked with the wind. When his right calf muscle cramped, he ducked into a doorway. With his back against glass, he caught his breath and rubbed his face. Metal signs creaked overhead. An unseen lid banged open and shut. Doors blew open.

Closing his eye halfway, he returned to the storm force. A newspaper wrapped itself around his torso, and he pulled it away. The chains on a closed newspaper stand rattled against the metal gate that protected its contents.

Jake gazed at the Tower to his right: all the lights had darkened, except in the two-story lobby, and uprooted trees were piled on top of each other on the patches of grass separating the sidewalk from the building. The water in the fountain overflowed.

Straight ahead, the Flatiron Building rose to the sky. Only the lights in the lobby and on the top two floors glowed in the darkness.

The rainfall softened and stopped. With his hair plastered over his forehead and water dripping off the end of his nose, Jake staggered to one side, regained his balance, and righted his course, each footstep producing a splash. Thunder rumbled within the clouds. Then a sound like bacon sizzling in a frying pan filled his ears, and countless golf balls ricocheted off the sidewalk.

Lumps of ice shattered on the sidewalk. Jake cocked his left arm over his face, shielding his eye. A hailstone struck the top of his head and almost knocked him unconscious. Another struck his left temple, drawing blood. He fell forward, then raised himself on his right arm, gasping for breath as the ice pellets attacked his back and fingers. At least it wasn't raining frogs.

He lifted one knee and stood, then continued forward, passing one closed business after another. Cracks formed in the display windows around him. Walking on the hailstones was like walking on marbles, and he went down on one knee again and remained there for a moment, like a boxer taking advantage of the count to regain his breath. Rising once more, he leaned against the wind and used both arms to protect his head from the hailstones.

At last Jake reached Broadway. A horn blared, and he leapt back as an ambulance sped by with its siren and strobes off. Looking both ways, he crossed the avenue and reached the Flatiron Building. He staggered to the main entrance that consisted of glass two stories high, with a curved top. Drawing a breath, he entered.

Jake stood in a lobby with white marble walls. Behind him, the hail stopped falling. As he walked to the security station lightning flashed behind him and the thunder that followed split the sky with a sharp cracking sound. Jake stopped at the station and stood dripping before the uniformed security guard.

"May I help you, sir?" the guard said.

"I'm here to see Lilian Kane."

"Do you have an appointment?"

"Yes."

"Your name, please?"

"Jake Helman."

The guard consulted her computer screen. "I'm sorry but I can't find your name."

Jake eyed the security cameras mounted on the glossy

walls. "Will you call her for me, please?"

"I'm not allowed to do that."

Jake sighed. He didn't intend to walk back to his building.

The telephone on the desktop buzzed, and the guard picked it up. "Yes, ma'am, he's here right now," she said after a moment and then set the phone down. "Ms. Soto left your name. You can go up now. Just sign in first."

Jake signed his name on the clipboard and listed Lilian Kane as his contact.

"Take the elevator to twenty-two," the guard said.

Nodding, Jake walked to the gleaming elevator doors and pressed the call button. A door opened and he boarded the car, then pressed the button for his destination. The elevator rose, and he used the time to wipe the blood from his temple and from the corner of his mouth, which had somehow split.

The elevator reached the twenty-second floor and settled, but the door failed to open. Jake glanced at the ceiling, then at the floor, fearing the elevator might plummet to the bottom of the shaft.

The door opened and he stepped into a white corridor lined with flower displays that reminded him of Lilian's estate. Turning right, he approached a glass partition with a wide glass door in its center embossed with the Eternity Books logo. Through the glass, he saw a receptionist with long dark hair behind a curved Italian desk. Standing at the door, he debated whether to ring the doorbell, but the receptionist looked in his direction and pressed a button, unlocking the door.

Jake opened the door and crossed the tile floor, noting book displays around the lobby and light globes hanging from the high ceiling. His fingers twitched as he approached the desk.

The receptionist, who he guessed was Vietnamese, smiled and spoke with a French accent. "Good morning, Mr. Helman. Ms. Soto will be with you shortly. You're welcome to have a seat or look around the lobby. Help yourself to some coffee."

Jake tried not to register surprise. "Thank you but I'm already caffeinated."

He turned to the oversize windows facing the Tower across the street. The hailstorm had ended, and flurries sliced the sky at a diagonal angle.

Snow in July, he thought.

He stared at the Tower's top floor, where he had confronted Old Nick, Kira Thorn, and Cain. He had moved to the Flatiron District to keep his eye on that building and its occupants, convinced that Tower International would somehow resurrect itself. Now it resembled any other skyscraper: glass, steel, and faceless. It had never occurred to him that the horror would come from a landmark across the street.

"Mr. Helman?"

Jake turned at the sound of Harla Soto's voice. She stood in the doorway on the other side of the reception desk, wearing gray slacks and a short-sleeved jacket buttoned over a low-cut black top.

He walked over to her. "We meet again."

"You look better than you did yesterday."

"Thank you for offering me that water."

"What can I do for you now?"

"I actually hoped to meet with Ms. Kane."

"Without an appointment? She doesn't do that. Neither do I."

"And yet here we are, reminiscing about old times. I'm willing to bet she'll do the same."

"Why don't you come into the VIP room and we'll see about that?"

"I'm honored." Jake followed her through the doorway and along a wide aisle flanked by several empty offices. "Where is everyone?"

"Haven't you heard? There's a storm coming. We're operating with minimal staff today."

Harla led him into a room that took him aback: silk hung from the windowless space one quarter the size of a gymnasium. Casual contemporary sofa beds of all shapes and sizes faced a round pedestal upon which an egg-shaped chair sat. Two statues of lionesses with jeweled eyes sat on either side of the modern throne, and statues of owls on pedestals overlooked the beds. Wall sconces cast soft lavender light, and liquor bottles along an illuminated black bar glowed.

"Is this where you hold office parties?" Jake said.

"When we're in the city it is," a voice said behind him.

Jake turned as Lilian entered the room. She wore a light green dress.

"Thank you, Harla. I'll call you if I need you."

Harla gave Lilian a slight bow and exited, closing the door behind her.

Lilian approached Jake, her eyes never leaving his. "I didn't expect you to come alone. If anything, that should have been Erika's play."

"She wanted to turn herself over to you. I wouldn't let her."

Lilian circled him. "If you're here, it's because she wanted you here."

Jake turned his body to keep it facing hers. "I don't think so. I make my own mistakes."

"Then why come? You must realize there's no way you can stop me."

"I don't believe in many things, but I do believe in rolling the dice."

She moved closer. "You're being disingenuous. You believe in a great many things that others would refuse to accept."

"Seeing is believing."

"What makes you so confident?"

"Call me Jake the Giant Killer."

One end of her mouth turned up. "I know who you are: a pawn in the great dimensional war. Use your remaining eye to look at those scars on your face in a mirror and that stump where your hand should be. By the time you've finished fighting the good fight, nothing will be left of you. And that's not even taking the emotional toll into consideration. If you manage to die of natural causes, you'll do so as a lonely, broken man."

"You know me well."

Lilian raised one finger, a diamond ring sparkling on it.

"I know Erika well and she knows you well. We're linked to that degree."

"You only know my thoughts through the time you kidnapped her."

Her smile appeared genuine. "I'm not concerned with your thoughts, though I'm not used to anyone knowing so much about me."

"I know the feeling. You know I was investigating the Order of Avademe the last time she read me."

"Karlin Reichard and his brotherhood of cranky old men."

"As opposed to your stylish sisterhood?"

"You have to admit they're nicer to look at. I assume you're the one who killed those old bastards, just like you killed Nick Tower."

"Since Laurel's shared my memories with you, you know I also brought down Katrina and her army of zonbies."

"You defeated a vodou slut and an army of dead slaves. I'm not impressed."

"I didn't kill all the members of the Order of Avademe, but the ones I offed weren't the only ones I killed during that caper."

"There was that assassin you buried upstate."

"Think bigger."

Lilian stopped moving. "Go on."

"Adam and Eve are gone and so are their mutant children." It felt good to boast.

Lilian narrowed her eyes a fraction. "I sensed their deaths, but I have difficulty believing you were responsible for them."

"I had a little help from your grandchildren."

Her expression showed no reaction. "Qayin and Havel worked together and with you to slay their own parents?"

"You have quite a dysfunctional family . . . Lilith."

The woman who called herself Lilian Kane parted her lips in a manner that conveyed amusement and danger. "You're lucky to be alive. I've never known the higher powers—from either party—to permit a human to know so much about their existence."

"We're old friends now on both sides of the fence. Abel told me all about you."

She stared deep into his eye, which he found unnerving. "Oh? What did that dear angel say?"

"That you were Adam's first wife, and Adam drove you off after you slept with the serpent, then married your daughter Eve in your place."

"Eve was Adam's daughter, too, which is why Havel is every bit as much of a monster as Qayin. They were born corrupt. My husband didn't drive me off. I left him because I have a mind of my own, and I wouldn't allow him to control me. I was created the same way he was, so I demanded to be treated like an equal. He was obsessed with worshipping our creator, and such men tend to treat their women as inferiors.

"Adam was also a lousy lay, not that I had anyone to compare him to in those days. All he ever cared about was getting himself off and procreating, and he even had the nerve to command me to lie beneath him while he shot his seed into me. As for the Serpent, he was beautiful and taught me real pleasure. The great Shaitan"—her tone took on sarcasm—"offered me knowledge of the dark arts in exchange for my body, and he kept his word."

Jake was not reassured that Lilith had opened up to him. "Satan cast Adam and Eve out of hell and condemned them to suffer here instead. Now that they're dead again, you're the oldest being on earth."

She paused before answering, as if weighing the meaning of everything he said. "Their passing saddened me; it's possible to mourn a worthy foe, even a pigheaded ex-husband and a twisted daughter. I visited them upstate once to make sure we didn't step on each other's toes with our different endeavors. Imagine my surprise when I saw they had no toes, just tentacles the length of telephone poles. Adam was pleased to see me, but my daughter seethed with jealousy. Such monsters. But then they always were, which I'm sure is why Shaitan banished them from the Dark Realm."

So she didn't know everything. Had Shaitan shut her out of the loop? "You're easier on the eyes than they were."

Her indecipherable smile returned. "Don't mistake me for being human, and don't think you can play me."

Careful, he told himself. *She's mercurial.* "Clearly not. The first known Cro-Magnon remains date back forty-three thousand years. If you're as old as those old bones and fossils, you're holding up surprisingly well. Old Nick would have been envious."

Lilith stepped onto her pedestal, sat in the egg, and crossed one leg over the other. "I did Shaitan's bidding without question, serving as his mistress and pupil. His attentions were extreme, but I must have pleased him because he used his powers to keep me alive during our lovemaking. He granted me eternal life and taught me his dark ways, making me the first witch. I got my powers from him and sowed their seeds around the world as his ambassador, all while catering to his desires. As you can imagine, a fallen angel has quite an ego; satisfying his imagination proved traumatic for me. But I've never been afraid to express myself.

"In time, we both grew tired of his efforts to make me subservient to his whims, and he used me in his games here on earth, sending me to seduce men on different continents and stir the flames of chaos. As I grew more powerful, I also grew more opinionated. Shaitan became weary of me just as Adam had, but I had no intention of subjugating any man, here or in the Dark Realm. Eventually, he lost interest in me and left me alone. I've continued to work my magic on earth, while his presence has diminished. Since my goals will never align with those of the Light, he's allowed me to live as I wish."

Maybe he didn't want you in the Dark Realm. "You brought magic into the world?"

"Black magic through Shaitan. Those choirboys on the other side found their own vassals to introduce white magic, which is as impotent as it is boring."

"Did you know Old Nick?"

She took a moment. "Not in my present guise. In another incarnation we met at a party. He had no idea who

258

I was, and I had no idea he would one day join the Order of Avademe only to strike out on his own. The man he was then didn't interest me; the pursuit of material wealth alone is crass. And I already had more money than his precious empire ever made."

"Then you didn't even miss the money Laurel stole."

"It doesn't matter how much she took. It was *mine*. It's the principal. Remember how Poseidon punished Odysseus for hurting Polyphemus?"

"They were gods."

Lilith stared daggers at him. "It would take me a human lifetime to tell you my story, and you don't have that much time left. I've answered your questions. Now you answer mine. How did you discover my secret? Erika never learned it."

"She knows you've lived several lifetimes, and that was enough to start with."

"Using Tower's Afterlife project? I wouldn't mind getting my hands on that."

You and everyone else who knows it exists. "I focused my search on witchcraft used to control storms, and I struck out until I found a very vague reference to a mythological Mesopotamian creature, a storm demon called Lilith who knew how to control the wind. This led me to an entire section devoted to you: Lilit, Lilitu."

She tilted her head to one side. "I'm disappointed it was so easy."

"Tower made it easy, and Abel's tale supported what Afterlife suggested. It was just a hunch on my part; I wasn't sure until now."

She rose from her throne. "There are so many myths about me—so many untruths—from the Babylonian Talmud to the Mesopotamian texts to the *Alphabet of Jesus ben Sirach*. You must have been overwhelmed in your research."

Jake shrugged. "It's funny how each interpretation paints you as a demon."

"Adam's ego couldn't handle that I wanted no more to do with him, even after he took our daughter into his bed. He decided I was Shaitan's succubus whore, and that's what he told his scores of children, who embellished his story in tales they told to *their* children."

"So you haven't strangled infants in their cribs and stolen children, and you didn't give birth to one hundred demon babies in a single day?"

"I did many things for Shaitan during our first centuries together. His lust left me barren, and I didn't want to ruin my figure anyway. Eve was such an ungodly mess by the end. Can you imagine?"

"According to one legend, you have a scorpion between your legs."

She smiled. "Would you like to see if that's true?"

Jake formed a mental picture. "No thanks." *I like to leave something to the imagination.*

"I'm flattered by the stories told about me, that I've been credited with inspiring men's wet dreams and women's miscarriages, but these are old husbands' tales."

"In medieval times the church advised people not to sleep alone or you might get them, and monks slept with their hands over their genitals, clutching crucifixes." Jake had been tempted to do the same the night before, but he didn't own a crucifix.

"I'm delighted with my place in culture: the paintings, the statues, the literature. Did you know there's a sculpture of myself, Adam, and Eve in the base of Notre Dame? Or that there's a music festival named after me? I'm a symbol of feminism—so richly deserved."

Jake had to drag her away from her reverie for herself. "Children may be safe, but apparently female icons in the entertainment world aren't."

Lilith's demeanor cooled. "I'm curious how you've survived this long. How can you possibly believe that revealing how much you know about me *to* me is a smart tactic?"

"The only thing that matters to me is the hurricane that's on the way. I don't want any more innocent people killed."

"Then you're running out of time to turn Erika over to me."

"I don't plan to do that."

Her irises flashed like lightning and thunder exploded outside. "That bitch stole from me."

"We'd like to make good on that."

"How can you? She gave most of my money away to *charity*."

"She has at least two million left, and there's still the building."

"That building's worth five million at best. What about the other ninety-three million?"

"Write it off as a bad investment."

"You must be joking."

"I'm sure you already claimed it on your taxes, so you've

already broken even. Nothing good will come of this war."

"War? Try *massacre* . . . an extermination. You're insects to me. I wouldn't let Erika go even if she had the whole hundred million. I'm angry to have lost that money but not as angry as I am to have lost *her*. I want her body back alive."

Jake drew a breath as he would when aiming a gun. She wasn't giving him a choice. "I don't think so."

"Do you know how easy it would be for me to relieve you of your skin right now? You're in no position to bargain with me."

"I think I am."

Lilith wiggled her fingers before her like snakes. "Give me a peek into that brain of yours."

"Knowledge is a dangerous weapon in the right hands."

"You don't know one hundredth of my story, and what you do know you could never prove; no one will believe you. If I allow you to live and you try to expose me, they'll lock you away until your dying day."

"You ordered Laurel—Erika—to murder a man at your mansion."

"She committed that murder, not me."

"Under your direction, after you got her drunk or high. Then all of you kept quiet about it. That's conspiracy. The RICO Act put Charles Manson away. It could do the same to you. I'm sure you could do a life sentence standing on your head."

"There's no body."

"There's at least one witness."

"A thief. Erika would go down with me."

"She wants to atone for her actions. Do you?"

"I'll never give her that chance."

"There's also the matter of industrial espionage committed against The Love Book. You destroyed Alicia Dormeyer's livelihood."

"I'll do worse to you."

Time to push some buttons. "Oh, and there's the matter of your being a centuries' old witch who's committed God only knows how many atrocities against men."

"I'd like to read that police report. Too bad you'll never get to file it."

"I've already created a report. I stayed up all night writing it. I'm sure Laurel—sorry, Erika—can add a great deal to it. As you say, difficult to prove. But can you imagine the publicity? The scrutiny? We live in the age of the twenty-four-hour news cycle when stories are reported with little or no need for hard facts. I wonder how your disciples will react to the news."

Lilith's face tightened. "I could level your building, burying her and that account."

"Destroying her body in the process."

"I'm more than capable of making difficult choices."

"Then there's the matter of who I may have shared that report with before I came over here this morning: lawyers, police officers, reporters. As an ex-cop, I know a lot of people."

"As a witch who absorbed your memories from a psychic, I can figure out who those people are. I bet two of them left your building last night after the show."

Don't let her get to you. "That's a lot of busywork."

"It's too bad I can't just take them all out in one big storm. Oh, wait. I can and I've already created one—the storm of the century." She looked at a clock on the wall. "It's due to hit in just about two hours, and it should have been upgraded to category 4 by now."

Jake offered her a disappointed look. "I guess we've reached an impasse."

"I don't see it that way."

"Here's my proposal. First, you let me walk out of here with all my limbs and organs intact. I go back to my building. As a sign of good faith, Laurel wires the funds she has into your Swiss bank account, and you call off this storm. The next day, from an undisclosed location, Laurel transfers ownership of that building to you. You sell the building or keep it, whatever makes you happy. We go our way; you go yours. Laurel disappears and you remain the Queen of Romance."

"Just like that?"

He held out his hand. "No fuss, no muss."

Lilith turned her back to him. "That's some proposition."

Jake stared at his open hand, so close to his shoulder holster. *What would happen if I pulled a John Wilkes Booth on her right now?*

His hand tensed, ready to reach for his gun.

That's what she wants so I'll tip my hand. He clenched his fist, resisting the urge to act, then opened it again.

She turned back to him. "But I have to reject it."

Jake swallowed. "Why don't you at least call off this storm and take twenty-four hours to think about it?"

Lilith made no movement or gesture; she didn't even blink.

Jake's legs flew out from under him, and he crashed to the floor and stared up at her.

"For one thing, these things that you promise will be mine anyway after I claim Erika's body as my own. For another, I know how your mind works."

With his arms spread apart, Jake flew to the ceiling, grunting as he slammed its plaster with dizzying impact. She had pinned him to the ceiling just as she had Laurel.

No candles are necessary because she's right here, he thought.

"You know I would never honor such an agreement. You just want me to call off the hurricane to buy you some extra time. Maybe you want to blow up this building with me in it?" She turned away. "I'm sorry to disappoint you."

Jake plummeted to the floor fifteen feet below, his back absorbing the brunt of the crash, and cried out.

Lilith faced him, her dark eyes ablaze. "How dare you come in here with so little to offer me. It's insulting. Get up on your hands and knees."

Wincing, Jake rolled over and got on his hand and knees.

Did I mean to do that?

"Are you a man or a dog? Play like a dog and maybe then I'll let you play like a man."

Jake crawled in circles, his disability hampering his movements.

What the hell is happening to me?

"I think you're a dog but not much of one. You're incomplete, and maimed animals are usually put out of their misery. Stop playing."

Turning to face her, Jake allowed his tongue to hang out of his mouth.

"Good doggie. Now beg. Beg!"

Jake stood on his knees with his hand and stump raised to his chest and panted. *I'll kill you for this, lady.*

Lilith stepped before him, taunting him with her close proximity. "Good boy." Leaning forward, she scratched behind his ear. "Good boy. You're such a *good* doggie. Yes, you are. What would you like? Would you like a treat?"

Trying to answer her, Jake gagged.

Lilith reached inside his jacket and pulled his Thunder Ranch from its holster. "Why, this is so small. I thought men carried big guns to make up for their small dicks. I don't want this." She held the gun out to him. "You take it."

He took the revolver from her and froze.

"Stand up, doggie."

Jake rose and faced her, his arm remaining in the same outstretched position the entire time.

"You look angry. Would you like to shoot me?"

His arm straightened, aiming the revolver at her face.

"Go ahead. This is a freebie."

Jake's finger tightened on the trigger, but his arm jerked in his direction as the gun fired, the loud shot painful to his ears in the enclosed space. Before he knew it, the smoking barrel pressed against his right temple.

"Too late, too bad. Maybe you'd rather kill yourself than see what I'm going to do to this city because of you."

The door behind Lilith burst open, and Harla ran in

with two other women with alarmed expressions. Jake recognized Chloe Sanderstein and Jada Brighton from World Book Expo and their profile pictures on the Eternity Books website.

Lilith didn't turn to face them. "Close the door, Chloe."

The blonde closed the door.

"Come here, sisters. Mr. Helman was just about to blow his brains out."

The three women—Lilith's angels—moved beside her.

Jake's hand trembled as his finger tightened on the trigger again. His lips twitched and sweat beaded on his forehead.

Don't . . . do . . . it!

Tears formed in his eye.

"On second thought," Lilith said, "why don't you ladies give him the VIP treatment?"

The three subordinates smiled at Jake and undressed. Nude, they swooped around him, caressing his stomach and back, unbuckling his belt and pulling his trousers down, peeling his clothing like skin from an orange. Still holding his revolver against his head, he stood exposed before Lilith, who shook her head at his slack penis, which had shrunk in his waterlogged pants.

"I've sensed something in him since I first met him, something that goes beyond the memories he shared with Erika. He needs some Magic in his life."

Still smiling, Chloe strutted to the polished bar and opened a stainless steel drawer. Jake ignored her round buttocks and full breasts. She returned with a glass pipe with a round bowl at the end. The bowl contained what appeared to be dark ashes.

Jake's pulse quickened.

Lilith returned to her throne. "You recognize that, don't you? Nod."

Jake nodded.

"I knew it. I saw it in your eyes right away. Hand the gun to Harla."

He gave the gun to Harla, and she set it down on one of the pedestals displaying the owls. Jada kneeled before him and took him in her mouth. Harla moved behind him, sliding her hands along his sternum and down his stomach muscles. Chloe slid the pipe between his lips and sparked a lighter, holding it beneath the bowl.

"Suck Magic, Jake," Lilith said.

Jake drew Black Magic into his lungs, igniting his senses and returning him to life.

"That feels so good, doesn't it? Your eyes were almost clear. It's been too long."

She's right, he thought.

Releasing his erection, Jada stood before him. Only she had transformed into Katrina.

Lilith is doing this, not the Magic.

Standing behind Katrina, Chloe had become Sheryl. And when Harla moved around him, she wore Maria's face like a mask.

"Come on, baby." Sheryl stuck the pipe between his lips again.

He took another hit of Magic. This time he held the foul smoke inside him longer before relinquishing it.

Maria pushed him onto a round bed, and Katrina and Sheryl crawled beside her, the three of them probing him with their tongues and fingers.

Jake didn't need Lilith to tell him what to do next.

TWENTY-TWO

Laurel lay on the cot staring at the ceiling in Jake's bedroom. She felt uncomfortable around Carrie and Ripper even though they didn't know the full circumstances of her situation.

The suspense of waiting to hear from Jake gnawed at her insides. She didn't believe he stood a chance against Lilian, but she knew he would not be dissuaded from facing her. For a time she had fantasized about him saving her from Eternity Books, but that was just a daydream.

Outside the wind howled and rain lashed at the windows; at least the snow had stopped. Rising into a seated position, she wrung her hands. After years in self-imposed exile, she had become Lilian's prisoner, and now she was Jake's. Her thoughts kept returning to him.

Frustrated by the waiting, she stood and left the room. In the office, she glanced at Jake's safe.

Keep walking, she thought.

She poured herself a cup of coffee in the kitchen and wandered into the reception area, where Carrie and Ripper sat watching the news on TV. Food wrappers and empty glasses were scattered all over Carrie's desk. Ripper glanced at her, then back at the TV.

On the screen a heavyset weatherman held on to a microphone with one hand and his hat with the other while the wind wrapped his poncho around him and rain drenched him at a sixty-degree angle. An orange metal garbage can rolled away behind him.

"Marissa, the wind is blowing seventy-five miles per hour. Wind must reach seventy-four miles an hour to be classified as a hurricane, and Daria hasn't even made it to us yet. A category 1 hurricane, the least destructive on the Saffir-Simpson Hurricane Scale, has wind speeds of seventy-four miles an hour to ninety-five miles an hour.

"Daria has been upgraded to category 4, which means winds will reach at least one hundred thirty miles per hour or higher. You won't find me out here when that happens. In fact, I'm getting ready to come in now. And remember, every time that category goes up, the sooner Daria arrives."

The camera switched to a Hispanic woman at the anchor desk. "Thank you, Leon. Except for a brief respite for hail and—I can't believe I'm saying this—*snow* in July, rain has fallen almost nonstop for fifteen hours. Subway stations are shut down, and area airports have canceled five thousand flights."

The broadcast cut to a wide shot of vehicles creeping across the George Washington Bridge.

"Tunnels are also closed, and there's been a steady exodus of residents fleeing the city via bridges and thruways. New York State Governor Durick has joined Mayor Krycek in urging people who haven't already left their homes to stay put."

The camera cut to the news anchor again. "The White House has issued a statement that FEMA is standing by to assist residents as needed once the hurricane has passed."

Carrie turned to Laurel with deep worry in her eyes. "Jake's been gone almost an hour and a half. That building isn't even a ten-minute walk when the weather's copasetic."

"But the weather isn't copasetic," Laurel said.

"It shouldn't have taken more than an hour to say his piece. He isn't coming back, is he?"

Laurel bit her lower lip. "I don't think so."

Carrie stood. "Maybe you should go check things out."

Laurel's heart skipped a beat. That was the next logical step. Or she could always run. "Maybe you're right."

Ripper stood as well. "Forget it."

Carrie raised her voice. "Ripper . . ."

"Save it. Jake said he wants her to stay here, so that's what she's doing."

"Jake could be dead because of her. She should have gone instead of him."

"He made his choice. We're sitting tight—*all* of us."

Blowing air out of her cheeks, Carrie threw herself into her seat and folded her arms. "Sometimes it's hard being the smartest person in the room."

"Maybe you're too smart for your own good," Ripper said.

"There's another option," Laurel said. "We can send someone else after Jake."

Standing beside Bernie in the upstairs corridor of Sloane House, Maria expected Alice Morton to answer her condo door. Instead, Shana opened it with the chain lock on and looked up at her from the height of the doorknob.

Maria's heart warmed to see the little girl so soon after their brief talk at the playground. "Hi, sweetie."

Shana looked at her with fear in her eyes.

"Shana, you better not be at that door."

Maria's muscles tensed at the sound of Alice's voice. Shana's eyes pleaded with her for help.

Alice's features filled the space above the chain lock. Frowning at Maria, she pulled Shana back from the door and closed it. "Go get in your room now." Then she removed the chain lock and opened the door. Unlike most people facing two detectives who had come to their home, she exhibited zero nervousness. "What do y'all want? This is getting to be a habit. I thought I told you to leave me alone."

Maria resisted the urge to slap her. "I already explained to you that my previous visit was unofficial, just a friendly call to make sure Shana was okay. This is different. This is official."

Alice shifted her gaze to Bernie and her frown deepened. "Is that why you brought super cop?"

"May we come inside?" Bernie said.

"No, you may not." She nodded at Maria. "I don't want this one anywhere near my niece."

"Do you know a man by the name of John Coker?"

Turning to Maria, Alice made a confused face. Maria knew the woman was just stalling while she decided how to answer.

"Maybe. I'm really not sure."

"I bet you know him by his street handle, Ramses. He's the gentleman I saw leaving here yesterday. We spoke about him?"

Alice's face hardened. "What do you want?"

Maria took an envelope out of her wet coat and removed a digital print of John Coker dead on a slab in the coroner's office. Regulations prohibited detectives from showing photos of DOAs taken at the scene of their death to their next of kin, so she and Bernie had waited for the meat wagon to deliver the stiff to its destination, then went there and took the shot. "Mr. Coker's dead. We can't track down any next of kin. Will you identify the body?"

Alice swallowed. "That's him. What happened?"

"He was shot in his SUV on Avenue B. Four hoppers working a spot there were killed, as well as three shooters. It was quite the O.K. Corral. But you wouldn't know anything about that, would you?"

"No, I would not. Ramses didn't deal no drugs. He was a churchgoing man."

"Did he stay here last night?" Bernie said.

"He was here but he didn't spend the night. He has his own place."

"Thanks for identifying his body," Maria said. "I think you know that I don't give a shit what happens to you, but I do care what happens to Shana. You better pull some muscle off the street to watch your back." Turning to Bernie, she nodded to the elevators. "Let's go."

They made to leave.

"Detective Vasquez."

Maria turned back to Alice.

"Thanks for your condolences." She closed the door and the detectives boarded an elevator.

"That was touching," Bernie said as the elevator descended.

"She already knew Ramses was dead," Maria said. "She had plenty of time to get into character for us."

Maria's cell phone rang and she checked the display: Helman Investigations. She debated whether or not to take the call.

"Who is it?" Bernie said.

She pressed the Talk button. "What is it, Jake? I'm busy."

Bernie rolled his eyes.

"This is Carrie."

"Oh," Maria said with surprise in her voice. "What do you want? Is Jake all right?"

"I don't know. He's kind of missing."

"What?"

"Just come to the office, okay? Alone. We need your help."

"I'm on my way." Maria ended the call as the elevator

reached the ground floor and they got off it.

"What is it?" Bernie said.

"Jake might be in trouble."

"How unusual."

Alice entered the living room, where Kevin Wilmont and Sapo waited.

"Just a minute," Alice said. She walked into the hallway and opened Shana's bedroom door.

The little girl sat on her bed with her legs straight out, a children's book open on her lap. Shana looked up at her with expectant eyes.

"I've told you to stay away from that door," Alice said. "Don't you ever answer it again. You hear me?"

Shana nodded.

"And I've told you I don't want you talking to that policewoman."

"I didn't talk to her," Shana said in a meek voice. "I didn't even say hello."

Alice gave Shana the kind of look she saved for underlings who had won her disapproval. "You'd better be telling me the truth, or it will mean the belt."

Shana sat still, saying nothing.

Alice closed the door and returned to the living room. "Did I tell you to sit down on my new furniture?"

Kevin jumped to his feet but Sapo took his time. Alice knew she had to watch that one.

"The police are all over Ramses's execution."

"We heard," Kevin said.

Alice held her temper in check. What was she going to do with these ignorant fools? "Here's something you didn't hear, smart mouth: they know those shooters were Raheem's boys."

"What you want us to do?" Kevin said.

"I'm getting to that, if you'll let me finish. First, I want you to drive around to all our spots and tell our crews to hold their ground. Raheem ain't taking what's ours."

Kevin and Sapo traded looks.

"That hurricane will be here in an hour," Kevin said. "We can't drive around in that."

Alice snorted. "You gonna let a little rain and wind scare you? Are you men or little boys?"

"I'm just saying, I don't know why we can't just call the crew bosses and tell them what you want."

"Because they might run like scared rabbits, just like you're talking about doing. You can bet your motherfucking ass those fiends out there ain't going to let elements keep them from getting their fixes. They need our product, and that means we have to stay on our corners. If our people walk away because of a little bad weather, Raheem will take them from us without firing a shot. Then we have to take them back when we should be concentrating on taking more corners away from him. You need to show our people that we're still in control, even without Ramses on the street."

Kevin sighed. "So you want us to tell them to stay at work. What if they ask what we're doing to protect them?"

Alice stepped closer to him. "You tell them we're taking care of business, and they better do the same." She glanced at Sapo, then back at Kevin. Neither one of them was smart enough to fill Ramses's shoes. "I need y'all to step up and take the slack."

"What's in it for us?" Sapo said.

Alice looked at him from the corner of her eye. At least he was ambitious. Too bad his eyes were clouded from too much weed. "What do you want, a promotion?"

Sapo shrugged. "Yeah."

"Well, what the fuck do you think this meeting is about? You two been triggermen for Ramses. Now I need you to be my enforcers, like he was. You know what that means? A piece of the pie. But first you gotta prove you're up to the task."

"How?"

"You do what I say *when* I say it. You don't question my authority. If I want your opinion I'll ask for it, which isn't damn likely. So without further commentary, take your asses out in that rain and check on my spots. Keep those boys and girls in line."

"Can we go inside after that?" Kevin said.

Alice slapped the back of one hand in the open palm of the other. "This storm's gonna shut this city down. That means it's going to shut five-oh down, too. There ain't gonna be a better time for action."

"You want us to take out another one of Raheem's spots?"

"Fuck Raheem's spots. I want you to take *him* out."

Bernie drove downtown with Maria beside him. They crawled at twenty miles an hour with the downpour producing spray on the hood and a cacophony on the roof.

With near zero visibility, he leaned over the steering wheel. "What time is it?"

Maria took out her phone. "Ten thirty."

"We've got half an hour before Daria hits."

"I know."

"I'd like to be back at the station by then."

"It's a short ride from Jake's office."

Bernie turned onto Twenty-third Street. "Be my navigator."

Maria lowered her window and squinted in the rain, which slapped her face. "It's up ahead. Okay, pull over."

He did and Maria raised her window.

"Do you mind waiting while I see what's up?" she said.

"Sure, just don't take your time."

Maria stepped out of the car and into a gale force wind that wrapped her raincoat around her hips and legs. She didn't even bother with her umbrella. The wind snatched the door, which bounced on its hinges so hard she feared it would come off. She had to lean against it to close it, and then she ran for the building.

A man with white hair and a droopy mustache stood there, dressed in a navy-blue engineer's uniform. He held the door open and she sprinted into the vestibule. The inside door was propped open behind him.

"Thanks," she said.

He smiled. "You're welcome. What are you doing outside?"

"I'm a cop. I'm here to see Jake Helman."

"Did he kill someone?"

She liked his dry demeanor. "I hope not. I'm a friend of his."

"He's up on the fourth floor."

"I know. Thanks." Maria hurried to the elevator, which opened as soon as she pressed the call button. She got on and pushed the button for the fourth floor. What the hell had Jake gotten himself into now? The door opened and she hurried to Jake's door and rang the bell.

Ripper opened the door and stepped back from it. "Come on in." He looked even more like a thug when he wasn't covered in dust.

"Thanks, Jeeves." She entered the suite.

"Huh?" He closed the door and turned its locks.

Carrie and Laurel waited for her in the reception area, leaning against the front of Carrie's desk.

Maria surveyed the mess. Wind rattled the window, and on the TV, live footage showed enormous waves smashing against the dock at the South Street Seaport, drenching the asphalt around it. Peering down the hall at the open door to Jake's office, Maria saw his empty desk chair. "Where is he?"

Carrie and Laurel traded nervous expressions.

Waving her hand before her face, Maria snapped her fingers three times. "Ladies, come on. I don't have time for games. Where's Jake?"

Laurel pushed herself off the desk. "Can I speak to you alone in Jake's office?"

Maria raised her arms and dropped them to her sides. "Sure, why not?"

Laurel led Maria into the office and Maria closed the door. Outside, the wind howled.

"My partner's waiting for me downstairs, and we'd really like to get out of here before this hurricane hits."

Laurel stood before Jake's desk. "I think it's too late for that. I'm afraid it is, anyway."

Maria crossed the floor and stood before her. "Spit it out. Did your slumber party go awry?"

"Jake went to the Flatiron Building to see Lilian Kane."

"The romance publisher? What does Jake want with her?"

"Lilian is a witch."

Maria blinked.

"She's the head of a coven, and I've been hiding from her for over two and a half years."

"Son of a *bitch*."

"She's also behind this hurricane."

"Get the fuck out of here."

"I know what happened on Pavot Island—"

"Well, isn't that sweet?"

"—because I read Jake when he rescued me from Lilian's mansion yesterday. She's threatening to turn this city upside down if I don't turn myself over to her."

Maria folded her arms. "So naturally Jake went to talk to her on your behalf."

"He wanted to strike a deal with her so she'd stop the hurricane. He said that if Daria hit, we'd know he failed."

"What does Lilian Kane want with you?"

"My body and my identity."

"I guess Jake wants the same thing."

"Jake isn't interested in me. Like I said, I read him. I know he only has feelings for you. This isn't some romantic triangle; I'm just worried about what Lilian will do to him—what she may already have done." Laurel picked up a hardcover book from Jake's desk and held it out to Maria. "He got this for you."

Maria took the book from her: *Love Knows No Lust* by Lilian Kane. She opened it to a flowery handwritten inscription:

Maria,

You're a lucky woman. Jake's got your back. Maybe we'll meet in person someday.

Eternally yours,
Lilian Kane

When Maria looked up from the book, she noticed Laurel staring across the office. "Is there something in that safe I should know about?"

Laurel raised her eyebrows. "No, I was looking at the security monitors."

Maria studied the screens. One showed the maintenance man crossing the lobby.

"That man is a friend of mine. I'd prefer he didn't know Jake found me."

"Whatever." Maria closed the book and tossed it onto the desk next to a replica of the Maltese Falcon. She gave Laurel a hard look. "I'll be back with Jake."

Maria strode past the kitchenette and through the reception area.

"Are you going after Jake?" Ripper said.

She faced him from the door. "Yes."

Ripper picked up a holstered .38 and slid it into his pocket. "Then I'm going with you."

Carrie's eyes widened and she ran to his side. "Ripper, no! If you're going, I'm going, too."

He held her at arm's length. "Uh-uh. Jake said for us to stay here and make sure Psychic Lady doesn't leave. One of us has to listen to him."

"To hell with her."

Ripper looked at Maria.

"Suit yourself," she said.

TWENTY-THREE

Sitting in the front seat of the Cavalier, Bernie ran the windshield wipers just so he could glimpse the traffic light ahead bouncing up and down on its cable.

"That bad boy's coming down," he said to himself, wondering how many others would do the same.

The front passenger door opened, and Maria leaned forward, rainwater cascading from her head and shoulders. She unlocked the doors and got in. "Turn around and drop me off at the Flatiron Building."

"Can I ask—?"

The back door opened, and an Asian man with dreadlocks and hardened features got in behind her.

"I hope he's with you," Bernie said.

She stared straight ahead. "Yes."

"If we're taking him in he needs handcuffs."

"I'm not under arrest," Ripper said.

"So, what, we're giving him a ride somewhere?"

"Please drive," Maria said. "He's with me."

"Oh, well, that explains everything."

"Bernie, meet Ripper. Ripper, this is my partner, Bernie."

"'Sup?" Ripper said.

"Is Ripper an Asian name?" Bernie said.

Ripper didn't answer Bernie, who pulled into the street and executed a slow, wide U-turn through six inches of water.

"I think I like Jake better," Bernie said. "How is he?"

"That's what we're going to find out."

"Of course." His cheery tone turned dour. "It's almost eleven."

"I know."

The car rolled forward, water jetting out from under its sides.

"This is like going through a car wash without the wax job," Bernie said, squinting. "That looks like a red light ahead."

"Go through it. The street's empty."

"I had a feeling you'd say that." He steered the Cavalier straight ahead. Through the rain, a vague outline blotted out the sky. "We're almost there. We passed this tower on the way down here, you know."

"I knew as much as you did then."

"You know more now?"

"Turn left on Broadway so we can get out."

Bernie frowned. "We never talk anymore." He pulled over to the curb. "Don't be long."

"If we're not back in fifteen minutes, leave without us."

The wind rocked the car.

"If I *can* leave in fifteen minutes."

Maria got out and slammed the door, and Ripper did the same.

Bernie couldn't even see them disappearing into the building. He glanced at the car's clock.

As soon as Laurel heard the front door close behind Maria and Ripper, she went to the reception area, where Carrie wiped her eyes.

"Are you all right?" Laurel said.

Carrie nodded, her features unseen by Laurel.

"I'm going to close this door and give you some privacy, okay?"

"Sure, whatever."

Laurel slipped back into Jake's office and closed the door. With her hand still on the knob, she pushed in the button lock and turned to the safe. The window shook, sheets of water rattling its glass.

Afterlife, she thought. Through Jake, she had already experienced some of its contents, but she wanted to know more. When he had offered to let her keep it, she had demurred. In the hands of a witch, the information in that research file could become deadly. It had been difficult for her to refuse even then; the research might have given her an edge over Lilian.

Now things had changed: if Maria didn't return with

Jake, Laurel would be on her own. Carrie and Ripper—if Ripper survived—would be useless to her, even if they offered to help, which she doubted.

More likely they'd deliver me to Lilian tied in a bow. She couldn't blame them if that happened.

Jake had said she'd know what to do if he didn't return.

Down on one knee, she caressed the safe's gray metal surface, creating friction against her skin. She slid her fingers up to the first dial and closed them around it. Jake had not changed the combinations since returning, and she shared his memories. She didn't have to think about the combination; she just twisted the dial on instinct. Three turns to the right, passing zero each time, stop at forty-two; two turns left past zero, stop at fourteen; one turn right past zero, stop at twenty-three.

Separating her palm from the metal, she dragged her fingertips down to the next dial.

The turning of the doorknob caused her to jerk her head toward the door even though she had locked it.

Laurel rose and walked to the door, which she unlocked and opened. Carrie looked up at her.

"Yes?"

"Why was the door locked?"

"I gave you your privacy. I wanted some for myself."

Carrie looked at the safe, then back at Laurel. "If you need privacy, lock the door to Jake's bedroom, not this one. I'm his office manager. I need access to his office."

"Whatever you say." Laurel opened the door wide, then walked to Jake's desk, sat, and booted his computer.

Carrie returned to the reception area, and Laurel's focus returned to the safe.

Accompanied by Ripper, Maria exited the elevator on the twenty-second floor of the Flatiron Building. She had only needed to show her shield to the doorman to get in. Their wet shoes squeaked on the polished floor as they approached the glass partition and door leading to Eternity Books. No one sat at the reception desk inside. Maria pulled on the door handle, which caused a sharp clanging sound, and Ripper pressed the doorbell.

A woman with auburn hair walked into the lobby and opened the door from the inside. Her hair had an unkempt, morning-after look.

"Can I help you?"

"Yes." Maria took out her shield. "I'm Detective Vasquez. We're here for Jake Helman. Bring him to us now."

One corner of the woman's mouth turned up. "I'm sorry?"

Maria returned her shield to her pocket. "What's your name, dear?"

"I'm Harla Soto, the president of this company."

Maria folded one flap of her raincoat back, revealing her holstered Glock. "Harla, Jake's here. He belongs to me. I want him."

"What's going on out here?" A woman with a perfect

figure and fashionable bangs stood at the threshold. Maria thought Lilian Kane must have a daughter who bore a remarkable physical similarity to her. She wore a designer dress and pumps, perfect for stormy weather.

"This woman says—"

Maria stepped past Harla, and Ripper followed her into the lobby. "I want Jake Helman."

Lilian smiled. "Maria."

Maria made sure not to react to Lilian's familiarity with her. "Thanks for the book."

"Jake bought it for you. I just personalized it."

"I'll thank him once you've returned him to me."

"You make it sound as if we abducted him. He came here on his own." She shifted her gaze. "Didn't he, Ripper?"

Ripper said nothing.

"You have one minute to produce him," Maria said.

"Or what?" Lilian said.

"Or I'll bring a tactical team in here, and you'll be all over the news at noon, five, six, ten, and eleven."

"I doubt it: look outside."

Maria turned to the wide windows. The downpour whipped across the sky at an almost horizontal angle, blotting out her view of the Tower across the street.

"I think the police and the news teams will be unavailable for some time."

"The clock's ticking," Maria said.

Lilian pretended to shudder. "I like your style. Harla, bring Jake out for Maria."

Harla nodded to Lilian and walked past her.

"At least you were smart enough to bring someone with you," Lilian said. "Not that it would matter if I chose to keep Jake for myself."

"It's hard to imagine him appealing to someone as sophisticated as yourself."

"I find you much more interesting."

"I'm just a lowly civil servant. I don't belong up here in the clouds."

"You're probably right. I'd invite you to visit me sometime and give it a try, but I don't think any of you will be alive for long."

"That kind of talk is no way to impress a girl."

"It depends on the girl."

Harla and two other women, one blonde and one black, hauled Jake into the lobby, his feet dragging beneath him and his head slumped forward. Maria thought they all looked like they had crawled out of a brothel for breakfast.

They stopped beside Lilian, who sank her fingers into Jake's hair and pulled his head back, revealing his face. His skin was pale, which emphasized the circles around his dark, glassy eyes, which failed to acknowledge Maria. A strand of drool rolled over his lower lip, and he blinked.

Maria's heart sank and she felt a knot in her stomach. She had seen Jake strung out on Black Magic before on Pavot Island.

Lilian released his head, which bowed again. "Put him on the floor, where dogs belong."

The women tossed Jake onto the floor, but Ripper jumped forward and dropped to one knee, catching him in his arms.

He stood and draped Jake's left arm over his shoulder.

"You can have him back now," Lilian said. "We're through with him. Wouldn't it be something if Harla, Chloe, and Jada all became pregnant at the same time? I'd have to create a nursery here."

Maria's jaw tightened as she gazed at each of Lilian's subordinates, who wore shit-eating grins.

"Tell Erika I sent Jake back as a token of my generosity. She's to take his place here on her knees or I'll flatten this island."

Maria pushed a button to unlock the door, and then she held it open for Ripper, who dragged Jake through it. She followed him into the corridor, allowing the door to lock behind her, and joined them at the elevator. She draped Jake's other arm over her shoulder and pressed the call button. Only then did she look at the four women standing in the lobby of Eternity Books, staring at her.

An elevator door opened and they boarded the car. Pressing the button for the ground floor, she prayed they made it there in one piece.

Bernie sat in the Cavalier with the engine running, listening to police calls. The wind howled on both sides of the car, rocking it back and forth. A splitting sound made him think of thunder until a tree collapsed in front of the car, blocking Broadway.

He reached down to shift the car into Reverse when the

rear passenger doors opened. Ripper shoved Jake into the backset while Maria, on the street side, pulled him into a somewhat upright position. Ripper got in beside Jake and closed his door.

Maria ran around the front of the car and slid in beside Bernie. "Let's get the hell out of here."

Bernie looked over his shoulder at Jake.

"It's not what you think."

"It sure looks like what I think." Bernie knew that Jake had resigned from the force rather than submit to a drug test in the wake of a shoot-out in which he had slain two armed robbers.

"Those witches were fine," Ripper said to no one in particular.

"Did you just say witches?" Bernie said.

"Drive," Maria said in a flat tone.

A bolt of lightning struck the tree in front of them, severing limbs and igniting leaves.

Bernie recoiled. "Jesus!"

The rain extinguished the flames and the tree branches smoldered. Bernie backed the car up through six inches of water, made a three-point turn, and got back onto Twenty-third Street. The car bounced on its shocks, the wipers sloshing rainwater from side to side, wind roaring.

A metal sign slammed onto the sidewalk and skidded away. The wind blew waves west across the flooded street, smacking the car. A dislodged tree from the grassy area surrounding the Tower sailed through the air in front of them, striking an apartment building on their right and dropping to the sidewalk.

"So this is what I've been missing not living in the Caribbean," Bernie said.

A flagpole dragging an American flag struck the other side of the street like a spear thrown from above.

"Whoa," Ripper said.

A streetlight crumpled over. An awning over a restaurant collapsed amid the twisting of metal. As they passed Madison Avenue, Bernie lowered his window. Two blocks away, a crane atop the skeleton of a skyscraper under construction dangled from the top of the structure. He raised the window and Maria lowered hers.

"We're almost there," she said.

Bernie pulled over to the curb in front of Jake's building. "What now?"

"I have to help get him upstairs."

Grimacing, Bernie looked outside. "Do you want me to wait again?"

"No, I want you to get back to the station safe. He needs me."

"He needs Betty Ford. What should I tell L.T.?"

"Tell him I decided to hole up with some civilians. Or tell him the truth."

"I'm glad I don't know what the truth is."

Maria got out, closed her door, and opened the rear passenger side door for Ripper, who slid out and pulled Jake after him.

Then the door slammed shut, leaving Bernie alone again.

TWENTY-FOUR

Maria and Ripper dragged Jake into the vestibule of the building, and Maria watched Bernie drive away. The water flooding the street spilled over the sidewalk. Ripper pushed the buzzer for Jake's office. Maria noted the building engineer had left his post, and a moment later the door buzzed open.

They carried Jake to the elevator. Maria pressed the button and the elevator door opened. They boarded the elevator and Ripper pushed the button for the fourth floor.

"Thank God the power hasn't gone out," Maria said as the elevator rose.

"I'd hate to carry him up four flights of stairs." He looked at her. "It's Black Magic, isn't it? He looks like a scarecrow."

"Yeah."

"Too bad he isn't as light as one."

The elevator stopped and the door opened, and they

carried Jake to the office door.

Carrie opened it. "What did they do to him?" Bringing Jake inside, Maria ignored her question.

"Never mind," Ripper said.

Carrie closed and locked the door, and Maria and Ripper dropped Jake onto the sofa bed.

Laurel ran to Jake's side and, grasping his face, turned his head left and right.

"How bad is it?" Maria said.

"They definitely knew his weakness," Laurel said. "A trip to the ER won't do him any good."

"Good thing. The ambulances will be out of commission soon. Can you handle this?"

"Yes, just like Mambo—"

"—Pharah—"

"—did on Pavot Island. I can't say I'm looking forward to it."

"What are you talking about?" Ripper said.

"I'm a psychic healer. I can absorb the Black Magic from Jake's system."

Carrie grasped Ripper's hand. "But then it will be inside you."

"Yes, that's why I have to expel it as fast as I can." She looked at Maria. "Help me get his shirt off."

Together, they took off Jake's wet shirt, which Maria tossed aside.

Laurel turned to Carrie and Ripper. "I need to concentrate."

"We'll be quiet," Carrie said.

"I prefer you wait in Jake's office with the door closed. Turn the TV off on your way."

"Shit." Carrie picked up the remote, turned off the TV, and led Ripper into Jake's office, where she closed the door.

"Now I need him facedown."

Maria helped Laurel roll Jake over onto his stomach. Then Laurel climbed onto the bed and straddled Jake's buttocks.

Maria stared at her.

"This is how I work," Laurel said.

I bet, Maria thought.

Laurel pressed her fists into the small of Jake's back, then pushed her palms up to his shoulders and drew her fingertips back down to his waist. She pressed her fingers into his muscles, kneading them like dough, and he moaned.

Maria dug her fingernails into her palms.

Laurel stopped moving, then snatched her hands away as if she had contracted a contagious disease. Her eyes opened wide. "No . . ."

"What is it?" Maria said.

"*Lilith.*"

"Who the hell is Lilith?"

With tears forming in her eyes, Laurel resumed her task. She worked Jake over and then moaned as well, swaying, and Maria realized she had become high from the Magic in Jake's system. Sweat formed on Jake's face and his breathing became regular. Laurel's body quivered. She toppled off him, falling from the bed into a heap on the floor.

Maria kneeled beside her and helped her up. "Are you all right?"

Covering her mouth with one hand, Laurel staggered to the bathroom, closed the door, and vomited.

Maria kissed Jake's cheek. "You're a stupid son of a bitch."

His eye fluttered open.

She brushed the wet hair out of his face. "A lucky one, too."

Jake closed his eye, and Laurel continued to vomit in the bathroom.

Maria crossed the reception area and opened the office door.

Ripper and Carrie turned to her.

"Help me get Jake into the bedroom."

"Is he okay?" Carrie said.

"As far as I can tell."

The three of them went to the sofa bed, and Maria and Ripper pulled him to his feet and supported him between them. As they walked him toward his office, Laurel emerged from the bathroom, looking nauseous and fearful.

Jake looked at her, then his head slumped forward.

Carrie opened the bedroom door, and Maria and Ripper dropped him onto his cot. Maria made him comfortable and drew the sheet over him. Laurel stood in the doorway as silent as a shadow. Thunder rumbled and crashed.

"How much rest does he need?" Maria said.

Laurel spoke in a low voice, almost a whisper. "At least a few hours."

"All we have to do is wait out this hurricane," Carrie said. "Right?"

Laurel touched her forehead. "This storm isn't going to

end until Lilith gets what she wants."

"You mean Lilian, right?"

"Her real name is Lilith, and she's going to kill you all."

Ripper moved closer to Laurel. "As in Lilith from the Bible?"

Laurel's eyes rolled up in their sockets, and she collapsed onto the floor. Ripper and Carrie ran to her side. Moaning, her eyes fluttered open without focus.

"Get her some water," Maria said.

"Yes, ma'am." Carrie ran to the kitchen.

"What do you know about Lilith?" Maria said to Ripper.

Cradling Laurel, Ripper helped her sit up. "She's a succubus or a demon or something."

Maria's body turned numb. She had seen the demon Kalfu in a summoning circle on Pavot Island, and Jake had mumbled about Cain and Abel in his sleep. She glanced at Jake, unconscious on the cot.

Carrie returned with a paper cup filled with water, which she held out to Laurel. "Here."

Laurel gulped the water and sighed. "I need to lie down."

Ripper helped her to her feet.

"We're going to run out of beds," Carrie said.

They were halfway across the office when lightning flashed, thunder boomed, and the lights went out, including the TV screens. An emergency flashlight plugged into the wall behind Jake's desk fired a beam at the ceiling, the light reflecting on their faces.

"The emergency generator should come on in a minute,"

Laurel said in a drowsy voice.

"Wrong," Carrie said. "Jackie checked up on us while you were passed out, and he said the basement's flooded. That generator isn't coming on."

"Then we'll just have to use candles," Laurel said. "Get some out of Jake's bottom desk drawer."

Maria unplugged the flashlight and aimed it at the desk. She opened the bottom drawer and removed a shoe box, which she set on the desktop and opened, revealing white candles in brass holders piled on top of each other.

"It's creepy how you do that," Carrie said to Laurel.

Maria picked up the phone on Jake's desk and listened for a dial tone. "The telephone lines are down, too." She pointed the flashlight at the doorway ahead. "Let's get her down and light these."

In the reception area Maria shone the flashlight on the sofa bed, which Laurel climbed onto.

Carrie lit a candle and set it on her desk, then lit more. "This whole office is going to smell like vanilla."

Maria took out her phone and pressed a number.

Bernie answered midway through the first ring. "Hello?"

"Just making sure you got back okay."

"I'm wringing myself out as we speak."

"What's it like there?"

"Crowded, just about everyone from the precinct who's on duty is here. The power went out but the genie kicked in. What about you?"

"It's crowded here, too. No power."

"How's Jake?"

That's a good question, she thought. "Resting but better. Did L.T. ask about me?"

"He accepted my explanation at face value when I told him you were helping civilians. He's got a lot to deal with."

"I want to save my phone's power."

"Copy that. Stay dry."

"You, too." Maria ended the call, then shone the flashlight at Laurel. "Fill us in on Lilith."

Laurel raised one hand before her eyes, shielding them from the light, which Maria aimed at the ceiling for reflection.

"In Jewish mythology, she was Adam's first wife. She refused to obey him and became a demon known for stealing infants from their cradles and causing pregnant women to miscarry. She appears in several religions, always with a different history and purpose. I never suspected that Lilith walked the earth in human form."

"Now you know that's her story because you read Jake?"

"He figured it out last night, but he didn't tell me."

"Why not?"

Laurel swallowed. "He doesn't trust me completely."

"That's great," Carrie said. "We're in this mess because of you, and Jake doesn't even trust you."

"You can ask him to explain his motives. None of it matters now."

"I'm not buying it. No one can be that old."

"And no one can control the weather. You can refuse to accept it if you want, but that won't change our situation. It's just a matter of time before Lilith kills everyone in this office."

"Except you."

"She wants me alive."

"Then the answer seems pretty simple to me."

"She'll assume you know her secret, and she can't allow that. Even if I give her what she wants, she won't allow you to live."

"I knew I should have stayed in school." Carrie went over to the window, where lightning silhouetted her.

"It's not just us," Maria said. "Other people were killed by those tornadoes yesterday, and more will die in this hurricane."

"I know," Laurel said in a weak voice.

"I'm not going down without a fight," Ripper said.

"What *is* that?" Carrie said at the window.

Maria joined Carrie, followed by Ripper. Gazing through the rain striking the window, she saw a dark shape as wide as a semi moving through the water, which had risen high enough to hide the tires of the cars parked below.

Two feet deep and rising, she thought. Which meant the water on the sidewalk was a foot and a half deep.

The dark patch within the water moved west, like a submarine. The rain continued to slam the water like gunfire, but the surface of the water above the moving shadow writhed with a life and texture of its own.

"Rats," Maria said.

"*Hell* no," Ripper said.

Carrie shook her hands in the air. "Ew, I hate rats."

"The flood must have driven them out of the subway tunnels and the sewers," Maria said.

Laurel sat up. "There are eight million of them in New York."

"I heard there are four rats for every person," Ripper said. "That makes thirty-two million."

A billboard on the roof of a building adjacent to the New York Edition Hotel blew over, balanced on the building's edge like a teeter-totter, then slid off, tumbling end over end until it struck a streetlight, then whipped down at an angle, demolishing a parked Camry with a sound akin to thunder.

Pressing her forehead against the windowpane, Carrie squinted. Lightning flashed and she screamed.

"What is it, baby?" Ripper said.

Thunder shook the building.

"Look down there!"

Maria pressed one side of her face against the glass for a better look and waited for another flash of lightning. When it came, a nauseous feeling seized her stomach: a dark wave clung to the wall of the building, ascending it at a steady speed. Only when the wind blew dozens of scurrying black shapes off the building's façade did she realize the army of wet rats had already reached the second floor.

Leaning over Carrie with his hands on her shoulders, Ripper stared below them. "There are hundreds of them."

"They're really hanging on, what with the wind and rain in their ugly little faces," Maria said.

"Maybe they're just trying not to drown," Carrie said.

"This is the only building they're climbing, and hundreds more of them are swimming with the current," Ripper said.

Laurel joined them at the window. "Rats have small brains so they're easy to control. Lilith sent them."

Maria unlocked the window and raised it. Raindrops ricocheted off the sill and struck them.

"What are you doing?" Ripper said.

"There could be any number of ways for them to get in here," Maria said. "I don't intend to let them turn us into Swiss cheese, do you? You take this window. I'll take the one in Jake's office."

"What about me?" Laurel said. "I can handle a gun."

"Really?" Maria turned to Carrie. "Give her the .22."

Carrie pulled the .22 from its holster. "I was just getting used to it."

"Keep it. I can handle bigger." Grabbing two candles, Laurel went into Jake's office.

"Okay, then," Maria said. "Carrie, you stay here with Ripper, and Laurel and I will take the other window. Don't waste ammo. Wait until they reach the third floor before you start shooting."

One candle burned on the safe and the other on Jake's desk when Maria entered. Laurel removed the painting from the wall and plucked a Beretta from its mount inside the wall. She selected a magazine from the mini-shelves beside the gun racks and slapped it into the Beretta's grip.

"You have handled guns before," Maria said, staring at Jake's hiding place.

"I've never fired one in my life, but I have all Jake's experiences at my fingertips."

"I didn't need to hear that. Bring the ammo over here." Maria raised the blind and then the window, and the roaring wind blew rain inside at her.

Laurel set two magazines on the floor and stood beside her.

Maria stuck her head outside, and the wind plastered her wet hair to her skull. The rats had passed the second floor and were just reaching the third.

Ripper watched her from the other window fifteen feet away, his dreadlocks dancing in the wind like Medusa's snakes.

Nodding to him, she drew her Glock and crouched with it in both hands, her armpits pressed against the window's edge as the rats clawed their way past the third-floor windows.

Lightning filled the sky, illuminating the rodents and lighting their eyes. Their heads bobbed up and down, their motion making it almost impossible for her to separate them, their squeaks rising on the wind, which buffeted her. The sky went dark and she fired into the oncoming horde. Blood spewed from the undulating mass, and a rat jerked into the air. Thunder cracked, and the wind carried the black shape away, depositing it into the water below.

Ripper fired as well and another rat dropped. Crouching beside Maria, Laurel fired, blowing a rat through the air.

Jake emerged from the bedroom. "What's happening?"

"We've got a rat problem," Maria said.

Laurel drilled another rat, and Maria fired again and again, blasting wet furry creatures from the wall.

"So we're hiding from them in the dark?" Jake said.

"We've also got a power problem."

Laurel fired again, exploding a rat's head. Before the creature hit the water, she picked off another. Ripper and Carrie opened fire at the same time, whittling down the rats' ranks.

Jake stood before his exposed secret compartment. "Where's my gun?"

"It's in the front room somewhere, but you're sitting this one out," Maria said. She and Laurel fired in tandem, wasting vermin. Still the rats advanced, their scaly claws digging at the stone façade. "Shoot faster!"

The guns barked, spilling blood, and rats fell spinning into the water. Others surfaced, replenishing their numbers. The howling wind devoured the sound of the gunfire.

Maria's gun clicked. "Reloading!"

Carrie ran into the office and almost collided with Jake. "Ripper needs more ammo."

Jake took out his last box of ammo for the Thunder Ranch and handed it to her.

"So do I," Carrie said.

He handed her two more magazines for the .22. "That's all I have."

"Reloading!" Laurel said as Carrie took off running.

At the window, Maria made a disgusted sound as four large rats crawled closer to the window. She and Laurel picked them off, blood spraying into the falling rain, but she got a good look at the rat's black eyes and sharp teeth and wanted Jake to take over. A fat rat crawled up the wall between the two windows as if they couldn't see it.

"Don't shoot," Ripper yelled to Carrie.

"I've got it," Maria said.

Turning in the window, so her back was over the bottom of the frame, Maria targeted the rat, which had clawed its way above the window, just as it leapt into the air, diving at her face. The dark shape blotted out the falling rain for a moment, and she squeezed the trigger, tearing the rat to pieces and altering its trajectory so it fell away from her.

Laurel stopped firing and grabbed Maria's shoulder. "Get up!"

Turning her head, Maria glimpsed three rats within two feet of her. With her heart hammering, she twisted her body away from the window.

Laurel fired until her gun clicked again. "Reloading!"

Maria took up her position again as half a dozen rats reached the same point two feet below the window, their black eyes reflecting the lightning and their squeaks piercing. She opened fire, cutting their number in half, and then she ran out of ammo as well. She slapped her last magazine into her Glock. "Reloading!"

Ripper threw his right arm against the wall and fired a series of shots that decimated three more rats. "Reloading!"

Laurel returned to action first, just as a rat climbed onto the window and hissed at them. She aimed at the rat at point-blank range and blew it into the rain.

Maria shot the remaining two and took out several following in their claw steps.

"I'm out," Carrie said.

"Reloading!" Ripper said.

Jake opened the safe and took out his Glock.

"You don't need that," Maria said, massaging one wrist. "They're gone."

"And we're practically out of ammunition," Jake said, "which was Lilith's plan."

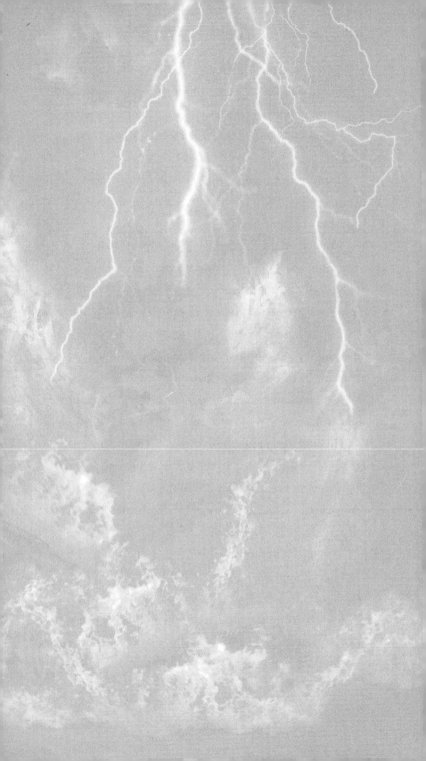

TWENTY-FIVE

Alice sat watching the news on TV, and Shana lay on the floor, coloring a page in a Dora activity book. The wind howled, rain pattered the windows, and the lights in the condo flickered. Shana didn't know what a hurricane was, but she didn't like thunder and lightning. When her mother was alive and they lived together in Far Rockaway, they cuddled at night during storms. Now that she lived with Aunt Alice, she slept alone no matter how frightened she became; Alice didn't want to cuddle with her, and Shana felt the same way about her aunt.

"One hour after Hurricane Daria landed on Manhattan, most of the island's east side is without power, city streets are flooded with two feet or more of water, and the entire subway system within the borough's limits has been shut down. In a surprising development, so far the hurricane's effects are restricted to Manhattan. Projections that Daria would cause havoc in the outer boroughs have not been realized, and meteorologists are at a loss to explain why the storm is moving in a circular pattern around Manhattan proper, making escape and rescue impossible."

Clucking her tongue, Alice reached for the remote control. "What the hell are they talking about?"

The next station showed a radar map overlooking the region as a weatherman said, "As you can see, we have rain across the city, but miraculously the hurricane itself is confined to Manhattan, which it appears to be circling—"

The screen turned black, and the lights went off, reducing Alice to a silhouette.

Shana sat up, a tremor of fear running through her body.

"Goddamn it," Alice said. A moment later the blue glow from the screen of her phone illuminated her face as she rose from the sofa. "Stay here."

Enough dull gray light shone through the windows for Shana to see her aunt as the thick woman crossed the hallway and entered the kitchen. Shana sat on her heels and waited.

Alice opened and closed cupboards. "Where is that flashlight? Did you put it somewhere?"

"No, Aunt Alice."

Shana missed her mother more than ever and found it impossible to shut out the mental picture of her father, Papa Joe, shooting her in the head so the zombies wouldn't get her. He would have killed Shana, too, if her older cousin Malachai and his beautiful girlfriend, Katrina, hadn't stopped him. Both her parents were killed that day.

Alice jerked a drawer open and rummaged through its contents. "Here it is. I don't know how it got here." She switched on the flashlight and swept a bright beam across the kitchen, then returned to the living room and held out her cell phone. "Take this in case you need to go to the bathroom, but make sure you don't drop it. Break it and you'll be in for a world of pain."

"Yes, Aunt Alice."

A banging on the front door caused Shana to jump.

"Who the hell is that?" Alice headed back into the hall, disappearing along with the light.

Shana rose and padded over to the edge of the hall and peeked around the corner as her aunt stood at the door.

"Who is it?"

"Kevin," a muffled voice said.

Alice turned the flashlight so it filled Shana's face, blinding her. "Go to your room."

Aunt Alice always sent her to her room when she had visitors, except for Ramses, who stayed here often. Shana knew better than to disobey, and, as she hurried to her room using the phone for guidance, she heard Alice draw the chain lock across the door. Shana entered her room and started to close the door but stopped, leaving it open a crack so she could see Alice's visitors.

Alice aimed her flashlight in the faces of the two young men who had been here earlier: Kevin and Sapo. Shana knew *sapo* was Spanish for "toad," and the ugly little man looked like one. She powered down Alice's cell phone, killing its glow so she wouldn't be seen.

"How did you get up here?" Alice said as the men entered the condo.

"There's no doorman downstairs," Kevin said. "Your lobby's flooded."

Alice locked the door. "I don't believe this shit. I'm paying for doorman service, and he just let *you two* up here? Please tell me you checked on our spots like I told you."

"Everything's good," Kevin said.

"But I bet you didn't cap Raheem yet, did you?"

"No, but we saw him."

"So why didn't you cap him?"

"Because he had other ideas," Sapo said.

"What—?"

Kevin slipped behind Alice, putting her in a choke hold, and Alice dropped her flashlight.

Shana could no longer see anything, but she heard awful juicy wet stabbing sounds, followed by a dull moan and gurgling. Her heart pounded for what felt like a full minute, and then a dark shape fell to the floor, blocking the flashlight.

"Stupid bitch," Sapo said in the darkness.

"Go find that little shorty," Kevin said.

One of the men picked up Aunt Alice's flashlight, and Shana felt her eyes bulging in their sockets as the beam swung in her direction. Sucking in her breath, she closed the door and pushed the button lock. She ran to her closet and opened its door, then entered it using Alice's phone for illumination.

Five feet away, the doorknob turned.

Shana closed the closet door and turned to her left, where

a wooden clothes hamper had been built into the wall. Parting the clothes on the rod, she faced the surface of the hamper, which appeared to be part of the closet's construction.

In the hall, one of the men pounded on her bedroom door, causing her to jump.

She removed a board in back and set it over the one in front. Then she scrambled on top of the hamper and moved between the clothes hanging on the rod above it, trying not to disturb them.

The bedroom door burst open.

Shana crawled through the opening into the hamper and pulled the loose board back into place just as the closet door opened. Crouching low to the floor with Aunt Alice's cell phone clutched in one hand, she held her breath in the darkness.

Through the floor she felt the vibrations from footsteps. The man jerked her clothes across the rod. She pictured him pulling on the first board, which would have held fast. Then he walked away and she let her breath out.

"Where is she?" the other man said.

"I don't know, not in there."

Their voices grew too muffled to hear.

Careful not to bump the hamper with her head or elbows, Shana sat. She pressed the cell phone until the light from the screen came on again. Using the glow from the screen, she searched her hiding place for the business card Maria had given her.

Jake sat on his cot with his hands clasped before him and Maria sitting beside him. A single candle on the end table beside them highlighted their features in a soft glow.

"How do you feel?" Maria said.

He thought about it. "Contaminated. I've felt that way ever since we got back from Pavot Island."

"The Magic?"

He nodded. "I feel like it's coated the inside of my skin and my brain."

"Why didn't you say something?"

"It's hard to articulate the craving to go out and score a drug that can turn you into a zonbie. There aren't any support groups like AA for it, either."

"That's why you need to confide in the people around you."

"It's been so long since I had anyone I could confide in. I've been carrying around secrets for years, one lie after another. With Sheryl, it was the coke and dirty money. With Edgar, it was all this supernatural shit and killing the Cipher. With you, it was that Katrina had turned Edgar into a raven."

"You also lied about sleeping with Laurel, but I've decided to give you a pass on that one for now."

"Every time I get dragged into something, there's always someone like Geoghegan around to give me the third degree, and all I can do is lie through my teeth. It's become a way of life for me. Laurel was the only person I could talk to."

"Maybe you want to rephrase that," she said.

"You dogged me for almost a year. A person obsessed with proving you did something you didn't do is the last one whose shoulder you want to cry on. Now I don't even want to spill my guts to Laurel."

"That doesn't seem to matter. She just takes whatever thoughts you don't care to share."

"It's not like she can help it."

"She said you don't trust her."

"I never told her that but it's true. When Katrina turned Edgar into a raven, Laurel never told me that one of Ramera Evans's blood relatives could reverse the curse. I had to find that out on my own." Even in his time of confession, he couldn't tell Maria that information had come to him via Sheryl.

"Maybe she didn't know."

"I'm tired of her knowing everything about me."

"Confronting Lilith like that was stupid."

"I just wanted to buy the city more time."

"Did they hurt you?"

He thought of Lilith commanding him to behave like a dog. "Just my pride."

"That isn't all they did, though, was it?"

Avoiding her eyes, he shook his head.

"This is some world you live in," she said in a low voice.

"If anything happens to me, get the hell out of New York."

Maria stared at him for a moment before speaking. "Why? Lilith has seen me. She already knows who I am. I find it hard to believe she's behind this hurricane, but I'd be stupid to discount she's a witch after what I saw on Pavot Island. If she's as powerful as you say she is, she can destroy me anytime she wants, can't she?"

He closed his eye. How had it come to this so fast? "Yes."

"Then we're better off facing her together."

He stared at the candle. "We're not on Pavot Island. You'd think being on our home turf would make this easier, but it doesn't. She has us right where she wants us."

Maria looked at the window. "How long can she keep this up? Long enough to starve us out?"

"Noah's flood lasted forty days."

"God's flood, not Noah's. Whatever Lilith is, she sure as hell isn't God. There has to be a limit to her powers or at least to her temper. She can't be willing to destroy the entire city."

"She sure seems committed."

Someone knocked on the door.

"Come in," Jake said.

The door opened, and Carrie stood before them holding a candle. "You'd better come out here."

Jake and Maria followed Carrie through the office and into the reception area, where Ripper and Laurel sat staring at Ripper's phone. Jake's Thunder Ranch lay on the table.

"The power's out across most of the city," Ripper said.

Jake, Maria, and Carrie sat around the desk.

"The hurricane is moving in circles around Manhattan," Laurel said.

"That's impossible," Maria said.

"That's what the weathermen are saying, too," Ripper said.

"She's using it to keep anyone from getting out or in," Laurel said.

The light from his phone lit Ripper's face from underneath. "The mayor just ordered martial law, the governor's sending in the National Guard, and the president's declared Manhattan a national disaster area."

"The National Guard isn't getting in here," Jake said.

"Well, then maybe the coast guard."

"This is on us."

"Team Helman?"

Before Jake could answer, Maria's phone emitted a half ring.

"Text," she said, taking out her phone.

Jake wondered how long it would be before their phones stopped receiving data.

"I'm not in the proper frame of mind to lead any troops."

"You got us into this mess by rescuing her"—Carrie nodded at Laurel—"so you can damn well be the one to get us out of it."

Maria stared at her phone. "Oh, my God."

"What is it?" Jake said.

She showed him the message. "Shana."

Help. They killed Aunt Alice. I'm hiding in my closet.

Maria started to key in a reply.

But Jake grabbed her arm. "A response could expose her to whoever she's hiding from."

"Who's Shana?" Carrie said.

Shoving her phone into her pocket, Maria stood. "I

have to go."

Jake stood, too. "You don't even know where she is."

"Alice's condo is on Thirty-fourth and Ninth."

"How the hell do you expect to get there?"

"I'll take the High Line."

"That's all the way on Eleventh Avenue!"

"I'll find a way. That little girl's been through hell, and now she's in danger. Don't try to stop me."

"Then let me come with you."

Maria looked at the others, then back at Jake. "No. That will just ruin your chances against Lilith."

"What makes you think she'll let you go?" Ripper said.

Maria turned to Laurel. "If I stick close to the buildings she won't see me, right?"

"This storm is her creation. She could easily see you."

"I have to take that chance."

"Come into my office," Jake said.

"I don't have time."

"It will just take a second."

They went into the office and Jake closed the door. He took two cartridges for his Glock and handed them to her.

"You may need these."

She pocketed the magazines. "I hope not."

"I have something else for you." Crouching before the safe, he turned the combinations and opened the door, then took out his Glock and an object he had trouble seeing in the candlelight.

Standing, he held the Anting-Anting by its chain. "I don't know if this will offer any protection from Lilith because I don't know what the hell she is, but it's worth a try. In ancient times Jews wore amulets to keep her away. I didn't think to take it with me this morning; my mind hasn't been working too well."

Maria gazed at the Anting-Anting, which Jake had worn when he outsmarted Kalfu. "You keep that."

"No." Raising the chain over her head, he placed it around her neck. "You can give it back when you see me."

She touched the amulet, then looked at Jake and kissed him.

Returning to the reception area with Jake behind her, Maria squinted at Carrie, Ripper, and Laurel in the candlelight. "Good luck to all of you. As soon as I get this little girl someplace safe, I promise to come back."

"Good luck to you, too," Laurel said.

"You've got my number," Jake said.

"You've got that right." Maria winked and left.

Carrie stared at Jake with a dumbfounded expression. "You shouldn't have let her go."

"He did the right thing," Laurel said.

"She'll be safer out there than in here," Jake said. "This way my feelings for her won't trip me up, and she can't get in the way of what I have to do next."

"What's up, chief?" Ripper said.

Jake picked up the Thunder Ranch. "Except for what's in this and in my Glock, we're out of ammo. But I have plenty of ammo for that big gun that's in my car, so I'm going to get it."

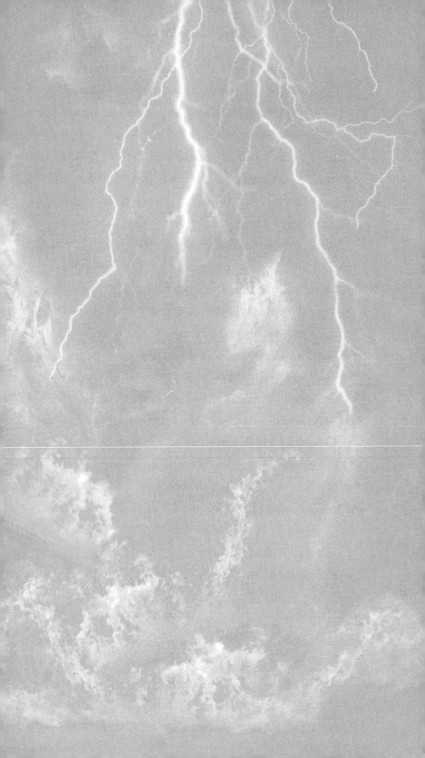

TWENTY-SIX

Using her Maglite for illumination, Maria took out her cell phone as she descended the stairs of the building and pressed a number.

"What's up, kid?" Bernie said.

"Raheem had Alice killed, and Shana's holed up in their condo. The triggermen may still be in there."

"How do you know that?"

"Shana sent me a text from inside her closet."

"Holy mackerel."

"I'm leaving Jake's building now to go there."

"How the hell do you expect to get to that building?"

"I don't know if I can, but I sure as hell aim to try. I want you to call the 10th Precinct and see if they have anyone in the vicinity they can send to help."

"No one's going anywhere. This city is locked down: no cars, no choppers, no friendly neighborhood patrolmen."

"You never know. Penn Station's right down the street."

"It's underwater, darling."

"Hell, there could be an off-duty PO who lives in that building."

"On a cop's salary?"

"I'm hanging up. Life and death, okay? Make the call." She ended the call and made another one.

Five minutes later, Maria stood on the last landing before the lobby. Water had filled it three feet deep, engulfing all but the last step. She descended the stairs and waded into the cold water up to her hips. The lower panes of the glass doors had broken from the pressure, allowing the water inside.

She prayed she would see Jake again, but she told herself that every adult in his office had made the decision to be there and Shana was an innocent child with no say in her predicament. Maria would give her life to save the little girl's, and she didn't intend to allow Lilith or anyone else to stop her.

Wading across the darkened, flooded lobby, she couldn't help but search the water for rats. If Lilith had sent them scaling the front of the building, she could just as easily send them to gnaw her to pieces at street level.

She gazed outside at the rain, which struck the water's surface in great sheets and rendered visibility almost nonexistent. It was just after 2:00 p.m., but it might as well have been nighttime. She couldn't see the Flatiron Building or the Tower, and across the street the New York Edition Hotel loomed like a monolith, its limestone surface gray in the rain.

Maria stepped outside, and the wind slammed her with such force that it knocked her backwards into the water, submerging her. The current dragged her and she flailed her arms. Her right hand caught the building's edge, which she grabbed with her left hand as well. Pulling her body forward, she raised her head, gasping for air. Then she pushed herself forward with her legs and held on to the front doorframe. This was going to be harder than she thought.

Three shapes bobbing in the water ahead caused her to reach for her Glock, ready to battle rats if necessary. As the shapes moved closer, she recognized the hands and head of a human corpse dragged by the current. Memories of the zonbies on Pavot Island bubbled in her brain, and she held her breath until the male corpse had floated by.

Using her left arm to shield her eyes from the onslaught, she tried to discern the corner of Twenty-third and Park Avenue ahead, which proved impossible. It occurred to her that if she hadn't clawed her way back into the entrance, the wind and current would have carried her straight to the Flatiron Building.

And beyond it, she thought.

The corpse had already traveled halfway down the block.

That's it.

Maria took her sunglasses, phone, and a scarf from her jacket pockets and slid the phone into her pants pocket. She unclipped her holster from her side and secured it to the back of her belt. Then she peeled off her jacket and tossed it inside the lobby. She slipped on the sunglasses and tied the scarf tight around her head.

Taking a breath, she faced the current and kicked off the sidewalk. The river took her but did not submerge her. She rolled over onto her back, attempting to float. The rain struck her face with such volume that she had to blow it out of her nostrils. Her heels tapped the pavement, and her legs swung up again, causing her face to disappear beneath the surface. She let out a slow exhale so she didn't take in water, and her face broke the surface again.

I'll get the hang of it, she thought.

When her heels touched the pavement, she gave a gentle kick, just enough to move her toward the middle of the street, so she didn't have to worry about colliding with a building. The hardest part was dealing with the rain, which stung her face, drops ricocheting inside her nostrils. She inhaled through her mouth and exhaled through her nose to compensate.

Out of the corner of her left eye she glimpsed a gray mass blotting out the sky: the Tower. Just a block to go before she reached the Flatiron Building. Hopefully she would float right by it.

Jake put on the dusty nylon camouflage outfit he had worn to infiltrate Lilian's estate. The jacket still reeked. He strapped his hunting knife around his right boot and holstered his Thunder Ranch. Then he went into the reception area and handed his holstered Glock to Ripper.

"I'm going with you," Ripper said.

"No dice. I need you to stay here with the ladies."

"You can't swim with one hand," Laurel said.

"I can. It will just be hard."

"Take Ripper," Carrie said. "We'll be fine here."

Jake pulled the Thunder Ranch from its holster and held its butt out to Laurel. "Then you take this. Ripper will have my back."

"That sounds fair," Carrie said.

"This shouldn't take more than an hour."

Ripper fastened the Glock's holster to his belt. "I'm ready."

"Please be careful," Carrie said. "Don't get eaten by any rats."

Sliding his heels apart, Ripper kissed her.

"Don't make me come looking for you," Laurel said to Jake.

Maria ceased all motion as she floated on her back past the Flatiron Building. She spread her arms and thrust her belly as high as she could to avoid sinking, but water still washed over her face, and she blew air out of her nose to keep from breathing it in. A coughing fit would expose her if anyone watched from the building.

Since she couldn't see through her sunglasses or the windows, she closed her eyes, controlled her breathing, and attempted to reach a Zen-like calm. The deafening roar of the wind and rain became soothing.

After what felt like five minutes, she opened her eyes but remained still otherwise. She had passed Fifth Avenue, and the outline of the Tower loomed on her left and the Flatiron on her right. With her arms still wide apart, she felt safe enough to nudge the street with her heels, but her feet made no connection, and she dipped beneath the surface. The water had become deeper.

Fighting the urge to panic, she waited for her body to rise. As soon as that occurred she kicked just enough to gain some propulsion, which helped her stay afloat without splashing. One more long block would take her to Sixth Avenue, and then she could swim harder.

Hang on, Shana.

Jake and Ripper waded through the lobby.

"It's almost four feet deep," Jake said.

As they neared the front doors, Ripper picked up a piece of clothing floating near one wall and held it up. "Isn't this Maria's jacket?"

"Check the pockets," Jake said.

Ripper turned the pockets inside out. "Empty."

"She's up to something, then."

Between the rain, the dark sky, and the lack of any electric illumination, Jake couldn't even make out the New York Edition Hotel across the street. He had become so accustomed to seeing the Tower, the Metropolitan Life North Building, and the hotel lit up like jewels that he now felt as if he had slipped back through time to the Middle Ages.

Ripper stood motionless beside him. "That current looks strong, J."

"I bet Maria used it to her advantage. You can swim, right?"

"Hell, yes. In a swimming pool."

"We just have to make it one block."

"Yeah, in a hurricane."

"You have my gun, so I can't have it against your head."

The body of a woman swept past them.

"I wonder what happened to her," Ripper said.

"It's only going to get deeper the longer we wait."

Ripper gestured for Jake to lead.

"The door to Laurel's parlor is recessed into the façade like this one, so there's at least some shelter, and we saw that car go through its front window. Try swimming underwater. That way we'll just be battling the current and not the wind, too."

"Whatever you say."

Taking a deep breath, Jake plunged into the water. The current slammed into him, and he kicked harder than he anticipated needing to. He swam with both arms, even though he had only one hand to cup. He caught the corner of the entrance to Laurel's parlor and kicked faster. When his head broke the surface he pulled himself into the alcove next to the door.

Ripper surfaced, gasping for breath, and Jake helped him in.

"Piece of cake, right?" Jake said.

"Damn, that water's cold."

"Let's cheat for the next leg." Jake stepped into the current again but went through the cave mouth where Laurel's picture window had been. The water was calmer inside the flooded interior, where Laurel's chairs and table floated.

Ripper got inside and surveyed the room. "Can you imagine how much damage this storm's already done to the city?"

"Not really." Jake waded across the parlor. "Watch your step. The floor is sunken." He waited for Ripper to catch up to him. "My favorite restaurant is next door. Same deal. We should be safe from the current as soon as we reach the doorway."

He dove into the water and swam beneath the surface. This time he found it harder to pull himself into the alcove.

Joining him, Ripper shook his dreads, casting off water as a dog would.

Jake slid through the broken glass door and entered the flooded Cajun restaurant. He doubted he would ever eat here again. Although the booths were bolted to the floor, dozens of chairs and tables bobbed on the surface, along with plastic dish trays. Ripper followed him to the far end of the missing picture window. A neon sign dangling from the ceiling blew back and forth.

"I hope the juice doesn't come back on while we're in the water," Ripper said.

"Don't think about it. The furniture store is next. It's a longer swim to the doorway, but then it's a longer walk inside, too."

Jake dove in and swam even harder than he had before because he wanted to get as far as he could before exhaustion slowed him. He passed a standpipe set in the sidewalk. Halfway to their destination, Ripper passed him.

Son of a bitch, Jake thought. He kicked faster and harder but seemed to move slower. He heard the wind and the sound of his own heartbeat. *Where's that damn doorway?*

He found himself moving backwards until Ripper seized his collar and guided him into the next alcove and through the broken furniture store window. Inside, gasping, Jake turned around. Cushions floated, mattresses bobbed, and wooden bed frames drifted along the expansive interior.

"Let's keep moving," Ripper said. "The water could be over our heads when we come back."

"But the current will be on our side then."

"Maybe."

They made circular motions with their arms to make walking easier and push the cushions out of their way. When they reached the last window space, they swam to an optometrist's store.

"Why couldn't there be a scuba diving shop on the block?" Jake said, his chest heaving.

"What's next?"

"That yuppie coffee shop. It's our last stop before the garage."

"We should have tried the roofs."

"In this wind? We'd have blown away. Besides, the rooftops are different heights, and there are no fire escapes on this side."

They swam to the coffee shop. Inside the dark interior the water churned broken glass.

"I can't believe we made it," Ripper said.

"Don't get cocky."

They half walked and half swam across the coffee shop, and Jake saw the buildings on the opposite side of Lexington Avenue. "The wind is traveling perpendicular to us now. No sheets of rain."

"Check this out." Ripper pointed at a large jar filled halfway with coins next to the cash register.

"Bring it. I'll explain what it's for when we get to the garage."

The water along Park was still compared to Twenty-third Street, the only turbulence created by the downpour. The buildings blocked the wind.

"There is a God," Ripper said above the roar of the rain.

They reached the parking garage with comparative ease, but the water reached the ceiling above the ramp.

"What now?"

"I swim down there."

"You'll never make it."

Jake slid the backpack from his shoulders. "Sure, I will. We parked close to the ramp." He handed the backpack to

Ripper. "Open that for me."

Ripper tucked the money jar under one arm and undid the backpack straps. Jake took out a flashlight and what appeared to be an oxygen mask from a hospital, with a clear plastic bag attached to the front of it.

"What is that?"

"I made this myself out of curiosity. It's based on a design used at an old job of mine."

"What was it used for?"

"You don't want to know."

Ripper examined the oxygen mask. "You won't get more than a minute of air out of it."

"That's all I need. As long as I can reach my car, I'll be okay."

"The air in the bag will work against you; it will make it harder for you to reach the bottom."

"That's why we stole from Jerry's kids." Jake took a pair of thick rubber bands out of the backpack, which he used to secure the flashlight to his stump. Then he pulled the oxygen mask over his head but not over his face. "If I'm not back in five minutes, leave without me."

"Don't worry. I will."

Jake took a deep breath, pulled the mask over his face, then took the money jar from Ripper, who gave him a thumbs-up. Grasping the jar, he dove into the water.

TWENTY-SEVEN

Traveling at ten miles an hour, Joyce inched along Queens Boulevard through Long Island City. Edgar couldn't see the Fifty-ninth Street Bridge through the downpour, even with the windshield wipers at full speed. The wind rocked the vehicle from side to side. Martin sat in the backseat, his face glued to a window.

"This is crazy," Joyce said. "You're crazy. Jake's crazy. Maria's crazy. You're all crazy."

"I can't help it," Edgar said. "I owe them."

"For what? According to you, they had nothing to do with you coming home."

"You know better. I owe them." He left it at that.

"This hurricane's tearing the city apart. Roosevelt Island is *gone*, and you want to walk across that bridge."

"It beats swimming."

"What if the bridge comes down?"

"Then I'll have to swim."

"This isn't funny. We just got you back. Do you want us to lose you for good?"

Edgar glanced at Martin, who continued to stare out the window, then turned to Joyce. "You're not going to lose me. But these are my friends and they need my help. I'd do this even if I didn't owe them."

"What about us?"

"I love you. Both of you."

"Then don't do this."

"I don't have a choice. That's not who I am."

"Is it always going to be like this?"

He considered her question. "No."

"What are you even going to do if you make it to Jake's office?"

"I can't tell you that." He didn't know the answer.

The rain abated as she pulled under the elevated train tracks of Queensboro Plaza. "This is as close as I can get."

"Then this is where I get out."

Joyce held up a tied plastic bag. "I made you dinner."

He smiled. "Thanks." He lifted one flap of his clear rain poncho and slid the food into the black canvas bag he carried, the strap crossing his chest.

"I've got something else for you." She handed him the gun case containing his off-duty Glock. "Jake gave it to me when he brought your stuff over. I kept it in a safe place."

Edgar was tempted to let her hang on to the weapon to show her she had nothing to worry about, but he knew he might need it, so he took it and put it into his shoulder bag.

"Thanks." Turning to Martin, he raised one fist between them. "Hey."

Martin looked at him, then bumped his fist.

"Don't worry. I'm coming back."

Then he kissed Joyce and got out of the car. The roaring wind seized the door and almost ripped it from its hinge and wrapped the poncho around him like Saran wrap. He closed the door and jogged away from the station toward where he knew the bridge to be. He did not turn back; the sight of Joyce and their son driving away might have changed his mind.

The strobes of two police cars came into view, then the outlines of the vehicles. He backed up until they became impossible to see again and jogged in a wide circle around them so the officers inside would not see him. He encountered more strobes and veered left to avoid them.

Two men waved air traffic control lights. They stood next to an army troop transport truck, the canvas stretched over it flapping in the wind.

National Guards, Edgar thought.

Moving closer, he saw another transport truck idling behind the first one and a third truck beyond that.

The men waving the traffic control lights shouted something, but he couldn't make out their words over the roaring wind.

Edgar bypassed the guards and saw others serving the same purpose. He found it impossible to tell how many there were. Then he came alongside a wave of people walking away from the bridge. Refugees from Roosevelt Island or Manhattan, he supposed. The soaking wet men, women, and children looked miserable.

He jogged in the opposite direction of them for fifty yards, searching for an opening, then cut through them. "Excuse me."

"You're going the wrong way," a woman said.

"Turn around," a man said.

Ignoring them, Edgar continued toward the bridge, where cars blocked the entrances to both the lower and upper decks of the cantilever truss structure. As he moved closer he realized all the vehicles had been abandoned.

Walking into wind and sheets of rain, he boarded the lower deck, which offered some relief from the storm because the upper deck acted as a roof. The bridge spanned seven thousand five hundred feet counting its approaches, and the refugees crowded the walkways on both sides of the bridge, somewhat protected by chain-link fencing.

The abandoned cars took up all five lanes and faced in his direction, which was not the way the bridge operated. Seeing no path through the pedestrian traffic, he set off between the cars.

TWENTY-EIGHT

Jake swam down the ramp, the jar of coins making the trip easier. No water seeped into his replica of the mask that Marc Gorman, the Cipher, had used to steal souls, including Sheryl's, for Nicholas Tower. Jake hoped his soul wouldn't wind up in the replica. There was no regulator in the mask, so all he could do was breathe as evenly as possible, cognizant that he would have to discard it soon.

The water grew darker, and when he aimed the flashlight bound to the jar at the garage below, the murky depths swallowed it. He leveled it at the ramp, tracing the surface of the blacktop, the oxygen bag attached to the mask pressing against his throat. He swam two feet above the pavement, conscious of the structure above him. At the bottom, shrouded in darkness, he set his feet on the ground. The weight of the jar held him in place, though his body tried to rise. The air inside the mask already felt warm.

Jake swung the jar from side to side, trying to locate a signpost, and found his way when the beam reflected off a white column to his right. He swam in that direction, wishing he could discard the jar, but the last thing he wanted was to get pinned against the ceiling without air. When he reached the column, he set his feet on the ground again. The air in the mask grew stuffy, his breathing labored. He searched for his car, which he knew had to be close. The water devoured the light, and he narrowed his eye, his rhythmic breathing filling his ears.

A figure as white as a ghost lunged into the light in front of him, and Jake screamed. The man's eyes and mouth were open, his hair undulating like a swimming squid's tentacles, clawed fingers reaching for Jake, who recoiled and dropped the jar.

As the jar pulled the flashlight to the ground, Jake lost sight of the man and his body rose. Now in pitch-black darkness, he collided with the man, his fingers poking soggy flesh. Using his stump and hand, he shoved the man upward, which also propelled him to the ground. The beam of light pinpointed the location of the jar, which he seized. Crouching on the concrete floor, he swept the flashlight back and forth, slicing through the darkness, until it illuminated the drifting corpse, dressed in the blue slacks and shirt of an attendant.

Dead, he thought. *Of course.* He could only imagine the death the man had faced when he was trapped by cascading water.

A pair of arms encircled his neck, and his heart leapt.

Twisting in his attacker's grip, he aimed the jar at the ceiling, illuminating the snarling features of a dead woman with black hair, her eyes open. It stood to reason that if Lilith had sown the seeds of black magic in the world, she had also reaped the rewards of Black Magic and had created the first zombie. Was Lilith watching him now through the woman's eyes?

The woman seized his throat in one hand and clawed at his face with the other.

He twisted his head away, repulsed by the touch of her wrinkled fingertips. His body rose, and he knew that if he reached the ceiling he was doomed.

Jake grabbed the woman's hair and jerked himself downward, then released his handhold to pull his hunting knife from the sheath strapped to his boot. Clapping the jar between his boots so that his position and the column of light before him remained steady, he stood face-to-face with the dead thing, which clawed at him like a wild animal, trying to reach his throat again.

Without a second hand to fend her off, he had no choice but to encircle his left arm and stump around the back of her neck and pull her close to him in a tight embrace, the flashlight illuminating both their faces. Forcing his left shoulder under her jaw, he pressed the tip of the knife against her cranium and drove it through her flesh.

The dead woman struggled, as if she knew what his actions meant, but he held her tighter and drove the knife through her skull and into her brain. She turned spastic, and he tried to wiggle the blade to inflict as much damage as possible to her organ, but the slot he had created in her head would not crack, so he made a sawing motion, sliding the serrated blade out and shoving it back in several times.

Her eyes rolled in their sockets, she belched air, and her body turned still. A series of flashes erupted around her body, causing Jake to look away.

When he turned back, the woman's flickering soul rose from her body and faded. Pulling the knife free, he shoved the corpse with his stump and watched it float away leaking brain fluid. It disappeared into the darkness.

Jake retrieved the jar, but panic set in: he had run out of oxygen. Leaving the mask on to protect his eyes, he held his breath. He might make it to the surface if he retreated, and he would probably not make it all the way to his car and then to the surface, but a retreat would make the mission a failure and the lives of his friends depended on its success.

He had only one chance. Ripping the flashlight free of the jar, he swam to where he knew his car must be. Sure enough, the beam struck the windows of the Maxima and bounced back at him. He kicked faster, but his body rose and he corrected its trajectory. Reaching the passenger side, he jammed the flashlight under his left armpit and gripped the door handle. Then he realized he needed his hand free just to get his car keys out of his pocket.

Damn it!

Jake exhaled some of the oxygen in his mouth and pulled himself down to the floor again. He dropped the flashlight and used his stump for leverage against the floor. Rotating his body, he slid his legs beneath the car's underbelly, then let go of the handle and pushed his chest beneath the car as well. At least the mask prevented him from breathing in water.

He removed his keys from his pocket, then felt along the car door until he found the handle and the lock. As he unlocked the door and opened it, he heard a reverberating rushing as trapped air escaped.

Jake seized the flashlight, maneuvered his body out from under the car enough to sit up, and set the flashlight on the front seat. Grabbing the passenger seat belt, he swung his legs out from under the car and got inside, aiming his head at the inside roof. His forehead struck the dome light and he flattened his face against the metal and sucked in air from a trapped pocket.

He burst into maniacal laughter, then lowered himself below the surface, grabbed the flashlight, and returned for more air. He reached into the backseat and found the strap for the ATAC 3000, which he slung over his head and one shoulder.

Jake took several more breaths, calming his heart rate, then used his stump to push himself down to the seats, where he shone the flashlight into the face of a dead parking attendant, whose eyes did not dilate from the sudden light.

Jake's heart rate soared again. He had no idea if the ATAC would fire underwater—most machine guns did not—and he had no intention of wasting precious time or oxygen freeing the weapon to find out. The attendant clambered inside the car, and Jake set the flashlight on the front seat pointed in his direction. He planted both feet flat against the driver's side and pushed off, streamlining straight into the zonbie and knocking him out of the car and against the inside of the door.

Wrapping the passenger seat belt around his left ankle twice, Jake stepped halfway out of the car, grabbed the outside door handle, and yanked his left foot out. The zonbie turned to engage him, and he slammed the car door against its head, pinning it against the edge of the car's roof and producing a reverberating sound, the water slowing his action.

Jake pulled the door back six inches and slammed its frame against the zonbie's head again and again and again until the zonbie's head split open and chunks of brain escaped, rising like jellyfish. The man's soul flickered in the water, rose, and faded.

Swinging the door open, Jake twisted the silhouetted dead man's shirt around his fist and sent the corpse toward the ceiling. Then he climbed back in and gulped the last of the air.

No time to rest now, he thought.

Grabbing the flashlight, Jake pressed his feet against the car and kicked off. He shot forward like a torpedo fifteen feet, then kicked with fury, riding his momentum. Only when he slowed did he engage his arms. He passed the column with ease and prayed he would find the ramp without trouble.

When Maria reached Seventh Avenue, she rotated onto her

front and swam freestyle. She sliced left against the current and made for the corner, where she wrapped her arms around a streetlight and set her feet atop its base. The rain continued to assail her, and she had difficulty breathing.

Four more blocks to the High Line, she thought. Three more long blocks. Uncertain whether she could make it, she pulled her phone out of her pocket. Maybe Bernie had some luck with the 10th Precinct. The phone's screen came on, but so did a message: No Signal.

"Damn it," she said to the storm. Twisting her head from side to side, she looked behind her at a pharmacy.

It's summer, she thought. Then she swam for the broken front doors.

Despite the pressure in his head from the lack of oxygen, swimming up the ramp was the easy part for Jake. When his head broke the surface, he was not surprised to see that Ripper had left him.

I would have done the same thing, he thought. *No, I wouldn't.*

The water seemed six inches deeper, and rain striking the surface ricocheted into his face.

"Over here," a trembling voice called out. Ripper leaned out of the last window in the coffee shop with his head just above water.

Gasping, Jake waded toward him. "I told you to leave after five minutes."

Ripper shrugged. "My phone isn't getting a signal, but I think it's only *been* five minutes or less. Shake a leg."

"I'm too tired." Jake glanced over his shoulder to make sure no zonbies swam after him.

"Any trouble?"

"None."

"Then why do you keep looking behind you like that?"

"Habit." Jake entered the coffee shop, which they made their way through.

"That's a sharp-looking firearm you're packing," Ripper said, his teeth chattering.

"This old thing? I only put it on when I've got nothing else to wear."

A feeling of discomfort came over Jake as they approached the front picture window on Twenty-third Street. The wind continued to blow spray off the unnatural river.

"Just remember the current will be on our side this time," Jake said.

"Unless we miss your building and it delivers us to Lilith's doorstep."

I'm going to wind up there eventually anyway, Jake thought.

They stood within the empty space where the picture window had been, holding on to the inside frame.

"You go first," Jake said.

"Why?"

"So you can catch the doorframe of my building with one hand and grab me with the other if you have to. That's the main reason I brought you."

"Then here I go." Ripper dove into the water, disappearing. Seconds later, his head reappeared and he swam freestyle, the current speeding him along.

Jake jumped in after him, and the current carried him away, the wind adding propulsion. Rain needled the back of his neck as he moved closer to the buildings. The wind pushed him underwater, and when he surfaced it drove him down again, like a giant invisible hand. He passed the furniture store, then the Cajun restaurant, and before he knew it, Laurel's ruined parlor. His heart beat faster as he worried he would be swept away.

Ripper leaned out ahead, holding on to the doorframe with one hand and reaching for Jake with the other. Jake raised his stump and Ripper caught it, then pulled him to the doorframe, grimacing from the strain. Jake wrapped his right arm around the frame and coughed. Then they forced their way into the dark lobby, and Jake took out his flashlight.

Maria's jacket still lingered in the water inside, and they waded toward the stairs.

Halfway there, Jake felt the water pushing toward them. "What the hell?"

Ripper slipped and went under, and Jake dropped the flashlight to grab his outstretched hand. He turned toward the door as Ripper raised his head out of the water and grabbed Jake's wrist with his other hand.

Behind Ripper, the water in the lobby rushed at them,

channeling through the broken doors. Jake's feet flew out from under him, and he slipped underwater. Rolling over, he swung his left arm through the empty space within the inside doorframe and held on by the crook of his arm. Cascading water slammed into his face and he bowed his head, screaming loud to hear himself.

Closing his right hand into a fist, he realized Ripper had let go of his arm, which he swung at the doorframe, his fingers clawing at the metal. With great effort, he turned to see Ripper clinging to the outer door with both arms. The wind increased, its roar deafening. The water level shrank in the lobby and on the sidewalk, and both men's legs rose above the surface, extended in midair.

A whirlpool had formed in the center of the street, and Jake's arms ached from resisting its pull. A mammoth waterspout rose into the sky, dwarfing the Edition. Jake's legs slapped the wet sidewalk, and Ripper's did the same. The waterspout widened, filling the street from sidewalk to side-walk and sucking in debris as the tornado had the day before.

Jake and Ripper ran into the lobby at the same time, their sopping wet clothes weighing them down. They slid across the wet floor, then scrambled up the stairs.

Clinging to an inflatable pool mattress and kicking with all her strength, Maria had passed the corner of Eighth Avenue when the wind reversed direction, forcing her to look away. The water's current reversed course as well.

"Not now," she said in a desperate tone. "Not now!"

As the water drew her back east, she turned around and kicked toward a beauty salon on her right. She threw the poor mattress through the picture window space, hauled herself up, and climbed inside. The mattress sailed past her before she could stop it, the water inside the salon rushing out. She hugged a marble countertop as water cascaded around her, returning to the street, then climbed atop it and gasped for air.

Maria studied the devastated salon. Dislodged furniture cluttered the window space she had just climbed through, and the remaining water, level with the bottom of the window, stilled. She hopped off the counter into the remaining foot and a half of water and staggered to the missing window to investigate. Outside, the water receded as low as two feet, as if sucked down a giant bathtub drain.

Stepping over the beauty chairs, she clung to the wall and looked outside to her right. What she saw made her body stiffen: an enormous cyclone of water had risen beyond the Tower. It sucked up the water, expanding and growing taller.

When Jake and Ripper staggered into the office, Carrie turned from the window with a terrified look on her face. "You have to see this."

They rushed to the window, which endured a continuous blast of water, and Jake gazed in disbelief as the waterspout moved north, directly into the Edition. At first the impact caused the speeding water to gush in all directions, raining down on the street below. Then the hotel's clock tower sheared off, and the entire fifty-story skyscraper came crashing down, a dense cloud of smoke rising as debris filled the street and smashed into the base of the waterspout, tilting it at an angle.

Dust blew against the window, clinging to its wet surface and preventing them from seeing anything else. As soon as the rain washed it away, more dust clumped on the glass.

A louder, longer rumble shook the building, and Jake knew the Metropolitan Life North Building adjacent to the New York Edition Hotel on Madison Avenue had come down as well.

"Get back," he said, and they ran to the far wall just as the windows in the reception area and office exploded and water gushed inside, slamming furniture across the room and pinning them against the wall.

Climbing through the window in the salon, Maria stumbled into the water on the sidewalk, which was only one foot deep now, and stood in stunned silence as the Edition Hotel toppled into the Metropolitan Life North Building. The art deco structure collapsed as well, no doubt crushing smaller buildings along Madison Avenue. At the same time, the waterspout exploded, drenching the buildings on both sides of the street and disappearing. Tremendous clouds of limestone-colored dust billowed out of the disaster site in all directions, swirling in the storm.

Maria prayed the buildings had been empty due to the storm but knew that was impossible: lives had been lost. Had Jake's building toppled as well? She couldn't see through the swirling mud storm.

She took a step forward and stopped. If the building had collapsed, she could do nothing about it. Even if she went back to look for Jake, she would have to pass the Flatiron Building and Lilith. She told herself that Jake and his companions had made the decision to stay where Lilith knew they were, and she had come this far to rescue Shana. Tears welled in her eyes, and she took another step toward Jake.

Then Maria looked down. The water rose as if the tide had come in, and the current had reversed itself. Looking up, she knew the decision was no longer hers to make: a great wave rose at Seventh Avenue, heading in her direction. Turning once more, she ran west. She would rescue Shana, and then she would worry about Lilith.

Carrie screamed. The water sloshed back and forth between the walls and then settled, four inches deep. Rain and dust blew through the window, so Jake closed the twisted blinds, which had several broken slats, but the wind just blew the blind at him.

Jake hurried into the office, his every footstep splashing water, and closed the tattered remnants of the blind in there as well. Then he checked his bedroom, which had no window, and rushed back into the flooded reception area, where Carrie now sat atop her desk, Ripper stroking her hair.

"Where the hell is Laurel?"

"She left ten minutes after you did," Carrie said.

Jake's spirits sank.

Carrie clung to Ripper. "She took your gun and said she was going to kill Lilith."

Jake's voice tightened. "And you let her go?"

"Hello? She had the gun. I don't believe that's where she went, though. She saw her chance to run and took it."

Jake looked around the dripping wet room. His chest rose and fell, his soaked clothes clinging to him. "I'm going back out there."

"To look for her?"

"To put a bullet in Lilith's brain before any more civilians get killed."

"Then Ripper's going with you," Carrie said.

Ripper gave her a questioning look. "We're lucky we made it back alive just now."

"You're right and you don't have to come," Jake said. "But I'm going."

Carrie's expression grew cross. "Tell him you're going with him."

"Why don't *you* go with him?" Ripper said.

"Because I can drown in four feet of water, and I'm not a tough guy like you."

"I'll make this easy," Jake said. "Nobody's going with me. I'll make it to that building alone."

"And then what?" Carrie said.

Jake said nothing. He had no answer, no plan. But he did have an ATAC 3000.

"I'm going," Ripper said, setting the Glock on the desk. "But I'm carrying the big gun."

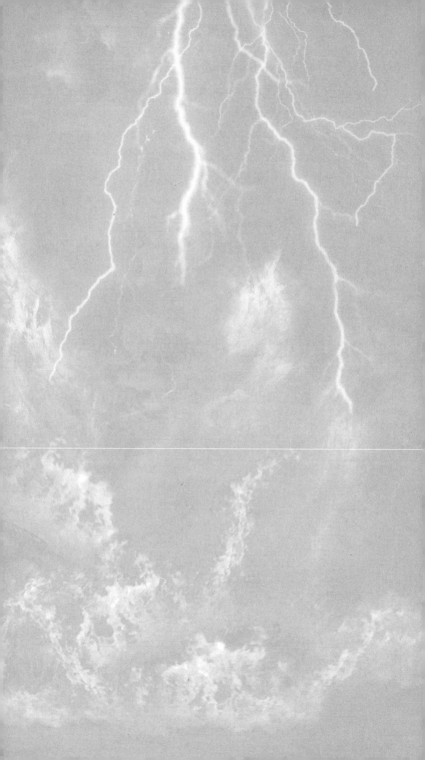

TWENTY-NINE

Maria was halfway across the block when the oncoming wave rose to as high as the second floor of the buildings on West Twenty-third Street. It broke at the corner of Eighth, and churning, foamy water raced forward, knocking Maria from her feet and carrying her farther west at a fantastic speed.

She tumbled head over heels and fought to get her head above water, and when she succeeded the wave left her in four feet of water at the intersection of Twenty-third and Ninth. The water continued to rise. She could try to wade or swim eleven blocks uptown or two blocks to the High Line and walk eleven blocks on the elevated train line, then travel one block through the water back to Ninth Avenue. It wasn't much of a choice, and she followed the wave to Tenth Avenue.

Edgar's feet and legs ached as he approached the end of the bridge. He hadn't engaged in any exercise lately, and the bridge's incline was steeper than it appeared. On the bridge, he had gazed in wonder at Roosevelt Island below him, its streets flooded, houses submerged, and bodies floating between the upper portions of buildings still above sea level—all unreachable by helicopter and boat during the storm.

Displaced people continued to pour onto the bridge. The wind grew stronger and louder as he crossed into Manhattan above the cathedral-style vaults that housed the Bridgemarket. Still shielded from most of the rain by the upper level, he stared in dismay at the flooded streets below. A curved ramp on the lower level separated it from the upper level, and water gushed before him like a waterfall.

Raising his poncho, Edgar opened his bag, took out his gun case, and opened it. Fingers trembling from the cold, he plucked his Glock from its foam rubber compartment, picked up the cartridge, and slapped it into the gun's butt. Then he returned the case and the gun to his bag separately, zipped the bag, and stepped into the torrential storm.

The wind blew him sideways and he compensated, leaning into the force. With sheets of rain dousing him, he descended the steep ramp, continuing downhill on wet asphalt until he reached Sixtieth Street, halfway between First and Second Avenues. The fire hydrants were underwater and parked cars inaccessible; only the tops of the parking meters remained visible.

Edgar waded across the street, the blockish tram station barely visible on his right. With the wind at his back and the current helping him along, he waded to Second Avenue. He lost his footing and fell at the intersection, where he got up and followed Second Avenue downtown. To his surprise, the current diminished but the water grew deeper.

Jake and Ripper descended the stairs to the dark lobby. Shining a flashlight around the walls and at the floor, Jake estimated the water was one foot deep. Dust lingered in the air, and enormous rocks had piled against the front of the building, dislodging the doorframes and filling the vestibule. Jake wore his Thunder Ranch in its shoulder holster and his new sword strapped to his back; Ripper held the ATAC 3000 ready to fire, with the strap on his shoulder.

"We're lucky this building didn't come down," Jake said. *Maybe it still will.*

They went upstairs to the second floor, and Jake selected a door to an office facing the street and kicked it open.

"This place needs better security," Ripper said.

"Tell me about it."

They crossed the wet reception office, which must have looked better than Jake's before the windows had shattered and water flooded it. He went to the broken window, his rubber-soled boots sloshing through water, and gazed outside as Ripper joined him. The wind had blown much of the dust west, and the rain had reduced the rest to mud covering the remains of the Edition, which filled the street and hid the sidewalk. Limestone boulders reached halfway up to the second floor of Jake's building, rain pounding it.

Jake put the nylon hood on and pulled its drawstrings. "Walk softly."

He climbed into the glassless window, turned around, grabbed the sill, and dangled over the edge. The wind blew him like a flag, and when he let go he dropped at an angle but managed to land on his feet, bending his knees to absorb the impact, and not twist his ankle on the sharp abutments. It took only seconds for the rain to rinse the dust off his running suit and then the limestone residue that replaced it.

Ripper landed a few feet away.

Turning, Jake took in the scope of the destruction. The two-story layer of rubble covered Twenty-third Street up the block and beyond the intersection at Madison Avenue. A swirling haze permeated the air even with the wind and rain. Using his stump against the facades of the buildings for balance, Jake moved across the rubble, testing each step before setting his feet down. The rain seeped through the crevices in some areas and pooled in others but made all the limestone slippery. At least they didn't have to swim yet.

When they reached Madison Avenue Jake stopped. The debris covered the avenue beyond Twenty-fourth Street, and the haze coupled with the rain prevented him from seeing how many smaller buildings had toppled, but he guessed the immense Metropolitan Life North Building's collapse had taken out half the neighborhood. The lack of any response from emergency services or residents of the buildings frightened him.

How many lives?

Almost in response, lightning lit the sky.

Jake gazed at the dull outline of the Tower, which had survived unscathed.

Of course.

Thunder crashed, and they descended the rubble and waded into four feet of water.

The rubble acted as a dam, preventing the eastern current from taking hold for at least one hundred yards. They had one half of one long block to go. The Flatiron Building became visible, which was when Jake saw a gray shark fin gliding in their direction.

By the time Maria reached Eleventh Avenue, she was too exhausted from swimming to veer to the sidewalk entrance to the High Line. She stopped kicking altogether, hoping to body surf, but the rain pushed her underwater.

Resurfacing, she forced herself to swim freestyle, gulping for air, and aimed for her destination. She managed to get above the sidewalk, then swim past the High Line's elevator and kick harder, propelling herself to the stairway's metal railing, which she threw her arms around. She stayed there for a moment, gathering enough energy to pull herself out of the water, then climbed up the stairs. When she reached the top, facing the second and third stories of buildings along the skyway, the wind chilled her wet body and she shivered.

Maria walked uptown, noting flooded streets, darkened windows, and no population. Did anyone inside the sky-scrapers see her? It didn't matter; she only cared that Shana and Jake were okay.

And Edgar, she thought. She had not put Shana or Jake in danger, but she had asked Edgar to go help Jake. If anything happened to him, it would be on her head.

She walked faster, breaking into a jog, the wind assailing her.

"Jesus," Ripper said.

The shark fin knifed past them and circled back.

"Move," Jake said.

They waded faster, bouncing toward a Jetta parked at the curb. Using both hands, Ripper sprang onto the hood of the vehicle, landing in two inches of water. He turned and grabbed Jake's outstretched hand with both of his. Jake set one foot on the Jetta's front tire as Ripper pulled him up, then the other on the hood. He looked over his shoulder as the shark fin submerged into the murky water.

Ripper climbed onto the roof of the car, and Jake scrambled after him. The wind knocked them to their knees, and they helped each other up. Ripper moved the ATAC 3000 into firing position, and Jake took his hunting knife from the sheath on his boot. Standing back to back, they turned in a circle on top of the car, searching the water for the shark, but the rainfall on the surface made that impossible. Ripper grunted, and Jake peered over the edge of the car. Lightning flickered; thunder growled.

The shark exploded out of the water, rocketing toward Jake and causing him to flinch. In the instant it took him to realize the shark had human arms and hands, the gray creature seized his throat, its momentum driving him and Ripper off the other side of the car. Before he struck the water, he saw the monster had long feminine hair, a shark fin protruding from its back, and a chest as flat as a boy's. From the waist up it appeared humanoid, and from the waist down it had the body of a shark.

A mermaid.

Cold water enveloped Jake, and his back touched the sidewalk with sandpapery fingers around his throat. The shark woman opened her mouth six inches from his face, revealing sharp teeth arranged in a jagged pattern, her eyes death black.

Jake pushed the shark woman's head away and drove the knife into her snout, drawing blood that clouded the water. Maintaining his grip on the handle, he held the head and its teeth back, and with his stump he knocked one of her arms aside, forcing her hand to relinquish his throat. He couldn't shake the other hand loose, but he twisted his body free and stood, raising his head above the water as Ripper scrambled back on top of the car.

The shark woman rose as well, still gripping Jake's throat with one hand. Lightning filled the sky, and Jake got a better look at her. Five gill slits sucked at the air on each side of her fat neck, and she had no chin. She swung her right hand at him, but he knocked it aside and locked her arm in his armpit, forcing her to struggle like a fish on a hook. Translucent shields slid over her eyes, protecting them. She released his throat with her other hand, which she clamped over his wrist, trying to force him to let go of the knife.

"Shoot her," Jake said.

Kneeling on the car's roof, Ripper struggled to aim the ATAC 3000. "I'll tear you both to pieces!"

The shark woman snapped her jaws at Jake, gnashing her teeth.

"Break the window," Jake said to Ripper. He jerked the knife out of her snout and plunged it into the gills on her left side. Blood spilled over them. The shark woman thrashed and Jake feared she would escape.

Dropping to his knees below the surface, he braced his stump against her flesh where a human female's pelvis would have been. Still gripping the knife, he rose once more, lifting the hybrid over his head.

Ripper smashed the driver's side window with the stock

of his weapon, and Jake hurled the monster six feet away, where it splashed. He still held the knife. Without waiting to see her reaction, he swam toward the car.

Ripper fired the ATAC over Jake's head, tearing up the water. "Hurry," Ripper said, wild eyed.

Setting his hand on the car door, Jake dove headfirst through the missing window. He raced to open the passenger door, hoping to trap the creature inside, but the shark woman vaulted in after him, her tail propelling her forward. He turned over on his back just as she landed on him, blood spilling from her gills.

Using his stump, he pushed her head back, then drove the knife up through her lower jaw and into the roof of her mouth, nailing it shut. The shark woman thrashed around, beating her tail against the steering wheel, and Jake reached behind him and opened the passenger door. He slid out from beneath her, pushing himself off the car underwater, and kicked the door shut.

Raising his head above the water, he saw that Ripper had climbed off the car and stood aiming the ATAC 3000 through the broken window. He opened fire, a burst of automatic gunfire strafing the shark woman's body, blood squirting through the punctures.

The creature continued to thrash, turning the water inside the car red. Then she stopped moving and sank, and when her body rose to the surface, it transformed: the fin receded into her back and the tail separated into legs.

Jake opened the door, sank his hand into the dead woman's hair, and yanked her head back. He recognized her because he'd had sex with her: Chloe Sanderstein, the VP of Eternity Books, who had appeared to him as Sheryl.

Ripper peered inside the car and gasped.

"Lilith has the power to turn people into animals," Jake said. Katrina had turned Edgar into a raven, and Lilith had turned men into cats.

Edgar had made it only five blocks down Second Avenue when he stopped at a streetlight to catch his breath. With rain pouring off the bill of his NYPD baseball cap, he reached inside his poncho, opened his shoulder bag, and removed the doggie bag Joyce had made for him: chicken-fried steak and black-eyed peas. He wolfed down the soul food in the middle of the hurricane, then discarded the tin tray and watched it wash away.

He checked his watch. It was 7:00 p.m. Two days ago at this time, the sun still shone; now darkness prevailed, made all the more pervasive by the lack of electricity in the buildings. He doubted he would ever have so much elbow room again in his life. He had no idea how he was going to make it all the way down to Twenty-third Street, then over to Jake's building between Madison and Park Avenues.

I'm not going to do it sitting here, he thought, his teeth chattering.

Disengaging from the light pole, he resumed swimming

toward Fifty-fourth Street.

Only thirty-one blocks to go . . .

Cold water slapped him in the face and he spat it out. He did the sidestroke, which he preferred, and switched sides after fifty yards. The water had reached six feet. Now it was harder to rest when he felt too tired to go on.

A droning rose over the furious sound of the wind and rain. It sounded like a lawn mower, and he searched the sky for a helicopter. Light swept over him and he turned around, treading water. The current struck him in the face, and he saw a spotlight heading in his direction.

A boat!

Edgar waved his arms over his head and called out, slipped beneath the surface, kicked off the sidewalk, and waved his arms again. The searchlight swept over him, and he continued to tread water at its center.

The boat drew closer, the light brighter, and the sound of the engine stopped as a small powerboat coasted toward him. The pilot, who wore a yellow rain slicker, threw a white life preserver on a line in his direction.

Edgar grabbed the preserver, and the pilot hauled him over to the boat, which rocked as he pulled him aboard, threatening to capsize. Edgar fell into six inches of water on the bottom.

"What are you doing out here?" the man said in a Cuban accent. "Getting a newspaper?"

Edgar clambered onto the bench near the outboard motor. "I'm going to help a friend. What are *you* doing out here?"

"Looking for dumb people to rescue."

"That's mighty kind of you, since no one else is bothering."

"I've seen NYPD boats in the water, but most of them went to where the storm hit the hardest. No one's out patrolling like me. Where are you headed?"

"Twenty-third Street."

"East or west?"

"Straight ahead."

"You want a lift?"

"Hell, yeah."

"I'm Carlos."

"Edgar."

Carlos set a metal coffee can before him. "Start bailing or we aren't going to get very far."

A lightning bolt jagged the sky as Jake and Ripper swam across Broadway to the construction awning attached to the Flatiron Building and grabbed the aluminum rods. The plywood that had surrounded the top of the awning had blown away, leaving corrugated metal. Limestone dust from the collapsed buildings clung to the plywood. Each man held on to a vertical pole and swung his legs onto a horizontal bar. Sitting above the sidewalk, with only their legs in the water, they faced each other.

"What do you think?" Ripper said.

"There could be a trap waiting for us in the lobby or in the stairway."

"She could turn us into one of those things, couldn't she?"

Jake remembered when he had discovered Edgar in raven form; Katrina had left a candle burning on a coffee table a few feet away from where the blackbird had revealed itself within a pile of Edgar's clothes. "Probably."

"So?"

Jake looked at the corrugated ceiling, which the rain assaulted.

"You want to climb a twenty-two-story building during a hurricane?"

"Not the whole building, just one or two floors."

Sighing, Ripper stood on the bar and slid his hand up and down the vertical support. "I don't know about this. The metal is slippery."

Jake gestured at the water around them. "It's not like we'll hit the sidewalk if we fall."

"You go first."

"Very funny."

Ripper reached for a short, angled bar that supported the awning. "Get over here and help me."

Jake couldn't reach Ripper's section of the skeleton, so he hopped down, waded across the water, and climbed beside him. Ripper grabbed the support and walked up the vertical bar, taking the rain full in his face. Jake put his hand on Ripper's bottom and gave him a shove, and Ripper pulled himself up.

Jake swung his leg around the support, his back to the rain, and waited for Ripper to extend a hand. He squeezed the hand and walked up as Ripper had, and Ripper pulled him onto the awning, then they ran to the side of the building facing Broadway. The only problem was that the downstairs lobby was two stories high, so the next row of windows was another floor up. A lightning bolt stitched the sky and thunder coughed.

"Great plan," Ripper said. "I suppose you want me to go first again."

"I'll never make it on my own with one hand."

"I knew you were going to say that."

Lightning continued to flash as Ripper climbed the limestone face of the building, which had plenty of sculpted texture to grab on to: step, handhold, step, handhold, repeat. The wind scattered his dreadlocks but did not blow him off. When he reached the ledge beneath the second-floor windows he grabbed it and allowed his legs to dangle straight down.

Holy crap, Jake thought.

Ripper pulled himself straight up, his head passing the ledge, and worked his way up on his arms so his crotch brushed the ledge. He swung his right leg onto the ledge, and Jake thought he would fall. But Ripper leaned toward the large window before him, wedged his arms between the limestone around it, and stood on his right leg, dragging his left leg behind him. He turned and looked down. "It's a piece of cake, you asshole. Show me how it's done."

Frowning, Jake climbed: step, handhold, step, repeat. The

wind howled in his ear, but before long he reached the ledge.

"If I take your hand we'll both fall."

Jake squinted in the rain. "See if the window's open."

Ripper reached behind him. "Negative."

"Break it."

With slow, cautious movements, Ripper removed the ATAC 3000 from around his head and held the thick barrel in both hands. "If I don't do this right I'll fall anyway."

"So make sure you do it right."

Ripper drew a breath, then drove the weapon straight back into the window as hard as he could, shattering a portion of the window. Leaning forward, he balanced on the edge, then stood erect. He turned his back to the street, reached inside, and raised the window. Then he climbed inside and turned around.

The wind blew and his fingers burned with pain, but Jake did not lose his grip. It took him three cycles to reach the point below the ledge, and by then Ripper stood halfway inside the second-floor office with one hand extended. Jake had to let go of the limestone to grab Ripper's hand. If he missed he would fall. Even if he caught Ripper's hand he might fall.

"Don't be a pussy. I want to get dry."

Jake took three breaths, stared at Ripper's hand, then reached for it. Their hands locked.

Ripper grabbed Jake's wrist with his other hand. "I've got you."

Grimacing, Jake walked up the side of the building, and Ripper heaved him over the ledge. Ripper backed inside, pulling Jake in after him. Jake fell face forward onto carpet in the dark office, grunting from the impact. Grateful to be out of the storm, he gasped for breath.

Ripper turned his back to the window and became a mild silhouette. "Don't expect me to pick you up off that floor, too."

Jake sat up. "I got it."

"It's about time you started pulling your own weight."

A shriek filled the office.

Jake jumped and Ripper spun to face the window. A flash of lightning silhouetted a dark shape. A creature with an enormous wingspan reached inside with two clawed feet like those of a chicken and dug them into Ripper's face.

Ripper seized the creature's ankles and screamed as it beat its wings and retreated from the building, pulling him out the window.

Jake leapt for Ripper's legs but he groped empty air, then slammed against the window's edge, rain spattering his face.

Ripper and the Harpy spiraled downward with Ripper's scream trailing them.

Jake held his breath, waiting to see if Ripper would clear the awning below.

The Harpy's six-foot-wide wing smashed against the awning, which Ripper plummeted past.

Jake felt momentary relief until the rectangular top of a metal traffic signpost burst through Ripper's back, impaling him. On his knees, Jake recoiled and dug his fingers into the sill.

Ripper's body slid down the wobbling signpost into the water and half floated there. The Harpy splashed beside him, its wing broken, and thrashed. The she monster threw its head back and attempted to fly but couldn't.

Ripper's soul flickered and rose from his body and faded.

Golden light, Jake thought.

Seizing the ATAC 3000 from where Ripper had left it, he switched on the scope's night vision function and located the monster below.

The distorted face of Jada Brighton, the director of business development who had impersonated Katrina, snarled between the wings, her hands located halfway along the top of each wing. Her angry eyes reflected the lightning flashing in the sky.

Jake squeezed the trigger, shooting her with enough rounds to reduce her monstrous wings to tattered flaps of flesh. He continued to fire until the ATAC clicked.

The broken Harpy unleashed a single tortured scream before falling facedown into the water. The current swept her winged corpse away like a downed kite.

Pulling his hood off, Jake gazed at Ripper's corpse. The rain washed away whatever blood there was. He had grown to like the man, and even if he hadn't, Ripper had saved his life more than once.

Another innocent life for Lilith to pay for, he thought.

But first he had to deal with Harla. And Ripper had the only ammo for the ATAC.

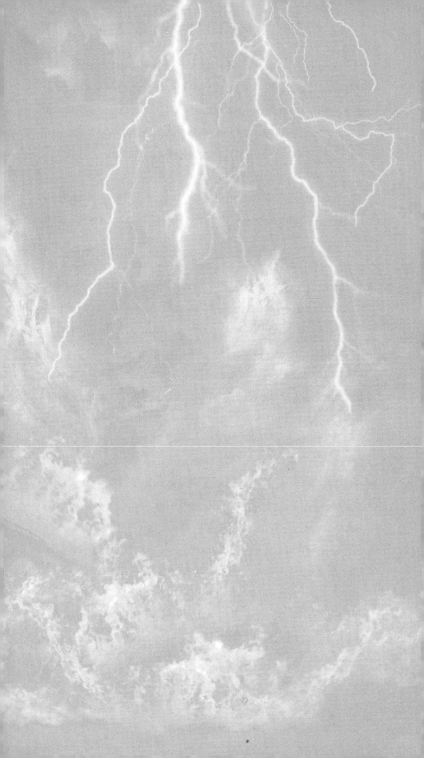

THIRTY

Maria sank to her knees from despair as much as exhaustion when she reached the end of the High Line. The top of Sloane House was visible a block and a half away, but it was uphill. Floodwater gushed down to the Hudson Yards development, and she knew she couldn't fight the current all the way.

She took out her phone, which still wasn't receiving a signal. The streets were deserted, and through the rain it was impossible to tell which windows in the buildings had candles glowing within them. Pocketing the phone, she made her way down the stairs and waded into the water, which had become deeper than she could stand in.

Taking a breath, Maria kicked off the handrail and streamlined into the current, then swam to a pole supporting the golden arches of a McDonald's. From there, she went to a car wash and noted cars abandoned on both sides of the street.

That's it, she thought.

She swam across the street, battling the current with everything she had, then climbed onto the first car. Water cascaded on either side of her as she crawled across the hood and sprawled out across the roof, gasping. Lifting her head, she squinted as water sprayed her face.

Just one block.

And then the intersection.

Rising, Maria slid down the back window of the car on her bottom, dropped to the street between cars, and climbed atop the next vehicle. When she reached the other end of that one, she leapt onto the next, praying the wind wouldn't carry her away, and slammed onto its trunk.

Holding the empty ATAC in firing position, Jake walked with his eye pressed against the scope, using the weapon's night vision to see the deserted second floor. He had attached his knife to the barrel like a bayonet. His nylon clothes made rubbing sounds, and his wet boots squeaked on the floor, the circle of light from his flashlight bouncing around the walls and doors.

He turned a corner and then another before locating the stairwell. He had to set the gun down to open the door, then he picked it up, stepped inside, and closed the door softly. Raising the gun's scope to his eye, he scanned the stairs above, listening.

Nothing moved. Nothing made a sound.

Jake climbed the stairs, stopping twice to rest. Two-thirds of the way to the top floor, he thought he heard something and his body stiffened. He aimed the scope at the stairway above him and listened. As far as he could tell, nothing moved up there. Climbing again, he heard the same sound and stopped. The sound stopped as well. He resumed his climb but stopped again as soon as he heard the sound: a wet hissing that continued for one second longer than the faint echo of Jake's last footstep, which was all he needed to confirm he was not alone.

Trying to subdue his breathing, Jake stared at the stairs and landing ahead, made luminous green by his night vision scope. An inhuman shadow glided across the concrete wall and disappeared. He continued moving at the same pace, so as not to alert Harla—whatever she had become—that he knew she waited for him. He reached the landing, which was now deserted, and stopped.

Dead silence greeted him.

Jake allowed the ATAC to fall, knowing the leather strap over his left shoulder would catch it, then opened the door, stepped into the corridor on the sixteenth floor, and slammed the door shut. He gripped the doorknob and held it, waiting for Harla to make her move. How strong could she be?

The knob twisted in his hand, but Jake wouldn't allow the door to open. A sound like a metal puncher in a factory reverberated in the corridor. A dent shaped like a cone—or the tail of a serpent—formed in the door, just grazing Jake's face. Harla punched the metal door a second time, then a third.

Jake let go of the knob and ran for his life.

The door crashed open behind him, and the sound of hissing filled the corridor, drowning out the sound of his footsteps.

Jake skidded to a stop and raised the gun to his shoulder. Through the night vision scope he saw a creature with the upper body of a woman and the lower body of a snake bearing down on him at an incredible speed. He aimed the gun in the other direction and saw a corner fifty yards ahead. Dropping the weapon on its strap he sprinted, his boots pounding the tile floor.

Harla's hiss grew louder and more frantic.

Jake turned the corner and slid to a stop. He freed the ATAC's strap from around him and raised the weapon to his shoulder. Through the scope he saw Harla whip around the corner and look in his direction. He lowered the barrel over his stump and lunged forward, thrusting the knife on the barrel's edge.

The knife cut into something solid, and Harla unleashed a hideous sound. Jake drew the blade out and thrust again, cutting into her sternum a second time. He pulled the blade out again, but this time something smacked the ATAC out of his hand with a whiplike snap, and he knew Harla had used her snake body to disarm him.

Jake backed up, ready to run, but something ensnared his ankles and jerked his legs out from under him. He landed on his back with a grunt, then clawed at the floor as Harla dragged him toward her. Lightning flashed outside the windows, illuminating Harla as she released Jake's ankles and wrapped her snake body around his legs and torso, pinning his arms to his sides.

The corridor turned dark again, and for a moment he recalled Avademe's tentacle encircling him. Harla squeezed the air from his lungs like an anaconda. Kicking his feet, he connected with her head, provoking an angry hiss. With the toe of one boot he located her neck, and then he crossed his legs around it and scissor kicked them together. Harla gagged and Jake locked his legs, strangling her while she crushed him.

Jake threw his body from side to side, trying to loosen her grip on him, but it was no use. He couldn't breathe, couldn't see, couldn't move, couldn't call for help. Thunder exploded. His life did not pass before his eyes, but he did pray that Maria rescued Shana.

Then Harla's body quivered, and a flash of lightning revealed she had stopped moving. The snake body slackened and Jake sucked in air. Struggling to get free of the tail, he found himself entangled in the legs of a dead woman.

Jake couldn't stand without bracing his hand against a wall for balance. Lightning illuminated the corridor, and Jake saw the knife wounds in Harla's torso and the blood pooling around her corpse. He staggered toward the ATAC.

Three down, Jake thought. *Now to deal with the head dragon.*

Reaching the end of her makeshift bridge of cars, Maria stood on the hood of an SUV parked at the intersection of Thirty-Fourth and Ninth. She would have to swim against the current to reach Sloane House.

I can't do it. I don't have the strength.

Had she come so far for nothing?

She sat on the roof and held her knees together. The wind blew her hair and the tears in her eyes. She knew she couldn't survive this exposure for long, so she would have to try to swim across anyway. If she failed, she would find temporary refuge uptown and look for an alternative method to reach Shana.

Maria stood on the roof, and the wind knocked her off her feet. Her body slammed into the roof, and she clawed at the edge so she would not go into the water.

"Damn it!"

The sobs came harder and faster until she discerned a light down the street: a red beacon.

A police strobe, she thought.

The strobe grew brighter as a harbor patrol boat became visible through the rain. Maria didn't recognize the first sound that escaped from her throat, a cross between a grunt and a moan, but she did recognize the laughter that followed.

Exercising caution, she rose on the roof and waved her arms. "Over here!"

Lightning slashed the sky and thunder cracked as Jake exited the stairwell on the top floor of the Flatiron Building. Holding the ATAC's scope to his eye, he approached the glass door leading to Eternity Books and opened it.

He stood before the wide window for a moment. A lightning bolt zigzagged through the sky, and a horizontal bolt formed in front of the window. The double thunder blast that followed shook the building.

Jake moved down the main corridor beyond the reception desk, passing deserted glass-faced offices. He opened the door to the VIP room where he had engaged in the orgy with Lilith's witches, and his gaze settled on a stone table shaped like a mushroom. In the center of the table lay the glass pipe he had used to smoke Black Magic, and his heart beat faster at the sight of it. Moving closer, he focused on the pipe: there was still some Magic left in it. Kneeling before the table, he held the machine gun butt out and struck the table with blind fury until he heard the glass break.

Raising the scope to his eye once more, he walked to the office at the end of the corridor, determining from its size that it belonged to Lilith. Jake counted four mirrors in the office, none of them small.

On the floor, he found what resembled a silver pancake: the molten remains of his Thunder Ranch revolver, which he recognized by its hard plastic grip. True to her word, Laurel had tried to kill Lilian. Lightning illuminated the office and thunder rattled it. He knew Lilith was close by.

She's on the roof.

The harbor patrol boat cut across the intersection of Thirty-fourth and Ninth and pulled perpendicular to Maria, facing uptown. Three crew members wearing life vests stood in the cabin, and one of them escorted a fourth figure into the back of the boat.

Maria laughed. "Bernie!"

"Where's your umbrella?" Bernie said over the wind.

"Where's yours?"

The crew member tossed a life preserver to her, and she caught it.

"Come aboard," the crewman said.

Pulling the preserver over her head and arms, Maria jumped into the water and popped right back up. The current dragged her away, but the crewman pulled her back, and he and Bernie helped her into the boat.

"Thank you so much," Maria said.

"Let's get into the cabin," the crewman said.

They went into the relative shelter of the cabin, and the captain piloted the boat uptown, turned around, and headed back to the intersection.

"Where's the rest of the cavalry?" Maria said.

"Busy trying to cope with the collapse of those buildings on Jake's street," Bernie said with suspicion in his voice.

"Were you going in here alone?"

"You didn't give me much choice."

She bowed her head against his life vest. "Thank you."

He rubbed her arm. "Let's get Shana out of there."

The captain drove the boat through the water over the sidewalk along Sloane House. A crewman put a life vest over Maria's head and secured its straps.

"We'll be back in half an hour," the captain said. "If you're not down here then, we're moving on."

"We'll be here."

Bernie climbed over the side of the boat and dropped into the water. "Cold! Cold, cold, cold."

Maria jumped in after him. "I wish I'd had this vest on my trip up."

They swam to the door, where Bernie powered on the light on his rescue helmet, and then they entered the flooded, deserted lobby. Cushions from the furniture floated on the surface, and the doorman's station poked through the surface.

"I can touch bottom here," Bernie said.

"There are two steps at the front of the lobby," Maria said. "We're on a raised level."

Like astronauts on the moon, they hopped toward the stairway.

Jake emerged on the roof and saw two women standing with their backs to him as they watched the lightning dancing in the sky. The wind continued to howl, blowing their hair, and the rain slashed at their dresses.

Laurel and Lilith, he thought.

But the woman who might have been Lilith had white hair, and the woman who resembled Laurel from behind wore the same dress he had seen Lilith in earlier.

He dropped the ATAC and drew the sword from its scabbard on his back.

Laurel turned in his direction. Lightning bolts arced behind her and her eyes flashed.

"Laurel?"

She smiled.

The old woman beside her faced him. It was Lilith or Lilian Kane or maybe her mother—sixty years old if she was a day, raindrops clinging to her wrinkles. "It's me. Laurel."

The being who had taken on Laurel's body said, "You're too late. What made you think you could beat me?"

Holding the sword, Jake swallowed.

Lilith circled him, and he turned like a top to keep his eye on her. "I am Lilit. Lilitu. Lilith. I've walked this earth longer than anyone, and no one's even come close to defeating me. Erika tried and failed."

"I'm sorry, Jake," Laurel said.

"Maybe no one's had as much motivation to stop you as I have," Jake said. "I'm sure hundreds of people died today." He glanced at Laurel in Lilith's aged form. "I know at least one person did. Ripper."

"And you killed three of my disciples," Lilith said.

"You shouldn't have sent them after me. Your bad."

"The girls found my methods extreme, so I gave them a chance to reconsider. It doesn't matter. I have what I wanted."

"Then call off this storm."

"As soon as I've finished with you." She approached Laurel from the other side now, her circle complete. "She came back to me, as I knew she would. As I knew you would."

"Lilian Kane will be found dead of natural causes, and Erika Long will pick up her mantle?"

Lilith glanced at Laurel. "Something like that."

Jake charged at Lilith, swinging the sword. She didn't even have to look at him to freeze him in place just short of reaching her. He struggled to move, but his entire body had become as rigid as a statue.

Lilith moved closer to him. "Maybe I should allow you to live as a pussycat in my home. Would you like that?"

No, Jake answered in his mind.

"No, you're not a pussycat, are you? You're a doggie, a mutt." Lightning flashed in her eyes and thunder ripped the sky. She glanced at his sword. "That's a hell of a lightning rod you've got. Maybe I'll just leave you here on the roof like a lawn jockey and see what happens."

"You have us both," Laurel said to Lilith. "You won. I know what's in store for me, and I accept it. There's no need to torture Jake. Just let him go."

"No. You took my money from me, and he took you from me. Someone has to pay."

"This entire city's already paid."

"I need more personal satisfaction."

"Then strike him down and put him out of his misery."

Thanks a lot, Jake thought.

"There's no need to torture him," Laurel continued.

"Torture is exactly what I have in mind for him," Lilith said. She clasped one hand over Jake's and looked deep into his eye. "No man fucks with me."

A shock wave traveled Jake's body from his toes to his skull, and he heard a cacophony of cracks and snaps as every bone in his body broke. His ribs collapsed and his hips split and his vertebrae popped; his fingers bent backwards and his feet shattered. The pain was excruciating, more than he could ever have imagined, and in his mind no one had ever experienced worse.

His body folded in on itself, like a deflated Christmas Santa, his skin a sack for his muscles and broken bones, his punctured organs sloshing around without an infrastructure, his muscles linking the different components like sausages. He came down as quickly and as definitively as the Edition had. Fissures split his skull. The lightning storm was nothing compared to the raging pain that exploded in the nerves throughout his body and the neurons in his brain. Yet his mind remained intact, his audiovisual senses functioning.

Dear Christ, let me die! A gurgling sound escaped his lacerated throat.

Laurel's shapely leg, which he had stroked just months earlier, filled his vision, and Lilith crouched beside him. "What's that you said?"

Just let me die! He gurgled again.

"I can't understand a word you're saying, which must be frustrating for you."

Please! Gurgle.

"Now, where did that eye go?" Lilith made a show of looking around before zeroing in on his eye. "There it is." She pushed the wet hair out of her face and leaned forward. "I can only imagine what's going through your head, the pleading. I won't allow you to die—at least not yet. I want every cell in your body to experience the price for interfering with my plans. I'm a living god and even Shaitan knows it." Turning to Laurel, she rose. "Your *champion*."

With a horrified expression Laurel ran to Jake's side and pressed both hands against his quivering flesh.

In his mind, Jake screamed a thousand times; outside his body, he gurgled and drooled blood.

Lilith tilted her head back and issued a haughty laugh as Laurel massaged Jake's lumpy form. "So that's true love?" she said, sneering. "It's just as foolish and logic defying as I'd imagined."

Laurel's healing power spread through Jake's body like a warm drug, and the neurons in his brain reignited with agonizing pain as all the bones in his hand and in each foot reformed. *Don't do it! Don't do it!*

Lilith circled them with a look of fascination in her eyes. "Go ahead, Erika. It's just as painful for him to be reassembled as it was for him to be broken. You're doing a great job."

Laurel continued to massage Jake's body. Her arms trembled and she wept.

Jake's head vibrated and his face snapped together.

All the king's horses
And all the king's men
Couldn't put Jake Helman together again.

His ribs rose with the breastbone, reconstituting his chest, and his breathing returned to normal. The bones in each limb rejoined, and the bones in his skull came together. Lying on his back with tears streaming from his eye, he unleashed the primal scream that had been building inside him. Pain burned every nerve ending in his restored body.

Groaning, Jake rolled over onto his side and got up on his hands and knees, every movement torture. His glass eye stared at him from the roof's surface. He grabbed it and held it between his thumb and middle finger, allowing the rain to cleanse it, and popped it into his waiting socket. He raised his left leg, then drew himself to his full height. Every inch of his body tingled.

I'm alive, he thought. The only pain was an echo in his brain. His bones felt fine.

The same could not be said for Laurel: she had taken Jake's place on the roof, her body broken, her face shattered from within, no longer human in appearance, a long, strangled gasp escaping from her lips.

Kneeling beside her, Jake reached out to her but stopped, knowing his touch would cause her pain.

She turned toward him, tears rolling from her eyes.

He looked at Lilith. "I'll do anything you ask. Just save her."

Lilith's face turned cold. "It's too late. She's already dead."

Jake returned his gaze to Laurel. Her eyes had stopped blinking.

Oh no.

"Without my power preserving her life as it did yours, she couldn't survive the pain."

He closed Laurel's eyes. "Then why didn't you keep her alive?"

"She made the choice to sacrifice herself to save you, her final insult to me. I allowed her to have the final gesture, but it was a gesture of futility. She gave her life for yours, which has a decidedly short expectancy."

Standing once more, Jake balled his hand into a fist. "You'll have a hard time explaining her body and those of your witches to the world."

"The most miraculous storm since the great flood has left mankind in a quandary. Tomorrow the people of this world will have much weightier issues to worry about than the bizarre deaths of four women who worked at a romance publishing house."

"Erika Long may have a difficult time reclaiming public favor."

"While Lilian Kane's followers mourn her tragic

demise, Erika Long will resurface at her mentor's funeral, easing all that pain. At least that's what I've outlined so far."

Jake retrieved his sword.

"What do you think I'll allow you to do with that?"

A gust of wind knocked Jake off his feet. Shaking his head, he got up again. "You made me beg like a dog before, but here I am, standing before you: a man."

"We'll see."

Without intending to, Jake dropped to his knees.

"Let me teach an old dog a new trick."

Jake held his sword before his face.

"They say guns are phallic extensions, but I think that applies to swords as well."

Jake extended his arm before him, pointing the sword at the sky.

"As a true romantic, I prefer blades over guns."

Jake tilted his head back and bent his elbow just a little, aiming the sword at his face, the tip an inch from his flesh. The blade moved to his remaining eye and stopped.

"Shall I gouge your eye out and leave you blind?"

The tip moved down to his mouth.

"Or make you swallow the sword whole?"

After the pain he had just endured, Jake found he did not fear death at that moment.

"How about neither?" a masculine voice said.

Lilith spun to the doorway as a gun fired. An instant later a crater opened in the back of her head.

Jake dropped the sword, which clattered on the roof, and rose.

Lilith turned away from Edgar, who stood in the doorway with a smoking Glock in both hands. The entry wound in her forehead resembled a third eye that did not blink, and blood flowed from the hole. Lightning flashed and thunder boomed at the same time. Her head made little jerky movements like a windup doll. She took a single step toward Jake, grimaced, then pitched facedown to the roof and lay still.

Jake looked at Edgar. "I owe you one."

Edgar lowered his gun. "Let's call it even, okay?"

"Yeah." Jake eyed the sky. The storm continued.

Lilith drew one arm back, her palm sliding through the water. Edgar raised his eyebrows.

Lilith drew her other arm back. Edgar aimed his gun. She pushed herself up, and he shot her in the back, dropping her again.

"The storm is still going," Jake said. "She isn't dead."

Lilith coughed, then pushed herself up again. Edgar took aim but Jake lifted his hand, stopping him. Lilith raised her head so that she stared at Laurel's corpse. "Erika . . ."

Jake picked up the sword and moved closer to Lilith, who turned her head to him. Her eyes reflected lightning flickering in the sky. Jake raised the sword and brought it down in a wide swing that separated her head from her shoulders, the gaping wound in her neck coughing dark blood as her corpse collapsed.

Thunder boomed and the rain and wind stopped, and Lilith's head and body disintegrated into clumps of dust that turned into mud and swirled in the bloody water.

"Now she's dead," Jake said.

Lowering his weapon, Edgar crossed the roof. "I hope so."

A sphere of concentrated black light rose from the spot where Lilith had perished. Jake had never seen such a dark soul.

"What the *hell* is that?" Edgar said.

Jake turned to Edgar, his pulse quickening. "You see it, too?"

Edgar aimed his Glock at the sphere. "It's there, isn't it?"

The sphere spun faster and faster, four feet off the ground, then rocketed toward Edgar.

Jake tackled his friend, knocking him to the wet roof, and the sphere sped through the space where he had just stood and shrank until he could no longer see it.

"What is it?" Edgar said.

"Her soul. She wants to kick your ass, or she wants to possess you. I don't like either option."

The sphere ricocheted off four imaginary walls, drawing their attention to each point on the roof.

Jake sprang to his feet. "Get behind me."

Edgar stood behind him and Jake held the sword. The sphere shot in their direction, and he swung the sword. The sphere stopped an inch shy of the sword's point and hovered, spinning in place. An appendage burst from its rear and rose three feet into the air, comprised of five segments and a stinger the size of Jake's hunting knife. Jake recognized the appendage as the tail of a scorpion. The tail lunged at him, and he deflected the stinger with his sword.

Edgar moved off to the side and aimed his Glock at the shape-shifting sphere while Jake parried the stinger with his sword.

"Come, woman."

Jake glanced in the direction of the voice and saw a man wearing a rain slicker and matching hat.

"Carlos?" Edgar said.

Jake looked at Edgar.

"Uh, he gave me a lift here in his boat."

The appendage disappeared inside the sphere, which retreated across the roof.

Carlos raised one hand, stopping it. "I SAID COME."

The thunder had returned.

Carlos's body expanded beneath his slicker, and he threw his hat aside, revealing salt-and-pepper hair. His skull and bones split apart as a monstrous figure grew out of his tattered body. The figure tore the slicker from his frame with throbbing hands and revealed the volcanic blood and pulsing black light within his transparent body, two pinpricks of light centered within the sockets of his polished black skull. He stood seven feet tall.

"YOU'VE GONE TOO FAR, LILITU. YOUR TIME IS AT AN END." Cain beckoned to the sphere with both hands. "COME TO ME. SERVE OUR MASTER."

The sphere floated to Cain in starts and stops. He spread his arms wide and absorbed her into his chest. His body trembled and he sank to his knees, throwing back his head and releasing an orgasmic moan that caused Jake to shudder. Then he bowed his head, stood, and looked Jake in the eye. "THAT WAS GOOD. SHE WAS THE BEST EVER."

"I don't think I want to hear it," Jake said.

Cain looked at Edgar. "BIRD MAN."

A seam opened in the air behind Cain, sucking him through it, and he vanished.

Edgar blinked. "What the fuck?"

"Lilith pissed off the very forces that gave her power. They wanted her gone, and they wanted me to do the deed, but they didn't think I was in any shape to do it alone, so they helped you get here to give me a hand."

"You've encountered these forces before?"

"It will be better for you if you don't know any more than I've already said."

"I think you're right." He looked at the mass of flesh on the roof. "Who was this?"

Jake swallowed. "Laurel."

Edgar stared at her. "That's too bad."

"How much of that did you see?"

"Enough. Maria told me as much as I could handle and told me to go to your office, but when me and Carlos saw those ruins we didn't think we'd get close enough. Then I saw your friend with the dreadlocks, so I came up here."

"Good thing for me you still have your cop instincts and that Maria called you. And that you got a little help—"

Edgar raised both hands. "Don't say it."

Helicopters droned in the distance.

"Let's go," Jake said. "This street is about to become the biggest news in the city."

Edgar gestured to the corpses on the roof. "What about them?"

Jake shrugged. "It's not my responsibility to cover this stuff up. Maybe it's time people started learning the truth about the universe."

"Laurel deserves a decent funeral."

"Which one would you bury? And how would you transport the body without implicating us both? This city isn't going back to normal anytime soon."

THIRTY-ONE

Maria sprinted through the carpeted corridor ahead of Bernie, relieved to set foot on dry flooring again. His flashlight cast eerie shadows on the walls. Drawing her Glock, she stopped at Alice's unit and pounded on the door. She pushed the doorbell, knowing it wouldn't work, and pounded on the door again.

"Shana, open up! It's me, Maria."

Bernie looked at the other doors. None of them opened. He drew his Glock.

Maria kicked the door but it didn't open. Aiming the gun at the lock on the door, she looked away. "Fire in the hole."

She fired, the round sparking the lot and ricocheting. She fired again, this time at the doorknob's joint, and the door opened at her touch. Bernie moved closer to her, and she took the rescue helmet from his head, put it on hers, and almost tripped over Alice's corpse, which lay in a pool of blood.

"Score one for Team Raheem," Bernie said.

Maria ran down the hall with her gun held before her. "Shana!"

A bedroom door at the end of the hall opened, and a small figure stepped out, blinking at the light on Maria's head.

"Don't shoot," Shana said.

Maria holstered her weapon. "No one is shooting anyone. It's me, Maria."

Shana stood in the doorway, her chest heaving. "Y-you came . . ."

Kneeling before the girl, Maria cradled her. "Of course I came, sweetie. I promised you I'd be there for you if you needed me."

The child sobbed. "I didn't know if you got my text, and I was afraid they'd hear me if I called you, and I didn't know if you could get here in the storm—"

Maria shushed her. "I know. We're taking you away. Let's get your things from your room, okay?"

Shana nodded.

Maria wiped the tears from her eyes, then turned to Bernie. "Find some garbage bags in the kitchen so we can put her clothes in them."

Bernie gazed into the living room. "It stopped raining."

"Really? Then it's over."

Jake won.

At least she hoped so.

Jake and Edgar exited the Flatiron Building, and Jake stood looking at Ripper's corpse for a moment. Edgar wore the ATAC 3000 on his back, and Jake retrieved the ammo clips for it from Ripper's pockets.

"He was a good man. I'm not looking forward to telling Carrie the news."

They moved on through the still water. Garbage and furniture floated around them. At least four helicopters circled the immediate area, sweeping the disaster site with searchlights.

"You said that thing was Lilian's soul," Edgar said.

"I'm afraid you'll see more things like that," Jake said. He hoped he was wrong. "Chalk it up to Katrina's curse on you."

By the time they reached the mountain of debris between Madison and Park, an entire fleet of rescue boats roared past Broadway, and dozens of uniformed police crawled over the debris across the street. The two men scrambled up the limestone rock pile, anxious to get inside before any authorities stopped them.

"Give me a boost," Jake said. He had said the same thing to Edgar what felt like a lifetime ago when they had sneaked into Katrina and Prince Malachai's Black Magic and zonbie factory in the Bronx.

"This is getting to be a habit," Edgar said.

Edgar laced his fingers together and gave Jake a boost to the same window Jake and Ripper had used to exit the building. A searchlight pinned them as Jake helped Edgar inside. He counted the strobes of six boats passing the Tower and six more behind them. He and Edgar retreated into the office before the police in the chopper could respond.

In the corridor, Edgar discarded his poncho and took a flashlight from his shoulder bag. He wore Timberlands, blue jeans, and a T-shirt beneath a light jacket.

They climbed the stairs to the fourth floor, and Jake unlocked the door and opened it.

Edgar whistled at the sight of the office.

Jake splashed water; Carrie hadn't mopped any of it. "Carrie?"

She didn't answer.

Jake grabbed a candle burning on Carrie's desk and sloshed through the reception area to his empty office, then checked his bedroom. "She's gone."

Edgar stood in the office doorway. "Maybe she got scared and took off. Can you blame her?"

Staring below the monitors on the wall, Jake crossed the office, a sick feeling growing in his stomach. He kneeled in the water and dialed the combinations on the safe, then opened the door and held the candle inside. He felt as if he had been punched in the gut.

"What is it?"

"She stole my files," Jake said. "She sent Ripper with me so she'd be alone in here." *She sent him to his death.*

"Anything important?"

"Old Nick's Afterlife project."

"What could she want with that?"

"I don't know."

But the possibilities terrified him.

Jake entered Detective Bureau Manhattan on East Twenty-first Street two hours later. The lights were on thanks to the generator, and about a hundred civilians crowded the stairway. He made his way between the people, some of them sleeping. A baby he didn't see cried.

A female PO stood at the top of the stairs. "Can I help you, sir?"

He appreciated that she didn't recognize him. "I'm here to see Maria Vasquez."

"You know her?"

"We're friends."

"I'll tell her you're here. What's your name?"

"Jake Helman."

The woman's expression turned queer, but she walked in the direction of the squad room.

Jake gazed at the miserable-looking people below.

A moment later Maria appeared with the PO.

"What time do you get off work?" he said in a joking tone.

"No time soon." She took his hand and led him around the corner, out of sight of the crowd, and embraced him. "I'm so glad you're okay."

He had missed the feeling of her warmth. "Me, too."

"How did you get here?"

"I swam. It's cheaper than taking a taxi."

"Is our problem solved?"

"Of course. That's what I do: solve problems." He lowered his voice. "Our friend the raven helped me. He's trying to find a way back to Queens. We didn't think it would look good if we both walked in here."

"Good idea."

"Ripper's dead and Carrie flew the coop with my computer files. She took Afterlife. That's one reason I'm here—to file a report."

Maria raised her eyebrows. "You'll walk out of here with a report number and nothing else. No one has time for something like that."

"At least she'll be in the system. You've got power here. I don't. Maybe you can be of assistance in that area."

"Don't expect me to risk my job for one of your crazy situations." She cast a furtive glance both ways. "Why would the little schemer want Afterlife?"

"I don't know but it can't be good. I'll file a legit report, and if you feel like helping out, no harm done. How's Shana?"

Maria nodded inside the squad room, where Jake saw Bernie Reinhardt showing a little girl a card trick. Papa Joe's daughter, Alice Morton's niece, Prince Malachai's cousin— quite a bloodline.

"She's okay, thank God. Raheem's people killed Alice right in front of her."

"Did she get a look at them?"

"It was too dark."

From the tone of her voice, Jake gathered it would have been too dark even if the lights had been on. "You did the right thing going to her."

"I hope so. We're waiting for social services to come get her." She paused. "I hate to see her go."

Jake tried to read the look in her eyes. "Maybe you should foster her."

"On a cop's schedule? Right."

"Get your mother to help. She's been bugging you for grandkids, right? Make two birds happy with one stone."

"You want to meet her?"

"Sure."

Maria led him into the squad room. "Since me and Bernie found Alice's body, we're investigating her murder, which ties in with some others we're working on."

"I feel sorry for Raheem."

"I always get my man."

Bernie looked up at Jake, who sensed the man's dislike for him.

"How's it going?" Jake said.

Standing, Bernie offered his hand. "Helman."

Jake shook his hand. "Jake will do."

Maria took her seat. "Shana, this is my friend Jake."

"Are you a police detective, too?" Shana said.

"No, he isn't," Bernie said a little too fast.

"I'm a private eye. You know, like on TV?"

Shana nodded.

Jake offered his hand. "Anyway, I just wanted to say hello."

The little girl shook his hand.

"Aren't you going to help me with that problem?" Jake said to Maria.

"Oh, right." Maria stood. "I suppose you want me to help you jump the line."

"Something like that."

Maria led him across the squad room.

"Do you want a roommate for a few days or weeks?" he said. "My place isn't exactly livable."

"It will be days before I can even get to mine."

"What are you going to do until then?"

"We've got cots here."

"That will give you time to weigh my finer qualities."

"I already know what those are. Where will you stay?"

"Maybe I'll find someplace shady tonight and hike to Joyce and Edgar's tomorrow."

They passed Mauceri. "Helman?"

They turned to him in unison.

"Hey, L.T.," Jake said.

The lieutenant looked at them together, then shrugged and clasped Jake's shoulder. "It's good to see you." Then he walked away.

Jake smiled at Maria. "Do you think he'd mind if I crashed in one of the interview rooms?"

It turned out the interview rooms had been converted into

dormitories for the precinct cops, who had also taken over the roll call room.

It wasn't hard to find a place to crash for one night. Except for storefronts with metal security gates, all the buildings in Manhattan had broken glass doors, and Jake found an evacuated one on Madison and Twenty-sixth. He didn't like breaking and entering, but he ended up staying in a decent one-bedroom apartment with a lovely view of the Tower.

Out of respect for the missing tenants and out of fear for his own health, he slept on the sofa in the darkened apartment, surrounded by black-and-white photos of screwball comedy stars and clutching his flashlight, with his hunting knife beneath the cushion serving as his pillow. Howling wind did not keep him awake, but the sounds of helicopters and motorboats did, and on occasion search-lights shot through the broken windows.

Jake didn't know what time he finally fell asleep, but when he awoke in the morning it pleased him that he hadn't dreamed of Avademe. He helped himself to cereal and cof-fee, then pulled on his wet shorts and headed out.

The water level had receded to three feet deep, and hundreds of police officers, firemen, engineers, and city workers waded around the disaster areas. Helicopters circled the sky, and Jake found it too difficult to count the number of boats spread out in the water around Madison and Twenty-third.

As he approached a human barricade comprised of National Guards, he studied his building; all the windows were broken. Laurel's parlor and the front of the building were buried in limestone.

"No one is permitted beyond this point, sir," said one of the guards.

"I'm a tenant in that building," Jake said.

"You're still not permitted beyond this point."

"I can't conduct business without documents in my office."

"How are you going to get in? The entrance is blocked."

Jake gestured with his hand. "I could climb up those rocks and enter through the second floor."

"That's unlikely. Besides, no one is going into any of those buildings until the engineers say it's safe to do so. Any one of them could come down."

"Just make sure no one else goes in there, okay?"

The guard said nothing and Jake waded away.

"Jake!"

Jake turned to see Jackie.

"This is some shit, huh?" he said, a cigarette dangling from his mouth.

"I'm glad you're still with us," Jake said. He looked around at the people milling about in the water, shooting photos and gawking at the destruction. "I have some bad news for you."

Jackie gestured at the building. "Worse than this?"

"I'm afraid so; Laurel's dead."

The ruddiness drained from Jackie's features. "How do you know?"

"I saw her body with my own eyes. Her death may become public knowledge, but I need to be left out of it."

Jackie nodded with a distant look in his eyes. He drew

a folded sealed envelope from his back pocket and held it out to Jake. "I've been carrying this around since she disappeared. She told me to give it to you if her death was ever confirmed."

Jake tore open the envelope, unfolded the documents inside, and skimmed them. He raised his eyebrows, then handed the paperwork back to Jackie. "Congratulations. You're the proud owner of one building in serious need of repair."

Jackie raised his eyebrows as well.

"Laurel was Eden, Inc.," Jake said. "This document transfers ownership of Eden to you. That building's got to be worth four million dollars."

Jackie read the paperwork. "It says here that you get to keep your office for one dollar a month for twenty years and her parlor for the same length of time."

"You take the parlor. I can't use it. But rent it out to a deli, will you?"

Jackie shook his head. "You rent it out to a deli. If you don't want the parlor, the proceeds of its rental go to you, not me. I can live with that."

Jake grunted his surprise. Laurel had provided him with a free office and an additional means of income. "So can I." He looked at the building. "I sure hope she carried flood insurance."

Three days later, Jake and Maria helped Edgar, Joyce, and Martin load their belongings into a U-Haul. The July sun blazed down on them, and they wiped away their sweat and drank lemonade. Queens had been spared the awesome fury of Hurricane Daria.

Joyce held her house keys out to Jake. "Take good care of it."

Jake pocketed the keys. "I will. I promise. And I'll find you a suitable tenant when my office is ready for me to move back into."

Joyce glanced at Maria. "I don't see that happening anytime soon."

The two women embraced.

Jake rubbed the back of Martin's head. "Stay out of trouble in North Carolina. Don't make me come down there and kick your butt."

Martin grinned. "Okay."

Martin hugged Maria and Jake hugged Joyce. Then Joyce and Martin got into Joyce's SUV.

Maria faced Edgar. "I guess this is it."

"Yeah. Keep this knucklehead in line, will you?"

"I'll do my best. Take care of yourself, partner. Thanks for teaching me to be a murder police."

"Thank God I did a better job with you than I did with Jake."

They kissed each other on the cheek.

"What do you think you're going to do down there?" Jake said.

"Find myself and spend time with my family. It's not like I'm going to Mars."

Jake looked away. "I don't know about that."

"This city's gotten too crazy for me. I need a slower train if I'm going to get back on track. I told Geoghegan where he can find me, but I'm pretty sure they don't plan to file charges against me for Katrina's death. You should think about going somewhere, too."

Jake shrugged. "I think I'll stick around."

"Then at least stop looking for trouble."

"It has a habit of finding me."

Edgar and Jake hugged, then patted each other on the back.

Edgar walked around the SUV and slid behind the wheel.

Jake and Maria waved to Joyce and Martin, then sat on the steps and watched the SUV pull out, trailer in tow.

"I'm happy for them," Maria said.

"Me, too." He turned to her. "Any luck with Carrie?"

Maria shook her head. "Most of our systems are still down, but if she's left the city she's got some damn good fake ID."

Jake scanned the neighborhood. "Then she might still be here somewhere."

"Maybe." She paused. "The building management company for the Flatiron found the bodies on the roof."

"Big news?" Manhattan still lacked power, and Jake's phone service hadn't reactivated.

"The decapitation by sword of the Queen of Romance and the unexplained death of Erika Long beside her? Small potatoes compared to the heavenly hurricane. From what I've seen on the news sites, the media's been taken hostage for religious debate." Maria set one hand on his thigh. "Forget all of that for a minute. What about you and me? Are we going to try to make this work?"

Meeting her gaze, he tried not to think about Carrie or Afterlife or how the world would react to the bizarre deaths of Erika Long and Lilian Kane. He tried to put the Realm of Light and the Dark Realm and Cain and Abel and Sheryl out of his mind. He just wanted to think about Maria and what she meant to him.

"Yes," he said.